"Paws down, o... time. A lively roman... heroine, a sexy leading man, and adorable dachshunds. No bones about it, this book is a real treat!"

— Diane Kelly, author of the Paw Enforcement series

"A satisfying blend of romance and mystery . . . Add the appropriate amount of playful banter and dog shenanigans, and you've got the makings of a promising start to a new series. A delightfully adorable mystery-romance with a well-planned plot. And dogs!" — *Kirkus Reviews*

"A fun and charming series . . . combines humor and romance with a dash of mystery, all while showcasing the author's determined heroine fighting for her dream. Settle in and enjoy, and keep the puppy treats handy!"

— *RT Book Reviews*

"Griffin's spirited, wholesome love story escalates into a deeper mystery offering playful comic relief en route to a revealing whodunit." — *Shelf Awareness*

"Who doesn't love a story with cute dogs, hot billionaires, quirky heroines, and a sweet HEA? I cannot wait for the next book in what is the start of a wonderful series to come."

— *Harlequin Junkie* (Top Pick!)

"Great characters and a lively and captivating plot make this a terrific read." — *Romance Reviews Today*

Also By Casey Griffin

MUST LOVE WIENERS
BEAUTY AND THE WIENER

A Wedding
Tail

Casey Griffin

St. Martin's Paperbacks

This is a work of fiction. All of the characters, organizations, and events portrayed in this novel are either products of the author's imagination or are used fictitiously.

A WEDDING TAIL

Copyright © 2017 by Casey Griffin.

For information address St. Martin's Press, 175 Fifth Avenue, New York, NY 10010.

ISBN: 978-1-250-08469-9

Our books may be purchased in bulk for promotional, educational, or business use. Please contact your local bookseller or the Macmillan Corporate and Premium Sales Department at 1-800-221-7945, ext. 5442, or by e-mail at MacmillanSpecialMarkets@macmillan.com.

Printed in the United States of America

St. Martin's Paperbacks edition /August 2017

St. Martin's Paperbacks are published by St. Martin's Press, 175 Fifth Avenue, New York, NY 10010.

10 9 8 7 6 5 4 3 2 1

Acknowledgments

I owe a *paw*sitively huge thank you to Rose Hilliard for helping me discover and unleash the best in this story. I appreciated all of your support and encouragement when things got hairy. I will never *fur*get you. Holly Ingraham, thanks for jumping on board this wiener with such enthusiasm and for seeing it through. And to Jennie Conway and the staff at SMP who have worked so hard to develop and promote the series, it's been a real treat working with all of you.

To Devin, my inspiration, my rock, and my heart, I wouldn't have made it without you. Pooja Menon, my stories wouldn't have been heard if you hadn't stuck by me and believed in me. Thank you to my criminal subject-matter expert Pat McCormack and to my cultural expert Kacy Inokuchi. And finally, a shout-out to the amazing Fredwardo, the most *special* dog I know. You've given me all the inspiration I could ever ask for.

And most of all, thank you to the fans of the series for your encouragement, dedication, and for sharing my silly sense of humor.

1

Top Dog

Zoe Plum stood in front of St. Dominic's church doors, greeting each wedding guest with a brilliant smile as they arrived, checking their names off a list on her tablet. However, she wasn't exactly smiling on the inside. Internally, Zoe was pacing and biting her nails, cringing at each new arrival that wasn't the guest she was hoping for: Levi Dolson. And boy was he going to hear it from her when he finally did arrive.

Just that morning, Levi had been upgraded from guest to groomsman—that's if he got there in time. The original groomsman had been hit with food poisoning late the night before—which Zoe suspected was more than likely a case of nerves, since everyone was on edge that day.

This wasn't a usual joyful wedding day. Her clients might have been the ones tying the knot, but it felt like the only thing in knots were Zoe's insides. No one would have guessed it, however, as she welcomed people up the steps and through the double doors with a confident smile.

Zoe could act like she was going for a facial while a zombie apocalypse was breaking out around her. But between each new arrival, she cast nervous glances down the street, wanting to throttle the fill-in groomsman who was running dangerously late.

A glance at her watch told Zoe there were fifty minutes until "I do" time. She just wished that when Levi did arrive, it would be on the back of a white stallion. Not because she secretly wanted a Prince Charming—that ludicrous fantasy was the last thing she dreamed of. It was because the bride, Juliet, had insisted on riding into the sunset—or at least the mid-afternoon blazing sun—with her new husband after the ceremony. Unfortunately, her assistant informed Zoe that the beautiful horse she'd originally booked had come down with a case of acute synovitis.

Summer was a busy time for the poor creature, what with the influx of tourists to show around San Francisco. The strain of pulling the cart for all those extra customers had put poor Puccini out of commission for the rest of the summer, and most annoyingly, for the wedding Zoe had been planning for the last year.

But it would all be okay. No. It was going to be *perfect*, just like every other event that Zoe had ever been hired to plan. She wasn't the best event planner in the city for nothing. And after all the added challenges that day had presented so far, she was really going to prove that by pulling it off without a hitch—or a hitch that anyone would know about.

The Fisher-Wells wedding was one of the more extravagant weddings she'd planned for that year, with a commission to match. Once it was done, she would finally have the rest of the down payment to buy her own place. A place to call her own, instead of renting a small apartment barely big enough for her. She couldn't wait to feel like she owned a little piece of the world.

What was better, she could finally prove to her mother that she could support herself without a man—as often as her mother tried to convince Zoe otherwise. Because if you could afford to buy a place in San Francisco, there was no doubt you had your life together. It was her final puzzle piece to having complete independence, that grown-up feeling of being a homeowner.

"Code red! Code red!" a panicked voice screamed out.

Zoe turned from the guests filtering in through the church's entrance. The disembodied voice carried around the side of the building and into the foyer. The guests exchanged worried glances.

Inwardly, Zoe cringed, but she maintained her poise. She smiled, like everything's cool. Nothing to see here.

A moment later, a plump blonde appeared at the bottom of the church stairs, ponytail swinging behind her, sensible flats slapping the walkway. When she saw Zoe's expression, she visibly gulped.

Zoe gave her assistant, Natalie, a quirk of her eyebrow and nodded her head inside. Obviously chastised, Natalie mimicked Zoe's "natural" air of confidence as she entered the church, past people congregating around the guest book. They ducked into a quiet vestibule so they were out of earshot.

The epitome of serenity, Zoe began rearranging a bouquet of roses on a carved wooden table. However, her insides had cinched together like corset strings.

"We can't handle a code red right now," she told her assistant. "We already have an MIA flower girl, a sick priest, a wild four-legged ring bearer, in-laws at each other's throats, and a sweaty congregation."

As usual, Zoe was the first to arrive at the venue that

morning, and it had taken her breath away. Literally. It
had been like stepping into a sauna. The church's air conditioning blew up the night before, and due to the heat
wave that had hit San Francisco that week, no available
repairmen could be found in time for the wedding.

After a few emergency calls, Zoe had found industrial
fans for rent that had blown the toupee right off the bride's
grandfather. Thankfully the fans came with protective
guards so the magical day didn't end with a magical am-
putation. That day was about joining two people together,
not a finger back to its owner.

The first crisis of the day averted, after that, everything that could go wrong had. *So what now*, Zoe wondered. "How bad is it?"

"This trumps everything." Natalie was practically
vibrating. She took a deep breath, but it didn't seem to
calm her. It only made her start hyperventilating. "It's
the dress."

Zoe froze. "What about the dress?"

Natalie hesitated, wincing a little. "It doesn't fit."

The rose stem in Zoe's hand snapped in two. The
words echoed through her mind as it emptied of all other
concerns. Family feuds she could squelch, flower girls
she could track down, rampant dogs she could bring to
heel, but this . . . And with *this* bride of all brides?

"What do you mean?" Zoe asked. "How can it not fit?
It was made for her."

Zoe hadn't even moved, but something in her voice
made Natalie take a step back. "I-I mean it won't zip up.
We're talking total back fat blockage."

Not on my watch, Zoe told herself.

She drew herself up and headed for the office building at the back of the church, or rather, the bride's temporary room. "We'll see about that. I'll make that dress

fit if I have to staple her into it." She imagined this was why corsets were invented, because at the last second, it was easier to make alterations to the body than the dress.

As Zoe skirted around the outside of the church, the afternoon sun beat down on her. And it was only one o'clock. It was bound to get hotter. She just hoped the fans could keep up.

Natalie remained close on her heel, her footsteps on the paved path matching the quick beat of Zoe's heart. Zoe couldn't wait until this day was over. Planning the Fisher-Wells wedding had been her biggest professional challenge yet. Amongst the bride's waffling desires, unrealistic expectations, and last-minute demands, Juliet Fisher had been a bridezilla from start to finish.

But no one deserved a crisis like this on their big day.

As they rounded the side of the building, Zoe hated to ask, "How is she doing?"

Natalie groaned. "Total bride meltdown."

Zoe had figured as much. She remembered the day the gold-embossed invitations arrived and Juliet's name had accidentally been placed last to read *Wells-Fisher*. To say the least, Fisher was not *well* that day. Somehow that had set the tone for their entire future marriage—something about feeling inadequate and her mother-in-law's strawberry rhubarb pie. It was all very difficult to understand once she'd broken down into full sobs.

As they made their way to the little office building where the bride was getting ready, Zoe mentally reviewed her to-do list.

Double check on bride's uncle (last seen nursing flask)
Find flower girl
Cough drops for priest

Leash for Juliet's golden retriever
Replacement horse
Levi Dolson

She added a new item to the list:

Get bride into dress

Zoe could feel her shoulder muscles relax beneath her stylish cobalt blazer as everything fell into place in her mind. She could get through this day. It was going to be okay. Heck, the year before she'd thrown a party where someone kidnapped dozens of her guests. They might have been of the four-legged variety. But still. After that, she was officially experienced with any disaster an event planner could face. Only, she'd never faced them all at the exact same time. And what was she going to do about that horse?

As Zoe and Natalie approached the separate building, they could already hear muffled screams coming from the other side of the door. They gave each other a look, like *Here we go.*

Natalie looked downright ill. Zoe figured they didn't both need to endure the impending abuse. So she turned to her assistant. "On second thought, could you please call around and find a horse for after the ceremony? Do whatever you can. Get me a zebra if you have to."

Relief caused Natalie's eyes to roll into her head. She nodded, her ponytail flicking. Another peal of swear words drifted through the door, and she scrambled away as fast as she could.

"Oh, and Natalie?" Zoe called after her. "If that Levi Dolson turns up, send him to me right away."

Zoe absently wondered what the weight restriction on ponies was, if it came to that. But there would have to be a ceremony before they'd need a horse, and the bride needed a dress before she could walk down the aisle. So tucking one of her stray jet-black locks of hair back into place, Zoe approached the "bride's room."

Automatically, she reached inside her utility bridal bag—well, truthfully it was a fanny pack. It may not have been as stylish as a Coach purse, but it was a necessity that no good event planner could do without—it had saved her butt more times than she could shake a bridal bouquet at. Besides, Zoe could rock anything and make it look like she was strutting down the runway. Even a fanny pack.

Unzipping a hidden pouch, she dipped her hand in. Her fingers brushed against super-soft polyester fur, and instantly, she could feel her worries melt away. She held the hidden object reverently, allowing its furry, comforting presence to sooth her. Because who could be upset when they were holding an adorable, lovable, huggable Fuzzy Friend?

The collectible line of stuffed animals was on the top of every child's Christmas list, and apparently on the list of stressed-out thirty-year-old Japanese-American women too. Or maybe that was just Zoe. While she couldn't explain it, the cuddly sack of beans was like a private solace to her during the worst of times—and simultaneously her most embarrassing secret.

Predicting a difficult day, she'd come armed with Pretty Puppy, one of her favorites. It was old and well loved, as evidenced by the multiple repairs over the years to seams, new eyeballs, and replacement plastic bean stuffing. It looked uncannily like her last dachshund, Buddy. While he'd died of old age more than a year before, the thought of him still brought those warm memories back.

Zoe missed Buddy. Even now, she still hadn't moved

on. While she continued to volunteer at the San Francisco Dachshund Rescue Center where she'd first adopted Buddy, she sometimes felt pangs, painful reminders of what she was missing in her life ever since he'd left her.

Ironically, she felt no such pangs of regret every time she attended a wedding, nor did she feel like she was missing a groom in her life. Certainly not the one that left her. She was better off on her own. In every way.

Zoe didn't need a man. There was only one thing a man could do for her and she did a better job of that herself. But that was the benefit of being a Pure Pleasure sex toy representative—an arsenal of free vibrators at her disposal.

She sold the popular toy line as a side business by hosting Pure Pleasure parties, pulling in an average of two thousand dollars a month. But the best part was the incredible discount and free samples that came along with the job. Which was a lifesaver, since Zoe was convinced she had a higher-than-normal sexual appetite— the amount of batteries she bought on a regular basis could attest to that.

She didn't only exude sexuality, she studied sex, understood sex, taught sex secrets and tips, threw sexucation parties to sell merchandise. Zoe was a sexpert in practically every way. Except, of course, for one tiny detail: She didn't have sex.

As she gave her Fuzzy Friend a final squeeze, she took a deep breath, preparing for what lay on the other side of that door before finally knocking.

"What!?" came a sharp reply.

Zoe braced herself and turned the handle. She cracked the door open just wide enough to check for airborne shoes or bouquets aimed at her.

When she saw the coast was clear, she poked her head

inside and found a cluster of brightly colored brides-maids, one for every color of the rainbow. They were huddled in the middle of the reception office, the desk and chairs pushed to the side of the room to make space for the wedding party.

"Can I come in?" Zoe asked.

At the sound of her voice, the rainbow turned in unison and seemed to part, revealing a billowing white tulle cloud in the middle. However, when Juliet spun away from the mirror to face Zoe, her expression looked as tempestuous as a hurricane. And she'd looked like she'd been through one too.

Mascara ran down her cheeks in black streaks from a pair of puffy eyes. Wisps of hair escaped her veil and clung to her sweaty cheeks. Her dress sagged off her body, half-zipped up. Her maid of honor struggled to hold it up while Juliet's body shook with sobs.

Zoe didn't skip a beat. "Look at you!" she gushed. "You look beautiful." Which was probably the biggest lie she'd ever told in her life, and in a church, no less—which was fine, since she'd always assumed she was going to hell anyway.

While she wasn't normally one to hold her opinions back, there were times that demanded truth and times that demanded an outright bald-faced lie. This was one of those times.

"No, I don't!" Juliet wailed, wiping her reddened nose on a tissue. "I can't go through with it. I'm calling the whole thing off."

"Why? What's wrong?" Zoe dared a few steps into the room. She needed to diffuse the situation, brush it off as though this kind of thing happens all the time—which unfortunately it did. But why, oh why did it have to happen to Juliet?

Juliet spun to face the floor-standing mirror again, elbowing her maid of honor out of the way. "Just look at my dress. It's a disaster! It doesn't fit."

She tugged at the beaded bodice futilely before giving a little stomp of her silk heel. Her bodice shifted and began to slip down again. The maid of honor lunged and held it up to prevent an accidental strip-show.

Zoe crossed the office full of tense bridesmaids. "I'm sure the zipper's just stuck. Let me have a look."

"See? I told you it was the zipper," Juliet snapped at the girl in the orange dress, then to Zoe she said, "I told her it was the zipper. She didn't believe me."

Zoe grabbed the two pieces of unzipped fabric at the back and pulled them together. Extra hands joined in the battle, tugging on the dress. As they were stifled, Zoe could feel beads of sweat form along her brow in the stifling, air-conditioning-less room.

Juliet sucked in, turning red, then purple, then blue. When she'd turned every color of her bridesmaids' dresses, it became obvious that Natalie was right. It wasn't going to close. Zoe stepped back to catch her breath.

She frowned at the gown. "Hmmm."

Juliet eyed her in the mirror. "Hmmm? What is that supposed mean? That doesn't sound like a good 'hmmm.' Like 'Hmmm, what kind of ice cream do I want tonight?'" she said sarcastically.

Zoe thought ice cream was likely the source of their dilemma. "It doesn't look like the zipper's the problem. But it will be all right," she added quickly. "We'll just have to make some emergency modifications to the design."

"How did this happen?" Juliet gripped her half-updo and tugged at her brown locks, making it more of a half-undo—yet, one more thing to fix. Her face screwed up. "It's probably the seamstress's fault," she spat.

Zoe was certain the seamstress wasn't to blame, but she wasn't about to suggest that in case Juliet started to cry again and they lost what little makeup they had left.

"Don't worry. These things can happen before the big day. It's totally not your fault at all."

"Of course it's not," Juliet said. "Stupid stress."

Assessing the expensive wedding dress again, Zoe ran through several options in her head like flipping through a wedding-dress catalogue. The whole room seemed to lean forward, awaiting her verdict. Juliet watched Zoe's reflection in the mirror, looking hopeful.

Zoe nodded. "I can totally make this work. But it's going to take stabbing several holes on either side of the zipper. How do you feel about a corset-style back?"

She dug through her fanny pack and drew out an emergency roll of thick, white silk ribbon and a small pair of scissors. Fanny-pack to the rescue!

Juliet's hopeful look darkened. "You want to ruin my dress?"

"Would you rather cancel the wedding and wait for a few months? And what's more important about today? The dress? The perfect ceremony? An equal number of groomsmen to bridesmaids? This specific location?"

"But it *had* to be this church," she whined. "My parents got married in this church."

"I know. I totally get it." Grabbing a tissue from her fanny pack, she dabbed at the mascara streaks on the bride's cheeks. "And we made it work, didn't we? Now we'll make the dress work too."

Emotions always ran high leading up to the big day,

and a good wedding planner knew how to maintain perspective, to be empathetic but remain neutral. Zoe could see the bigger picture. She was objective. She didn't get wrapped up in all the fantasy of romance and love. It was all bullshit anyway.

Forget the excitement of the day, the silk dress, the gardenia arrangements, the old family tortoiseshell kanzashi comb passed down by a proud mother. Because once you stripped it all away, there was just a man and a woman, and no amount of planning, organizing, and dreaming was going to make him walk down that aisle if he changed his mind. There were some things you couldn't control—like when her groom hadn't been waiting on the other end of that aisle for her. He'd been a no-show.

But Zoe knew better now, of course. She'd walked away a stronger person, more level-headed. And because of it, she could organize the best damned wedding a bride could ever dream of—at least *that* was in her control. She was going to make the Fisher-Wells wedding happen, come heat wave or missing groomsman.

"Today isn't about all the details," she told Juliet. "It's about getting married to the man you love. This is just the first day. It's the rest of your lives that really matter."

Whenever Zoe put it like that, it usually brought any errant bride back down to earth, because ultimately, their wedding day was about their union with the man they loved. Right?

Juliet's eyes, however, were still lit with an argument. Like when she'd argued about keeping the same venue even with the heat wave and lack of air conditioning. Like she'd argued about wanting to push her already-strained budget to accommodate the additional three tiers on the wedding cake. Like she'd argued about the first two dresses that seemed perfect to Zoe but Juliet ultimately ended up selling on eBay.

Finally, Juliet let out a breath like she'd been defeated. "Fine. I suppose. Do what you need to do." She turned her back to Zoe and faced the mirror.

Zoe checked her watch. Thirty-nine minutes until go-time. She'd have to make quick work of the designer dress.

She began to cut holes into the back of the dress on both sides of the zipper, careful to hide them beneath the folds of the ruching detail. Then with long, deft fingers, she began to thread the silk ribbon through the holes, crisscrossing them in a corset-style.

When Zoe had threaded the last hole, she instructed the bridesmaids to hold the bride steady. "Brace yourself," she told Juliet. Heaving on the ribbon, she cinched it tight, sucking Juliet snuggly into the dress.

The bride gasped with each jerk. Zoe grunted as she yanked and pulled, maintaining tension until she could put the final bow in place. Then she thought better of it and added a double knot.

Wiping her brow, Zoe stepped back to admire her handiwork. "There. That's better, isn't it?" she panted. "I think it adds a certain sexiness to it, don't you?"

The bridesmaids parted. Hesitantly, Juliet turned her back to the mirror and looked over her shoulder. Her scrutinizing eyes roved up and down the laced ribbon, eventually softening. After a few moments, it was clear she was unable to find another argument, and the collection of colorful bridesmaids released their held breaths.

Zoe had to admit, it looked pretty damn good. Unless you knew it was supposed to be a zip-up dress, you couldn't even tell. As she stared at her bride's reflection in self-congratulations, she caught a glimpse of something white streak across the mirror. Her eyes focused on the reflection of the room's open window as another white object soared by.

She spun just in time to see it clearly: white doves. Sure, they could be any old white doves. It was the outdoors, after all. But considering how the day was going so far, she just knew they were the white doves that were prepared for the newlywed's grand exit. The white doves that were supposed to be waiting in their cages around the side of the church.

Zoe gasped.

Juliet stiffened. "What? What is it? Is the fabric ripping?" The tulle skirt swished as she twisted this way and that to see what was wrong.

"No! It's nothing. I just thought I saw a cloud outside," Zoe lied. "I would hate for the weather to turn on us."

"Oh, no! I hope it's not going to rain." Juliet gathered her skirts and rushed toward the window.

Zoe lunged to block the way, throwing her arms out. She couldn't let Juliet see the doves and come up with yet another reason to call off the wedding. "No! I . . . I think I saw the groom outside. I wouldn't look if I were you." She shooed the bride away. "Bad luck and everything."

And they certainly didn't need any more of that.

The door burst open. Natalie practically fell into the room, a feather clinging to her bangs. She was wheezing for air after clearly running all the way there. Her wide eyes fell on Zoe, and she seemed to make an attempt—however poor—to act natural.

Zoe suppressed an eye roll. She was going to have to give that girl some acting lessons in cool.

"Sorry to interrupt, but—"

Zoe held up a hand before she could finish that sentence. The white feather waving in her hair said enough. "No, not at all. Perfect timing." She threw on a brilliant smile. "Can you please touch up the bride's hair and makeup for me? We've only got"—she checked her watch again—"thirty-three minutes."

As Zoe headed for the door, Natalie clung to her arm. "But the—"

"I know." Zoe plucked the feather out of her hair. "I've got everything under control."

Grasping the door handle, Zoe yanked it open, ready to deal with the next disaster. As it swung open, violent gusts of wind flapped in her face, feathers tickling her cheek and stirring her long hair.

Zoe cried out. She threw her hands up, swatting at anything that might come near. When the flurry in front of her disappeared and she could finally open her eyes, she saw two more doves escaping, headed east on Bush Street.

"What's wrong?" Juliet demanded. She turned to look just as Natalie held the eyeliner to her lid, effectively leaving a thick ebony streak across her face.

If the bridesmaids had noticed Zoe's feathered attacker, they were all too scared to say anything to their friend.

Zoe managed to rearrange her face into fake outrage. "Who put the rose topiary out here?" She gestured to the front steps. "This isn't where it was supposed to go. Do I have to do everything around here?"

Juliet rolled her eyes at Zoe's dramatics. "It's okay. They're just flowers. You know, you're kind of high strung."

Zoe grit her teeth. *Look who's talking*, she thought, but

managed to give her a confident look. "I'm here to make sure your wedding is perfect."

"Everything *is* perfect." Now that the most recent meltdown had been avoided, it seemed Juliet was the perfect picture of a blushing bride. "So long as you have the horse for after the ceremony, that is. You do, don't you?"

Zoe quirked her eyebrow at Natalie in question. But she gave a subtle shake of her head. Zoe's smile only wavered a little. "Absolutely. You can count on me." Although how she was going to pull it off, she wasn't sure.

As she turned to leave, Natalie called out, "Oh Zoe! I almost forgot. Levi Dolson is waiting for you in the foyer."

"Thank you. I'll take care of it." She shut the door behind her to go wrangle a seriously late groomsman and some damn birds. Yet another thing to put on the list for the day. *Bird herding.*

She found it strange that Natalie hadn't checked on the birds herself. After a year of working together, her assistant still hadn't learned to take a little initiative. Today, however, she seemed worse than ever, like instead of rising to the challenge, she was adding to it. How could so many things possibly go wrong with one event?

Zoe decided to take the shortcut through the sanctuary and nave. There wasn't much time to waste. Her heels clicked steadily on the hardwood floor, echoing off the vaulted ceiling.

"High strung," my ass, she thought. She was nothing if not level-headed, cool, and collected. Her emotions were always in check. At least, they had been ever since her own wedding day. That day itself, however, was an entirely different story. But who could blame her?

Since then, she'd vowed never to let herself lose control like that again. Especially not over a man. Instead, when she felt her temperature rise, her emotions start to bubble to the surface, she pushed them down. Deep, deep down. She imagined bottling them up and screwing on the top. Which sounded perfectly healthy, right?

Zoe never let her bottle-o-crazy get too full, however. She had a way of safely releasing the built-up pressure. Sure, it cost her a fortune in batteries, but what better way to prevent herself from blowing her top than . . . well, blowing her top?

To everyone else, she appeared tranquil, calm beneath that layer of ice. No one could make waves in waters they couldn't touch. More than one bitter man she'd turned down over the years had called her an ice queen. And because she was just so cool, they never had to know just how much it hurt. No one had to know what went on beneath her smooth, hard surface.

Marching through the church, she shooed doves down from curtain rods, from St. Mary's shoulder, and away from the topiaries. So far, she'd counted twelve feathered fugitives. The more she chased toward an open window or swished out a nearby exit, the more Zoe found her cool starting to thaw.

At least one problem was about to be solved. Her substitute groomsman had finally arrived and not a moment too soon. But when Zoe reached the foyer, chasing yet another dove away, there was no groomsman.

There was, however, a man in his mid-thirties, wearing ripped jeans and a wrinkly T-shirt. His hair stuck up in a blond tangle of gelled curls, mashed up on one side like he'd just rolled out of bed.

He turned at the sound of her footsteps, a dreamy smile lighting up his unshaven face, like he'd just stumbled out of his bedroom and not into a church.

For a second, she hoped the man was just sleepwalking and needed directions back to his bed, but then he said the words she dreaded to hear.

"Zoe Plum? I was told you're looking for me." He held out a hand. "Levi Dolson."

2

Stop the Music

Zoe stared at the rumpled man in front of her. She could feel her eyebrow twitch with annoyance as she took in his careless style, his bedhead hair, his sleepy half-lidded eyes that ran up her long, lean legs beneath her tight skirt. It was the kind of look a girl would dream about waking up next to, but at that moment, it was Zoe's nightmare.

"You're not Levi Dolson," she said.

He arched a pierced eyebrow. "I'm not?"

"You can't be. The Levi Dolson I'm expecting is a groomsman in a wedding. Not a candidate for a sleep study."

He ran a self-conscious hand over the stubble on his square jaw. "Hey, give me a break. I just woke up half an hour ago. At least I brushed my teeth."

"Too bad you forgot your hair," she said, only half-jokingly. The other half was dead serious. This was the last thing she needed. "Late night?"

"You could say that." He grinned, and Zoe assumed it might have had something to do with the cherry red lipstick mark still bright on his cheek. "You gotta grab life by the balls while you can, right?"

"Looks like it wasn't just life that had its balls grabbed last night."

His forehead creased with confusion. Zoe dug into her bridal utility bag and pulled out a makeup remover to-go cloth.

She waved it in question. "May I?"

He nodded so she reached up and wiped the red smudge off his cheek. She showed it to him, and he kind of shrugged sheepishly.

"Nice shade," she said with a smirk.

Reaching back into her bag, she pulled out a travel hairbrush. She held it up. After he nodded, she began styling his hair as best she could. It was a nice mix of honey and caramel. The sides were faded short but there was plenty of length on top to give it some style.

"Why are you so late?" she asked. "Were you planning on sleepwalking down the aisle in your Snoopy slippers?"

"I don't have Snoopy slippers. I'm a man, not a child. I have Batman slippers," he chuckled. "Besides, I only got Owen's text forty minutes ago that he wanted me to fill in. I came right away."

"But you were supposed to be a guest. Why weren't you already here, and"—she gave his curls a final ruffle to add some life—"showered?" She nodded appreciatively at his hair. He had nice locks—if only he'd done them before he came.

"Let me see?" He pretended to think. "Attend the stressful wedding of a guy I knew back in university or sleep in after a late night? Tough call. Besides, I was going to attend the reception. No big deal."

"Well, it's a big deal to the bride and groom. And it's a big deal to me. You're pushing us dangerously behind schedule." She checked her watch again. She couldn't stand tardiness.

Levi's attention suddenly shifted, following the path of something sailing over Zoe's head. *The nerve of this guy,* she thought. He wasn't even paying attention to her. He opened and closed his mouth a couple of times before he figured out exactly what he wanted to say.

"Are there more birds in this church than usual, or is it just me?"

Zoe gasped. "Crap. The doves." Spinning on her heel, she raced for the front entrance. "Come on!" she called over her shoulder. "We need to take a detour, and I'm not letting you out of my sight."

On the way by a replica painting of the Last Supper, she spotted Juliet's half-cut uncle slouched in a velvet chair. She stopped at the refreshment table in the corner and filled a Styrofoam cup with black coffee.

"Oh, that's awesome," Levi said. "I could really use a cup."

As he reached for it, Zoe swiped it out of his grasp. "If you wanted coffee, you should have woken up earlier. There's no time."

He gave her a pathetic pout. Despite how vexed she was with him at the moment, Zoe laughed, but she didn't relent. Although, that playful look did make her waver a little.

Zoe snuck up on Uncle Wally slouched over in his chair and wrestled the flask out of his hands before he could fight back. "I think you've had quite enough of that."

His bloodshot eyes opened half-way, blinking out of sync before landing on her chest. "But I'm celebrating," he whined.

"Save the celebrations for later. They're not married yet." She handed him the coffee and a Tic-Tac from her utility bag.

Zoe mentally ticked that item off her to-do list and returned her focus to the top priority.

As she weaved through the last guests filtering into the stuffy church to take their seats, Levi tugged on the neck of his T-shirt.

"Why is it so hot in here?"

"Air conditioning is broken," she said, trying her best not to sprint out the front doors as she saw another dove soar by.

"And they're still having the wedding here? Don't they know there's a heat wave going on right now?"

She rolled her eyes. "You're pretty sharp for a man who just woke up at the crack of mid-day."

Descending the steps, she took the paved path to a nook at the side of the building where she was keeping the caged doves until the end. As she rounded the corner, her eyes fell on a small devil in lace and braids, disguised as an adorable six-year-old flower girl. And she was reaching for the latch on the next birdcage.

Zoe fixed her with a hard stare. "And what do you think you're doing?"

The girl jumped and blinked up at Zoe. "They were sad," she explained. "They wanted to come out and play."

"But they will come out and play right after Juliet and Owen get married," she said. "You'll see."

But the flower girl jiggled the latch impatiently like that sounded way too long. "But I want to play with them now."

Zoe crouched down, ready to spring into action if she opened it. "You can even help let them out if you want. How does that sound? Hmm? Help create the grand finale?"

"Grand finale?" She eyed Levi like she smelled a trick. After a moment of serious consideration, the flower girl nodded.

Zoe clapped her hands together. "Great! Why don't we find you some cake to keep you busy for a while?"

The girl's eyes lit up. "Cake!"

There were already seven tiers on the oversized cake. She was sure Juliet wouldn't miss one little piece. "If I get you some cake, do you promise to behave and carry the flowers down the aisle like we talked about?"

"Uh-huh," she said around the drool forming.

"Do you think she could really use more energy?" Levi muttered.

Zoe snorted. "No, but I just need to get through the next"—she checked her watch—"twenty-four minutes until the ceremony begins. One thing at a time."

Taking the girl by the hand, Zoe led her around the side of the building to the parish hall where the reception tables were set up for dinner. She made sure Levi was following behind. "Sorry. This won't take long."

"No rush. I've got nowhere to be."

Zoe glared at him over her shoulder and saw his mischievous grin. Was he actually egging her on at a moment like this? Did he take anything seriously? This was a wedding. It was supposed to be the best day of the bride's and groom's lives, and he was acting like it was, well, no big deal.

But it was a big deal. Her entire job was to organize "big deal" celebrations.

"Cake!" the girl demanded.

"Okay, okay." Zoe steered her toward the kitchen at the end of the hall. "The cake is just in here."

But when she swung the door open, she got a lot more cake than she'd anticipated. Red velvet with cream cheese icing to be exact. Right in the face.

Zoe's head whipped to the side like she'd been slapped. The cream cheese icing slid down her cheek and onto her

silk blouse. She blinked the sponge cake from her eyelashes in surprise.

"What the hell?"

The flower girl gasped. "You said a bad word."

"You did say a bad word," Levi said in mock seriousness.

Zoe scowled at him. "What?"

The little girl grinned, and yelled, "Hell!"

"Don't say that." Zoe pinched the bridge of her nose.
This day was so not going according to plan.

Then Levi got a look inside the kitchen and he said,
"Holy crap."

"Crap!" the girl cried.

Zoe glared across the kitchen at the father of the
groom—or FOG, for short. Wedding cake coated his
right hand, the frosting smeared up to the elbow of his
suit jacket. By the looks of the mangled fifteen hundred
dollar seven-tiered cake, he'd tried a few times to hit his
target: the MOB, or mother of the bride. She, however,
was relatively cake free but for a few globs of icing that
clung to her permed hair.

"I'm so sorry," the FOG told Zoe. "I didn't mean to."
Then he frowned and spun toward the MOB. "This is all
your fault. You'd drive a priest insane!"

She was a short woman but somehow seemed to grow
taller with her fury at the balding man. "The way you
drove my daughter insane? Her ten-thousand-dollar dress
won't fit now because of you."

"Because of me?" His laugh sounded like a forced
bark. "I didn't force feed her all that ice cream. Just
because she has no will power—"

"Will power?" she screeched. "This wasn't her fault.
It was all stress induced."

"Yeah, stress induced by your crazy family." He
jabbed an accusing cream-cheesy finger at her.

"We're crazy? We're crazy!?" Her eyes bulged. "I'll show you crazy!"

She grabbed the engraved cake knife from the tray while Mr. Wells scooped a chunk from the next tier of cake and balled it up in his hands.

Zoe lunged between them. "Whoa! Whoa! That's enough."

They froze at the tone in her voice, eyes darting from their enemy to Zoe and back again. Neither seemed ready to be the first to lay down their weapon and yield.

Levi hovered close by, but stayed out of it. Maybe because he was afraid of Zoe too. Or maybe because he knew what was good for him, she thought.

"This day is not about you or how much you hate each other." Zoe's sharp gaze darted between the two of them. "This day is about your children and their happiness. So if you aren't willing to support them or be quiet witnesses of their love and happiness today, then you can leave."

Mrs. Fisher still glared, looking scarily like her daughter when she was mad—which was all the time. Her knuckles turned white as her grip on the knife tightened.

"And if you don't leave. I'll call the cops," Zoe added. "Now give me the knife." Zoe held out her hand.

Mrs. Fisher seemed to come to her senses and stared down in surprise, like the hand still clenching the knife belonged to someone else. After a moment, her fist relaxed and she passed the two-hundred-dollar cake knife to Zoe.

Zoe took a deep breath as she set it aside. Another potential crisis averted. She turned to Mr. Wells. "Now you go wash up. The bride is about to walk down the aisle in exactly"—she checked her watch—"seventeen minutes."

"Cake!" the flower girl cried.

Zoe spun in time to watch the girl ram a fist into the bottom layer of the cake. She pulled out a clump to shove in her face, effectively destroying what was left of the red velvet monstrosity.

Levi stared at the ruins. "Maybe you can still save it. You could, like, put a flower here." He pointed. "And here. And here." He swiped a finger over the icing and licked it off. "If it's any consolation, it tastes great."

Sighing, Zoe pulled out her phone to scroll through her list of cake bakers. When she found one, she sent Natalie a text to order an emergency replacement cake from Gimme Some Sugar Shop.

"Mrs. Fisher, can you please take the flower girl and get her cleaned up and to the doors ASAP?"

The MOB nodded and began to herd the sticky girl with two fists full of cake out of the kitchen. Before the doors shut behind them, Zoe remembered to yell out, "And keep her away from those birds!"

Zoe checked her watch again, but Levi placed a hand over it before she could see. "Don't worry. It will all work itself out."

"Work itself out?" She gaped at him. "Things don't just work themselves out because you want them to. Things will work out because I make sure they do. I have everything under control. I am in complete control," she said, as though to convince herself.

Without thinking, her hand found its way into her bridal utility bag. As her fingers brushed fur, her shoulders relaxed. When Levi began staring at her a little strangely, she pulled her hand out, afraid he'd discover her secret. But he continued to give her a funny look. Something between amusement and, well, she wasn't sure what.

His hand rose to her face, and she flinched away. She

hadn't realized she'd taken a step until her back hit the refrigerator.

"What are you doing?" she demanded.

He chuckled but closed the gap between them. Pressing herself against the fridge, she recoiled as his hand caressed her cheek. She felt his thumb gently brush her skin. It was a little rough, but his touch was warm and gentle.

When he pulled away, her eyes fluttered open. She wasn't sure when she'd closed them.

Belatedly, she slapped his hand away. "What do you think you're doing?"

He showed her his thumb. It was white with cream cheese icing. "You still had cake on your face."

His smiling eyes held hers as he sucked the icing off. Her gaze fell to his lips as he did it, watching the way his mouth moved around his thumb. The thumb that had been touching her a moment before. She stared at him as though he was licking the icing right off her body.

"You didn't think I was going to kiss you, did you?" He looked a little incredulous.

"What? No." Actually, she didn't know what she'd thought. They'd met only fifteen minutes before, and he was already touching her face. Well, she supposed she touched him first. In fact, she'd sort of groomed him. But that was different.

Levi hadn't backed off yet. "I've never seen someone so afraid of a kiss before."

She scowled at him. "I didn't think you were going to kiss me. And I'm not afraid." Then why was she shaking, she wondered.

Zoe may have been celibate, but it wasn't like she didn't touch people at all. She hugged her friends and her mom, shook hands with strangers. Pigs in bars thought slapping her ass was a reasonable substitute for a cheeky pickup line. Hell, she touched herself all the time. So what did it matter if he touched her cheek?

Levi was still standing so close, and she couldn't stop staring at his lips now. Mentally shaking herself, she pushed him away. That's when she caught sight of her watch.

She gasped. "Crap. We've only got fourteen minutes to get you ready."

"Well then, you'd better stop trying to make out with me."

"I'm not . . ." She sighed. Could he be any more exasperating? "I wouldn't kiss you."

"Really?" His eyebrows shot up. "Challenge accepted."

Rolling her eyes, she spun and headed for the sanctuary. She couldn't bring herself to turn around to see if he was following, in case he mistook her flushed cheeks as an invitation of sorts. Which it wasn't. She was simply stressed. And as the day went on, the church only seemed to absorb the afternoon heat. That was it. She was just hot. And *not* for Levi.

"You seem to have a pretty good handle on things," he said. He waltzed along beside her through the shortcut to the foyer, as though they were having a casual conversation, not trying to make a wedding happen in less than fourteen minutes.

"That's because I don't just let things work themselves out," she said, taking the next corner in the hallway as fast as she could without running. "That's what a good event planner does."

"So you don't just do weddings? What other kinds of things do you plan?"

"Anything really," she said distractedly, running over

the list once more in her mind. "I even throw Pure Pleasure Parties on the side to sell products."

"What kinds of products are those?" he asked.

"Sex toys."

His footsteps faltered, and she glanced back to watch him find his footing. She grinned to herself, happy that she could catch *him* off-guard for a change.

"Sex toy parties?" His cheeks were slightly pink, but he was grinning, his eyes practically twinkling with curiosity.

"If it's a party, I'm there," she said. "I plan it all. But as of next weekend, I think I'll be doing mostly weddings."

"Why's that?"

"The Wedding Expo is next weekend. It's the best place to promote your business for the upcoming season. I hear you walk away from that event with more clients than you know what to do with." And more than enough money for her down payment, she thought.

"Maybe I should try it out. I'm in the entertainment business." He slipped his phone out of his pocket, typing away as they neared the nave.

"You can't just 'try it out,'" she said. "This kind of thing takes planning. I've been preparing for months. Advertisements, promotional material, pitches—"

"There," he said. "I'm all signed up."

She came to a stop so fast that he ran into the back of her. "You're what?"

He showed her his phone. A message flashed across the screen: *Thank you for your participation.* "I've booked a booth at the expo."

She gaped at him. Was this guy trying to get on her last nerve? Her emotional bottle was going to need extra emptying that night.

Shaking her head, she ducked through the doors and into the nave. Most of the guests had already been seated. The priest was waiting front and center, coughing into the sleeve of his vestment. In the corner, the organ player stretched her arthritic fingers to stay limber for her big moment. Zoe vaguely wondered if she was the same organ player that performed the wedding march at Juliet's parents' wedding.

They skirted around the outside of the nave, past the pews jammed with hot guests waving the decorative fans Zoe had picked up earlier. Bright colors flashed as the folded paper moved back and forth in front of their flushed faces, wafting the muggy air around.

Reverently, Zoe snuck through the sanctuary, leading Levi to the vestry where the groom and his groomsmen were waiting to take their places at the front.

She knocked softly on the door and waited for an answer. A moment later, which seemed like forever with eleven minutes to go, the best man opened the door and she entered the small room. She waved Levi inside.

After greeting Levi, the groom and his six groomsmen resumed their positions in a quiet circle. Despite the row of stained glass windows casting bright, cheerful colors on them, the scene was a grim one. They all wore expressions as though this were a funeral and not a wedding.

Zoe honed in on the groom, Owen. The rest of the party may have been somber, but he looked like he was supposed to. Like this was the best day of his life.

She approached him, automatically straightening his bow tie. "How are you feeling? Are you ready?"

"Absolutely." He beamed. "I can't wait for us to be husband and wife."

She took in the euphoric look on his face and before she could stop herself, she asked, "Are you sure?"

Zoe clamped her lips shut, but it was too late. Since she'd begun wedding planning four years ago, she'd never asked a bride or groom anything like that. It appalled her that the words had slipped out. But out of the corner of her eye, she caught the groomsmen sharing a look, and she knew she wasn't the first person to ask the question.

She wasn't sure how she expected Owen to respond. Maybe with offense or indignation at her audacity. The look on his face changed slightly, but he was still smiling.

"Yes," he said. "I love her. And I'm ready to spend the rest of my life with her."

Zoe breathed a sigh of relief. "Good because she's just about ready for you." She patted him on the shoulder like a coach before the big game. "You don't want to keep her waiting." She clapped her hands. "All right, gentlemen. Take your places."

As they filtered out, she grabbed a tux from a hook on the back of the door. She thrust it at Levi. "Here. Hurry. You've only got six minutes."

"Can do." Reaching for the hem of his shirt, he pulled it over his head.

She blinked, and her eyes grew wide. Maybe the guy wasn't as much of a slacker as she thought, because he must have worked hard to get a body like that.

He grinned at her, but she was done letting him put her off her game. She tucked that mental image away for later that night and kept a straight face as she asked, "What are you doing?"

"You said to hurry. You can stay for the rest, if you'd like." He winked. "It only gets better."

Zoe snorted, making a show of her so-not-impressed reaction, but she could feel the heat running its fingers up her neck. Make that down her stomach to between her thighs.

Okay, so she was impressed, but she hid it beneath her composed mask and held his eyes as though there was nothing out of the ordinary. "If I thought there was much to see, I'd stick around for the show."

He cringed and his lips formed an "o" like he was in pain, but then he winked and reached for his fly.

There was a knock on the door, and Zoe turned reluctantly. It had been a long time since she got to see "the rest" in person. Six years to be exact. Vibrators just weren't the same.

Natalie poked her head inside. "Sorry to interrupt, but—" She hesitated. Her eyes focused past Zoe, probably wondering what exactly she'd interrupted.

"Oh God. What now?" Zoe asked.

After tearing her eyes away from Levi—with difficulty—Natalie pulled a face. "We're down an organ player."

"What? She was just there. I saw her." Zoe whipped open the door and peeked over at the organ as though she didn't believe Natalie. But because that was just the kind of day she was having, the elderly organ player was missing.

"What happened to her?" she asked.

"She's in the bathroom throwing up."

"Great. Awesome." Zoe took another deep breath and tried to remain positive. "I need to find an organ player. I can do that. No problem."

Her fingers itched, craving the touch of Pretty Puppy. Resisting a grope in her fanny pack, she turned back to Levi and suddenly had to fight the urge to grope something else, because he was wearing nothing but a dress shirt, staring down at the ends of the bow tie around his neck.

Zoe cleared her throat, trying to keep her eyes on his face. "Need help with that?" she asked casually.

"Depends on what you're referring to." His sleepy eyes narrowed as he gave her a wicked grin. "But actually, I might be able to help you."

Zoe couldn't help but glance down this time. The length of his shirt hid anything important, but by the way the fabric bulged at the front, she thought he'd be an excellent help. Forget carrying an emergency Fuzzy Friend around for support. She should have brought an emergency dildo.

Her eyes only lingered a second—okay, maybe two—before refocusing on his face. "And how can you help me?" Her voice became thick, layered with the double meaning.

And his response was the same. "I can play your organ."

There was just something about his voice. Maybe it was the timbre, the warm rumble, but it made her insides melt. God, the material this guy was giving her for later. That is, until his actual meaning hit her. She shook her head, clearing her one-tracked mind.

This time, Zoe's shock broke through her mask. "You play the organ?"

"Well, I don't know about an organ, but I play the piano. It shouldn't be too much of a leap."

Her heart which had risen at first, sank a little. "Oh, well, I don't really think it's that easy."

He shrugged, but smiled like he was being all heroic or something. "No big deal. I'll give it a shot."

She scoffed, but tried to remain patient, with only two minutes, no . . . make that one minute and fifty-nine seconds to go . . . fifty-eight . . . Her eyebrows rose a fraction. "No big deal? A shot?"

"Sure." That smile, that way-too-adorable smile, brightened just a little more like the angels in that stained glass were shining down on him.

He was still struggling with the bow tie. Sighing, she began to arrange it with practiced fingers. "No offense, but the bride's grand entrance hinges on you giving it 'a shot.' It actually is kind of a big deal."

Now that they were close, she realized how tall he was. Despite her Japanese genetics, she was five-foot-eleven, and Levi had a good half-foot on her, even with her heels on.

She loved a tall man. It meant that she had to tilt her face up to kiss him rather than down. Plus, it was far better for other things, like spooning—or more important, sixty-nine. At least, that's the kind of information she'd give clients during her sexucation talks. It's not like the fact that he wasn't wearing any pants was making her think that or anything. And certainly not at a time like this.

He slipped on his pants and as he tucked in his long dress shirt—and *himself*—she realized he'd been in so much of a hurry that morning that he'd forgotten to put on underwear too. She hadn't been that close to a wiener since Buddy died.

She gave Natalie a look, but her assistant just stared at her, as though waiting for instructions. Zoe gave her a wave, and she scurried off. With a final tweak of the bow tie, Zoe stood back like everything was perfectly normal, and handed him his vest.

"Relax," he told her. "Life's too short to stress about the little things." He shrugged himself into the vest, buttoning it up. "I'll go jump on the organ now to practice. It will all work out." He started to leave.

Relax? The little things? This was so not "little." Zoe stared after him. Did he think he was simply going to jump on the organ and give it a whirl? Yup, he was opening the door. Now he was headed for the unmanned organ.

Feeling the seconds tick by and her anxiety level rising, she stormed after him. She laughed incredulously, but kept her voice low as they passed through the sanctuary. "Look. I'm sure someone else here knows how to play. I'm not about to leave something this important up to chance."

"It's not chance," he said. "I'm a musician. I'll just wing it."

" 'Wing—' " Zoe closed her eyes and pinched the bridge of her nose. When she opened them again, he was already seated on the organ bench.

Marching over, she grabbed his arm—his surprisingly toned arm. "Okay, enough playing around. We've only got . . . one minute before go-time."

He gazed up at her pleasantly. "Well, then I guess you'd better *go*."

She scowled down at him. Oh, this was so not part of the plan. So far, she'd averted every crisis that day had thrown at her, kept everything going perfectly to schedule. She'd met every challenge head on. But this guy was more than a challenge with his "just go with the flow" attitude.

Hesitantly, Levi tried a couple of keys. It sounded like a cat walking across the organ. Zoe flinched.

"You'd better hurry," he said. "You only have fifty more seconds to go." He grinned up at her.

God, how she wanted to wrap the *Congratulations* banner around his neck at that moment. And yet she knew that cocky look was going to be starring in her silicone-induced fantasies later that night.

She checked her watch again. He was right. She supposed there was no helping it. Levi was going to play the organ.

Gritting her teeth, Zoe spun on her heel to go search for her bride, wincing with each incorrect note he played as he tried to "wing" it.

She remembered at the last minute to toss the priest a pack of cough drops and headed to the foyer where she found Juliet and her entourage already making their way through the hall. Makeup back in place, hair artfully re-arranged, Juliet looked like a picture-perfect bride, smile and all.

"Oh. You look wonderful," Zoe said. And this time she meant it. "Are you ready?"

Juliet squealed in excitement. It appeared as though she'd done a complete one-eighty since she'd last seen her. "Yes."

Zoe didn't have to ask if she was sure about her groom. She'd be crazy to not want to marry a man as patient and understanding—and maybe slightly oblivious—as Owen.

"Good," Zoe said. "He's already waiting for you. Let's go."

Juliet nodded and took her place at the end of the pro-cession line next to her father.

Zoe leaned close to Natalie. "Nice job on the makeup, by the way."

"All the fires put out?" Natalie asked.

"Not out, just maintained. Make sure the doves are outside the front steps for the end. Oh, and we need that new cake for the reception."

"I'm all over it."

A quick scan of those gathered outside the doors told Zoe the devil flower girl had made a break for it again. She was probably bouncing off the walls somewhere from all the sugar. But at least they still had Juliet's other niece to sprinkle rose petals.

The bridesmaids lined up like a rainbow outside the doors, and Zoe raised her watch to check it one last time just as it struck one o'clock on the dot. Poking her head into the nave, she glared at the blue bow tied groomsman sitting at the organ.

Levi was just hanging out, staring off into space. Didn't he know how critical this was? Or was everything "no big deal" to him?

Zoe waved her hand back and forth furiously before he finally noticed her and waved back. She moved her hand in a circular motion, trying to cue him to begin. He gave her a thumbs-up and raised his hands above the keys.

She resisted the urge to stick her fingers in her ears as she held her breath for the first note. But when his fingers hit those keys, it actually sounded in tune. And as they drifted over the organ, it formed a real song. *Canon in D,* she realized. Levi was playing a classical song. *How does one simply "wing" Pachelbel?*

Zoe watched in amazement. People didn't often catch her off-guard, but Levi certainly had. And that irritated the hell out of her. He was flaky, laid-back, unpredictable. She couldn't plan for unpredictable.

When heat began to rise above her blazer collar and over her cheeks, she realized the entire congregation had turned expectantly to her. There was a tap on her shoulder.

"Zoe." Natalie whispered behind her. "Zoe, we should begin."

"Oh right."

Jumping to action, Zoe opened the doors wide and backed out of the way.

She turned to the first person in line: the MOB. "Well, you're up first. Looks like everything is going well."

Mrs. Fisher smiled, her heavily eye-shadowed gaze fixed on Zoe's. "You'd better hope so."

Zoe's eye twitched, but she managed to ignore the implied threat. Stepping aside, she gestured for the woman to enter the nave. As she glided by at a measured pace, Zoe spotted a few pieces of red velvet cake clinging to her curls and smiled to herself.

All Zoe's hard work and planning came together in that moment. The parents marched first, followed by the bridesmaids who looked like a perfect rainbow arching down the aisle. The flower girl tossed her petals and Juliet's ring-bearing dog was actually bearing. Finally, the bride slipped her arm through her father's and she gave Zoe a nod.

The harmonious humming from the organ inside altered in an improvised segue into the traditional wedding march. Somehow Zoe didn't think her last-minute pianist just winged that either. But she didn't have time to think about that as she signaled the bride forward.

The room was hushed as Juliet made her way toward her future husband. Suddenly, the cake wouldn't matter, the horse was going to be a minor hiccup—she hoped—and the dress was forgotten. Because all the bride and groom could see in that moment was their partner. Their focus was on each other, where it should be. Not on the details.

And that's why Zoe did what she did. For that moment when everything came together and the bride and groom's day was suddenly perfect. She took satisfaction in knowing she helped give them the day she never got. Because no one should have to go through what she did. Not on what was supposed to be the best day of their life.

Zoe snuck in and quietly sat down in the back row. She preferred to be present during the ceremony in case anything went awry. Over the years, she'd had a fainting pastor, a narcoleptic photographer, and a father of the bride with a heart attack. By now she was prepared for practically anything a wedding day could throw at her. She'd developed some pretty mean photo and video skills and had taken advanced CPR and first-aid training. Hell, she'd even been ordained—just in case.

She sat back and listened to the priest recite the

same old routine that she'd heard a thousand times. By the time they got to the end, she began to think this disaster might actually work out. And not because things just magically worked out on their own, like Levi Dolson believed. It was thanks to Zoe being on top of her game. She was an expert, after all.

Zoe waited for the end of the ceremony with anticipation, and it wasn't because she was moved by the union, but because that's when her busy afternoon picked up again.

She zoned out for a few seconds, already running through the to-do list in her head. By the time she tuned back in, the groom stepped forward, Zoe thought to kiss the bride. Then she looked to the front. It wasn't the groom. It was the best man.

Confusion rippled throughout the room among both the congregation and the wedding party. The priest glanced between the bride and groom. Juliet and Owen shared a look.

Finally, the best man spoke, and because there was dead silence, it was clear as a wedding bell even to Zoe in the far back.

"I object."

There was a chorus of gasps and held breaths from around the room.

Oh, shit, thought Zoe.

She'd been so worried about every little detail that could destroy Juliet and Owen's special day that she'd never considered this possibility. It had never happened before. Usually all the objections were made by this point. And they had been—yet Owen was still determined to go through with it.

Her whole body tensed with the instinct to sprint up there and tackle the best man. Her job was to give the couple a perfect day, to sort out any issues, iron out the kinks. But this was one problem she couldn't fix. One problem that had nothing to do with the wedding planner.

The best man took a deep breath. "I'm in love with Juliet."

It was as though time had stopped. The priest looked confused, the bride shocked, the groom furious. As Juliet opened her mouth to respond, the double doors burst open. Everyone turned in the pews to watch as Juliet's uncle stumbled in.

His glazed eyes cast over the room before he yelled out, "Congratulations!" He raised one of the bottles meant for the wedding party table and took a deep swig.

Juliet began to cry, a full-on ugly cry. The groom seemed torn between comforting her and punching the best man's lights out. But whatever he was saying to Juliet was drowned out as the FOG and the MOB picked up where they left off in the kitchen. Their screams could be heard echoing through the cloisters and above the church bells that rang at the exact time the ceremony was *supposed* to finish.

The guests twisted and turned in their seats, their surprise and gossip a hum of constant noise that set Zoe's teeth on edge. She jumped to her feet, not even sure what she could possibly do other than usher people outside or call the police to prevent a murder.

As she pressed her way into the aisle, she watched the MIA flower girl scamper through the open doors and down the aisle screaming "Hell!" The flock of remaining doves released from their cages flew by her like she was the profane pied piper of birds.

The flower girl's timing couldn't have been better, Zoe thought numbly, because as the bride came sprinting down the aisle past Zoe, the groom hot on her heels, she realized that the wedding was, in fact, over.

One dove flew over Zoe's head and up to a chandelier,

it's poorly timed evacuation landing squarely on Mrs. Fisher's feathered fascinator—maybe in an animal-cruelty protest, of sorts. Excited by all the commotion, the ring bearer began humping a guest's fake-fur purse.

Zoe stared at the chaos in disbelief. How the hell did this happen? More important, how was she going to fix this?

Reaching into her fanny pack, she found her fuzzy strength. With a deep breath, she gathered her wits and began to make a mental list.

Tie up the dog
Shoo the birds out
Stuff cake into the cussing flower girl's mouth
Kick the best man in the balls
Coax the bride back in front of the priest

While on her way up the aisle to grab the dog's leash, Zoe noticed people starting to leave, probably because the doves were still lingering dangerously overhead. She held her hands up and addressed the congregation as a whole.

"Don't worry everyone!" she yelled in the most confident voice she could muster. "This is just a little hiccup. Please remain seated, and we'll be underway again in no time!"

But Juliet's partially deaf grandmother obviously never heard her because she shuffled out of the aisle, bumping into Zoe. Her cane crunched down on Zoe's foot.

Yelping, she leapt aside, hopping on one foot. She bumped into another guest. When she turned around, she found herself face of face with Levi.

"Well, I'm glad I didn't sleep through this wedding," he said like he was making casual conversation. "How can I help?"

The last thing she needed right then was a guy who thought this was all *no big deal*. "Just stand up at the front and be ready for a wedding." She began dragging the overexcited golden retriever down the aisle.

"Zoe!" he called over the crowd. "Are you sure?"

"I've got this," she said. "I have a plan!" But just as she was wrangling the dog out the doors with the promise of treats, she saw the bride racing through the church's front doors to wave down a cab.

Zoe ran after her, calling out, "Juliet! Come back!"

But she couldn't be heard over the loud *hee-haw* that blurted from the sidewalk. A man in a sombrero blocked her path down the steps. He yelled into the church doors like he was delivering pizza to a college rec room.

"I have a donkey here for a Zoe Plum!"

Zoe gaped at the donkey chewing on the shabby chic sign directing wedding guests into the church. It also wore an oversized sombrero and poncho. "Horse, Natalie. I said horse," she muttered under her breath. Smelly donkey just didn't have the same romantic feel while riding into the sunset.

"Hee-haw!" it said.

If only Zoe could talk to Juliet. The day might still be saved. So it didn't go as planned. So what? It was about the end result, right? No big deal?

But before she could push past the donkey, the cab's tires squealed. Burning rubber, it sped off.

Owen chased after it, his dress shoes clicking on the pavement. The train of Juliet's dress, which was shut in the door, dragged along Bush Street behind it, flapping in the wind.

Zoe watched in disbelief. How could things have gone so wrong so fast? She thought she'd been prepared for everything that could go wrong. She just never expected for *everything* to go wrong at the exact same time. How was it even possible?

She sensed someone come up beside her. For a moment, she expected Natalie or maybe even Levi. But the smell of bourbon and coffee invaded her nostrils before she even turned around.

A wobbly Uncle Wally raised his bottle of wine at the retreating cab. "You win some, you lose some." Then he bent over and vomited on her rose topiary.

3

Dog and Pony Show

Welcome to the Wedding Expo! The giant letters scrolled across the digital sign above the Hilton Hotel. The thrill of it had Zoe gripping her wheel in excitement as she pulled her van into the underground parking lot. Keeping an eye out for a free space, she wound farther and farther down. There were already so many vehicles there, which meant so many potential customers.

When she finally found a free space, she pulled in and parked. But she still hadn't seen her assistant's bright yellow car anywhere.

Grabbing her phone, she texted Natalie.

Just arrived at the expo. Are you here?

Normally, Zoe wouldn't have been worried, but Natalie had grown increasingly distracted over the last few weeks, letting things slip, being tardy, making personal phone calls while on the clock. Whipping out her tablet, she brought up her to-do list for the week and made a note to speak to Natalie about her recent performance. Zoe liked the girl, but business was business.

She leaned back in her seat and waited for a response, mentally going through her current to-do list. The song on the radio came to an end, replaced by the news on the hour.

"Our top story today, the San Fran Slayer has struck again. Last night at approximately eight-thirty P.M., an up-and-coming local jewelry designer was found stabbed to death in her shop. Police say the murder occurred just before the shop was to close for the day. Anyone with information about the crime is asked to call the police. In other news . . ."

Zoe frowned as she turned down the radio. The serial killer had been on a killing spree for a couple of years now. The lead investigator on the case was Bob, the boyfriend of the Dachshund Rescue Center's manager. While he didn't let on much about the case, Zoe knew how the Slayer was keeping the precinct busy. The whole country was watching.

She checked her phone again, but there was still no response from Natalie. There was, however, a text from her seamstress saying her bride's Marchesa wedding gown was ready. She replied, telling her she'd have Natalie pick it up that day, because she was as excited to see it as the bride was. This wasn't just any dress. It wasn't just any bride. It was her best friend, Piper Summers.

She cc'd Natalie on it and hit *send*. Sighing, she resigned herself to setting up the booth on her own and got out. A blushing bride beamed at her from the ad on the side of her van, about to throw her bouquet.

While her sex toy sales were good, there was big money in the wedding business. Since it paid more bills, she promoted her event-planning services more than her pleasure services. That, and because she thought a giant bride throwing a bouquet was more appropriate on the side of her van than a strap-on. Although, much less fun.

Loading up with supplies, she slung a bag of pamphlets and fabric samples over her shoulder before pulling out two mannequins dressed as a bride and groom. She set them on their feet and gave them the once over. They looked as ready as any couple would before walking down the aisle. In fact, she'd looked exactly like that on her wedding day, since it was her dress and veil the blonde mannequin wore.

Zoe stared down at her beautiful bride, at the tulle ball gown with the scalloped lace edging and bateau neckline. It had seemed a shame to throw it out after it had never even made it down the aisle. Or to burn it like she'd originally wanted to. Or to track down the missing groom, strangle him with it and set them both on fire.

Slipping the groom's top hat onto her head so it wouldn't end up on the ground, she grabbed a mannequin under each arm and headed for the elevator.

Potential customers liked visuals. They didn't want to hear about what Zoe could do for them as a wedding planner. They wanted to see it, to imagine themselves walking down that aisle under her care and guidance. She wanted them to be able to visualize their wedding day, to touch it, to smell it.

She'd prepared bouquets, place settings, photo albums, centerpieces, and other decor. She had everything, right down to two silver chairs with cute signs that said *Bride* and *Groom*. Her booth was going to be a miniature version of the big day.

It was certainly going to be better than Levi Dolson's booth. He probably wouldn't even have a sign, or business cards, for that matter. But the expo was so big, spanning over twenty different rooms in the conference center. There was a good chance she wouldn't even run into him.

She hadn't seen the pianist turned organ player since Juliet ran away from her wedding the weekend before. She'd lost him in the chaos after the ceremony fell apart. By the time the feathers had cleared, all that remained was a big mess to clean up. Zoe still couldn't understand how it all went so wrong.

But the expo was going to be a fresh start for her. The Fisher-Wells wedding was behind her now, and she had to focus on booking new clients to make up for the lost commission. She'd even had to cancel her appointment with the real-estate agent indefinitely until she could replace the funds.

The lobby was already choked with people, expo guests, she realized once she started reading the passes on the lanyards around their necks. They were already lined up at the doors, hoping for the early-bird specials, the best deals, the yummiest baked giveaways. As she shuffled through the excited throng, they eyed her bag of samples greedily.

She approached the guest services desk and dinged the bell. Or rather, the groom mannequin did, since her hands were full.

A moment later, a clerk slid behind the desk. "Yes, may I help you"—he hesitated as his eyes passed over Zoe—"three?"

"Good morning," she said. "It's my first year running a booth at the expo. Can you tell me where can I find the Grand Ballroom?"

"Oh, that's an excellent location for the expo." He took out a map of the conference center. "A very high traffic area."

"Apparently they reserve certain prime locations for up-and-comers, to help newbies build their business." Zoe could already feel the sweat starting to form on her brow from the weight of her supplies, but she couldn't help but gush. She was so hopeful this weekend's event was going to put her business over the top.

Zoe didn't consider herself a newbie, by any means, but she'd only been an official business for a few years now. Before that, her event planning was just a side thing she did for friends' parties and weddings. It was one of those rare instances that people complimented and celebrated her OCD tendencies instead of rolling their eyes. So in the end, she decided to put her blunt opinions to use and get paid for being OCD.

"What kind of business do you own?" the clerk asked politely as he took out a pen and a map of the facilities.

"I'm a wedding planner," she said.

"Excuse me," a girl nearby interrupted. "Sorry, but I couldn't help overhear. My name is Jessica, and this is Cole." She laid her hand on the chest of a young man next to her. "We're getting married."

The sparkling princess cut set in white gold made that obvious enough. But the way she'd said it, kind of nervously, made Zoe think they were only recently engaged and still getting used to the idea themselves. The girl gazed up at her fiancé like he was the only man on earth.

Zoe could remember looking that way once. Thinking there was only one man for her. What a joke that turned out to be. But that didn't mean she couldn't understand what it meant to her clients, that she couldn't put herself in their shoes.

It was her job to help them through the next several months of the lovey-dovey crap, before reality set in, before the harsh truth, the heartbreak. If they made it that far. Hell, she didn't even make it down the aisle before her world fell out from under her.

Shaking off her negativity, she smiled warmly at the couple, letting their joy infuse her with the ambition to take on whatever their hearts desired. "Congratulations. That's exciting."

"We were thinking of hiring a wedding planner," Jessica said.

Before Zoe could open her mouth to respond with some sales pitch, someone nearby cut in. "Then the last thing you want to do is hire Zoe Plum to organize your wedding. Or you might not get married at all."

The doe-eyed look left the bride-to-be's eyes. She turned and blinked at the newcomer. When Zoe saw who it was, the hinged joints of her mannequins squeaked as she held them closer in a supportive group hug.

"Juliet. What are you doing here?" she asked between clenched teeth.

The ex-bride's hair was a tangle of curls and grease, almost as though she hadn't washed it since her wedding day. In fact, she probably hadn't, since Zoe noticed she was still wearing her wedding jewelry—although, she was missing one teardrop earring.

"I'm just trying to prevent people from making the same mistake I did in hiring you." Dark circles ringed her eyes, but they were also puffy from crying. When she narrowed them hatefully, it looked as though she'd been punched in the face and she was sporting two black eyes.

Zoe took a deep breath, maintaining an air of complete professionalism, despite the silly top hat. "I'm sorry you were unhappy with how your wedding day turned out, but—"

"Wedding? You call that a wedding?" she screeched. "It was a circus. And you were the ring leader."

Zoe pressed her lips together to stop herself from saying that Juliet had been the clown. "I know things didn't turn out the way you wanted them to, but sometimes we need to be more flexible as in the case with, well . . . many of your requests."

"It was your job to make my dreams come true!" She jabbed a finger at her, nail bitten to the quick.

"No," Zoe said calmly. "It was my job to give you the wedding you asked for. And I did my job."

"Then why aren't I married!?" Grabbing a vase of flowers off the front desk, she raised it above her head and threw it on the ground.

The vase smashed at their feet. Glass scattered over Zoe's heels. Water sprayed Jessica, and she inched closer to her fiancé, but both of them seemed too shocked to move. If all the potential clients waiting for the expo to start hadn't noticed the confrontation before, they all turned their way now.

Juliet stood there shaking, stray wisps of hair falling around her face like Medusa. She let out a frustrated scream like a three-year-old having a tantrum. It sounded hoarse, like she'd been up drinking ever since the ill-fated day. Hell, maybe she had been. It certainly didn't seem like she'd gotten much sleep since.

Zoe noticed the clerk casually pick up the phone and press a button. He murmured into the mouthpiece, but one word was clear enough. ". . . security . . ."

Juliet seemed to hear it too. "Good. Call security!" she yelled. "Zoe doesn't even belong here. She spouts nothing but false advertising."

The young couple shifted uncomfortably, backing away from the scene. "Maybe we should go," Jessica said.

Zoe held up her hands. "No. Please. It wasn't how she's making it sound."

"It's true." Juliet scowled. "I didn't get married that day because of *you*."

Zoe had had enough of Juliet, of her demands, of her accusations, of her crappy treatment for over a year. She wasn't under contract anymore. It wasn't her job to keep her happy or sugarcoat things.

As she took a step forward, she thought that she could have really used a Fuzzy Friend right about then, but her arms were full with her bride and groom. So instead, she hugged them for support and drew on her years of practice maintaining her cool, of stuffing her unwanted emotions into her inner Zen bottle.

She stared down the bridezilla. "Because of me, you got everything you asked for. Every ridiculous, over-the-top demand. I bent over backwards for you. I did everything I could to get you down that aisle. All you had to do was say 'I do.'"

At some point, she hadn't noticed when, the young couple had slipped away and disappeared into the crowd. The onlookers gathered closer and closer out of curiosity and some even in mild horror.

Maybe it was the appearance of the distraught bride, still partially dressed from her wedding day in her jewelry and shoes, frozen in the moment that every bride fears might happen: the moment it all falls apart. By the glares that Zoe could feel fix on her, the crowd had naturally sided with the bride.

Whatever Juliet's reasons were for running away from that day, from her fiancé, Zoe couldn't begin to guess. Well, maybe it had something to do with guilt over whatever was going on with the best man, but that was none of her business. However, the situation had brought back memories of her own wedding day, of being left at the altar.

By running away, Juliet had done to Owen what Sean, her ex-fiancé, had done to Zoe all those years ago. And because of that, she just couldn't seem to find any sympathy for her. The girl obviously had some issues to work through, but she needed to work through them somewhere else.

Zoe sighed, hoping security would get there soon. "It

wasn't me who prevented you from getting married. You didn't get married because of *you*."

Juliet's chin quivered, but her eyes narrowed with fury. "How could I possibly say yes when I was so upset about the mess you caused?" She pulled an already-used tissue from her pocket and blew her nose. "I should sue you."

"Sue me for what? Out of courtesy, I waived my own fees." Which was more than she deserved after the way she'd treated Zoe.

"I'll sue for the cost of the wedding. Not to mention emotional damage."

Oh, you were damaged long before I came along, she nearly said aloud, but managed to bite her tongue to avoid further inflaming the situation.

"Is there a problem here?" A man's voice cut in. The crowd parted to reveal a rather beefy security guard for such a happy event. Zoe vaguely wondered how often wedding expos got out of hand.

"Yes. This woman is making a scene and running my customers off." Zoe pointed out Juliet, but by her appearance, it was obvious who the crazy person was.

The security guard crossed his arms, but considering the difference between Juliet and the beefy man, he didn't need to turn on the intimidation. "If this is true, ma'am, I'll have to ask you to leave."

"The problem isn't with me," Juliet told him, yet her very appearance said otherwise. Her voice began to rise, just in case the people on the other side of the lobby hadn't heard the commotion yet. "I came to warn everyone here that hiring this Zoe Plum as your wedding planner is the worst decision you'll ever make!"

"All right. Let's go," the guard said.

But Juliet wasn't going to go that easily. After a couple of attempts at avoiding capture, she obviously realized she wasn't going to win that battle. She gave Zoe a look that said, *This isn't over* before rag-dolling.

The security guard barely caught her before she hit the tiles, then proceeded to drag her out, dirty silk bridal shoes scraping along the floor. A couple hundred eyes watched her go, pity clear in their owner's expressions. Once the hotel lobby doors shut and Juliet's screams were muffled, their attention swiveled back to Zoe.

She pulled her top hat down ever so slightly and tried to ignore them as she reached for the clerk's facility map with the instructions. "You know, it didn't really happen like that."

The clerk's expression was cool as he passed her the map. "Good luck," he said like she was going to need it.

"Thank you." She tipped her head in thanks, the top hat dipping.

Raising her chin high, she headed back to the elevators in search of her booth and her dignity. So much for the Fisher-Wells wedding being behind her.

Zoe followed the map, making her way down a couple of levels, past rooms lined with eager vendors and wedding-circuit professionals. There was table after table offering all sorts of services.

She took note of a few stalls beginning to set up that she would have to visit later in the day, like handmade decor suppliers, and allergen-free flower alternatives. And she was definitely interested in listening in on a few panel discussions that were advertised on shabby chic sandwich boards everywhere. Such as *Wedding Traditions: Obligation or Obsolete?*

As early in the morning as it was, she was already dodging people, people just like her, rushing to get ready for the big weekend. There was an excited tension in the air. It was in the way people scrambled around their tables or lugged supplies back and forth, hoping for what every other business owner hopes for: success.

For Zoe, she hoped to finally show her mother that she was just fine on her own. To finally prove her wrong. Her own business, her own money, and, soon, her own home. Once she saw her name on that mortgage agreement, she'd have everything she needed in life. As much as her mother believed Zoe needed a man, she felt satisfied, complete, all on her own.

To Zoe's American born-and-raised mind, it was insane that anyone would still believe in such old-school ideals. Despite living in the United States for over thirty years, her mother's traditional Japanese beliefs were as ingrained in her as a thread in a *zanshi* weaving. Zoe wasn't sure she'd ever find common ground with her.

Finally, Zoe reached the Grand Ballroom. She passed through the double doors, beneath a thick arch of dripping lilacs that greeted guests with a fresh, powerfully romantic scent.

Her footsteps were softened by a wide aisle runner that had been rolled across the length of the room so the expo guests would feel as though they were already walking down the aisle on their big day. She gripped her mannequins in an excited hug. It was certainly going to be *her* big day.

Down either side of the main aisle, stands with giant bouquets of flowers were placed every ten feet or so. Each one was a different arrangement created by a variety of local florists showing off their talent. She assessed each one with appreciation as she headed for the middle of the room where her information packet told her she'd be located.

A glittering behemoth of a chandelier dangled above her, casting her with a warm light, like the heavens were shining favorably upon her. This was it. She'd arrived. This was where her business would reach new heights.

She slowly made her way past each table. Her gaze flit around the unoccupied spaces, scanning the place cards for her own company's sign: Plum Crazy Events. But her excitement gradually turned to confusion. Her name was on none of the open stalls.

Zoe's arms were growing tired, and if Natalie didn't show up soon, she'd be racing to set up her booth all by herself. Not wanting to waste any more time searching, she turned to go find one of the expo volunteers for help.

As she took a step, there was a rustle under her foot. She glanced down to find something stuck to her shoe. She tried to shake it off, hopping in her heels with the bride and groom, but it wouldn't budge. It just made her look like she was dancing in some kind of three-person ho-down.

Shifting her partners in her arms, she tried to get a better look. It was a discarded place card. The tape had adhered itself to her black suede heels.

Using her bride's bedazzled shoes, she managed to pry it off. The paper fluttered to the plush aisle runner, landing face up. She read the typeset: *Zoe Plum. Plum Crazy Events.*

"What the hell?"

"Zoe?!" A shrill voice called out. "Is that you? Oh, my gosh, it's so good to see you."

Zoe turned to find a skinny brunette approaching her with a haughty look on her pinched face. It didn't help that her bun was gathered so tightly to the back of her head that it looked to be pulling the flesh from her skin— something Zoe had been tempted to do on more than one occasion.

"Hello, Chelsea," she said, like she'd just stepped in gum with her heels. "I wish I could say the same about you." She gave her a smile, the kind that would never be mistaken for a real one.

Zoe's bride and groom were getting heavier by the second, and the last thing she wanted was to waste time dealing with her rival—a term she used loosely.

Chelsea didn't have a hope in hell of ever being as good as her. "Rival" was more of a self-proclaimed title that Chelsea gave herself. Maybe because she was jealous of Zoe. Maybe because she secretly hoped to be like her. Or maybe because she just wanted to make Zoe's life miserable every time they ran into each other.

Chelsea's pinched face puckered as she took in Zoe's models. "I see you brought your friends along. But if you want to make it look like your booth is popular, I don't think these two will fool anyone. Because let's face it. You're not that popular." She chuckled at her own joke.

She waved a hand in the direction of her own booth. A garish banner hung over it, screaming *Enchanted Events* at anyone who passed by. The backdrop of sequined curtains dripped with glittering hearts and streamers, oozing cheesy high school dance romance.

"My booth, on the other hand, will be the talk of the expo," she said. "Customers will be lined up all the way to the lobby."

Zoe was only half listening to her babble. She was busy counting the tables, trying to remember the layout in her information pack. By her third time counting, there could be no doubt.

She spun on Chelsea. "This is supposed to be my booth."

Chelsea's penciled eyebrows shot up to her hairline. "Oh no. How embarrassing. Didn't anyone tell you? You've been relocated."

Zoe narrowed her eyes at the woman. "To where?"

"Oh, I don't know," she said, her voice infused with

sweet innocence. "Somewhere way, way, way over there in the back corner." She gestured in an ambiguous "over there" direction.

Zoe gritted her teeth. She should have expected Chelsea to pull something like this. But this was bold even for her. "Funny that I've supposedly been relocated and you just so happen to be the one taking my place."

"The event coordinator told me first thing this morning. I'm just being cooperative." Her eyelashes fluttered. "I guess they decided to give the better space to the better planner." She pointed to her chest, in case Zoe didn't know who she meant.

Zoe half-hoped she'd accidentally stab herself with one of her ridiculously pointy gel nails. She shifted the mannequins in her arms for a better hold and turned to head back to the main lobby. "Well, I'll just have to go find him. Straighten this all out."

"Oh, sure," Chelsea said, casually. "I'm sure it's just a simple mix up. Make sure to ask for James," she called to Zoe's back. "James Carruthers!"

Zoe's footsteps came to a halt as the last name sank in. "Carruthers? As in Chelsea Carruthers?"

"Yeah, that's right. As in my cousin. What a weird coincidence, right?" She laughed like they were two besties sharing a good joke. "But don't let that stop you. I'm sure he'll side with you over his favorite cousin."

Zoe kept her face straight, except for a sharp eyebrow arch, but her insides were strung tight. There was just something about Chelsea that ruffled her calm, orderly feathers.

Her arms tightened around her bride and broom until plastic squeaked in protest. But Zoe quickly pushed the annoyance back down, screwing the cap tight on that bottle-o-crazy.

Chelsea wasn't worth the effort—not that Zoe had the

time to spare for it, anyway. The doors opened to the public in an hour and she still had to find and set up her booth. She'd just have to win over her clients because she could offer them more talent and skill than Chelsea ever could. Besides, who could ignore her kick-ass display replete with a bride and groom?

"Oh, Zoe." Chelsea clicked her tongue as she took in the bride's wedding gown. *Zoe's* wedding gown. "The dress is a bit outdated, isn't it? You know, you should really put your best foot forward for these kinds of events," Chelsea told her very seriously. "They'll really make or break you."

"It's a classic style," Zoe told her. Although, she wasn't sure why she was defending her style to the likes of Chelsea.

"Not with this lace it isn't," she said. "My own dress is going to be Chantilly. Nothing but the best." She smiled like she had a secret to tell.

Zoe realized Chelsea didn't mean for her display but for her own trip down the aisle. She'd obviously been looking for any excuse to spill the news. "You mean you've actually found someone to put up with you? Congratulations. I didn't think that was possible."

Chelsea bit her lip like she wanted to say more but then stopped herself for some reason. Instead, she fingered the fabric with distaste. She shuddered. "Is that polyester?"

Zoe used the groom's hand to slap hers away. "Hands off the merchandise."

Chelsea checked her watch. "You'd better hurry. You don't have long to set up, and it's a very long walk to your booth." Chelsea waggled her fingers. "Bye-bye."

Zoe sneered at her, but shook her head. "You're right. I don't need to waste my time with you. One day, all the things you pull will catch up to you. You'll get yours eventually." Not about to let her rival delay her any longer. With two lead weights in either arm, she could do little more than turn and trudge to the other end of the Grand Ballroom. Way, way, way at the other end.

After wandering around for what seemed like forever, she finally located a table with *Zoe Plum, Plum Crazy Events* hastily scribbled on a sticky note. She groaned as she set her bride and groom down, dumping the rest of her supplies onto the floor.

Once the feeling to her arms returned, she removed the top hat from her head and plopped it onto the groom's. She frowned and angled it by five degrees.

While she stood back to appreciate it, her skin began to prickle with the sense that someone was watching her. She slowly turned around and discovered her perv sitting at the table directly beside hers.

"You've got to be kidding me," she said.

Reclined in a plastic chair, feet propped up on the table with a guitar resting on his chest was Levi Dolson. "Miss me?"

4

Paws Off

Zoe tapped the edges of her pamphlets, setting them perfectly in line with her display. But that didn't look quite right. So she set them at an angle. A little more. A little more . . . Finally, she settled on fanning them out so each one could be seen.

She could feel Levi watching her from the next table over, but she was far too busy to pay any attention. She wasn't aware of his blue eyes running up and down her long legs. And she certainly didn't care why, out of all the tables in the twenty-thousand-square-foot venue, he was sitting next to her. Nor did she let the fact that he seemed perfectly at ease bother her.

As she rushed to put the finishing touches on her display, he sat back in his chair, feet on the table, strumming a guitar lazily instead of preparing for the rush of customers about to flood through the doors at any moment.

"Don't you have to get ready?" she asked, and realized that she actually was paying attention to him. In fact, he was so annoyingly present he was impossible to ignore.

Or maybe that was just her. "The expo's about to begin, and you've just been sitting there since I arrived."

"That's not true." He plucked a few strings. "I helped you in with all your stuff."

"Thank you for the help by the way," she relented. "I'm not sure what happened to my assistant. She was supposed to be here early to help." She checked her phone again, but there was still no text or call from Natalie. What was going on with her lately?

He eyed her display. "Why do you need so much stuff, anyway?"

"To advertise what I do, what I can offer my clients," she said, rearranging the brochures again. "The question is, why don't you have more stuff?"

"Because this is it." He waved a hand over his reclined body. "What you see is what you get."

Actually, what Zoe saw surprised her. If he wore T-shirts and crinkled jeans to a wedding, Zoe would have expected him to show up to the expo in pajamas. On second thought, he didn't seem like the PJ kind of guy. More like a boxers-only guy. Or maybe au natural. That would explain why he'd shown up to the wedding without his tighty whities. Zoe's eye automatically dipped down again.

But Levi had stepped it up a notch that day. He'd taken a razor to his stubble, the smoothness highlighting his full lips. His slate gray button-down shirt—with only a few wrinkles—made his blue eyes pop. In fact, that wasn't the only thing highlighting his eyes. It looked like Levi had smudged charcoal eyeliner around his thick eyelashes.

His fingers picked at the guitar strings in a random tune, nails painted black with chipped polish. His hair stuck up on his head as though he were caught in a wind storm. Zoe was certainly blown away. He looked like a regular rock star who just walked off stage. And was that eyebrow always pierced or had it been the other one?

After tearing her eyes away, she faked a scoff. "I'm afraid to tell you that you might want to improve your sales pitch or add some incentives." Although secretly, from what she'd seen so far, it was more than enough incentive.

Since she'd met Levi, every time she'd pulled out her toys for a little stress relief, her mind kept wandering back to that vestry in St. Dominic's church. To Levi standing there with nothing but a shirt on. *Oh,* then Levi on the desk. *Oh, yes.* Then she'd tried to imagine what he'd look like with nothing but that tie on. *Mmmm.* And in a church, no less. How naughty, how hot! And yes, yes, *yes!*

As Zoe's toy did its job, and imaginary Levi did his, she got closer, and closer, and then . . . it simply stopped. Her vibrator remained full of energy, yet she was the one who kept fizzling out.

It had been like that for the last week. It was unheard of. It had never happened to her before. Hell, considering her sexual appetite, she wouldn't have thought it possible.

Of course, she'd tried to imagine something else, anyone else. She'd even blown through her Pure Pleasure porn collection. But every time she got close, it was Levi's face that kept popping back into her head.

It's just curiosity, she told herself. She wondered what he'd done to deserve that red lipstick kiss, what he'd been doing all night that kept him up so late. And what was under that shirt?

If she could only satisfy her curiosity, she was sure she'd get her mojo back. What would he do if she asked him to simply whip it out? A slow smile crept across her lips.

Obviously she'd been staring at him too long because he stood up and walked over, as though she were giving him "come-hither" eyes. Or maybe it was because she'd been staring at his crotch.

"We could always team up," he suggested. "I can sing romantic songs while you go through your sales pitch. Like background music. It will really put the customers in the moment, you know?"

Perching on the edge of her table, all dramatic-like, he played a couple of riffs while making some nonsensical warbling noises with his deep voice. He gave her a goofy grin.

She shoved him off the table but found herself laughing at the image of him serenading her clients. "You can definitely stay out of my moment."

Wandering behind her table, he popped the top hat off the mannequin's head and slipped it on his own. "Why are you so worried, anyway?"

"I'm not worried. Everything will go perfectly." She snatched the hat off his head, placing it back on her groom. "I'm prepared, I'm confident, and my reputation is known throughout the city—despite the wedding from hell last weekend," she added. "The expo is going to be an absolute success for my business."

"Then why do you need all the stuff?"

Zoe groaned and flopped into her chair just as a voice boomed overhead through the speaker system.

"Attention. The doors will be opening in five minutes."

"What are you really doing here, anyway?" she asked Levi.

"It's lovely to see you again too," he said, and his pleasant smile supported that claim.

"It's always lovely to see me," she informed him. "But what are you doing *here*?"

"I'm a musician. I do a lot of wedding gigs. It's my bread and butter. You know, until I make it big," he said it like it was only a matter of time.

"Last time I checked, the organ wasn't highly requested on the radio."

He grabbed the chair meant for her MIA assistant like the decision to "team up" was already made. "So you admit I can play the organ."

"I'll admit you did . . . pretty good," she said.

He seemed to consider her reserved answer before nodding. "I was pretty amazing, wasn't I?"

Zoe laughed. Actually, he had been amazing. He'd really saved her, but she wasn't going to tell him that. He didn't need any more encouragement than he seemed to be finding all on his own.

Despite her standoffishness with him, he didn't even seem to notice. He was relentless with his flirting. Heck, he'd even signed up for the expo. And while he said it was for his own business, it was a little too coincidental that he was assigned to the table next to her.

Okay, so maybe she'd been guilty of flirting back. But in a very dry, so-not-impressed way. Well, maybe she was impressed, a lot, but she wasn't about to let him know that either.

Over the years, it wasn't like men hadn't tried to get close to her, but they never stuck around for very long. No man had ever been able to win out against her cold shoulder. Maybe because she knew none of them could win out against her vibrator. Because what else could she need them for? Certainly not a relationship, since she was so much happier on her own.

No more flirting, she told herself. It wouldn't be right. She'd only be leading Levi on. Besides, once the expo weekend was over, she'd never see him or his rock-hard abs ever again.

"You know, I find it a strange coincidence that out of all these conference rooms and halls, and the few hundred expo participants, we're assigned to booths side by side."

"So weird, right? It's like fate or something." He batted his eyelashes at her.

Zoe puckered her lips, thinking fate probably had nothing to do with it. She'd heard that line before too. But "fate" had never been able to beat her cold shoulder either, so she wasn't worried.

Before she could dig into the real reason they were neighbors, her first customer arrived. She turned with her best you-can-count-on-me smile, but it wasn't a customer, it was her assistant. Her smile vanished, replaced by her no-nonsense business face.

"I am so sorry I'm late," Natalie said. "My car broke down, and I had to call to get a boost."

"The tow truck delivers flowers now?" Zoe asked, indicating the giant arrangement Natalie was setting in the center of the table. Right on top of her fanned out pamphlets.

"Oh yeah. I just so happened to break down next to a flower shop, so I thought I'd get us a nice centerpiece for our booth to make it up to you."

"Peonies. Very nice." Zoe did find her irritation level shrink because of the gesture.

She spotted the business card tucked into the blooms. It was from a florist she often used on 16th Street called Pushing Daisies. However, she knew Natalie lived in North Beach. She wouldn't have been anywhere near that florist on the way to the expo.

Zoe figured it was none of her business how she got there, just that she was late. However, she was there now, and it wasn't really the time to address it. Saving the rest for later, she said, "Thanks for the flowers, but next time

I expect a call or text. I had enough to deal with after running into Chelsea Carruthers and Juliet Fisher."

Natalie blanched slightly. Her face took on that wide-eyed, groom with cold feet look, like she'd worn the day of Juliet's wedding. She didn't blame her assistant, because even Zoe was still having nightmares about the day. But Natalie wasn't exactly made of the toughest stuff, either. The girl wouldn't have lasted twenty seconds in a bouquet-toss fray.

"Don't worry," Zoe told her. "Security dragged her away. But not before she managed to turn half the expo guests against me."

Natalie sighed with relief. "Don't worry. There are going to be so many people coming this weekend that it won't even matter."

Zoe gave her a grateful smile. "Thanks. I hope you're right."

Only those in the hotel lobby had witnessed Juliet's blow up. And it was just the first day. Within a couple of hours, the witnesses would be replaced by all-new expo guests eager for her business. Even now she could see new faces circulating around the area in time to the music from the overhead speakers, like a game of musical chairs. Someone was bound to end up in her silver bride and groom chairs.

And just as she thought that, a woman passed by her table and curiously picked up her business card. Zoe smiled, thinking things were already turning around.

She opened her mouth to greet the woman, but the music was suddenly interrupted, replaced by a female voice. A voice that had Zoe reaching into her purse for Darling Dolphin.

"Testing. Testing. I have an announcement to make," Juliet declared. *"Zoe Plum is the worst wedding plan-*

ner ever. She ruined my wedding day. Don't hire her. She's—"

"*Give me that,*" a male voice demanded.

"*Hey!*" she yelled.

"*Stop . . . Don't.*"

There were sounds of struggling and muffled banging. A loud electronic squeal had the entire ballroom covering their ears. A bridezilla scream blasted through the speakers, one Zoe knew all too well.

"*Ouch!*" the male cried.

Zoe's potential customer dropped her card on the table and walked away. Finally, the air went dead—as dead as Zoe's schedule for the upcoming season was going to be.

5

Leader of the Pack

Zoe marched down an aisle suffused with the sweet scent of flowers, purposeful steps falling in time with the sounds of Prince's *Kiss*. Flanked by her two besties, Piper and Addison, her confident stride held everyone's rapt attention as she passed, because she was the woman of the hour, the star of the show. Zoe was San Francisco's premier wedding planner, and she was planning one of the most anticipated weddings of the year: the Summers-Caldwell wedding.

It was time to put Juliet's botched wedding behind her. So what if everyone at the expo heard about the matrimonial mess? So what if they were avoiding her booth like that weird uncle the bride's mom forced her to invite?

Zoe was looking toward the future. Aiden and Piper's specifically. Their epic wedding was going to boost her promotion power by gossip and word of mouth alone. Juliet Fisher who?

Hands reached toward Zoe as she passed each vendor's stall, thrusting Venetian veils, demo reception play-lists, personalized place cards, and everything a wedding planner could need.

But Zoe declined all the free swag and samples. She already had everything she needed to pull off the most legendary wedding of all time. After all, she'd practically been planning it since the day Piper met Aiden, the young CEO of Caldwell and Son Investments.

The couple met when Aiden had bought the old Dachshund Rescue Center and Piper was still working three jobs to put herself through veterinarian school. When she'd lost two of those jobs, Aiden had offered her a position as his dog walker. And the rest was history.

Okay, well, it hadn't been quite that simple. But it all worked out in the end because they got a beautiful new rescue center where Piper could do surgeries and procedures on the sick pups that came in, and they were now tying the knot. It was going to be nothing short of the best for her bestie.

Reaching into her purse, Zoe pulled out her tablet to consult a numerical, color-coded, categorized list she'd labeled *Piper's Dream Wedding*. She swiped down the exhaustive list with a manicured finger.

With only two weeks left to go, the seating had been arranged, the flowers were ordered, the caterer booked and informed of Piper's sesame-seed allergy, the dress altered and ready for pickup. All that remained was to fill an annoying last-minute cancellation by the salsa instructor.

Her eye twitched involuntarily. Nothing annoyed Zoe more than a glitch in her well-organized plans. Zoe was perfectly aware that the instructor didn't break his leg on purpose. It's not like she could blame him for falling off that horse—not completely, anyway.

"Zoe!" Piper called out to her.

Zoe paused and turned around to find her friends lagging behind. Not only did she not like to waste time, but she was considerably taller than her friends, and her long strides always left them in the dust during their frequent shopping trips. Which wasn't always a bad thing when it was a flash sale and time was of the essence.

Piper took a deep breath when she finally caught up. "Can we slow down?" she asked Zoe.

"I second that." Addison squeezed between two women fighting over the last wedding cake sample from a bakery vendor. She stumbled forward. "My feet are killing me. These are new shoes I'm breaking in. Fifty percent off. I just couldn't say no." She grinned sheepishly.

The backpack strapped to Piper's shoulders shifted and writhed until a black-and-tan head snaked out of the open zipper. Piper never went anywhere without her doxie, Colin, and by the way his tan eyebrows furrowed at Zoe, it was obvious that he was tired of her quick pace too.

His look seemed to say, *What's the deal? People are trying to nap in here.*

"Sorry," Zoe said. "But we don't have much time. We've got a schedule to maintain. There are too many entertainers to interview." She brought up the list she'd compiled on her tablet based on the expo brochure. "Four gymnasts, eight dancers, including belly, flamenco, ballet, and jive. Not to mention eleven artists, a magician, three gymnasts, two acrobats, and one fire breather."

Piper blinked. "Fire breather?"

"I threw that one in as a wild card. I wanted you to have options. And besides"—she winked—"he performs half naked. His abs have abs. It's really just an excuse to check him out."

Piper's eyes wandered, taking in the endless booths.

"What if we just perused the entertainment section? Maybe something will catch my eye."

Zoe snapped shut the cover on her tablet and shifted, blocking her bride's view. She pointed to her own eyes, locking gazes with Piper. "Look at me. Stay focused. It's a battlefield out there. It can be overwhelming. If you have any ideas, I'm all ears, but it's best if we keep our blinders on and stick to the original plan. Besides, the longer we wait to book someone, the less options we'll have. We need to make our move now, before it's too late."

Piper swallowed hard at the look in Zoe's eyes. "You make it sound like war."

"It is," she said. "The wedding industry is cut throat. It's not for the weak hearted. Now, let's get a move on. I'm sending Natalie to pick up your dress from the seamstress in an hour." She released Piper and made sure Addison was close by. "Are we ready, soldiers?"

Addison and Piper saluted.

Flicking her auburn hair back, Piper tried to fan it out to hide Colin from sight. He disappeared back into the depths of her backpack, probably sniffing out any remaining crumbs left from the treats she'd thrown in there to keep him quiet.

Zoe opened up her list again and ran her dark eyes over the alphabetized notes. "Okay, we'll work through the entertainment section systematically. Let's start on the right-hand side and—" But when she glanced back up, Piper and Addison were enthralled with a nearby balloon artist.

Rubber squeaked as the man twisted and spun a long white balloon into several bulges and placed it around Addison's neck like a pearl necklace. Next, he fashioned Piper a wiener dog that looked strangely like the one poking his head out of her backpack again to see what all the squeaking was about.

Zoe sighed but gave into the whims of the bride-to-be as Piper haphazardly zigzagged her way through the aisles. Tucking her tablet into her purse again, Zoe followed behind, her heels squishing into the aisle runner. She reminded herself that while she might have been there as Piper's wedding planner, she was there as a friend first.

It was sometimes hard for Zoe to fight her borderline OCD nature, but the bride's happiness always came first. If they wanted a hot-air balloon for their wedding, they were going to get it. If they wanted a jousting competition, Zoe would buff the lance herself.

They wandered around the endless rows of booths, but the hour passed and Piper still hadn't made a decision. It was a no to the dancers, a no to the artists, a no to the acrobats.

"What about the fire breather?" Zoe asked as they returned to her booth.

Piper gave her a look. "Definitely no fire breather."

Zoe sighed extra dramatically. "Oh, but those abs. You're missing out."

Before they got to her table, Levi suddenly popped in front of Zoe, blocking her path. "Talking about me again, I see. You know, if you want to see my abs again, all you have to do is ask."

Addison's wide eyes flicked from Zoe to Levi. "Again?"

Levi gave Zoe a childish smile, plunking his guitar strings in a playful tune.

Zoe sighed. "No, we were talking about finding an entertainer for my friend's wedding." She gestured to Piper as evidence.

Levi's fingers froze, the strings humming off key. "Wait. What about me?"

Zoe stared at him. "What about you?"

He sidled closer to her until she could smell his cologne. "I've been told I'm very entertaining." His voice lowered with insinuation.

She rolled her eyes. "You most certainly are that," she said, not unkindly. One would even say it bordered on flirting.

No flirting, she reminded herself.

Piper eyed Zoe and then Levi. She crossed her arms with an amused look. "Okay. Show us what you've got."

"Pipe." Zoe widened her eyes in a secret message.

Piper just gave her an innocent eyelash flutter. An entire hour perusing San Francisco's best collection of entertainers and *now* she was showing interest? In *him*?

But Levi didn't seem to notice Zoe's irritation. He cleared his throat dramatically and strummed his guitar.

"Oh, Zoe Plum!
You make my legs go numb.
My brain goes dumb.
Every time you're near, my heart goes ba-ba-bum-bum.
Ever since you saw me half nude,
I don't mean to be crude,
But you've got me in the mood,
Despite your cool attitude.
Miss Plum, you drive me plum crazy.
You make my eyes go all hazy,
And it's not because I need glasses to see.
My eyes are 20-20.
No-o-o-o! It's because you drive me plum crazy.
Miss Plum Crazy."

As he sang, he paused every so often, clearly making it up as he went along, but he made the pauses in his silly song seem dramatic, like they were on purpose. To top off the cheese, he strummed out a hardcore guitar solo that just didn't have the same effect on an acoustic guitar. He finished with a rock-star pose, his tongue sticking out like Gene Simmons.

The small crowd that had paused to listen clapped. Zoe hadn't even noticed them gather around as he serenaded her. At least they weren't glaring at her like she was a wedding wrecker anymore.

Addison and Piper laughed at his antics, clapping along with everyone else, impressed by his quick lyrics. Addison's wide eyes flicked between Zoe and Levi. She wore the same expression she did whenever they watched *Love Actually* every Christmas together.

Addison's eyes glistened with hope and romantic optimism, and probably fairies and rainbows too. But Zoe wasn't about to fall as easily as her hopeless romantic friend—emphasis on the hopeless.

"You know, she's the bride to be." She indicated Piper with her thumb. "You should be trying to impress her. Not me."

"Oh, you're definitely the one I want to impress." He waggled his eyebrows and his piercing flashed.

She pretended to yawn. "Is that all you've got?"

"The show's only just begun. I'm still warming up." Reaching into his messenger bag behind his table, he drew out a CD and handed it to Piper.

"Here's a demo of my band's stuff. You can book me individually or the whole band. Keep us in mind."

"Thanks," she said, checking out the cover. "I will."

Zoe snatched the CD out of her friend's hand and gave her a firm "no" look before slipping behind her table. But as her friends took a seat in her *bride* and *groom* chairs across from her, Levi just handed Piper another copy before settling back into his chair with his feet up.

Zoe turned to Natalie like that was the end of that.

"Thanks for looking after the booth for me. How did things go while I was gone?"

"Pretty good," she said. "I handed out almost two-dozen business cards to interested people."

"That's great," Zoe said. Although, she wondered if Natalie was just saying that to cheer her up because by the looks of her decorative cardholder display, not a single card was missing.

Zoe was about to toss Levi's CD aside, but then she glanced at the cover. In a bold typeface, the words *Reluctant Redemption* were scrawled across the cover. The band photo showed a group of four men dressed in your stereotypical rock-and-roll uniform: leather, jeans, faded shirts, tattoos etc. And in the center of the group was Levi.

Levi Dolson wasn't just a cheesy wedding singer-slash-organ player. He was the lead singer of a band. It was kind of hot, she had to admit. But compared to the man flashing her a silly, toothy grin from the next table, the dark, hardened man on the CD didn't seem to fit.

Piper leaned over the table and lowered her voice so she wouldn't be heard over Levi's strumming. "Why can't we hire this guy?" she asked. "Everyone hires a DJ. Maybe having a wedding singer would be fun. More personal than a DJ. We can still cancel him and hire Levi."

Addison nodded her head enthusiastically. "Besides, he's really cute."

Zoe gave her a look. "You're in a committed relationship, remember?"

"I'm not talking about for me," she said. "I'm just looking out for you."

Zoe rolled her eyes. "I can look out for myself, thanks." She began busying herself with rearranging the pamphlets on her table . . . just so.

Addison grinned at her. "I think he likes you."

"Who? AC/Chee-Z over there?" Her eyes flitted to his table.

She laughed. "Yes. Who else?"

Zoe rolled her eyes and smiled mischievously. "Well, of course he does."

"Oh, come on," Piper said. "Admit it. He's adorable."

"He's annoying," she said.

Addison flipped through some of Zoe's pamphlets with a wistful look on her face. She was probably imaging her own inevitable wedding to her boyfriend, Felix. "He isn't annoying. I think he's the kind of guy that gets under your skin if you *let him*."

Zoe huffed, unwilling to entertain the idea. "Yeah, gets under your skin like a tick. He's persistent, I'll give him that."

"You know what they say," Addison half-sang. "Persistence pays off."

"Well, not for him," she said, like that ended it.

Zoe and Addison didn't exactly see eye-to-eye when it came to love and relationships—and it wasn't just because Zoe was practically a foot taller.

Despite her history of bad luck with men, Addison still maintained her idealized fairy-tale view about happily ever after. And since she'd recently shacked up with her boyfriend, Felix, and his daughter, it seemed to be working out well for her.

But Zoe was far too practical for that fairy-tale line of thinking. Addison called her a cynic. She thought of herself as a realist.

What Zoe wasn't telling her friends was the real reason she didn't want to hire Levi. That she didn't want to see him again after that weekend. That she didn't like the way she felt around him. He got a rise out of her—both her emotions and her libido.

Used to hiding her feelings, sometimes she'd find the

good ones would get bottled up with the bad. She'd forget to laugh some days, maybe because she was afraid something else would slip out of her bottle-o-crazy with it.

But Levi's persistent, corny stand-up comedy show had her laughing even when she was trying not to. He made her feel good. Which was bad. So very bad.

And that was a whole different matter she wanted to hide from her friends. Even after all these years, she hadn't let on the extent of her reluctance to dating men. Of course, they'd heard her talk about men, watched her flirt with them, accept their numbers. But when it came to the details—of which there were none to share—she kept them in the dark.

Zoe suspected they assumed what a lot of people assumed. That she had *relations* without having *relationships*. And that was fine with Zoe. It kept people out of her hair, from looking at her like there was something wrong with her, because the truth would have made them think there was something to fix. And Zoe was just fine the way she was.

Her friends shared a meaningful glance, but she ignored them. "We'll find something else," she assured them. "You are the future Mrs. Caldwell," she told Piper. "You deserve to have your dream wedding. Besides, it's getting too late to make all these changes now. It's bad enough we need to find a new entertainer at the last minute."

Piper frowned. "But you have to admit, he's pretty good. And it might be fun to have live music at the wedding. We wouldn't even need an entertainer."

Zoe crossed her arms with a playful glare but one that also said she meant business. "Look. You hired me to plan you a wedding fit for the kind of swanky guests Aiden will be inviting. And that means no cheesy wedding singer. I promise you, you'll have the classiest wedding in town or I'll quit the whole damn industry."

"But—"

"Trust me."

"Do I detect trouble with the Summers-Caldwell wedding already?" A high-pitched voice cut through the air like a spoon clinking a glass at a reception. And it had the same response too. Everyone froze and turned to the sound.

Among the crowd there was a flash of platinum blonde hair and a pink lemonade pantsuit.

Over the hush, someone hissed, "Is that Holly Hart?"

The Holly Hart from Channel Five News emerged from the gathering crowd. Her hand rose, like she was inviting applause that never came. The other hand held her shivering Chinese Crested, Jasmine. The dog's pink hairless skin almost blended in with Holly's outfit, the white tuft of hair on its head almost matching Holly's over-processed color.

Nearby, a woman cried out as Holly's cameraman nearly barreled over her. He struggled to keep up with all the equipment strapped to him, sweat rolling down his flushed cheeks.

Zoe didn't actually know the cameraman's name. Although she'd had a few run-ins with the local news team, she'd only ever heard Holly call him "Hey, You." Not that she cared to get to know the guy. The only time she'd ever spoken to him was to utter explicit threats to his nether-regions because he and Holly were harassing Piper.

Holly's eyes landed on the three friends. Her hand flew to her mouth and she gasped in shock. "I don't believe it. Piper? What a complete coincidence to see you here," she said in a way that made Zoe think it wasn't a coincidence at all.

Holly had been writing stories about Piper's fiancé

long before she became a legit news reporter. Back when
she'd worked for the gossip mag *The Gate*, she'd followed
Aiden along his trail of sordid escapades—pre-Piper, of
course. But that wasn't him anymore. He'd found the
woman for him and was ready to settle down. And definitely ready to give Holly the shake, once and for all. But
Holly had other plans.

The local reporter had been hounding Zoe for wedding details on Piper and Aiden's wedding ever since the
announcement was made in the entertainment section
of the paper. Now she'd managed to track down Piper
herself.

"My, my," Holly cooed. "If it isn't the future Mrs.
Caldwell herself."

"Well, I was thinking of hyphenating," Piper mumbled, clearly not as pleased to see Holly as she was to
see her.

As though Colin could sense who was there, he began to growl inside the backpack.

But the reporter ignored both of them. "So. The count-
down begins. Only two weeks until the big day. So, tell
me, Piper. Any pre-wedding jitters? Cold feet perhaps?"

"No. Just a cold shoulder." Piper shifted in her chair
to turn her back on the reporter.

Zoe shared an eye roll with her friends. "Why don't
you guys just get out of here before this gets ugly? I
need to get back to work anyway."

She stood up, ready to play defense so her friends
could escape, but she felt a weight on her shoulders as
Levi slung his arm around her.

"Aren't you going to introduce me to your friend
here?" He indicated Holly with a chin thrust.

Zoe flung his arm off her. "Why would I do that?"

"I thought we were a team."

She rubbed her temple. "We're not a—"

"Levi Dolson, front man for the band Reluctant Redemption." He gave Holly a winning smile, holding out his hand to Holly. "You've probably heard of us. And before you ask. Yes. I'd be happy to do an interview."

Her tiny dog began to growl, its white teeth flashing. He pulled his hand back an inch.

Holly glanced down at his hand but didn't take it. "Never heard of you. And no one wants to hear about your little a cappella group."

He frowned. "Rock band. Been around for years. On the precipice of breaking out. Nationally. No, globally." He spread his hands as though enacting the sensationalism. "We just need a little exposure, is all. You want in on the action?"

"I can find my own action," she told him.

He shrugged. "Your loss."

"I don't think it is."

"Trust me," Zoe said to Levi, "you don't want to get mixed up with Holly Hart."

"Ouch," Holly said in mock hurt—although, Zoe didn't think the reporter had actual feelings to hurt.

"Is this any way to treat an old friend?" Holly asked the three girls.

Zoe laughed in Holly's face. "Friend?"

Holly held a hand to her chest like she'd just been shot. "Addison, who helped you get your business back on track when you were accused of stealing all those show dogs last year?"

Addison stood up so she could glare at Holly. "You were the one who accused me of stealing them on national television in the first place."

The reporter had taken the accusations of a few angry dog owners and ran with it, turning San Francisco against Addison. A two-minute-long smear segment and her dog-spa business and promising Fido Fashion line had been facing obliteration.

Holly barely skipped a beat. "Any publicity is good publicity. Besides, you got your boyfriend Francis out of it all."

"Felix," Addison corrected.

"Whatever." She held a hand up like she'd had enough. "And Piper, you got all those donations for your precious Dachshund Rescue Center thanks to my amazing reporting skills and enormous viewership." She gave her a light punch on the arm and chuckled genially. "You're welcome, by the way."

"That's true," Piper relented. "But the reason your viewership is so enormous is thanks to us and your exploitation of our misfortunes." She slipped her backpack on carefully, ready to leave.

"Now no one likes a bragger." Holly held up a finger. "Let's not quibble about semantics. So Zoe, what do you say about an exclusive?" She nudged her with a chummy elbow. "A sneak peek of the wedding? You know, a few spoilers of the happy couple's big day?"

"I'm a contender for the entertainment," Levi offered.

"Is that so?" Holly turned to him with a flash of interest.

"No, he's not," Zoe said.

"Then give me *something*," Holly said.

Zoe raised an eyebrow. Which said more than enough—she had mad eyebrow game. "I don't think so."

"Oh, come on," Holly persisted. "Think of the mutual benefits. Maybe there could be a couple segments leading up to the big day. Imagine the promotional opportunities for your event-planning business." She plucked a pamphlet off the table and began flipping through it.

Zoe rounded the table and snatched it back. "My business is doing just fine, thanks."

Holly frowned. Or rather, she tried to frown if not for all that filler and Botox. She looked pointedly around at all the clients not lined up for her booth. "Well, remember, it's tit for tat. You scratch my back, I'll scratch yours. You know where to find me." She winked before heading back the way she came. With a snap of her fingers, she beckoned Hey, You and disappeared into the crowd again with her dog.

Addison watched her go. "After what she did to my business last year, I'd never trust her. She'd as soon stab you in the back as scratch it."

"Trust me," Zoe said, replacing the pamphlet on the table. "The last thing I need is to tango with Holly Hart. Good PR be damned."

"I appreciate it," Piper said. "God knows Aiden and I have taken up enough real-estate in the papers. We just want to keep the wedding as quiet as possible, you know?"

Zoe raised her hands. "Absolutely. Low key. Private. Everything will be perfect. I promise."

"I know." Piper wrapped an arm around Zoe. "Because you're planning it."

Zoe gave her a grateful look for the confidence. And she was going to do everything in her power to earn that look. Especially after what they'd been through over the years.

She remembered how Piper had been there for her when her father died. Piper had gone through it all herself when she was in high school, so she understood what Zoe was experiencing and was there to help her through every rough moment of it.

Now it was Zoe's turn to be there for her, to begin to

show Piper just what her friendship meant. To give her the perfect wedding. "I won't let you down. I promise."

"Oh!" Addison sniffed as she began to get teary and pulled them in for a group hug.

"I love group hugs," Levi said, pretending to lean in. "Oh, you mean just the three of you. Okay. That's cool. I'll just be over here."

The girls laughed. Even Zoe. Addison was right. The guy was persistent.

Just as she started to relax, thinking the weekend might still turn around, she spotted Holly standing farther down the aisle. With two fingers, the reporter pointed to her own piercing eyes, and then at Zoe, in an "I'll be watching you" gesture.

6

⚭

Same Song and Dance

Zoe pressed the *down* button for the elevator. It dinged and the Hilton logo on the doors split open to a blissfully empty elevator. It had been a long day with little to do in her far, far, far corner at the expo. By the time most people reached her booth, they'd already found a wedding planner.

She stepped inside and chose the level that her van was on before leaning back, her head falling against the mirrored wall. A *ding* rang out as the doors slid closed, followed by a yelp.

Her eyes flew open in surprise to see a hand poking through the nearly closed doors. They jerked apart again, and Levi stood on the other side, his guitar bag strapped to his back. He looked as tired as she felt, but when he saw her, his face reanimated.

"Hey."

"Hi," she said. "I thought you went home already. How was the rest of your day?"

"It was great," he said. "I started working the room.

You know, wandering around the place, serenading random people. Got a few contacts, some interested customers. How was it for you?"

She blew out a breath, watching the floor numbers light up as they descended. "I didn't sign a single contract today. I need a new plan. Today was a complete bust."

"That's not true," Levi said. "You got to see me again."

"Of course." She smiled. "How could I forget that? Considering you were strangely assigned to the table next to me. Somehow. Randomly," she fished.

But he wasn't biting. "It's true. I'm unforgettable," he said humbly.

"You are that. But mostly because you don't ever seem to go away." She grinned mischievously as they got out of the elevator to let him know she was kidding. Which was a first, really.

Mostly when she told men to screw off—and that was often—she meant it. But Levi was different from most guys who hit on her. Sure, he was a flirt, but in an entertaining way. It wasn't the smarmy propositions that she got any time she and the girls went out on the town.

"Well, you'd better get used to it," he told her. "Because once you listen to my CD, you'll discover how amazing I am and you'll have to hire me."

"Don't hold your breath. I won't be calling you any time soon."

She started heading for her van and he walked with her. She doubted they happened to be parked next to each other—unless he'd somehow set that up too.

"I'm a patient man," he said.

"Well, you'll be waiting a long time, my friend," she threw back at him.

"I know when something's worth waiting for."

Zoe laughed. "Do those lines work on the girls at your

gigs?" She imagined that for some girls, all he had to say was "I'm in the band" and their clothes just magically fell off. Well, Zoe was not one of those girls.

She didn't want to hurt Levi, but he just didn't seem to be getting the hint. She wasn't interested. In *anyone*. Sure, she'd considered doing the no-strings attached thing on more than one occasion. In fact, Levi had been making her reconsider that as an option. But maybe that was just her built-up sexual frustration talking.

Just because she chose to be single, didn't mean her lady parts had any say in the matter—in fact, they were downright pissed with her. But then she'd bust out her toys and the urges would disappear. No one knew her body better than she did. She didn't need a man. Just batteries.

Well, that usually worked. But ever since she'd met Levi, things had changed. Just one more reason to leave the guy in the dust. So things could get back to status quo.

"Come on. Just give me a shot," he said. Not in a desperate way, but in a "you don't know what you're missing" way. He must have forgotten she'd seen him without his shirt on. So she had an inkling of just what she was missing.

"Nope. Sorry."

"Are you saying no to the musician? Or the man behind the music?"

God, he just couldn't take a hint. How cold did she have to get? She pulled a face. "I have to be honest. Your music is a bit amateur."

His smile widened, like she'd just given him the best news. "So the man has a chance."

She snorted, but smiled despite herself. "I didn't say that. It was more a comment about your music skills."

"Honey," he said, undeterred, "I've got skills you've never seen before."

"Trust me," she shot back. "You've got nothing I haven't seen before. Besides," she said with finality, "we don't need a musician. Just the entertainment. We've already hired a DJ."

Levi shrugged, but she could sense the disappointment as he turned away. She wasn't sure if it was because she was rejecting his services or him. Either way, she felt a pang of guilt.

"Well, keep me in mind if your DJ breaks a leg too," he said.

While he'd acted overconfident and persistent with her since they met, the look of hurt made her wonder if his intentions weren't more sincere than she'd first thought.

Zoe wanted to say something, but she wasn't sure what. When they rounded the corner where her van was parked, it seemed too late. Besides, what would she say that wouldn't give him the wrong idea, wouldn't lead him on? Maybe she'd been too harsh, but obviously he'd taken the hint. That's what she wanted, wasn't it?

She shook it off. Of course it was. She'd been sure of it for years. That didn't change just because some sexy musician walked into her life. Or just because she hadn't been able to make herself climax without imaging them back inside that vestry with the door locked. It didn't change a thing.

"Well, this is me," she said, already taking her keys out.

But her escape was hampered by a group of hotel guests lingering in the middle of the parking area, blocking access to her van.

After a long day of being stuck in the perfect ogling position next to Levi, she wanted to put some distance between herself and the rocker. To get some perspective. Out of sight, out of mind, right?

"Excuse me. Excuse me." She tried to maneuver

through the crowd, weaving through them. They didn't seem to be doing anything. Just standing around.

Then a woman on her phone noticed Zoe and covered the mouthpiece. "Is this your van?" she asked.

"Yes," Zoe replied a little hesitantly, because she wasn't sure she wanted it to be yet. A bad feeling crept over her.

"Don't worry," the woman said. "I'm calling the police now."

"Calling the police about what?" Frowning, she pushed forward to get a better look.

People began to move out of her way, kicking up something white that fluttered over the pavement like fresh snow. When she looked down she saw it was silk flowers. *Her* silk flowers, she realized. They were scattered over the pavement like a flower girl had passed by.

Her heart began to race as she followed the trail. The last of the gathered looky-loos made way for her, opening up the scene like curtains drawing. But it was a tableau of a tragedy.

Her van's back doors had been pried open, the windows smashed in. The contents spewed out as though it had vomited a wedding day.

Her ivory aisle runner draped out of the back, mud and old oil stains soaking through the delicate fabric.

Zoe's mouth dropped open, and she stepped closer. Something crunched under her heel. She glanced down to find broken glass. No. Not just glass. Crystal. Her vases and candle holders lay in bits and pieces on the pavement, shattered beyond repair.

Décor, spare fabric, table runners, photo props. All smashed or torn. But that wasn't the worst. What made her heart stop dead in her chest was the white gossamer and lace fabric hanging out of the back and down the bumper like a dead body.

"Oh, my god." Zoe automatically reached out for it.

Someone grabbed her hand and held it back. It was Levi. She hadn't even realized he was still there.

"Don't touch it," he said. "The police are on their way. You don't want to disturb the crime scene."

Instead of pushing him away, her own hand tightened around his. "But the dress," she breathed. "It's ruined."

"It's okay," he said. "You can order another one."

"No. You don t understand. Wedding dresses are ordered months, sometimes a year in advance. The wedding is in two weeks." What bad luck. Why did the dress have to be ready that day? Why did she have to send Natalie to pick it up?

Piper's dress drooped lifelessly, the tattered shreds dangling on the greasy pavement. It had been perfect. A Marchesa. There was no replacing that dress. Not with only two weeks left to go. To get a dress in that time frame, Zoe's best friend, who was marrying one of the richest men in San Francisco, was going to have to resort to getting a dress—she gulped—off the rack. It was a disaster.

There was the telltale click of a camera going off on someone's phone. Zoe turned to the sound and found Holly Hart taking a photo of the wreckage.

"That wouldn't be Piper Summer's dress, would it?" She grinned like a kid with a bowl of ice cream. "Delicious."

Zoe swiped at the phone, but Holly danced away before she could grab it. Her fingers were already moving in a blur as she typed something on the screen—probably a new post about how Zoe just ruined her best friend's wedding.

Zoe's fists clenched as she marched after her, but Levi blocked her path. "Just ignore her. She's going to write about it either way."

She glared at the reporter, but relented. "You're right. I don't want to give her more material against me."

When she glanced back at Levi, he had this passive look on his face as though he was just hanging out. She checked her watch. It was past eight o'clock. Surely, he had some gig to get to or band party to attend.

"Don't feel like you have to stay," she told him. "The police are on their way."

He shrugged, his usual easygoing response. "I thought you could use a ride."

She stared at him in surprise. It was only five minutes ago that she'd been rejecting him, and here he was being so nice. "No. That's a really kind offer, but after I answer their questions, I might just wait for the cops to finish up so I don't have to bring a taxi here tomorrow."

"They could be a while, and you look like you could use a coffee." When she shook her head, he said, "Dinner? How about that drink?"

She laughed humorlessly. "I could definitely use a drink, but I think it will take more than a couple to end this day on, so I'd best wait until I get home."

"Great. I'll drive." He proffered his arm for her to take.

She let his arm hang there "You don't give up, do you?"

"Should I?"

She frowned. "What?"

"Do you want me to give up?" he asked. "Because you pretend like you do, but I can't tell if that's just an act. You strike me as a pretty direct person. So give it to me straight."

He stiffened, shoulders drawing back, chest out like he was waiting for her to hit him with it. But hit him with what?

She opened her mouth, unsure of how to answer that. Hadn't she been cold to him? Hadn't she basically rejected him both personally and professionally? Wasn't it obvious enough? But for some reason, she couldn't find a simple answer. Like "Yes. Give up."

Zoe's phone rang in her hands. "Hold that thought."

She read the screen. It was a number she didn't recognize, which made her worry all the more. It was just one of those days. "Hello?"

"Hello. Is this Zoe Plum?" a male voice on the other end asked.

"Speaking."

"You're listed as the emergency contact for a Junko Plum."

The name rang in her ear for a second as she tried to think of any other Junko Plum that she could possibly know. Anyone else at all. Anyone that wouldn't make her heart clench as a torrent of worst-case-scenario visions flashed through her already-overwhelmed mind.

When she could think of no other Junko Plum, she took a steadying breath and said, "Yes. She's my mother. What's happened?"

"She's had an accident. She's in the emergency department at SF General Hospital."

"I'll be there right away. Thank you." She threw her phone into her purse and, without thinking, headed to her van, but the sight of it brought her up short.

She hesitated, shifting from foot to foot as she thought what to do next, but all that she could focus on was that her mother was in the hospital. *The hospital.* She needed to get to her right away.

When she turned around, for the first time since she'd met Levi, he looked dead serious.

"How about that ride?"

7

Dog Days

The air in the emergency room of San Francisco General Hospital reeked of antiseptic, of sterile linen, and cool indifference. Zoe hated that her mother was in there, being taken care of by strangers. Her legs twitched with impatience, wanting to move faster, but it seemed Nurse Derrick was determined to move at a glacial pace.

She hadn't bothered to stick around and wait for the police. She'd have to catch up to been later. The van had been the least of her worries when the only trying she could think about was getting to the hospital to be with her mother.

Levi had been really sweet on the drive to the hospital, trying to distract her, making small talk like everything was cool. No big deal. But she could tell he was rushing because his van's tires squeaked around a few corners, and she noticed a few lights turn red before they left the intersection.

Maybe that was just his way of being. The more serious things got, the more relaxed he became. A way to balance the situation out. It had certainly helped balance out her erratic emotions.

Once they arrived, she thanked him and said she'd get a taxi back to the Hilton. However, he insisted on staying. But of course he had. There was just no getting rid of the guy. At that moment, however, Zoe found that she didn't mind the company so much, knowing he was sticking around waiting for her.

The nurse paused at a privacy curtain pulled across a stall and peeked inside. "Mrs. Plum, your daughter is here."

Too anxious to wait for an answer, Zoe grabbed the curtain and whipped it aside. When she saw her mother lying on the stretcher, it brought her up short.

Tucked under the stiff hospital blankets, her mother looked so small and helpless. Her cropped, graying hair was lifeless and unkempt, and she didn't have a stitch of makeup on, which was why her swollen, black eye stood out stark against her pale skin.

Her mother had always seemed like some wound-up ball of energy, a force to be reckoned with, feisty, and full of life and sharp spirit. Seeing her this way was like seeing her for the first time in ten years, because she looked older than fifty-three.

After a stunned moment, Zoe rushed to her bedside. *"Kaasan."*

"Zoe." Her mother reached out for her hand.

She took it and squeezed tightly. Maybe it was just her imagination, but it felt like her mother's hands had become smaller, frailer. She grabbed the plastic chair next to the bed and dragged it closer before sitting down.

"How are you feeling?" Zoe asked. "Are you all right?"

Junko waved away her daughter's concern, like it wasn't her idea to be there hooked up to various beeping monitors and whirring machines. *"Daijoubu."*

Zoe frowned. "You're not all right, Mom. You're in the hospital. What happened?"

"Zoe." Her eyes flicked meaningfully toward the nurse who was writing on a clipboard at the end of the bed. *"Nihongo de."*

She gave her mom a look. "It's fine. He's the nurse. We can speak English."

Her mother's mouth pressed into a firm line. Gripping the stiff hospital sheet, she pulled it up to her chin like this could protect her from prying ears.

Zoe knew how prideful her mother was. As sad as it made Zoe to see her mother like this, her mother probably felt just as ashamed. Like it was her fault she was in there.

"Nihongo de." Her mother widened her eyes intently.

"Okay," Zoe replied in Japanese. *"What happened?"*

"I just had a little fall."

"You fell? How?"

"I felt tired, is all. I must have tripped," she said. *"I'm fine. I'm fine."*

"You're not fine. I mean just look at this black eye." Zoe touched a gentle thumb to the dark patch around her eye, and her mother flinched.

It was as though her mom thought she could hide what was going on, like the ambulance attendants who brought her there hadn't caught on, like the tests they ran wouldn't have told them everything. The IV dripping into her arm, the monitor displaying her vital signs, it was all just a precaution.

"Ever since dad passed away, you've had ailment after ailment," Zoe said. *"And last month, you locked yourself out of the house for five hours."*

She smiled at the mention of her late husband. *"Your father kept me young."*

"Well, Dad's not around anymore. You can't keep going on like this. I'm worried about you."

"It's you I'm worried about." She placed a hand on Zoe's cheek. The nurse slipped out then, but she continued to speak in Japanese. *"One day, I'm going to be gone, and you'll be all alone. You're well into your thirties."*

Zoe rolled her eyes. *"I just turned thirty."*

"And unmarried," she said like she didn't hear. *"Who is going to take care of you?"*

"I can take care of myself. This is the twenty-first century. I don't need a man." She sat back in her seat, suddenly annoyed at having the same old conversation at a time like this. *"And how did this become about me?"*

Her mother picked up the spare blanket at the foot of the bed and began to fold it. Knowing her, she probably felt like a burden and wanted to be helpful to make up for it. *"I had hoped that Sean was the one."*

"Well he wasn't," Zoe said.

"He almost was."

"Almost? It's not like there's a fine line between showing up for your wedding day and leaving your bride at the altar. It's pretty cut and dry."

"Zoe." Her mother fixed her with a hard stare. *"I am your mother. You will listen to what I have to say."*

Zoe suddenly straightened in her chair. Conversations with her mother were usually so puzzling, a minefield of poorly masked guilt and jokes that weren't really jokes. Yet today, she was being rather direct. Maybe it was because she was too tired to put on false pretense. Or maybe, Zoe worried, it was because her mother knew something about her health that she didn't yet.

"I think it's time we discussed the deal we made after your father died."

Zoe blinked in confusion. *"What deal?"*

"You agreed that if you were still single by the time you turned thirty, you would consider letting me set you up."

Zoe gaped at her mother. *"You're sitting in a hospital bed right now, and you want to set me up on a blind date?"*

"Not at all."

Zoe relaxed against the stiff plastic backrest.

"I was thinking more of an arranged marriage."

"What?" Zoe laughed as though her mother was joking.

But her mother's expression remained firm beneath the oxygen tube running into her nose. Zoe's laugh petered off into a groan. Her heart sank as she realized that she had, in fact, made that promise—more or less.

It had been two weeks after her father's death. Her mother was holed up in their home. Zoe recalled her mother's subdued state. She'd seemed so lost without him, wandering restlessly around the house like she didn't know what to do now that he was gone.

To see her like that, to see her alone, it stirred something in Zoe. Add that to her own sense of loss, of loneliness without her father, and the rejection that still stung from being left at the altar less than a year before, and Zoe felt crippled with fear. Fear that maybe she would end up alone, that she'd struggle through the rest of her life on her own.

She let that fear expose her, leave her vulnerable to her mother's poking and prodding, her little lighthearted comments and jokes about being single—although Zoe understood her mother well enough to know she wasn't really joking.

In the end, when her mother proposed an arranged marriage, the idea seemed to be the only thing to free her of the fear. If her prospects in life hadn't improved by the age of thirty, then she was guaranteed to not end up isolated and destitute.

Of course, time heals all wounds, and Zoe soon forgot her promise. Forgot her terror of being alone. In fact, it became easier to trust in that loneliness. If she never found a man, she'd never be susceptible to abandonment, either by choice or by death. She couldn't grieve what she never had. She could continue in a single life of status quo.

But her mother was the master of manipulation, taking advantage of situations, even laid out in a hospital bed. It was all out of love, of course. She was looking out for Zoe's best interests, or rather, just her own version of it. Surely she didn't expect for Zoe to make good on a promise she'd made five years ago.

"His name is Taichi Kimura," her mother said.

Apparently she did expect it.

"Your aunt in Kyoto is very good friends with his mother. He is a celebrated architect. He went to university here in America and is now looking to move to San Francisco and start his own firm here. He has lots of potential a good wife could help him fulfill."

Zoe ran her hands though her hair. Her mother actually had someone picked out. *"Mom, arranged marriages are archaic."*

"They are still widely practiced," she said matter-of-factly.

"Maybe in Japan."

"You're Japanese. Or am I so unwell that I'm hallucinating and you're not my real daughter?" Her mother laughed.

Zoe didn't find it very funny considering her current state. *"I'm also half American."*

"And you're also thirty," her mother said. *"And single."*

And there they'd come full circle. This was the kind of roundabout conversation she was used to having with her mother. She wanted to point out that in America, thirty wasn't unusual to still be single. People were getting married later and later—she was the expert on that. But that excuse didn't apply to her since she didn't plan on marrying at all.

"*Whatever happened to marrying for love?*" she asked evasively.

"*Love can grow in time. But you need a good part-ner if you want to build a strong foundation.*"

"*But you married Daddy for love. Weren't you happy?*"

"*Very happy. And I got a wonderful daughter out of it. Most days,*" she joked—sort of.

Zoe rolled her eyes.

"*Give it some time,*" her Mom said. "*There's some-thing to be said about a man who you know will be there for you, will take care of you.*"

"*Ahh!*" Zoe said suddenly. "*Technically the deal was I would agree only if I couldn't support myself by the time I was thirty. If my prospects and situation hadn't improved from when Sean left me.*"

Zoe very clearly remembered her promise had noth-ing to do with romance, with craving male company—it had been the last thing on her mind after Sean.

Her mother's lips puckered thoughtfully. "*And what is different about your life now compared to five years ago?*"

Zoe took a breath, preparing to give her a long list of all the ways she'd become more self-sufficient, more fi-nancially stable, more independent. She had her own thriving business now, after all. Well, it was supposed to be thriving, but ever since the Fisher-Wells wedding, it had been going downhill. And the expo wasn't really the hit she'd been hoping for.

Of course, there was always the home she was about to buy . . . when she'd replaced the fees she waived for the Fisher-Well's wedding.

The silence seemed to drag out, the rhythmic beeping from her mother's monitors marking the seconds that passed like a timer counting down. When she took too long to answer, her mother laid a hand on her arm.

"You've tried very hard," she said. *"But this marriage will be beneficial. You will see. Don't think of it as a marriage. Think of it as a partnership. A business relationship."*

She was already talking as though it were a done deal. How did she always manage to turn these conversations around?

Zoe opened her mouth to say that she didn't want either of those things. Not from Taichi Kimura. Not from anyone. But then the curtain swished open, interrupting them.

A woman in a lab coat stepped into the partitioned space. Her thick brown hair was piled on top of her head in a sloppy bun, glasses resting on the end of her nose as she read what Zoe assumed was her mother's file.

She glanced up, her eyes landing on Zoe. "Oh, hello. You must be Junko's daughter, the wedding planner we've heard so much about."

Zoe eyed her mom, wondering just how much she'd told them. "Yes." She held out a hand. "Zoe."

The doctor shook it. "Dr. Neilson. Your mother said it would be all right if I update you on her condition. Would you mind just stepping outside with me for a moment?"

"Sure." She looked at her mom before following, but she was averting her gaze.

Zoe met the doctor outside where nurses and physicians rushed from one curtain to the next, answering phones, and jotting notes in charts. Dr. Neilson found a quiet corner before turning to Zoe.

"So your mother had quite the fall outside her home this evening," she said. "I guess a neighbor called the ambulance. We're still in the process of doing tests, but I'm fairly certain the cause was due to a transient ischemic attack or a TIA."

"What is that?"

"It's like a miniature stroke, a temporary lack of blood flow to a part of the brain."

Zoe swallowed hard. She thought her mother would stick around forever. Who else was supposed to guilt trip her about men? Something was really wrong with her mom. She had an actual diagnosis and everything. It felt far too real.

"A stroke?"

"With TIAs, the symptoms are usually temporary," she said reassuringly. "So far, your mother's symptoms have mostly resolved, but this is usually a warning sign of an impending stroke if no action is taken."

Zoe wanted to grip her by the collar and yell, *Well do something!* "What happens now?"

"I've ordered a few more tests to determine the cause. I suspect it's partially due to her high blood pressure, but her readings could be off because she seems fairly anxious with everything going on."

"Yes, I'm sure she's not that comfortable here."

"I understand, but to get a better picture of what's going on, I'd like her to stay in hospital over the weekend so we can keep an eye on her. It's important to properly diagnose and treat her, but she seems rather resistant to the idea." By the look on her face, Zoe knew she probably meant something more along the lines of "stubborn as a mule."

Zoe cringed. "My mother can be pretty obstinate. She's very private and doesn't like to be a bother to anyone."

"Well, if you can convince her to stay, that would be my recommendation."

Zoe nodded, ready to strap her mother to the bed if needed. "Of course. I'll try. Is there anything else I can do?"

"Well, there will be the long-term care to consider," Dr. Neilson told her. "It's important that she follows doctor's orders, takes her medications, makes changes to her lifestyle, that sort of thing. While her symptoms will be fully resolved by the time she returns home, she may need a lot of support to help her during the changes. Does she live with anyone?"

"No. She's lived alone ever since my father died."

Dr. Neilson nodded and made a note in the file. "Once she's at home, it would be a good idea if someone keeps a close eye on her."

"I pop in regularly," Zoe said. "Maybe a few times a week. Do you think I'll need to stay with her for a while?"

The doctor seemed to consider this for a moment before making a vague sound. "It's hard to say. If she's independent and able to take care of herself, then I don't see why you would have to. Every situation is different."

Nurse Derrick approached then. "Sorry to interrupt, but the patient in bed five has returned from medical imaging, Dr. Neilson."

She gave a curt nod. "Thank you." She turned back to Zoe and closed her mother's file. "For now, the best thing you can do while she's recovering is ensure she remains as stress free as possible."

"No stress," Zoe assured her. "I can totally do that. Thank you."

"We'll be in touch. Excuse me," she said, already moving away.

"Sure."

Zoe returned to her mother's bedside. When she slipped through the curtain, her mother's eyes were closed, her breathing deep and slow as she napped. She must have been tired if she was able to sleep through all the racket in the emergency department.

As she took a seat in the cold plastic chair, she stared at her mother's bruised face and felt a twinge of anxiety about the potential loss. The possibility that she could lose the last family she had felt too real in that moment.

That old fear of being alone crashed over her, and for a second, she thought that if she was hooked up to those same vital-sign monitors, alarm bells would be ringing. Her hand slid into her purse. The moment it wrapped around Darling Dolphin, the uneasiness washed away just as quickly as it had come on.

Her mother stirred, groaning as she shifted beneath the stiff hospital blankets.

Zoe leaned over her. *"Kaasan. Daijoubu?"*

"I'm okay." She smiled sadly and held a hand to Zoe's cheek. *"I only worry about you, dear. If only I could rest knowing you'll be okay when I'm gone."*

"Kaasan . . ."

"It's okay. I won't be around much longer to worry about you." She closed her eyes, as though she was ready to cross over to *Anoyo,* the other world, right there and then.

Zoe rolled her eyes, ironically ready to strangle her mother who she knew was playing up her illness. Besides, if she really did pass on, she was certain her mother would forgo the forty-nine day journey to *Anoyo* just to remain a spirit here in *Konoyo,* the world of the living, to continue to pester Zoe about finding a man.

Stress free, the doctor had told her. Zoe gritted her teeth. If that was the only thing Zoe could do to help her mother, then she'd do it. Before she had time to think about what she was saying, she blurted out in English, "I'll do it. I'll go on a date with Kimura-san."

Her mother's eyes fluttered open. She searched for Zoe's face, squinting as though she couldn't quite see her from two feet away. "You'll consider the arranged marriage?" she asked weakly.

Zoe took a deep breath. "Yes. I'll consider the arranged marriage."

"Oh, well, it means nothing to me, but if that's what you wish," her mother said offhandedly. She closed her eyes again and looked as though she were sleeping, but Zoe knew she was faking it because she could see a hint of a smile on her lips.

Annoyed, Zoe left before she began ripping those cords out of the wall at random. *No stress. No stress. No stress.* Instead it was Zoe who was stressed.

But as she headed back to the waiting room to find Levi, she knew her mom was right—but she would make the trip to *Anoyo* herself before she ever admitted it to her mother. If she allowed herself to think about it, really honestly think about it, she'd been lonely ever since her doxie, Buddy, died.

She knew it was time that something changed in her life. That did not, however, mean she needed a man. What she needed was to figure out a way to turn her recent bad luck around and book some clients, make some money, and buy a house. Once and for all, she had to prove to her mother that she was just fine on her own. Before she wound up walking down the aisle herself.

8

Well, Dog My Cats

The dark streets of San Francisco went by in a blur outside Levi's van. Zoe stared out the passenger window unseeing, distracted by the memory of her mother lying in that hospital bed, not to mention the reminder of her upcoming date with her potential future husband.

It was ridiculous. It was absurd. Her heart began to pound, her fingers wrapping around the door handle, ready to dive out and run away as fast as she could. The moment she began to resent the entire setup, an image of her mother's black eye popped into her head and she resigned herself to the date once again.

That day alone had filled her emotional bottle to the brim, and then some. She craved the release in tension that was waiting for her at home in her night stand. After the day she'd had, she was going to have to bring out the big guns.

"How is your mom doing?" Levi asked as they approached the Financial District. She suddenly realized that she hadn't said a word on their drive all the way back to the Hilton.

"She's okay," she said. "It was a mini stroke, so the doctor says she'll be all right with treatment. It might take some major changes in her life, but I'll be there to help her through it."

"That's good," he said. "You seem close with your mom."

"She's the only family I have. I've had to look out for her since my dad passed away five years ago from a heart attack."

"I'm sorry."

They'd stopped at a red light, waiting for it to turn. She could feel his eyes assessing her from the driver's seat, but she avoided his gaze.

"Thanks," she said, dismissively, not really wanting to talk about it. "This is definitely going to take some re-adjustment for the both of us, but once she's on her feet again, I think she'll get back to being independent. She does pretty good on her own, all things considered."

"What do you mean?" he asked her.

The light turned and he finally had to look away. As he took off, Zoe could hear instruments jostle around in the open back, ready for his band's next gig.

"I think she relied pretty heavily on my dad, so I've taken to doing a lot of his jobs now. It sounds like I'll be taking on a bit more until Mom gets back on her feet. Maybe I'll even move in for a while."

Zoe cringed, wondering how her mother would turn that one around. First, her plans to buy a home had been delayed, now she was moving back home at the age of thirty? Yeah, that looked great. Just what every indepen-dent woman strives for.

Levi pulled up to the door to the Hilton's underground

parking. When it rose, he pulled inside and began the downward spiral to where her van was parked. "Sounds like you've got your work cut out for you."

Her van came into view. All the yellow police tape had been ripped down, the contents stuffed back inside and the doors shut. They'd called her an hour earlier to let her know they'd finished with it.

She wondered if they'd found anything. Evidence that pointed to Juliet. Or maybe even the bridezilla's mother. She couldn't forget the implied threat she'd made before walking down the aisle. Maybe she blamed Zoe for the wedding falling apart just like her daughter did.

Of course, she'd informed the police of all this over the phone. They understood her not sticking around for them, but she had to go into the station at some point to give an official statement.

Levi eyed her van as they drew close. "Strange that it was only your van that was hit."

"It wasn't a coincidence. I suspect it was Juliet, but there's no way to know for sure. On the phone, the police said the only security cameras are placed at the entrance and exit to the place, but not inside the parking garage itself." Zoe frowned. With all the extra traffic the expo had brought in that day, the vandal could have been anyone that attended the expo.

"You don't think it could have been a random attack?" he asked.

"No way." She shook her head. "That dress was a Marchesa. It was worth over eleven grand. Instead of stealing it, they mutilated it. They wanted to send a message, make a point. This is a wedding expo, after all. Chances are, whoever did this must have known its worth or at least had some idea."

Levi pulled into the space next to her vehicle. Putting his van in park, he leaned back and stared at her in the silence. "Someone out there trying to sabotage you? Sounds scandalous."

The word "sabotage" had Zoe second-guessing her revenge theory. Could it have been a rival trying to cause trouble for her? The first person that came to mind was Chelsea.

Levi was still staring at her. "Well, from what I saw at the wedding last weekend, something tells me you'll be able to handle whatever's going on."

"You're damned right, I will," she said. "I can handle anything."

"Anything? Can you handle me?"

Zoe snorted. "Oh, I think it's you who can't handle me, rock star."

He smiled, his eyes softening a little. "Try me." His voice kind of rumbled, deep and low, like when he sang.

That tone, that look, had Zoe anxious to get home to her toys. The man certainly knew how to turn on the charm when he wanted to. He could be the king of cheese one minute, making her stomach ache from laughter, then the next he'd have her aching in an entirely different place.

His easygoing nature seemed to find ways to open her up, to tell him things she hardly discussed with her friends. But as he gave her that daring, seductive look, the one he probably used to make his groupies swoon when he was on stage, she could feel herself opening up in a whole new way. She felt herself tempted toward things she normally ignored. Maybe Addison was right. Levi's persistence was paying off.

The mere thought of him the night before had left her vibrators inadequate, as though her body was telling her it needed the real deal. And from the sneak peek she'd gotten in the vestry at Juliet's wedding, she suspected he was as real as it got.

Would it be so bad to give in just this once? she wondered.

She bit her lip. Levi glanced down to watch her mouth, his own lips parting as though he wanted to be the one to bite it.

Oh, she wanted him. Bad. Her recent sexual frustrations could attest to that. But it was such a slippery slope. Could she stop with just the once? Or would she crave him again and again? And then how many times before the lines began to blur, before they grew comfortable with each other, started staying the night, met each other's family?

No. She shook her head, chuckling. "Try you?" she repeated. "Sweetheart, I'd leave you crying the blues." Zoe reached for the door handle and hopped out of the van.

She needed to put distance between herself and Levi, to get home and relieve that building temptation. But he had other plans. As she rounded the back of his van, he hopped out and blocked her path.

"If you leave me hanging, that won't be the only thing blue." He slid his hands over her hips and around her waist.

Zoe's knees buckled slightly, and she braced herself against the van, like everything was cool. She was cool. Not at all affected by that cocky smile or the feeling of his large hands on her.

"I can sell you some merchandise that will help you out with that."

"Oh, right. The sex toys." Obviously her acting skills had failed her because his gaze darkened beneath his charcoal eyeliner. "I might need a demonstration."

"Sorry. I'm not a hands-on instructor." She dug through her purse for her keys.

"I'd even settle for an oral explanation," he said.

His teeth flashed as he brought his face close, his mouth within inches of her neck. He didn't kiss her, but she could feel his five o'clock shadow tickle her, scraping against her skin deliciously.

Leaning her head back, she closed her eyes and imagined what it would feel like rubbing over her body, down her stomach, between her legs. Zoe tried to shake it off, to shove him away, and yet, she couldn't seem to stop herself from sliding down that slippery slope that would surely end in Levi's bed.

The thought brought an eager smile to her lips. "I have been told I have quite the mouth on me."

"How about putting that mouth on me?" His body pressed against hers, and she could feel what a mouthful he would be. She half-moaned at the mental image it conjured.

Levi smelled amazing, especially as it replaced the harsh hospital scent still trapped inside her nose. She inhaled him like something she wanted to devour. His lips hovered close to her neck, her jaw. All she had to do was turn her face and kiss him. To grab him. To tear off his clothes in that parking garage.

Before she'd consciously made the decision, her arms came up. But instead of embracing him, she pushed him away. She didn't even realize she'd done it until he was stepping back, a surprised look on his face. As surprised as she felt.

What was that? Maybe it was instinct after so many years. Maybe she wasn't even capable of letting herself have sex with a man anymore.

Belatedly, she laughed, like she was being playful and not totally screwed up. "Thanks a lot for the ride. I really appreciate it, but I think we'd better stop." She fished out her keys. Turning her back on him, she rushed to unlock the driver's-side door.

"Do you want me to?" he asked, finally.

Her hand froze on the door handle. "What?" She glanced back at him, still feeling dazed, torn between her body's need for Levi and her decision to remain unattached.

"Do you want me to stop?" He stood with his hands in his pockets where she'd pushed him away. He waited patiently for her answer, like he really wanted to know.

As persistent as he'd been, he'd never been pushy, or overbearing, or handsy like some guys could get when they flirted with her. He'd never pushed farther than she'd allowed him to. Than she'd invited with her own actions. And here he was giving her a genuine choice, an invitation to make her desire clear. All she had to do was say "no" and she had no doubt he would back off.

No. She'd said it a hundred times to a hundred guys before Levi. It was easy. *No.*

But right now, her desires weren't even clear to her, and obviously Levi was picking up on that. Well, maybe her physical ones were as clear as crystal champagne flutes, but it was nothing her vibrator at home couldn't take care of. That's what she'd normally do and not think twice about the guy she turned her back on.

And yet, as Levi's open invitation for rejection hung in the air between them, the word "no" just wouldn't come to her lips.

Instead, she opened her door and hopped behind the wheel. "Thanks for the ride."

"That's not a no!" he said, the amusement ringing clear in his voice.

She slammed the door shut but grinned to herself as she started up the van. She wasn't sure why she was letting this back and forth flirting to go on, getting sucked into it. Maybe because it had been so long since she allowed herself to flirt, to bask in the attention of a man.

But that was wrong, she told herself. It's wasn't like she was going to let it go anywhere, and she certainly couldn't keep stringing him along. She had to be absolutely, 100 percent clear with him. They still had two more days at the expo together, after all.

The radio was barely a whisper, but the familiarity of the voice coming through her speakers caught her attention. She turned it up. It was Bob. He was making a statement about the most recent San Fran Slayer killings.

"*. . . can assure you that we are doing everything we can to bring the person to justice before they hurt anyone else. We encourage people to keep calling in with any information that might help us solve this case. Thank you.*"

Zoe turned the volume down. Bob was good at hiding it while he was hanging around the rescue center, but as a person who was good at masking her emotions, she knew the case was getting to him.

She pulled out of the parking space. In her mirror, she saw Levi start after her in his van, following up to the street level and out.

When she slowed down to turn onto Washington Street, her foot hit the pedal wrong because it took a second too long to come to a stop. She regretted not changing her heels before getting behind the wheel—wardrobe changes were a necessary inconvenience when you wanted to look as fabulous as she did.

There weren't many cars cruising the Financial District this late at night. It was mostly a nine-to-five neighborhood. But traffic or no traffic, she thought she should pull over and put on different shoes because she just couldn't seem to hit the brake properly. And considering San Fran's notoriously steep streets, that wasn't something you wanted to mess around with.

The intersection ahead lay at the crest of a hill. The light turned red. This time, when her foot came down on the brake pedal, she realized the problem wasn't because of her footwear. The pedal gave a little resistance before slowly sinking toward the floor.

Her van approached the stop line, crawling forward like it had a mind of its own. Her heart thudded against her rib cage. She pressed harder, but it was metal on metal.

That moment seemed to freeze inside her cab. Everything felt so quiet, so serene, as her van gracefully rolled through the intersection like she intended it to do so.

Lights glared into Zoe's side window. The car coming through the green light honked its horn. Tires screeched as it slammed on its brakes.

Zoe's fingers tightened around the wheel, the leather squeaking in her grip. She braced for impact. But the car skidded to a stop inches from her door.

She imagined the person yelling and swearing at her inside their cab. She waved her arms frantically at them, but even if they could decipher her spastic gestures, what were they supposed to do?

A few more horn honks and she coasted through the intersection. Zoe focused on the path ahead. Her breath caught in her lungs as she saw the severe downward slope before her. She instinctively pumped the break a few more times, but she might as well have been tap dancing. The metal clicked against the floor.

After a stunned moment, she remembered the parking brake. She lifted her foot and applied it steadily, but with no effect. Now she really began to panic.

Her eyes darted from one side of the road to the other, automatically squeezing shut as the van sailed through the next intersection. A painful heartbeat, a gasp of air, and she was through unharmed.

Options flashed through her mind. For a panicked moment, Zoe considered diving out of the van while she was still going slow enough, but in the time it took her to think it, the van's speedometer rose by ten miles an hour.

She wondered if she should crank the wheel and pull a quick U-turn. *No*, she decided. At that speed, it would probably roll the van.

Staying the course and hoping to slow down at the bottom wasn't an option, either. Too many intersections, too many possible T-bones. And this was San Francisco. Who knew when the hill would taper off?

The Financial District may have been quiet on the weekend, but it was only a matter of time before she ran out of less-busy streets. And luck.

Bright lights, colorful banners, and dangling lanterns farther down the hill caught her eye. Chinatown. Flashes of headlights whizzing though intersections told her it wasn't a quiet Saturday night. But when was it ever?

"Come on, Zoe." She gritted her teeth and gripped the wheel tighter.

As she came to the next intersection, she saw a figure silhouetted by the lights. She laid on the horn, blasting a warning. The pedestrian's head whipped toward her.

She saw the whites of their eyes before they leaped out of the way. Zoe winced as intense headlights poured in through her passenger window. A horn honk. An angry shout.

Once she was safely through, she drifted the van to the side, inching it closer to the line of cars parked along the street. With a nudge of the steering wheel, she planned on grazing the side of the next car, just a gentle kiss. But when the van connected, it was more like a wham-bam-thank-you-ma'am.

Metal scratched against metal. Plastic siding crumpled.

Zoe yelped in surprise as she was thrown to the side. Her head cracked against her driver's-side window, stars bursting before her eyes.

The wheel jumped beneath her hands. She clamped down and braced for the next vehicle. And the next one. Each time, it threatened to throw her off course, but Zoe held it steady, glancing the van off each one to create friction—not to mention a long list of insurance claims.

Gradually, her vehicle began to slow, but not quickly enough. The busy streets of Chinatown were coming up. Erratic shadows and flickering lights hinted at crowded crosswalks.

The next intersection came too soon. A long delivery truck was passing through, and she was on a direct collision course with it.

There was no other choice. At the corner, she cranked the wheel for a sharp right turn.

Rubber chirped on pavement. Body slamming against the door, she felt the tires lift off the ground. For a heart-stopping moment, she thought the van would roll. Then the wheels set back down, slamming her back in the seat.

The steering wheel tore out of her death grip, the van taking off with it. Her world spun. When it came to a stop, Zoe was staring down the grill of the approaching delivery truck, headlights blinding her.

A deep horn reverberated through her brain. The truck's tires skidded on the pavement, its cab juddering, rubber smoking.

Zoe's hands flew up. She cringed, expecting glass, flying debris, or a whole truck to come crashing through her windshield.

She held her breath, her eyes clenched shut. The moment seemed to drag on forever, and then they connected.

She felt a sharp jolt, some rocking. After a few seconds, she opened her eyes, wondering if she'd find herself in a hospital. Maybe her mind had blocked out the rest of the tragedy. But all she saw was the delivery truck's grill and her completely intact van.

Trembling, she leaned forward and glanced up through her windshield at the truck driver in his cab. He removed his *Sharks* ball cap and ran a hand through his thinning hair. For a moment, they just stared at each other in silent communication, like, *Holy shit. Did that just happen?*

The oddly serene moment was broken when Zoe's door squeaked open.

"Zoe!"

She jumped at Levi's loud voice in the sudden quiet. Where the hell did he come from? Did he follow her all this way?

"God! Are you okay?" Levi leaned into the cab, automatically reaching out for her.

Rattled and confused, she moved into his embrace, only to realize that he was reaching for the drive shaft. He threw it in park and turned off the engine. He reached down to push the parking brake.

"It doesn't work," she told him.

His wide eyes took in her expression, searching her face. "Are you okay?"

"I-I don't know," she stuttered. "I think so. The brakes wouldn't work."

"Come on. Let's get you out of here."

Zoe didn't argue as he unbuckled her and helped her out of the van. Since her limbs were as sturdy as cooked ramen noodles, her knees buckled and she slid toward the ground.

Levi caught her, wrapping his arms around her. She

let him support her weight until they were safely on the
sidewalk. Sinking to the curb, she sat with her head between her knees and took deep breaths.

Something fell around her shoulders and she looked
up to find Levi wrapping a leather jacket around her. She
hadn't noticed she was shivering, but now the cold began to set in. But there was a heat wave going on. Numbly,
she realized it must be shock.

Turning her face to the side, she inhaled the scent of
cologne imbedded into the silk lining. Cinnamon and
wood. It felt strangely comforting. So did the feeling of
him touching her hair as he swept it to the side so he
could zip up the jacket.

He grasped her shaking hands in his hot ones and it
felt like they'd been tucked into her mother's freshly
baked *anpan* bread.

"Put your hands inside the jacket," he said. "Keep
them warm. I'll be right back."

There was something in his expression as he stared at
her. A look that made heat creep across her cheeks. With
his scent lingering in the air and his jacket hugging her,
it made her feel as though his own arms were around her.

His look softened, like she was something fragile to
be taken care of, not the strong, independent woman she
was. Obviously, it annoyed the crap out of her.

However, instead of taking charge of the situation, she
realized that, at that moment, maybe she should let someone take care of her. As a compromise, she took a deep
breath and stood up. She stumbled slightly and had to
brace herself against a lamp post, but she felt a little less
like a weakling.

People were starting to crowd around, getting out of
cars to help out. Or maybe they stopped because they had
no other choice—Zoe's van and the delivery truck were
blocking the entire street.

She watched as Levi weaved through the people and jogged back to her van. Easing himself onto the ground, he wormed his way along the pavement until his upper body was beneath the van.

Someone stepped out from the crowd, holding a cell phone to their ear. "Hey! You should wait for the police to come," he told Levi, even as the sirens began to wail in the distance.

"I'm not touching anything," Levi said. "I'm just having a look." Slipping his phone out of his pocket, he shone the light from the screen around the dark undercarriage.

The truck driver approached Zoe, looking almost as shaken up as she felt. "Are you okay?"

She nodded. "I think so. You?"

"Yeah. You scared me half to death." And she could believe it, because he still looked a little pale. "What happened?"

"That's the question of the day."

Levi got to his feet, wiping his hands on his jeans as he returned to the sidewalk. His brow furrowed, and his mouth turned down.

"What's wrong?" she asked him.

That concerned look was back, stronger than ever. For a moment, Zoe wondered if this time, he really would hug her. And strangely, she wanted him to.

"Someone cut your brake lines."

9

Howling Mad

Zoe tapped her blank "I do" notebook with a pen that was becoming increasingly gnarly with her anxious teeth marks. She glanced at her watch again. The expo doors had been open for an hour already. Saturday was supposed to be the busiest day of the whole weekend, and yet none of the customers who had found their way to her far, far, far little corner had shown any interest in her booth.

Her hopefulness for that weekend's results had turned to desperation overnight. The expo started out as a way to finally buy her own home, to feel like the responsible grown-up she was trying to convince her mother she was, to advance her business. Now those desires had mutated into needs.

She *needed* to buy a home to prove to her mother she was a success. She *needed* to get out of that arranged marriage without causing her mother stress. She *needed* to undo the negative word-of-mouth created by Juliet's wedding.

There seemed to be so much more than her pride riding on that weekend. If only there wasn't someone out there possibly trying to sabotage her. Or kill her.

Between Juliet's tantrum and Chelsea's scheming, she was desperate for anyone to stop by her table. Things hadn't been a total bust, though. There were all those business cards that Natalie had handed out the day before. Maybe one of those interested people would pop by that morning.

At the thought of her assistant, she checked her watch again, like it was going to be drastically different from two minutes ago. Ten o'clock and still no sign of her.

Zoe knew she had to have a serious talk with that girl. Either that or she was going to have to get a new assistant. Zoe added it to the growing list in her head.

Replace assistant
Find new dress for Piper
Buy new wedding supplies
Find out who's trying to kill me

Zoe stared off at nothing in particular, the beats of her pen growing louder and faster. The strum of a guitar interrupted her fretting. Levi perched on the edge of her table, directly in her line of sight.

"Zoe's eyes sparkle like bay.
A smile from her blows me away.
But I don't get one today.
Because she seems kind of gray.
Hey, hey, hey . . ."

Zoe cut Levi's crooning off. "Did anyone ever tell you that your tunes are cheesy?"

"They're not cheesy. They're honest." He feigned

offense, but considering the ease with which he played around on his guitar, something told Zoe there was a lot more talent he was hiding beneath his cheap rhymes.

"Did you have a chance to listen to my demo CD?" he asked.

"No. I didn't exactly have time between my mother landing in the hospital, someone trying to sabotage my business, nearly dying in a car accident, and answering police questions until one in the morning."

He didn't let her sarcasm rattle him. "Right. Well, I'll forgive you. This time."

"Look. We don't need a musician for the wedding," she told him flatly. "Now if you'll excuse me, I have a booth to run."

Zoe turned, as though she expected someone to approach at any second. It was mostly so she didn't have to get sucked into another flirt session with Levi.

After waking up from yet another steamy dream about the musician, she was done entertaining his advances. An hour, three vibrators, and a cold shower later, she was ready to strangle him—no matter how illogical it was.

Maybe it was simply the stress of the night before. Or maybe it was the memory of his hands on her body, the concern in his eyes after her van careened out of control. Or was it the fact that he hadn't held her once he'd discovered she was okay? Or more concerning, that she'd wanted him to.

However, that didn't explain all the other times she'd failed to climax in the past week, since she'd been unable to think of anyone but him. Not even Ryan Reynolds was doing it for her. Everyone's face ended up transforming into Levi's.

As the pressure on her business was building, so was the pressure inside her already too-full bottle. And for some reason that she couldn't—or rather refused to—explain, her one release was, well . . . not *releasing*.

She felt ready to explode. She just needed to get through that weekend and everything in her life would go back to normal. Without Levi Dolson.

Levi glanced both ways down the aisle, taking in the complete lack of customers vying for her attention. "Don't you have an assistant to help you?"

"I'm supposed to, but she hasn't exactly been very reliable lately."

A woman turned down their quiet corner. Her eyes shifted over the row of booths before finally landing on Zoe's. Recognition passed over her face and she headed that way. She was probably one of the people who Natalie gave a card to the day before, Zoe thought.

Zoe sat up straight and pointed. "See? There. A customer," she told Levi in an 'a-ha' tone of voice. "I have a customer. Now if you'll excuse me."

Levi returned to his chair, guitar resting on his chest as he strummed at random, but she could tell he was paying close attention.

As the middle-aged woman approached, Zoe smiled. "Hello. Can I help you?"

Her eyes darted around Zoe's display, as though still not sure if it was the right place. "Actually, I wanted to talk to the other wedding planner that was here yesterday."

So did Zoe, but she imagined for different reasons. "Actually, I'm the wedding planner for Plum Crazy Events. That was probably my assistant you were speaking to yesterday. I'm sure I can take over where she left off with you." Zoe gripped her pen and held it eagerly over her notebook. She wrote down the date, just to make it official.

"Plum Crazy?" The woman frowned. "Actually, I'm looking to hire the girl who works for Enchanted Events. I spoke to her here yesterday. Her name was Natalie."

Zoe blinked, trying to make sense of what she was saying. "Natalie is the name of my assistant, but I can assure you this is the booth for Plum Crazy Events. If you're looking for Enchanted Events, that booth is somewhere over there. Way, way, way over there." She gestured vaguely. "But my services are quite competitive. I can give you a quote to keep in the back of your mind for comparison sake."

The woman stared at her like Zoe was playing some kind of trick on her. "No. I'm certain this was the right booth. I remember that ugly wedding dress." She pointed at Zoe's mannequin.

Zoe's eyebrow arched in annoyance, but she kept the smile on her face in the hope of at least one interested customer that weekend.

The woman rifled through her purse and pulled out a pink business card. "Here it is!" She waved it in Zoe's face like *I told you so*. "Natalie. Natalie Evans."

Zoe gaped at the card. After a second, she reached out. "May I see that?"

The woman handed it over, all smug. Zoe could feel Levi reading over her shoulder, but she didn't care. The words on the card were all she could see.

Natalie Evans. Enchanted Events. At the bottom was her title: *Wedding Planner.*

Zoe read the silver embossed lettering three times before it began to sink in. By the time she was finished, her hands were shaking.

"See? She was at this booth offering her services yesterday." The woman tapped Zoe's table insistently. "Are you a smaller affiliate or branch company?"

Zoe's eyelashes flickered at the unintended slight. A

sort of cold calm blew over her, but it felt more like the eye of a storm.

Natalie hadn't been lying when she said she'd handed out two-dozen cards. It just wasn't Zoe's cards. It had been her own. Natalie was jumping ship. And not just to anyone's ship, but Chelsea's.

She thought back to the day before when Natalie showed up late with a bouquet of flowers from the opposite end of town from where she should have been. Had her car really broken down or had she been placing an order for a wedding she was planning? *Is that where she is right now?* It was Saturday, after all. And she'd used *her* florist.

Zoe didn't know why that fact cut at her the most. People were free to use any florist they wanted, but Zoe had been using that one for years. She used them almost exclusively in exchange for a VIP discount. And Natalie was probably benefiting from that discount, since they knew she worked for Zoe—or rather, *had worked* for her.

Zoe had taught Natalie everything she knew, showed her the best retailers, how to get the best deals, all the industry secrets. And she'd taken those secrets and run straight to her competitor with them.

The betrayal was like a garter toss shot to her face. It stung.

Zoe's mind ran over the last couple of months. The private phone calls, the weddings she hadn't been available to assist for, the tardiness.

Her fist clenched around the pink card, crushing it.

"Hey, I need that," the woman complained.

"Trust me. You don't." Zoe tossed it in her purse. "Anything would be better than Enchanted Events. And everything Natalie knows, she learned from me." She stood up so fast she knocked her chair over. "Now, if you'll excuse me. I have to go find someone."

Zoe wasn't aware of anything else but her hatred for Chelsea or the feeling of soft fur in her hands as she dug desperately into her purse for the solace of her Fuzzy Friend. She couldn't focus on the booths she passed, the potential clients watching her storm by, or Levi following close behind. He was saying something, but she couldn't hear him over her anger. All she saw, all she knew, was red.

When she'd turned down the main aisle and Chelsea came into view, Zoe squeezed the life out of Gentle Giraffe. But it had little effect at the moment.

Strangely, as their eyes met, Chelsea looked as furious as Zoe felt, which was pretty difficult, since Zoe was irate.

"You!" Zoe said like it was an accusation. "You're trying to ruin me."

Chelsea planted her fists on her hips. "Really? And how the hell am I doing that?"

Zoe risked letting go of Gentle Giraffe to count on her fingers, if only to keep her hands busy so they didn't find their way around her rival's neck. "First you stole my booth. Then you stole my potential clients. And now you've stolen my assistant."

"Oh that." Chelsea waved it off like it was old news. "Obviously she wasn't happy with you. She moved on to greener pastures."

This brought Zoe up short. It was hard to imagine Natalie not being happy. Zoe treated her not like just an employee but almost like a friend. She'd gone to her grandfather's funeral to show her support, and even helped her move when her boyfriend was treating her like crap. Zoe gave Natalie regular raises, Christmas bonuses, paid vacation.

Confused by the sudden betrayal, Zoe narrowed her

eyes at Chelsea. It felt so personal. "What did you say to her? What did you offer her?"

"Just some independence," Chelsea said. "Her talents have been smothered under you. I've given her a position as wedding planner. She's overseeing one as we speak."

"She's not ready for that," Zoe said. "She can barely show up for work on time." Heck, she thought, she could barely tell the difference between a horse and a donkey.

The memory of Juliet's wedding was the final puzzle piece. She inhaled sharply. "Did Natalie sabotage the Fisher-Wells wedding?"

Chelsea shrugged a bony shoulder. "How would I know about that? I was nowhere near it."

Zoe's body became rigid with fury. If that wasn't an "I can't be held culpable" statement, she didn't know what was. But how was Zoe supposed to prove she was set up, if that's even what happened? There were so many ways Natalie could have accomplished it without leaving so much as a fingerprint of evidence behind.

Chelsea's earlier anger seemed to return. She crossed her arms. "So is that why you retaliated? To get back at me for stealing Natalie?"

"Me?" Zoe laughed. "What did I ever do to you?"

There was a gasp and murmurs of surprise behind her. She spun to see those around them all facing the same direction, snapping photos, or whispering behind hands.

"Oh, my gosh!" someone said. "Is that Holly Hart?"

Zoe's glare landed on her other least-favorite person. The platinum blonde swept down the aisle as though she could smell a story brewing. Her hairless Chinese Crested sniffed the air from Holly's arms as though she could smell it too.

Holly's sights honed in on Zoe and Chelsea, her sharp gaze flicking between them. The moment suddenly interrupted, Zoe realized Holly wasn't the only one paying close attention. Being in the best location at the expo, their argument had attracted quite a crowd.

"My drama radar is going off," Holly said. "Do I detect a story here?"

Chelsea ran to her side, grabbing her arm. "Holly Hart. Holly Hart. I'm so glad you're here."

The dog growled, bearing its fangs like *back off, bitch*. She seemed as mean as her owner.

"Watch the suit." She shook her off. "It's Gucci."

Chelsea patted the bun on top of her head, making sure every hair was in place for the camera. "Have I got breaking news for you."

"I'll determine what's breaking news," Holly said, petting Jasmine. "What happened here?"

"Sabotage. That's what. By Zoe Plum." Chelsea's face looked as though it was lit from within. As though this was the moment she'd been hoping would come along.

Zoe rolled her eyes, but by the confidence in Chelsea's expression, she was almost too afraid to ask what she was talking about.

Holly looked like she was practically salivating. "Ohhh, delicious." She twirled her finger in the air and Hey, You materialized from seemingly nowhere, his camera aimed at Zoe.

"Little Miss Perfect here couldn't handle her jealousy of me," Chelsea said. "Look what she did to my booth last night." She waved her arm awkwardly, as though they were on some kind of game show and she was inviting the camera to take a panorama.

"What?" Zoe started, completely thrown by the turn of the conversation. "What are you—" Then for the first time since her tunnel vision had cleared, she caught sight of Chelsea's booth or rather, what should have been *her* booth.

The ostentatious banner was ripped in half, dragging on the floor, sparkling hearts littered the aisle runner, crushed like they'd been stomped on. Décor samples and photo albums were cut to shreds.

After taking in the destruction, Zoe finally shook her head. "How could I have done this? I've been nowhere near your booth. I've been over there." She pointed to the corner. "Way, way, way over there. Remember?"

"It happened sometime last night," Chelsea said. "I just spoke to security and they said you came back to the hotel late after the expo closed. You were caught on camera leaving the parking garage around ten o'clock."

"I came back to pick up my van. So what of it?" Zoe planted her hands on her hips. Not exactly the image of sweet innocence, but well, she *was* innocent, so she didn't need to pretend. Besides, maybe Chelsea already knew that because she was the one who broke into her van.

"So you probably snuck in here and destroyed my booth," Chelsea said.

"Oh please." Zoe rolled her eyes. "What proof do you have?"

"You threatened me yesterday. You said 'You'll get yours.'"

Zoe heard murmurs ripple throughout the crowd. Hey, You snuck closer until the camera was practically in her face. She shoved the lens away.

"I was there," a woman manning the next table over piped up. "I heard her say that."

"Yeah. Me too," said another vendor.

Zoe groaned. "I was talking about karma. I didn't mean I was going to do anything myself. Why on earth would I want to do this?" She gestured to Chelsea's booth.

Chelsea leaned against her table, the perfect resemblance of justified righteousness. "Because you're jealous of me."

"Jealous?" Zoe laughed. "What would I have to be jealous of you for? You're a terrible wedding planner."

Chelsea made a show of heaving a big sigh, as though she was growing weary of having to spell it all out for Zoe. "Not because of my wild success. Because of my recent engagement."

Zoe laughed. Like she gave a damn. "Congratulations. You finally found someone to put up with you. You're a real dream come true."

It was like they'd switched roles. Zoe was usually the cool one in any confrontation, but she was feeling anything but at the moment. Whereas Chelsea's calm demeanor just made Zoe look even guiltier by comparison.

Zoe decided not to feed into her game anymore and turned to head back to her corner. She wasn't wasting any more time or room in her emotional bottle on Chelsea's crap. But the camera stuck with her, Hey, You backpedaling in front of her.

"Well, obviously I'm more of a dream than you," Chelsea called to her back. "Because he left you and traded up."

Zoe's steps faltered. "Traded up?"

"What? Don't tell me you didn't know." Chelsea laughed, each giggle hitting Zoe's back like tiny little daggers. "I'm about to marry the man who left you at the altar."

The world fell out from under Zoe's heels, and she had to hold onto a nearby table for support. Before she'd even meant to, she reached back into her purse hoping Gentle Giraffe's comforting power would take effect quickly.

Her breaths came faster and faster until she felt like she was going to pass out. Slowly, she spun back to face Chelsea, and the rest of the gathered crowd. Holly looked delighted.

"What did you say?" Zoe asked, although it was too quiet to hear over the beating pulse in her ears.

Chelsea spoke her next words very slowly, very clearly, just in case Zoe, or the camera, might miss one heart-wrenching word. "I'm the future Mrs. Sean Wilson."

Zoe took these words and, with every last ounce of patience she had left in her, stuffed them deep down, then took a breath before speaking.

"You two deserve each other." And she meant every word of it—but not in a good way.

Chelsea grinned like a joyful bride to be, coming in too close for anyone else to hear. "You're right. We do. Obviously *you* didn't deserve him, or you'd be with him right now." She laughed, her happy expression at odds with the venom behind her words. "I guess things really do happen for a reason. If he actually showed up to your wedding day, he'd be married to you right now. And he wouldn't be marrying the woman he belongs with. *Me*."

Gentle Giraffe's head popped off in Zoe's hand. Beans spilled into the bottom of her purse, the same way she could start to feel her emotions spilling out of that carefully sealed bottle.

Her fists clenched, her body shook, her breaths came in hard pants like a bull about to charge. Someone screamed, a fierce, painful wail from the gut. Zoe suddenly realized it was her.

She could see it all happening, see herself losing control as everything she'd pushed deep down inside herself was erupting. It was as though she was outside herself, watching it all unfold. And she felt like there was nothing she could do but sit back and watch it all go down, just like on her wedding day.

That day had been a culmination of months of wedding stress—the planning, the calls, the meetings, the details—that seemed to explode out of her in one epic moment of grief and anger. All that work was supposed to be for one single, joyous purpose. It was supposed to be a celebration of her and Sean's love, of their eternal union.

But it was all for nothing. Instead, the purple-and-chartreuse theme seemed to mock her. So when she couldn't get revenge on her fiancé, she took it out on all that planning.

She shredded the freesias, tore paper lanterns from the ceiling, threw cupcakes, and all in front of the entire congregation with their pitying eyes and whispers. Zoe had lost her mind. No. Worse. She'd lost her heart, like a part of her had been removed when she'd heard the words "He's not coming."

And now, standing in front of a gloating Chelsea and all those people, she felt that day come back to her, the sharp stab of rejection. Sure, it was duller now, but she felt Chelsea's announcement like a boot crushing that old scar, stepping on her chest where her heart had been ripped out.

As surprised murmurs and hushed exclamations rippled through the crowd, humiliation rang in Zoe's ears like the whispered rumors of the congregation on her big day.

"How scandalous."

"How awful."

"Poor Zoe."

She wanted to fight back, to repel the idea that she was that weak, "poor" Zoe. She was strong, and she wasn't going to take it lying down. Nor was she going to stand for Chelsea's accusations or poisonous attitude.

Legs that didn't feel like hers moved toward her rival, hands balled into fists. She didn't know what she was going to do. It almost frightened her, as though she couldn't do anything to stop it.

Suddenly, arms wrapped around her from behind, preventing her from taking another step. She struggled against them, but they wouldn't budge. They were firm and unyielding so she couldn't escape, yet so gentle, so reassuring. Like a strong hug holding her together, preventing her from falling apart in that moment.

"Zoe." Levi's deep voice hummed in her ear. "Just let it go."

It had been so long since a man had hugged her. In fact, she couldn't remember the last time she was in a man's arms since her father died. The touch unarmed her. And for some reason, it also infuriated her. Not the fact he was touching her, but what it did to her.

Her eyes suddenly began to sting. She didn't need a man. And she certainly didn't need Levi.

She ripped free and pushed him away. "What are you doing?"

"Trying to help you," he said, holding his hands up to show he was backing off.

"I don't need your help," she said.

"Obviously you do," he said calmly. "She's just egging you on. Walk away. It's not worth it."

"Oh, yes it is."

But she felt more aware of herself now and of everyone watching, watching her lose control. Something Zoe didn't do. She was above all that now. Above caring. Above being hurt, especially by her ex-fiancé, Sean.

"Oh, what a fabulous story," Holly purred from the sidelines.

Zoe shook her head, feeling the humility weigh down her rising emotions. "No story. Ancient history."

Holly shrugged. "Well, it will have to do. It's been a slow weekend at the expo. Too much lovey-dovey crap for me."

She snapped her fingers in the air, and Hey, You was

at her side in an instant, lugging the equipment through the crowd. He handed her the mic, and she stood next to Zoe as though about to interview her.

But Zoe wasn't sticking around. She slipped away and headed for her booth. All she wanted to do was run, to disappear for the rest of the weekend.

So many curious customers lingered around them, blocking her path of escape. She desperately pushed her way past them all, ignoring their cries when she stepped on a foot or accidentally bumped someone too hard. Breaking through the other side of the thick circle, she nearly stumbled into a bakery booth with a precariously balanced five-tiered pink cake.

"Hey, where do you think you're going?" Holly chased after her. Her nails dug into Zoe's arm as she tugged her back. "You're not going anywhere. You're my story. Like it or not, it's happening."

Zoe felt dazed. She just wanted to get out of there.

Levi wedged himself between the two women, like he was protecting Zoe. And she was actually grateful for it. "I'm still available for that interview, if you'd like. You know, we've got a big tour of California coming up."

"The people don't want to hear about your little boy band."

"Rock band," he said.

She swept him aside. "They want Zoe's misfortunes."

"But I didn't do anything," Zoe said. "I couldn't care less about Chelsea and her sad personal life. And I didn't vandalize her booth." She glared down the reporter. "And if you think for one second that I'm going to let you try to ruin my reputation like you did with Addison, then you've got another thing coming." She took a step forward. "I'm not as nice as Addison."

But Holly wasn't deterred. "Well, one way or another, I

need a story out of this boring weekend. So what story am I running?" She pretended to think, fluffing up the little tuft of white hair, like bangs, on Jasmine's head. "Maybe something along the lines of *Always a Wedding Planner, Never a Bride*. Think of the damage control you'll have to do. How can you plan other people's weddings when you can't even make it through your own?"

Zoe closed her eyes. *Great,* she thought. *What else can go wrong this weekend?* "Please don't."

Holly took a moment to look her up and down before reconsidering. "Well . . . there's only *one* other story I'm more interested in." She grinned mischievously. "And that's the Summers-Caldwell wedding."

"Of course." Zoe laughed humorlessly. "I see your angle here."

"Little old me? An angle?" She bit her lip and fluttered her eyelashes innocently.

"I'm not throwing my best friend under the bus," Zoe told her.

"No, no, no. Nothing as scandalous as that. People just want to feel connected, like they're involved in the monumental occasion." She inched the microphone closer to Zoe's mouth. "Just a tidbit. A morsel. Nothing more. I promise." Another eyelash flutter.

Zoe glanced back at Chelsea. She was no longer alone. A man hovered anxiously next to her, a boss-like arrogance about him, a gold name tag on his lapel.

Chelsea heaved a sigh and laid a dramatic head on his shoulder. Zoe assumed he must be her cousin, the expo coordinator. Despite her overly visible anguish, when her gaze locked with Zoe's, she found a triumphant grin just for her. Zoe scowled back.

The coordinator turned to that beefy security guard who had dragged Juliet away the day before. The guard's eyes scanned the crowd before landing on Zoe. Whatever the coordinator had said to him made his eyes narrow and his nostrils flare when he spotted her.

Zoe felt her heart skip a beat. She automatically glanced over her shoulder as though her primal instinct for fight or flight was kicking in and she was searching for the easiest way out. But there was another security guard rounding on her from the other end of the aisle. She was trapped.

"Tick tock," Holly said. "Hey, You, are you ready to catch the take down?" she asked her cameraman. "I want the best angle for the five o'clock news."

Zoe groaned, feeling the decision pull at her insides, especially after Piper said she'd wanted to keep the wedding as quiet as possible. She cringed. "Just a tidbit?"

Holly nodded eagerly, mashing the microphone against Zoe's lips.

But Zoe pushed it away. "Off the record."

"Of course." She snapped her fingers and when Zoe glanced around, Hey, You had disappeared.

Zoe chewed the inside of her cheek, but on seeing Beefy charge her way, she said, "Fine. The dress is, *was*, a Marchesa."

"But it's a goner now, so what else have you got?"

"The theme is pink and navy blue." The colors weren't a big deal, Zoe reasoned with herself. It wasn't critical or anything. Not like the location.

"And . . ." Holly coaxed.

"And the dogs are their ring bearers." That factoid wasn't so terrible, either. They were dog lovers. It only made sense.

She glanced down the aisle to find the security guards closing in. "Happy?" she asked the reporter.

Holly's mouth tweaked, neither a smile or a frown. "For now." With a wiggle of her fingers in farewell, she backed off to the sidelines for a good view as everyone else seemed to converge on her.

Chelsea drew closer for a front-row seat as the security guard reached for Zoe's arm.

"Are you going to come quietly, or do I have to call the police?" he asked her.

"Oh, I'll come," she said. "But I won't do it quietly."

Chelsea scoffed at her, a self-satisfied look on her pinched face. "Just can't admit when you've been defeated, huh?"

"No. I just figure, if I'm getting kicked out, it's going to be for a good reason."

Reaching for the bakery table next to her, she jammed her hand into the pink sample cake. Before Chelsea or the security guards could react, she cupped a handful of the dessert and slapped it across Chelsea's smug face.

She gasped and sputtered, wiping the icing from her round, shocked eyes. "Screw you, Zoe Plum! I'll get you for this!"

"There," Zoe said, licking the remains off her fingers—*mmm, pink champagne cake*. "Now I'm ready."

10

✦

Tail Between the Legs

I know what you did. You're fired.

Zoe stared down at the words she'd typed to text Natalie. There'd be more to come eventually, but she needed time to wrap her head around it, to deal with the hurt so that she could act semi-professional when she finally did confront her. She was still in shock.

At the moment, she wasn't sure what else to say that could encompass the betrayal she felt, the anger for all the lies and deceit over the last few weeks—maybe even longer. She now understood why Natalie had been extra skittish recently. It was guilt.

Clutching her phone, she hit send with a flourish. But really, the firing was just a formality. The only one rejected was Zoe.

The bride and groom in her booth leered at her with their plastic expressions of marital joy. They were mocking her, turning their perfect noses up at her failure.

Annoyed, she ripped the tiara and veil off the bride's

wig and tossed it in a box, but they remained indifferent to her feelings. Now they were just trying to piss her off.

The happy couple watched as Zoe began dismantling her booth, one carefully, lovingly, thoughtfully chosen decoration at a time. The last of Zoe's leftover pamphlets and business cards made a weighty and demoralizing *thump* as she threw them into the box, along with her groom's top hat.

She looked around her booth, disappointed at how the weekend had gone. She'd had such high hopes. This had been her chance to really break out, to use some of the momentum from planning Piper and Aiden's high-profile wedding and let it take her business to a whole new level. One where she could be choosier about which events she took on, maybe charge a bit more so she could work smarter, not harder.

The expo had been her chance to ensure a down payment and steady income for the next year of mortgage payments. Maybe her mother might have even laid off the whole husband business and canceled her date with Taichi Kimura. And Zoe had blown it.

Security had allowed her to return only once the expo closed for the day. She supposed it was a blessing that mostly everyone had gone home by the time she returned. It meant fewer people to witness her walk of shame— although she didn't feel like she did anything to feel ashamed about.

Okay, so she did smash pink champagne cake in Chelsea's face. But, well, that was just satisfying, and totally worth having to pay for the cake—even if it was three-hundred dollars.

Zoe gripped the bride's head and ripped it clean off the body. It pulled out of the socket with a satisfying *pop*. She tossed it over her shoulder and it landed in a box.

"Whoa. Is that any way to treat a lady?"

Zoe jumped to find Levi watching her from the other side of the table, his mouth full of cake. He placed a second piece on the table and slid the plate toward her. The pink icing glared up at her judgmentally.

"Can you believe they were just going to throw this away?" He shoveled another bite into his mouth. "It's delicious."

She gaped at it. "You're eating the cake I threw at Chelsea?"

"No. That would be disgusting," he said. "I'm eating the part that wasn't thrown."

Zoe couldn't help but laugh, which she supposed was probably his goal. "Oh well, I can't have my cake this weekend, but it turns out I can still eat it."

She picked it up and dug in. It was actually pretty good. She needed a little pick-me-up after the day she'd had, as ironic as the choice in dessert was.

They ate in silence for a while before he asked. "So what was that all about earlier? Why does that woman hate you so much?"

"Usually it's just a little industry rivalry," Zoe said. "I think it all began when one of her customers was tired of her poor service and asked me to plan their wedding instead. Ever since then, Chelsea's hated me. She tries to bad-mouth me to people in the business."

"And today?"

"That was definitely something else."

It suddenly occurred to her that maybe Levi didn't know what to think about her run-in with Chelsea that morning. She'd been escorted out before she'd had the chance to talk to him. Maybe he thought she was as crazy as, well, exactly how she looked that morning. Heck, maybe she was a little crazy.

"I didn't ruin her display. You know that, right?" She didn't know why it was so important that he knew. Once she packed up and left the expo, she'd never see him again. But for some reason she couldn't walk away wondering if he believed that.

He gave her a look over his pink mound of sweet icing. "If I thought that, I wouldn't be here eating cake with you."

"No. I guess not." She smiled, happy to have one person on her side.

His expression grew serious, and she thought he was just enjoying his cake, but then he said, "You said that Chelsea's booth was originally supposed to be yours, right?"

"Yeah, why?"

"Your company's name would have been on the original expo map layout."

Her fork froze halfway to her mouth. "You think that the vandal might have thought it was my booth they were trashing, not Chelsea's?" Zoe grew quiet as she considered it. "Well, if the lights were off in the ballroom, they wouldn't have wanted to turn one on in case they were caught."

"And it would tie in with the damage to your vehicle." He gestured with his fork.

"So maybe the van wasn't a one-time thing." She gnawed on her lip. "Maybe someone is targeting me. Great. That makes me feel so much better." She took another comforting bite.

"Well, it's not a great theory, but it might help you get closer to figuring out who it is."

Zoe smiled her thanks. "You're right. The last thing I want is for anything else to happen. Any information I can give the police, the better."

All afternoon, Zoe had been running scenarios through her head, reviewing everything that had happened over the last couple of days. Heck, maybe even since Juliet's wedding. After learning of Natalie's betrayal, she instantly wanted to point a finger at her for everything that had gone awry. The very thought of her assistant had her reaching for her Fuzzy Friend. Then she remembered it was a pile of beans at the bottom of her purse.

But as much as Zoe wanted to blame Natalie and get some kind of vindication for the betrayal, she couldn't see the timid thing with a crowbar in her hands exacting violence on her van. Or for that matter, knowing where to find the brake lines to sever them.

At the end of the day, Natalie didn't exactly strike her as the cold-blooded killer type. Shoving a metaphorical knife into Zoe's back, however, was a different thing. She seemed to have no problem doing that. Besides, if Levi's theory was right and the same person was behind all of it, it couldn't be Natalie because she knew perfectly well where Zoe's booth was.

"Thanks for earlier, by the way. I'm glad you stopped me from doing anything stupid."

He waved away her appreciation. "You were understandably upset."

"No kidding. Chelsea can be antagonistic to say the least."

"Are you sure that's all it was?" he asked. "It couldn't have had anything to do with the fact that she's marrying your ex?"

The way he was looking at her made the cake in her mouth turn thick. Usually so cheesy and silly, he was staring in a way that cut right through her. Past the mask she put on every morning, deep down to where she hid everything she didn't want people to see.

"Oh that?" She swallowed hard. "It's ancient history. It was years ago. I'm over it."

"It didn't seem that way to me."

She pulled a face, like *that was ridiculous,* but her mask felt a little stiff. "It's not that I'm jealous, or anything. Chelsea just hit a sore spot."

Levi took another bite of cake, regarding her silently as he chewed. "If you say so."

Zoe rolled her eyes. She didn't know why she wanted to explain herself to him. It's not like it mattered once they finished their cake and parted ways, but still, something in his look compelled her to. "Sean left me standing at the altar."

He whistled. "That might leave a sore spot. Maybe more like a gangrenous festering wound."

"Ew." She wrinkled her nose. "No. It's healed by now. It's just not something you forget, you know? It stays with you. The questions. The doubts. I guess when Chelsea told me they were engaged, it caught me off guard." She shook her head as the news seemed to hit her for the tenth time that day. "God, Chelsea of all people. You can't help but make comparisons. He didn't want to marry me, but he wants to marry her? *Her?* What does that say about me?"

"It says you're too good for him," Levi said.

"Thanks." Zoe wasn't meaning to fish for a compliment, but there it was. And it felt good.

Of course, Piper and Addison had said that very same thing a thousand times over, in a hundred different ways. But they were her friends, it was right at the top of the friendship contract that they were supposed to say those kinds of things.

Levi didn't know her. He didn't owe her anything, but for some reason, coming from a guy—the same species as Sean—it felt less of a contractual obligation and more true. It's not like she'd ever really gotten a guy's perspective on it since then. In fact, she'd barely given guys much thought at all.

"For what it's worth," he said. "I would have been standing on the other end of that aisle."

A voice drifted toward them from around the corner, and Zoe couldn't mistake the owner of that high-pitched voice. Holly Hart.

"Crap."

Levi pulled a face, maybe a little pouty. "Okay, well I might not be what you're looking for. But, you know, I'm not exactly the bottom of the barrel. I have a lot of things going for me and . . ."

He continued to mope, but Zoe didn't have time to correct him. She was already searching around for an escape route. The last thing she wanted to do was endure another onslaught of questions about Piper's wedding. But her booth was backed up against the wall. There was no way out.

With the footsteps approaching and Holly's voice growing louder, Zoe dove for the only thing large enough to hide her—the headless bride. Hoisting up layers of semi-transparent fabric, she peeked beneath it.

Levi was still talking. ". . . I mean, I've been told I have a certain old-school gentleman quality to me, but—"

"No, no. You're great. Shhh." Zoe lunged for him and pressed a hand to his mouth. "I mean, 'crap,' Holly Hart is coming this way," she hissed.

"*The* Holly Hart?" Levi said a little too loud.

Clearly eager for his fifteen minutes of fame, he craned his neck to see down the aisle. But he never got a good look because Zoe grabbed his hand and yanked him down to the floor.

Lifting the dress's hemline, she shoved him under the billowing tulle and scurried in after him. The wide skirts created a tent beneath the white fabric, the mannequin's legs its center post.

"Why are we—" Levi began.

Zoe held a finger to her lips as the voices became clear, and Levi trailed off. Even through the multiple layers of tulle, Zoe could make out two figures passing in front of her stall. One was definitely Holly because she wouldn't shut up.

Zoe crossed her fingers, hoping they would move on, but they came to a stop right in front of their hiding spot. If she could see them, if they looked hard enough, they'd probably see Zoe and Levi.

". . . so get over it," Holly spat.

"But you were supposed to interview me, not her. This wasn't some crap episode of *Everybody Loves Zoe*."

Zoe's fist clenched as she recognized Chelsea's nasally voice.

"She ruined my booth and you acted like she was some kind of star. The focus should have been on me, not the person who was responsible for the damage."

"What can I say, sweetheart?" Holly said. "No one cares about your little stand with a few broken candlesticks."

"Do you have any idea how long I've been waiting for this weekend?" Chelsea asked. "How hard I've worked? This is the biggest promotional opportunity for wedding planners, and Zoe not only managed to ruin my chances of getting my business noticed, but then she overshadows me in the media?"

Holly clicked her tongue and spun to face her impatiently. "Who are you? You're a nobody." She gave her a once-over with her sharp gaze. "My job is to give the public what they want. And since I've been doing my segment, *Holly Hart's Hounds*, it's clear that the public wants Zoe Plum and her friends. Piper Summers is about

to marry San Francisco's most eligible bachelor. That's
what the viewers want to know about. Not you."

A high-pitched grumble started up, like a mini mo-
torcycle idling. It was hard to see through the dress, but
Zoe assumed Jasmine was cradled in Holly's arms.

There was a heavy *thump* like Chelsea stomped her
foot. "This is bullshit. I've been targeted."

But Holly wasn't paying attention; her gaze was scraping over Zoe's both.

Clearly she'd been on a stakeout ever since the expo
closed in order to corner Zoe again. It was as though
she could sense Zoe's presence, could smell her nearby.
Even hidden beneath the dress, Zoe shrunk in on herself
like that would help hide her beneath the sheer tulle.

"A crime has been committed," Chelsea continued.
"It's your public duty to tell the truth. This is an injustice."

After a moment that seemed to drag on forever, Holly
finally huffed and turned away from their hiding spot.
"I'll tell you what's an injustice," she said. "That dress."

Zoe rolled her eyes.

Chelsea banged on the table. "Pay attention to me,
damn it!"

"Then do something worthy of attention."

"But . . ."

Holly reached into her purse and drew out something
white. "Here's my card. Give me a call if you have any
real news to report." She handed it over. Casting a last
glance over Zoe's dismantled display, she turned and left.

Chelsea dipped her head to read the card. "Hey! This
is a coupon for the Dog and Bone." Tossing it aside, she
stomped after the reporter.

Zoe waited a few moments until she was sure the coast
was clear. Lifting up the wedding gown's heavy skirts,
she crawled out and held them up for Levi.

He popped up to his feet and wiped his brow. "It sure gets hot in there."

"Try wearing it for a whole day." Not wanting to risk Holly coming back, Zoe began stacking up boxes to take out to her van, ready to put the weekend behind her. When Levi grabbed the box of brochures, she said, "You don't have to help. I'll be fine."

"I know, but I have to burn off the cake calories somehow. Unless you have some other way to help me burn them off." He gave her a suggestive eyebrow waggle.

"You bet I do," she said, her gaze scraping over his tall, fit body. Then she stacked another box on top of his already heavy one. "There."

He grunted under the new weight. "Yup, that'll do it."

As they rounded the corner, she discovered the security guard hadn't gone very far. He'd been waiting around the corner for her to finish up. He followed them to the lobby and hit the elevator buttons for them.

"So what are you still doing here?" she asked Levi. "The doors closed almost an hour ago."

He tilted his head noncommittally. "Hanging out."

"Because you have nothing better to do on a Saturday night?"

"What better way than spending it with you?" He grinned at her over the boxes, but she couldn't tell if he was being serious or evasive.

When the elevator dinged and they got in, she selected the parking level the van was on. They rode down in silence except for Levi tapping out a beat on the box.

When they came to a stop, they all stepped out. The security guard waited there for them to return for the rest of Zoe's things, watching them struggle with the heavy boxes all the way to her van.

After her long day, Zoe decided to get straight to the

point with Levi. "You know you're barking up the wrong tree, right?"

"What could you possibly be talking about?"

Zoe sighed. Apparently he wasn't going to make it easy. "I'm not sure if you waited here for me or because you want to get hired for my friend's wedding, but neither one is going to happen."

He grunted as he shifted his hold on the boxes. "Damn. You mean I'm out twenty bucks for nothing?"

As they approached her rental van, she unlocked it. "What do you mean?"

"I paid the guy who originally had my booth to swap with me."

Zoe nearly dropped her box. "I knew it! I knew it couldn't have been a coincidence." The confession annoyed her, but at the same time it had her setting the box down so she could clutch her stomach since it was aching with laughter.

"Where was your original booth?" she asked when her giggles died down.

"Center aisle."

Zoe's head whipped toward him. He'd given up a prime location just to be next to her?

Levi's expression was unapologetic. "Oh well, I tried." But something told her he wasn't giving up that easily. "So, you want to get some dinner? My treat."

"I'm not going on a date with you," she said, but with a hint of an amused smile. She supposed those were the hints that were making him question if she really wanted him to stop pursuing her. She bit her lip to hide it.

"It's not a date. I figure we should probably get to know each other better," he said, way too casually. "We could talk business. We'll be working together, after all."

"Right." She laughed. "What makes you think I'd do business with you?"

"Because your big-shot client says you will."

Zoe's smiled faded. She gave him a questioning look. "Piper wouldn't . . ."

"She just called me." He waved his phone as though it was hard evidence. "Apparently she liked my demo CD."

Zoe dug her phone out of her purse again, ready to call Piper, but a message popped up on her screen at that very moment, as though reading her mind.

Hey! Aiden and I listened to Levi's demo CD. We think Levi's band would be fun and much more 'us' rather than a DJ. I've already let him know. Talk later. Lots of love!

But Zoe wasn't feeling much love at the moment. Except from maybe Levi who was beaming at her.

"Looks like you and I will be spending a lot of time together."

And by the way he said it, she wondered if her vibrators would ever work again.

11

Puppy Dog Eyes

Zoe pulled up to the San Francisco Dachshund Rescue Center in her rental van. The sun was out in full force, shining down on the canary yellow home. She'd always loved spending her free time volunteering at the center, but ever since Aiden had purchased the early 1910 farmhouse and renovated it to suit dogs, it truly felt like coming home.

Her time spent with her four-legged friends was one of those rare occasions when she felt her emotional bottle open and some of what was trapped inside pour out harmlessly. Of course, since Buddy had passed on, that solace didn't come nearly often enough.

So with everything that had happened recently, she was looking forward to an afternoon with a bunch of wieners that weren't fashioned out of silicone. Besides, she'd already tried *that* earlier, not to mention twice the night before. But she was still batting zero. Levi had definitely thrown her off her game.

Zoe hurried up the flagstone steps to the wraparound

porch. Thick floral scents enveloped her like a hug. As she pushed open the French doors to the reception area, the little brass bell above them rang, announcing her arrival. She was greeted with the Bee Gees playing through the speakers wired into the ceiling and throughout the rest of the house.

Marilyn, the manager of the center, stood behind the desk, poring over some adoption records. She glanced up at the pleasant jingle. "Oh, hi. I didn't expect you today."

Addison was mopping the upgraded laminate flooring. She did a double-take when she saw her friend. "Zoe?"

Naia, the five-year-old daughter of Addison's boyfriend, sat on one of the wingback chairs, putting together a puzzle on the coffee table. She waved when she saw her come in. "Hi, Zoe!"

"Hi, Naia," Zoe waved back.

It wasn't unusual to see her there on the weekend. Addison often brought her along to play with the dogs—and probably to give her father a chance to catch up on some sleep after working late on Saturday nights at the bar he owned.

Piper came into the front carrying a black-and-tan piebald doxie in her arms. "Hey! What are you doing here?"

"Why are you guys so surprised?" Zoe asked. "This is my normal shift."

She tossed her purse behind the reception desk, pretending she didn't understand everyone's reactions. Like what else would she possibly be doing? You know, other than trying to repair the damage to her business's reputation, preparing for her mother's return home, planning a wedding to a man she'd never met, or trying to figure out who was messing with her at the expo and who cut her brake lines.

Something rolled across Zoe's foot. She looked down

to find Marilyn's blue dachshund, Picasso, rolling around in his wheelchair. While he suffered from a severe case of intervertebral disc disease, the little doggy wheelchair helped him to get around pain free.

She bent down and gave him a scratch under his collar where he liked it. "Hi there, Picasso. How's it rolling?"

She noticed Piper share a glance with Addison. It didn't seem like her friends were going to drop the subject that easily, especially since she'd filled them in on everything the night before, including Piper's poor Marchesa dress.

"I figured with everything going on, you might skip today," Piper said. "Not that we don't want the help," she added hastily. "But we can manage without you if you need the day off."

"You mean because someone wants to kill me?" She waved a hand like *no big deal*, then she caught herself because it reminded her of Levi. "There's not much I can do until the police are done with their investigation. Right now they have no idea who cut my brake lines, so it's not like I can protect myself from everyone and anyone."

"What about your mom?" she asked.

"I already visited her this morning. She doesn't get released until after the weekend. And since I'm no longer in the expo, I had some spare time."

Piper frowned. "Are you sure you don't want the day off? You know, to relax? De-stress?"

Zoe groaned inwardly. If only she could relieve some stress. "I'm sure." She signed into the logbook as though that settled it.

Checking the chore list, she scanned it until she found something that hadn't already been done. Seeing the fish hadn't been fed yet, she ticked it off and grabbed the food. It was easier for her to do since she was the tallest of the bunch and the aquarium took up practically the entire wall behind the reception desk.

When she turned around, she could have sworn everyone was trying really hard not to look at one another.

"The girls told me about what happened with that woman yesterday," Marilyn said as she wiped down the counter. "Sounds like your ex has his hands full with that trollop. And in my opinion, your ex deserves what he gets."

"Marilyn, I'm shocked," Zoe teased the British woman, which she often did for her culturally quaint word choices. "Such language."

"Well," she sniffed, "no one hurts my girls. And if that woman was able to get a rise out of my Zoe and cause all that trouble, then she must be a real piece of work."

"Exactly," Addison agreed. "You're the coolest cucumber I know. What did she do to piss you off so badly?"

Zoe stood in front of the aquarium to watch the exotic fish dart around the tank like someone had dropped a box of colorful confetti in there. "I don't know. I guess she just hit the right buttons and I saw red." She snorted. "Or rather, pink champagne cake."

"Well, it's understandable," Marilyn said. "I'm sure it hurt to find out she's marrying Sean."

"That's not it. I don't miss him or anything." She laughed extra hard like that proved how ridiculous the idea was. "I'm not jealous, if that's what you mean."

Finished with the floor, Addison plopped the mop back into the bucket. "You may not miss him, but maybe you miss"—she hesitated, searching for the word—"*it.*"

" '*It?*' " Zoe arched a suggestive eyebrow. "Oh, I get plenty of *it* by myself."

Addison threw her a sour look. "Not pleasure. *Love.* It's been a long time since you've had a boyfriend."

Piper frowned. "Come to think of it, I don't think I've ever met any of the men in your life."

That's because there's never been any, she thought. But she kept that to herself.

It wasn't like she was lying to her friends. She was just keeping information from them. Information that, if they knew, they wouldn't drop it until they "fixed" her. Like they knew what she needed. What Zoe needed was to be left alone. Besides, she already got enough lectures from her mother.

"It doesn't mean that I'm missing something just because I don't have a serious man in my life right now." *Or ever.*

Piper clicked her tongue and set the piebald doxie down. His toenails clicked on the floor as he explored the room. She sat down on the edge of the settee next to the fireplace, as though settling in for a good, long talk.

"You know what we mean," she said.

"We?" Zoe's eyes flitted around the room and she realized all her friends had stopped working, their focus on her. *What is this? Some kind of romance intervention?* She crossed her arms. "No I don't know what you mean."

"Zoe how can you not be lonely for companionship?" Piper asked her. "For something more?"

"Because I have everything I need. I have your friendships, my mother, my businesses, and a little relief from my silicone collection. Besides,"—she plucked the doxie off the ground, cradling it in her arms—"what better companionship can you get than from a loyal dog?"

A dog would never leave you. They loved you unconditionally. Your love and affections were never wasted on them, never thrown away. It was always appreciated and returned with lots of kisses, cuddles, and tail wags.

The doxie gave her a kiss as though proving her point. *Nice to meet you,* it seemed to say.

Addison sat on one of the wingback chairs, joining the intervention. Naia automatically scrambled onto her lap, because apparently everyone was in on this.

"But you don't even have a dog," Addison argued. "Not since Buddy passed away."

It was true. Ever since he'd died, it left a wiener-sized hole in Zoe's life. She'd thought she'd move on by now. It's not like she didn't have an endless source of dogs to choose from at the center, but more than a year later, she was still returning to an empty home.

"I'm getting there," she said, finally. "I just haven't found the right dog."

"And maybe you haven't found the right man," Marilyn said.

Zoe laughed. "Isn't that an oxymoron? Do those even exist?"

But Piper wasn't laughing. "Remember who you're talking to. You don't have to be Miss Always-In-Control with us."

"I'm acting in-control because I am in-control." When they continued to give her a look, she relented. "I guess the news about Sean's wedding kind of caught me off-guard. But I'm okay. It's not about him," she said.

And it wasn't. Maybe it wasn't even about Chelsea. But her reaction had to do with someone. She just feared that the issue was more about *herself* than anyone else, that her bottle was getting too full to keep a lid on it.

"Well, I appreciate you coming in, Zoe," Marilyn said, thankfully changing the subject.

She grabbed her purse from the closet and checked her graying hair in the antique mirror above the fireplace. "Now that you're here, I might visit a couple of the usual kill centers to check for some guests."

Zoe knew that "guests" meant stray dogs, because the British manager liked to think of them only staying for a short period of time before finding a family. She also knew a trip to the other centers around the city meant Marilyn would be coming back with at least ten new guests.

The centers tended to fill up fast, and abandoned pups didn't do so well cooped up in a strange place. They would only be held so long before they were placed on the chopping block, and Marilyn just couldn't walk away knowing that. Zoe smiled, putting it on her mental to-do list to make sure spare cages were ready to accommodate Marilyn's outing.

The intervention officially over, Piper got up from the settee. "We're already dirty from chores, so Addy and I will go start baths." She took the doxie from Zoe to carry him to the back. "Do you want to cover the desk?"

"Sure thing," Zoe said.

For the next hour, she puttered around the house, picking away at the chore list. She was just doing inventory on the dog food when her cell phone rang. Craving a drama-free day, she was tempted to ignore it, but then she worried it had something to do with her mom, so she answered.

"Hello?"

"Hi, Zoe. It's Amber."

The voice gave Zoe a mental jolt. Amber was a client. Her wedding was still four months away, but her voice was halting, like something was wrong. Zoe always made her brides a priority, even when it meant turning her back on her own problems.

"Amber. How are you?"

"Oh, I'm okay," she said, but it didn't really sound like it.

"You sound upset. What can I do for you?"

"I just wanted to call to, well"—she hesitated—"to let you know that I've decided to go another way."

Zoe frowned. "What do you mean? Go where?"

"I mean"—she took a breath—"I've signed with another wedding planner."

Zoe stared at the phone, checking the call display as though this must be a wrong number. Finally, she found her voice. "Did I do something wrong?"

"No, no. You've been great. Perfect really. You've always been there for me," she gushed. So then why was she firing her? "It's just that our finances have kind of changed with Dean getting laid off and we've had to re-evaluate our budget."

"But you're still going with a wedding planner? We can always take another look at cheaper flower options as well as combining the venue for both the service and reception to save some money." She was already pulling her tablet out of her purse to open Amber's file.

"I'm sorry, but it just won't be enough. Another planner contacted us and offered us a lower rate."

"By how much?" Her file was open and Zoe was already doing mental calculations to see how much of a discount she could give them to keep the contract. She'd already put so much time and effort into planning their wedding. To lose them now would be a huge hit.

"Half."

Zoe nearly dropped her tablet. Her rates weren't expensive by any means, but there was no way she could compete with that price. But who possibly could? Who would undercut her by that much?

"Well, I'm sorry to hear that," Zoe finally said. "Do you mind if I ask who you've signed with?"

Amber kind of whimpered on the other end, and the line went quiet for a second. "Natalie."

Zoe gripped her phone until it squeaked under the pressure. But she'd let her emotions get the best of her enough lately, so she reached inside her purse, giving her

Loyal Lion Fuzzy Friend a good pat, and said, "Well, I wish you and Dean all the best."

"Thanks, Zoe. Again, I'm so sorry."

Zoe ended the call and rubbed her temples. She put her phone back in her purse, automatically seeking the comforting touch of microfiber fur.

So Natalie was coming out guns blazing. Of course she would offer introductory prices to build her client list and make a quick name for herself. And she was certainly doing that.

The wedding circuit was a small world. Soon enough, word would get around about her cheeky tactics and substandard pricing. She wouldn't make many friends that way, least of all Zoe.

The front bell rang, interrupting her thoughts. Abandoning the inventory, she headed for the front desk. When she got there, a man was already waiting, tapping his fingers on the wood countertop as he looked around.

"Can I help you?" she asked.

He jumped, as though he'd been caught doing something wrong. "Yes. I spoke to a woman named Marilyn on the phone earlier. She's expecting us."

"Us?" Zoe glanced behind the man, looking for the rest of his party.

The man bent down, disappearing behind the tall reception desk. When he reappeared, it was with a wire-haired dachshund.

He placed it on the counter in front of Zoe. What she'd mistaken as black and tan coloring turned out to be wild boar. He was a beautiful mix of brown and black, with a bit of gold highlighting over most of his body. Around his mouth, paws, and spots on his legs, however, tan hair grew, the color that, annoyingly, kind of reminded her of Levi.

"Hello, there," she said. "What's your name?"

"Freddy," the man offered.

"Hi, Freddy. It's nice to meet you."

Two tan eyebrows above his chocolate eyes quirked up. He tilted his head to the side, as though trying to suss Zoe out. His oversized ears stuck out to the side quizzically as he padded a little closer and gave her hand a sniff.

He was still a pup. By the disproportionate body, she figured he was less than a year old—not that one could ever accuse doxies of being proportionate with their stubby legs and stretched torsos. Which was why they were so damned cute.

Once he finished sniffing her, he gave her a lick of acceptance before exploring the rest of the counter. She ran a hand over his coarse fur, just to keep a protective eye on him as he checked things out.

"I'm sorry," Zoe told the man, "but Marilyn just stepped out. Maybe I can help you."

"Oh, okay." He frowned, glancing over his shoulder like he hoped Marilyn would come back soon. "Well, Freddy here will be staying with you for a while."

Not many people just waltzed in to show off their beloved dog and then bring them back home. They were a rescue center, after all. Zoe had assumed that's what the man was there for—that would explain his guilty behavior—but his evasive words chafed at something inside of her.

"You mean you're giving him up," she said, as though she were clarifying.

"We're not parting ways by choice," he said. "I have to. I'm moving into an apartment that doesn't allow pets."

"Of course." Zoe nodded understandingly. "It wouldn't be because Freddy's moving into a place that doesn't allow humans."

His forehead creased in confusion. "What?"

"Never mind." Zoe's eyebrows drew together. She bit her lip to stop from saying more.

This guy was acting as though the center was doggy daycare. A nice relaxing spa that Freddy could spend the weekend de-stressing in. The way he was avoiding the truth of what was really going on grated on Zoe, but it wasn't her place.

Any time she admitted new guests, she tried her best to think of Marilyn and how she would deal with it. Her manager always preached the importance of welcoming new guests warmly, and to not criticize their owner. Everyone had their reasons for giving up their pets, and maybe some of them were even good ones. She didn't pretend to be the judge of what happened in other people's lives.

Maybe the guy had lost his job and he had to downsize. Maybe he was moving in with his girlfriend and she gave him an ultimatum—it was her or the dog. Maybe his kid was allergic to dogs.

Focusing on the task rather than the person, she took out one of the record books and opened it to a new admission form.

"Is there anything special about Freddy that we should know about?" she asked him, pen at the ready. "Has he had all his shots? Any health concerns?"

"I already gave Marilyn all the information." He jingled his keys impatiently, like he had things to do, or maybe the situation just made him uncomfortable. "He's a good dog. A bit stubborn, maybe."

She snorted, flipping through the completed intake papers until she found the one Marilyn had prepared for Freddy. "He's a dachshund. That's to be expected."

"Right." He chuckled uncomfortably. "Well . . . thanks. See you, buddy." The man gave Freddy a scratch behind the ears before he turned and walked out the doors.

Freddy whined a little as he watched his master leave. He shifted from paw to paw as though he wanted to follow him right off the countertop. Zoe picked him up before he got any funny ideas.

When the door swung closed behind the man, the doxie squirmed in Zoe's arms. She murmured soothing things to him, petting him slowly. He tilted his face up, giving her actual puppy-dog eyes. Dachshunds were fiercely loyal to their owners. It was just too bad some owners didn't share the same trait.

"How about we find you a treat. Do you want a treat?" Whether it was the excitement in her voice, or he understood the word "treat" well, his tail slapped against her side, beating to the rhythm of Justin Timberlake playing on the radio.

She plied him with comfort treats as she entered Freddy's information into the computer. Freddy was a healthy dog. His shots were up to date, he'd been tagged, and clearly groomed regularly. He was a great option for someone to adopt.

Once she was done, she snapped a few photos of him to post on their website. Thanks to Holly Hart's news segments about the center the year before, they'd gained a lot of local notoriety and support. Most of their guests found families through the center's adoption page, which Zoe maintained and kept up to speed.

While she worked, Freddy explored his new surroundings. He sniffed at the fireplace, tested the plush sitting room furniture, and even ventured a step or two upstairs.

Zoe kept a close eye on him, but allowed him his freedom to check out the temporary digs. Most of the time, he seemed content to sit by Zoe's feet, staring up at the massive fish tank, big brown eyes following the tropical fishs' path back and forth. Even when she went to the kitchen to make some tea, he shadowed her.

Grabbing her steaming mug, she stepped out onto the farmhouse's wraparound porch. The property opened up into a beautiful sanctuary in the city. Tall privacy tress surrounded the green space, muffling the sounds of the San Francisco traffic. It provided ample room for the guests to explore and play, coming and going freely from their kennels in a longhouse if they'd been cleared to play with others. It was like a horse barn but with little doggy doors to each kennel.

Naia ran around in the middle of the enclosure, surrounded by a writhing mass of excited fur balls. She squealed as the dachshunds chased her until she threw a tennis ball. Their deep barks echoed across the yard as they raced for it, rolling in the grass as they fought.

"Do you wanna go play?" she asked Freddy.

He watched his group of peers romp, as though deliberating. After a moment, he huffed and walked over to join Zoe, his tail tucked between his legs.

Some dogs took longer to warm up to the center. Then again, he'd just been abandoned by the man he trusted most in the world. She didn't suppose that would instill a lot of confidence, either.

"Don't worry." She bent down and gave him a scratch under the chin. "I know exactly how you feel."

His foot began to jiggle, slapping the wood planks. Like *Oh, yeah. That's the spot. Scratch that itch.*

Taking a seat next to him on the top step, she gazed out into the yard and sipped her tea. With U2 playing softly in the background, they watched Naia chase the dogs around and get chased in return.

After the weekend from hell, the moment settled over Zoe like a calming breeze. She petted Freddy absently, feeling like they were having a wordless conversation there on the porch.

If she was honest with herself, she supposed her

friends were right about missing companionship in her life. She missed having someone to go home to, to watch TV with, to talk to, a breathing body on the other side of the bed. Maybe it was time to move on. And who better to move on with than a dog?

Dogs could fulfill all those roles. There were no complications with dogs. No fear of abandonment. Besides, if someone really was out to get her, having a loud watch dog might not be such a bad idea. A dachshund was better than any alarm system you could buy.

"What do you say?" she asked. "You want to come home with me? Huh, Freddy?"

Freddy licked her hand in response, like he really could understand her. He was so well behaved and calm. Exactly the soothing countenance she needed in her life. They were going to be the best of friends. The perfect match. She could just feel it.

Her phone vibrated in her pocket, and she pulled it out to find a text message flash across the screen.

Hi Zoe. It's Levi. I was wondering if you'd like to get together tonight and run over the playlist for Piper's wedding.

But there was one role a dog couldn't fill. And since Levi Dolson fell out of bed and into her life, she was having a harder time trying to fill that void with a vibrator. And now that they were going to be working together, it looked like it was about to get harder.

After six years, she was starting to wonder if it wouldn't hurt to give into that temptation, to scratch her own itch. Maybe it was finally time.

She hit reply.

It's a date.

12

∞

Love Me, Love My Dog

"Whoa! Stop! Heel! Bad dog!"

Zoe careened around the next hallway of Levi's apartment building in pursuit of Freddy, who, the moment she stepped out of the rescue center with him, seemed to be possessed by the devil.

She passed by a large plant that had a curious puddle next to it—even though she'd just tried to get him to pee outside—and followed the trail of shredded paper from a newspaper he'd decided to procure from someone's front door.

"Freddy!" she hissed.

Trailing him through the halls, she tried to keep her voice down, but one of the building's tenants must have heard their chase because an industrial-style metal door at the end of the hall slid open. Freddy apparently took this as an invitation because he veered toward it.

She lunged for the leash dragging behind him, scraping her knee on the hallway floor. The leash grazed her hand, but her fingers clamped down on thin air. Freddy slipped into the stranger's apartment and disappeared.

Zoe cringed. She didn't even know if animals were allowed in the building, and here he was inviting himself into random apartments. She was still on her hands and knees when the door slid open the rest of the way.

She glanced up. "Levi?"

Zoe had considered being in this position for him more than once in the last week. In fact, she'd been hoping for it all day. With far less clothes on, of course. When he gazed down at her, it was with a look that said he'd thought about it too.

He held his hands up. "All right, all right. You don't have to beg. I'll go out with you."

She laughed and reached out for his hand so he could pull her to her feet. "I'm sorry. My dog seems to be out of control."

"Is that the dark streak I saw fly through here?" he gestured over his shoulder.

"That would be him." She rubbed the bruise forming on her knee. "We're still getting used to each other."

He chuckled, stepping aside. "Come on in."

"Thanks." She slipped by him and into the apartment.

The space looked like the rest of the building: very industrial, tall ceilings with exposed ductwork, glossy cement floors, exposed metal beams. One entire wall was floor to ceiling warehouse-style windows. The place was spacious yet still comfortable and inviting with furniture that spoke of quality.

The open loft flowed from one end to the other, the kitchen leading into the dining area, which spilled into the living room toward a set of spiral stairs. It was dark up there, but she suspected that's where he slept. Beneath that space sat a collection of instruments, spaced out in a semi-circle. She assumed that's where his band practiced.

A rare loft like this in San Francisco didn't come cheap. Levi had said weddings were his "bread and butter." By the looks of his loft, he must have raided a bakery.

"Business must be good," she said appreciatively.

He shrugged—no big deal. "I get by."

He gestured to the sitting area. That's where she found Freddy tearing around the oversized area rug like he'd ingested a V6 engine on the way there—along with the mints in her purse, and, come to think of it, part of her purse too.

Levi chuckled. "What did you feed him? Jet fuel?"

"I think he's just overexcited. He was dropped off at the dachshund rescue center today where I volunteer."

Freddy took another spin around the carpet, pausing at her feet. His tongue lolled out as he stared up at her before tearing off again.

She sighed wearily. "I thought it was love at first sight."

"Hopefully it won't turn out to be a one-night stand."

She smirked to herself. *Funny he should mention that,* she thought. "I hope you don't mind that I brought him here. It was kind of an impromptu decision today. I'm taking him home for a two-week trial run to see if we're a good fit. He was much calmer at the center. I don't get it."

"Don't worry about it. I love dogs."

"All right, shall we get started?" Zoe said, wanting to get down to business. So hopefully they could *get down to business.*

"You can't just snap your fingers and ask me to perform like that. You have to be immersed in the experience." He gestured to the sofa. "Please, have a seat."

"All right." She sat down on the edge of the leather couch. Crossing her legs, she waited patiently.

He gave her a funny look. "You can relax."

"I am relaxed," she said.

"No. I mean, really relax. Or do you not know how?"

She frowned at him. She supposed he was the expert. Mr. Relaxed himself.

Maybe she was a bit nervous. She'd been imagining how their little meeting would go all day. Imagining what she would say to him, how she would broach the subject of a no-strings attached arrangement. It's not like she propositioned guys often. Or ever.

"I know how to relax," she said. Wiggling back on the cushion, she made an awkward attempt to lean back, but she slid down a few inches because of her tight skirt.

He snorted. "You look like it." Walking over to the coffee table, he picked up a piece of paper and handed it to her. "This is the list of songs that are usually big hits at weddings."

She scanned the list, pausing on one song in particular. "Sir Mix-a-Lot?"

"It's a beautiful song about a man's love."

She quirked an eyebrow. "For big butts."

He grinned. "Yes."

She gave him a flat look. "No."

"But it kills at the right moment. Usually about ten drinks in. I'll show you." He picked a guitar off a stand in the corner and perched on the arm of a chair across from her. He gave a slow, romantic strum of the strings.

"I like big butts and I can't lie. No, I cannot lie. I cannot lie. No, no, no. Mmmm . . ."

He pulled a boy band, emo-face as he drew out the so-not-romantic verse.

Zoe laughed at the serious look on his face. "Absolutely not," she said between giggles.

"Freddy seems to like it." Levi nodded to the middle of the carpet.

The doxie sat at his feet, staring up at him expectantly. Finally, he barked, like he was impatient for the next song. *Encore!*

Zoe frowned. "That's weird. I guess he finally burnt off all his energy."

"Okay. Let's see if he likes this one." He strummed out a new tune. At first, Zoe didn't recognize it, but once he started to sing, it turned out to be Adele.

As he ran through a couple of examples from his list, he didn't just regurgitate the same old pieces, but made them his own, speeding them up or slowing them down, adding his own style. Freddy certainly seemed to approve of the songs. Head resting on his paws, he listened to Levi sing, as captivated as a groupie.

Zoe had to admit, his voice was pretty amazing. Smooth and low, with just a tinge of a rumble that vibrated through her body, as though massaging her from the inside. He sang until every little knot in her back melted, and she really did relax.

For the moment, she put aside worries that someone was trying to hurt her, of arranged marriages, her shrinking savings, and Piper's wedding dress. Everything seemed to wash away, until all that was left was his voice.

A hand squeezed her shoulder. She opened her eyes, blinking at her surroundings. Levi stared back at her with that amused smile of his.

"Good morning," he said.

"What?" She jerked upright. "I slept all night?"

He chuckled. "Kidding. You just fell asleep."

"Oh, God. I'm sorry. I don't know what came over me. I guess it's been a busy weekend." She yawned, rubbing a hand over her face. She paused when she smelled parmesan and oregano. "What's that smell?"

"I just finished making dinner."

"What? How long have I been asleep?" She glanced at her watch.

"An hour."

"Oh, wow. Sorry." Tucking her hair back into place, she began to straighten her clothes. "I guess, we'll have to go over the rest of your playlist another day. You can stop by my office, if that works for you."

"Or we can try again after we eat. I made dinner for two," he said. "Besides, I've already taken Freddy outside for a walk, so you've got time."

Zoe glanced around the apartment to find the doxie curled up on one of the arm chairs. "I see he's still his calmer alter ego."

"He started to get a little excitable, so I threw on some music and he calmed right down."

Zoe tuned into the soft background music. "Jazz?"

"Classic. Smooth. He's been napping ever since." He held out his hand. "Would you like my meatballs?"

"What?" Zoe gaped at him. Her eyes automatically dipped to his crotch. Did he know what she'd been thinking when she came over? Had she been talking in her sleep?

"Spaghetti and meatballs." He gave her a cheesy smile "That's what's for dinner."

Dazed, Zoe took his hand and he helped her to her feet. When she followed him to the dining area, she saw he'd already set the table. Steam rose from the dishes of served spaghetti.

"You didn't have to go through so much trouble," she said. Secretly she wondered if he didn't sneak someone in there to prepare it while she slept.

"No trouble at all." He pulled out her chair.

Frowning, she sat down as he pushed the seat in behind her. She glanced at the table setting, the music, the candles. "Did you just trick me into a date?"

"Date? Me? Nah. We're just two people eating a meal together." He shook out his napkin—a fabric one, not paper—and placed it on his lap.

She narrowed her eyes. "Sure. If you say so." Twirling her fork into the pasta, she took her first bite. "It's not bad."

"Something I just threw together."

She peered over at the kitchen, looking for the empty cans of pre-made pasta sauce. But all she found was the remains of diced vegetables and spices. "You made this from scratch?"

He held an offended hand to his chest. "Don't sound so shocked. I can cook."

She took another bite and nodded. "You can cook pretty well. You struck me as a take-out kind of guy."

He hesitated before responding. "I don't know what that means."

She laughed. "Me neither, I guess."

"So why did you want to get into wedding planning?" Levi asked her while they ate.

Casual small talk, Zoe thought. The getting-to-know-you type of conversation. Now it definitely felt like a date. It wasn't exactly what she was there for, but she was hungry, and they were going to need their energy if she had her way.

"Originally, I just wanted to plan parties," she said. "It sounded so extravagant, nothing but fun and cocktails and fancy dresses. I never expected to be planning weddings."

"Why not? You don't enjoy the buildup, the excitement, all the mushy girly stuff?"

She shrugged. "Maybe it's like that for the bride, but all weddings are the same after a while. For me it's just business. I already let myself get caught up in all that crap once before."

"I suppose it would have put a bad taste in my mouth too, if I had your personal experience," he said, taking a sip of wine.

"So why do you work the wedding scene?"

"Because I like the mushy girly stuff." He laughed. "Call me crazy, but I think weddings are kind of nice. Sometimes you see some pretty romantic things."

Zoe's fork froze half-way to her mouth. She stared at him in confusion over the home-made dinner, the candles, the slow jazz, and wondered where her rock star went.

When she didn't say anything, he shrugged. "But it's mostly because it's where the steady money is, you know? Same as you, I guess. In a perfect world, our music would take off and the band would be filling the big venues. For now, I've got to be flexible."

She nodded. Now that she'd eaten and woken up a bit, she was ready to get back to the real reason she was there. Levi Dolson was a barrier to her main form of stress relief. If she couldn't do it herself, then Levi certainly seemed up for the job.

Ever since she'd received his text at the center, she'd gone back and forth about giving into her temptations, her desires fighting with her instincts to run far, far away.

She'd been avoiding men for so long that it seemed unnatural to consider spending the night with one. And yet her very nature was screaming for her to do it with Levi.

After a week of being unable to climax, she was more than ready to give into him. But instead of acting like a flirtatious, cocky rock star with a girl in his apartment, he was wining and dining her. How the hell was she going to get him in the mood?

"Sex in a pan?" he asked.

Zoe blinked. *That was more like it.* "I prefer a bed, or maybe a shower, or we can do it on the couch if you like."

He laughed, but she wasn't joking. "No. I mean dessert."

Grabbing their dishes, he headed for the kitchen. When he returned, he was carrying two plates loaded with layer upon layer of chocolate, whipped cream, pudding, and some kind of nutty base.

"Sex in a pan. Well, it's not in the pan anymore, but it was."

"Looks delicious."

"Shall we eat in the living room?"

He carried the dessert to the coffee table and she followed him. When she sat down and took her first bite, "delicious" didn't even come close. The man knew how to cook.

Again, she assessed him while he ate. There was still the faded T-shirt and ripped jeans, the chipped black nail polish, the piercing—which she was sure had been on the other side. Yet, Levi was acting like a regular Martha Stewart.

"Dinner seems a little less impromptu than you made it sound," she said.

"What?" He started guiltily. "You mean you don't have sex in a pan sitting in your fridge all the time?" When she gave him a look, he held up his spoon. "Okay, you caught me. I was hoping you'd say yes to dinner."

"Well, I'm glad I stayed." She made a moan of pleasure as she took another bite. "You make good sex."

"Thank you." He winked. "I knew I'd have you moaning in no time." His voice dipped low, teasingly.

Zoe put down her spoon, thinking the dessert she'd really come for was finally ready. She leaned in close. Close enough to smell his aftershave, close enough to run her nose across his stubbled cheek.

"And tell me," she whispered, her lips grazing his earlobe. "How do you plan to do that?"

He made a groan of his own before turning so his face was inches from hers. "First, I'll have to get you comfortable on this couch."

He leaned toward her, pushing her back until she was lying down. The cool leather caused goose bumps to rise on her skin. Or maybe that was Levi's hand gliding up her thigh. He toyed with the hem of her skirt, pushing it up an inch or two.

"Mmmm," she moaned as he ran his nose down her neck, inhaling her perfume. "And then what are you going to do?"

"Well," he said, "being a musician, I'm pretty good with my hands."

"Is that so?" She parted her legs, desperate to find out just how good. She felt his fingers creep higher. Shutting her eyes, she reveled in the touch of a hand other than her own for once. "Where are you going to put them?"

"I'm gonna put them all over your . . ."—his fingers trailed along the lace of her thong—"feet."

Her eyes flew open. "Huh?"

"I know how to give the most amazing foot rubs." His voice rumbled against her throat as he ran kisses up her neck.

Okay, she thought, *maybe he was a foot man*. She could do kinky. "I was thinking you could start by rubbing something else."

"Like your back?"

Her hips squirmed greedily toward his touch, but his fingers went no farther. She grunted in frustration. Her vibrators never teased. "Or we could always skip the foreplay," she said hopefully.

Pushing him aside, she shifted on the couch until she was on top, straddling him. She couldn't take it anymore. Popping the top button on his jeans, she unzipped his fly. When she tugged his jeans down over his hips, he was wearing boxers. They only gave her a teasing hint of what bulged beneath.

Greedy for more, she reached for the waistline of his shorts. Before she could pull them down too, he grabbed her wrists and drew her back up for a kiss. As his lips grazed hers, she pulled back in surprise.

Kissing was for romance. If she wanted romance, she'd be watching a chick-flick with Addison.

"We can't skip the foreplay. That's my favorite part," he said. "I'm good at it."

"Yeah? Like what?" She bit his chin playfully, feeling the scrape of his stubble against her teeth.

"Like flirting."

"Mmmm," she groaned. "You're good at that."

Reaching for the bottom of his shirt, she tugged at it, ready to rip it right off of him. Sliding it up, she exposed the smooth, hard chest she'd previewed in the vestry—and had imagined touching ever since. She ran her tongue against his hairless skin.

"And talking," he said, but she noticed his voice was a bit breathless.

"Yes." Zoe panted. "Talk dirty to me."

"And hand-holding."

Her lips paused against his tight stomach. "Umm. Yeah, okay."

"And texting thoughtful messages throughout the day."

"Like sexting?" She shook her head in confusion.

She was done with the talking now. It was torture. He'd been after her since the day they'd met, so now that she wanted him, why was he drawing this out? When she needed it the most?

He claimed to be the kind of guy who reached out and grabbed life by the balls. And now that she'd decided to do the same, he was playing hard to get.

Tired of playing around, she took a page from his

sheet music. Reaching out, she grabbed those balls—
literally. *His* balls.

Levi jumped, surprised by the touch. "Whoa." Before
she could feel anything more, he tugged his pants back
up. "Wait. What are you doing?"

"Grabbing life by the balls. Was I too rough?" she
asked. "You strike me as a guy who likes it rough." She
gave his ear a nip.

He laughed, but gently held her away so he could meet
her eyes. "I feel like you've misunderstood the ball-
grabbing theory."

"What are we waiting for?" she asked. "You're ready.
I'm ready."

"Ready for what?"

"Sex."

"Oh, we're not having sex," he said. "At least not tonight." Although by the way he took in the sight of her
straddling him, she thought he must be kidding.

She shook her head as though the sex fog clouding her
brain had affected her hearing too. "What?"

"It's too soon for that."

Zoe slid off his lap and back onto the leather. "Are
we on some kind of schedule I don't know about?"

He straightened up on the couch to face her. "I just
mean that we should get to know each other better first.
Hobbies, likes, dislikes, family. That my childhood's pet
name was Jujube."

She leaned toward him again, running her hands up
his chest with a coy smile. He couldn't be serious. "Why
get into all that when we're clearly attracted to each other.
Let's just have some fun."

"I'm trying to. But I want more first." He grabbed her
hand as though to hold it.

She pulled it back like he'd burned her. "How much
more?"

"Like a date. A few of them. Dinner at a restaurant. Maybe a movie. That new rom-com just opened up. I could take you to that on Friday night," he said hopefully.

Zoe wrinkled her nose. "A rom-com?" She laughed. Was this a joke? "Okay rock star. Let's cut the crap, shall we? I'm offering you sex with no strings attached. Except that if it's good, maybe I'll want to do it again."

Levi leaned back against the couch and gave her a hard look. "But I don't want that."

"Then what do you want?"

"I want *more*." He gestured to her, like he meant specifically more of her, not just her body.

"I don't *do* more. I'm not a relationship girl. To be honest, I don't even do this." She waved a hand at the couch. At them.

"We're not doing anything." He laughed, like she was being ridiculous.

The sound of it set her back rigid. She'd practically just thrown herself at him, and he was laughing? "You're right," she said. "We're not doing anything." Tugging her skirt back down, she stood up and gently picked her sleeping puppy off the chair.

"Wait a minute," Levi said. "What's going on? I don't get it. You seemed interested. I thought we had something going here."

"Yeah, so did I." Zoe grabbed her purse and headed for the door.

He laughed again. "Then what's the problem?"

"I don't want any of this romantic crap." She waved a dismissive hand at the dinner, and the candles, and the jazz music. "Come on. What's with the thoughtful texts and foot rubs? You're supposed to be Mr. Rock Star. You stay out all night and wake up with lipstick on your cheek in the morning. Are you being serious right now?"

He crossed his arms like she'd offended him. Maybe

as a rock star. Maybe as a romantic at heart. "I'd like to be serious about you. But unless you want the same thing, then I think we're done here."

"I think you're right. Come on, Freddy."

Zoe wrenched open the sliding metal door and stormed out of the apartment. It clanged shut behind her.

She didn't know what consumed her more: the humiliation at being rejected when she'd practically thrown herself at him or the frustration of knowing that her vibrators were going to be useless again when she got home. Either way, she wasn't getting any with Levi or herself that night. In a pan or otherwise.

13

Singing the Blues

Zoe pulled out of the Monday-morning traffic and into a free space in front of a brick office building on Folsom Street. The four-story, early 1900s structure was once a hotel that had been converted into an office building long ago. The quaint details of its previous life had been restored like the ad painted on the brick, advertising rooms for rent.

She killed the engine and the radio shut off. Freddy whined from the passenger seat, wondering what they were waiting for. Or maybe it was because he had to pee. Or because he was hungry. Or because he was simply being Freddy. Since he was proving to be a highly unusual dog, she thought it might take some time to get better at communicating with him. She supposed that's why all people who adopted dogs from the center were given a two-week trial run. Because not all adoptions went to plan.

He whined again, but Zoe was in no rush to get to work. After that weekend's fiasco at the expo, there wasn't a lot to look forward to. Just a lot of damage control.

With his two-second attention span, Freddy got fed up with waiting for her and hopped down from the passenger seat, sniffing his way into the back. A few seconds later, a *thump* made Zoe jump in her seat. She spun around to find Freddy buried beneath a pile of clean, pressed cloth napkins she'd just bought—or at least they *were* clean.

The pile shifted and twitched until a tan beard nudged out. Freddy spun in a circle. He dug at the pile a couple of times, burrowing like a true doxie before worming his way into the hole he'd built.

Zoe tutted. "Freddy."

The doxie laid his head on his paws as his tail slapped against his makeshift bed, in a totally-not-guilty way. *I didn't do it.*

Zoe rolled her eyes. She couldn't argue with that.

This wasn't the calm, well-behaved dog she'd planned on adopting. What if he never settled down? If he continued to act like a lunatic throughout their two-week trial period, she wasn't sure it was going to work out between them. Maybe they were just too different.

She had to admit, he had his moments. He'd been good the entire drive to her office, but now he couldn't seem to sit still. Maybe he just liked car rides. Or maybe, she thought, Levi's theory was right, and the dog liked to jam.

Turning the key until the radio tuned in, she peered into the back loaded with the new supplies she'd bought to replace her damaged stuff. It only took a few moments for Freddy to stop his relentless, and destructive, burrowing. Laying his head down, he kicked back like he was just chilling to some soothing Jack Johnson.

Pulling out her tablet, she made a note to pick up some

speakers for her office. The time at the top of the screen told her she was running way behind her usual schedule.

She'd popped by her mother's house that morning to stock the fridge with groceries before she was released from hospital later that day. And of course, her hour-long session with her toys that morning didn't help either. And like usual, it resulted in nothing but failure, dead batteries, and frustration.

Every time she'd gotten even remotely close, an image of Levi pushing her away would pop into her head. And every time, she would grow angrier and more furious with him, like he'd intended to steal her orgasms from day one. Like his penis was a giant pink eraser that had left her with a completely blank sexual page.

She had nothing left, it seemed, unless she was near him. Then her urges shot into overdrive.

And for some reason, compared to everything—her mom's illness, the expo, her van getting trashed, Piper's dress, her brake lines—that seemed like the worst thing at that moment. Because the one thing that could get her though all that stress had been stolen. By Levi Dolson.

Zoe wanted to scream and throw a tantrum, drive her rental van over him and then throw it into reverse and do it all over again. She didn't understand how she could want someone so badly and yet want to kill him at the same time.

The very thought of him made her both horny and angry. She groaned, banging her head against her steering wheel. The beautiful hate-sex they could have. If only he'd have sex with her at all.

The only other thing that was effective in putting her thoughts back into harmony was making lists. So Zoe leaned back in the morning sun shining through the windshield to mentally go over her to-do list for the day. Of course, Piper's wedding consumed her itinerary, since it was less than two weeks away. And at the top of the priority list was scheduling an appointment at a bridal store for a replacement dress. It was going to take a miracle to find one and have it altered in time.

Sighing, Zoe resigned herself to start the day and pulled the key out of the ignition. It was like a signal for Freddy to start snooping for something to chew on. As she reached to open her door, a figure popped up next to the van and rapped sharply on the window.

Freddy barked in surprise, running back up to the front, knocking over a box of blank thank-you cards. Then Zoe saw the bright pantsuit and over-processed blonde hair and nearly screamed.

Rolling down the window, Zoe shushed Freddy's persistent barking. Picking him up off the floor, she soothed him until his barks subdued into mumbled threats.

Bleached teeth flashing, Holly Hart leaned through the window. "Darling! It's so good to see you."

Zoe heaved a sigh. Holly was the last person she wanted to see right then. "What are you doing here, Holly?"

The reporter slipped her oversized sunglasses on top of her head. "I was in the neighborhood and thought I'd pop in for a little girl chat." She gave Zoe a not-so-subtle wink. "What do you say we go grab a coffee and catch up?"

"We don't have anything to catch up on." Zoe opened her door, shoving Holly out of the way with it.

Holly pouted. "Now don't be like that. We were like old pals at the expo, remember? Now where were we?" Her friendly smile melted and she fixed a don't-mess-with-me look on her plastic face. "Oh right. I was doing you a favor by not running a story that would have been super embarrassing for you, and you were telling me all about your friend's upcoming wedding. Now go ahead. Gush. It's just us girls."

Zoe ignored her and went to grab her supplies from the back, but when she rounded the van, Hey, You shoved his camera in her face.

She scowled at him and gave Holly a look. "Just us girls?"

"Oh, right. And him. But don't be shy. It's for note-taking purposes only." She waved him away like he was simply air. "Just ignore him. I do."

Zoe could have sworn she heard him huff in annoyance, but he never stopped recording for a second. She ignored both of them and wrenched open the back doors.

Holly took a seat in the back, crossing her legs super casually. Now Zoe couldn't get rid of her without physically tossing her aside or slamming the door closed on her—which were tempting options.

"Listen up," Zoe said. "I have nothing more to give you on the Summers-Caldwell wedding."

She picked up her bag, slinging it over the arm that wasn't burdened by a wriggling doxie. She began to close the van doors, hoping the reporter would take the hint.

Holly held out a hand to stop the door from shutting on her. She wasn't going to move an inch. "Don't hold out now, Plum. Remember? It's tit for tat."

Zoe's teeth clenched. "Yeah. I remember." She took a deep breath.

While Zoe didn't want to give her any sort of tit, she needed Holly's tat. Not only did she fail to gain new clients at the expo, but her run-in with Chelsea probably cost her some reputation points for the next season. However, she also wasn't about to go against her best friends' wishes to keep her wedding on the down low. She'd given enough info away at the expo.

"Look," she began, "I appreciate you not running that story on me—"

"Then show your appreciation and give me some

facts." Holly made a gimme-gimme motion with her manicured hand. "It's not a big deal, you know. If I search hard enough, I can easily dig up the same info. It would just take a few annoying phone calls," she said as though making a phone call was, like, the hardest thing to do in the world.

Zoe scoffed. "To who?"

"To florists, seamstresses, caterers." Her eyes rolled back into her head just standing there listing them off. "Eventually I'd find the right ones. But that sounds incredibly boring, so why don't you save me some time? No one has to know it was you."

Zoe cocked an eyebrow at the camera. "I bet."

Holly hopped out of the van and waved the cameraman away. Zoe saw the red light on the front dim before he lowered it and began packing up his equipment.

"Just give me some meaningless tidbits to keep my fans satisfied," she said. "The venue, perhaps?"

Zoe laughed, slamming the van doors and locking them. "There's no way you're getting the venue." *Or anything for that matter,* she thought.

She spun toward the office building where she could lock her door and be free from Holly's harassment. But Holly's heels clicked sharply on the sidewalk as she kept on her.

"Oh, come on. You can tell little old me. Where's it taking place?"

Zoe spun to face her, trying to use her extra height to look down on the sleazy news reporter. "I can't, *I won't* tell you. And certainly not the public. If I did, the place would be crawling with curious looky-loos. Or worse." She narrowed her eyes. "*You.*"

Holly pouted. "Fine. Then what about the florist?"

Zoe hesitated. She chewed on her lip as she thought about that one. She couldn't see any harm in it, not if it would get Holly off her back. Besides, her florist was like an artist. And Zoe believed strongly in cross promoting her contacts in the wedding industry. It was all about building a reputation. And what goes around comes around. Tit for tat, she supposed.

Finally, she relented. "It's Pushing Daisies on 16th." With that, she turned and grabbed the door handle, but Holly blocked her from opening it.

"And the person performing the ceremony?"

"I think you've got enough intel already. I don't need you harassing the justice of the peace."

Holly's eyes lit up. "Oh, so they're not going the religious route then?"

Zoe cringed. That wasn't something she'd wanted to reveal. It would be an entire post for Holly's blog all on its own. "Now if you're done harassing me, I need to get to my office."

"What do you mean harass?" Her mouth dropped open in offense. "I don't harass. I investigate."

Zoe ignored her and wrenched the door open, hitting Holly so she stumbled out of the way. Slipping inside, she let the door close behind her. She could still hear Holly yelling through the glass.

"Great talk! We'll have to do it again soon."

Freddy barked over Zoe's shoulder. *Good-bye!* His tail whipped back and forth against Zoe's blouse, like, *Wasn't she nice?*

Zoe waited until they were on the fourth floor before she set him down in the hall so he could sniff and explore his new surroundings. If she ended up adopting him, he'd be spending a lot of time there with her, so he might as well get comfortable.

In the past, the landlord had allowed her to keep Buddy there during her office hours, so she knew it would be all right to bring Freddy to work. Then again, Freddy wasn't quite the well-behaved dog her last one was.

She whistled, calling him as she headed toward the office with the deep plum-colored sign that read *Plum Crazy Events.* He trailed behind, sniffing dubiously beneath random doors. Thankfully, no one came out to see what all the snorting at their door was about.

She had no appointments booked with clients, so when she turned the corner to her office and a man stood there waiting, she gasped in surprise.

Then she saw who it was and felt even more surprised. "Owen. Hi . . . How are you?"

At her reaction, his lips curled into a smile, but the rest of his face didn't seem to want to join in. "Good. You know, all things considered."

"Still haven't patched things up with Juliet?"

He shook his head. "She won't even return my calls. I've sent her texts, e-mails, flowers, but she doesn't want to see me."

"I'm sorry to hear that. Sometimes these things happen," she said, apologetically. Because she was sorry. For him, mostly. Not for Juliet. "The weeks and days leading up to a wedding can be so stressful. Tension builds, adding to anxiety and fears. It can put a lot of strain on a relationship. Maybe her running off was a blessing in disguise," she suggested hesitantly. "I mean, if it's not meant to be, then it's better to know now rather than once you're married, right?"

Owen nodded with a frown. Clearly, it didn't surprise him to hear her say that. Maybe because it wasn't the first time he'd been told.

But what he said was, "It doesn't feel that way."

"I'm sorry it had to happen to you." She didn't say that she wished it hadn't, because it wouldn't be true. He seemed like a great guy. If the wedding had been a success, well, then he'd be married to *Juliet*. Enough said.

Zoe took a moment to give him the once over. They hadn't even gotten married and Juliet had already destroyed him. His eyes were bloodshot, his hair greasy beneath his ball cap. He looked as terrible as Juliet had when she verbally attacked Zoe at the expo.

Distracted by his thoughts, Owen was watching Freddy sniff around the hallway.

"So, what can I do for you?" Zoe asked.

"Actually, I'm here about Juliet. Or maybe on behalf of." He cringed with a bit of hesitation.

"Oh?" Zoe said. "I thought she wasn't talking to you."

"She's not, but I've been in contact with her mother. She tells me Juliet's been in trouble with the police. Interviews and such. I guess there was some vandalism."

Zoe nodded, beginning to see why he was really here. Now she was hesitant too. "There was. To my van," she said cautiously.

"She didn't do it. She couldn't have," he said simply, or maybe naively, she thought.

"I suppose it was a coincidence that she threatened me earlier that day, and then I suddenly find my vehicle vandalized?" She didn't say it unkindly, but she wasn't about to sugarcoat the situation for him either.

"I know it looks bad, and Juliet can sometimes be a little . . ."

"Frigging nuts?"

She decided to skip the expletives, even if she was a tiny bit annoyed that he was there trying to convince her to . . . what? Not pursue it? Not press charges? The guy had been through a lot recently, and at the end of the day, despite everything, he still cared for his bride. He was only guilty of being blinded by love.

"Well, yeah," he relented. "But she doesn't mean it.

She's like a cute little Chihuahua." His smile was real this time, kind of boyish. "She's all bark and no bite."

Zoe scoffed. She'd had enough experiences with Chihuahuas to know they could bite pretty hard. "Sorry. But I'm not convinced. And there's nothing I can do about it, anyway. It's in the hands of the police now. If she's truly innocent, then she has nothing to worry about and their investigation will turn up nothing."

Owen stared down at his feet, or rather, he stared down at Freddy who rolled onto his back to ask for a belly rub. He gave in, squatting down to pet him. Freddy squirmed like a writhing worm, trying to get the belly rubs and give Owen's wrist a lick at the same time. Like his slobbery kisses were tit for tat.

"I suppose you're right," he said. "It's just difficult right now. I can see that she's angry and hurt. I wish there was something I could do for her." Sighing, he stood up. "Well, I'd better go. Thanks for hearing me out. I'm sorry to bother you. I know your day didn't go exactly as planned either."

"It wasn't my day. It was your day," she said. "And again, I'm sorry."

He nodded, but his head sank as he trudged back to the stairwell.

Zoe saw the hunch in his back, heard his feet scuff like he just didn't have the energy to go on. She couldn't begin to understand what he saw in Juliet, but she couldn't ignore a problem to be solved. She loved a challenge. And God knew, Juliet was nothing if not challenging.

Rolling her eyes, she jogged back down the hallway after him. Freddy jumped and barked at her heels. *Why are we running? Are we going somewhere? I like going places. I like running too.*

When she reached the top of the stairs, she called out. "Owen!?"

A second later, his head poked back around the corner.

"Try a box of truffles from the shop at the ferry building," she called down to him. "They're the kind that she requested to be placed in your honeymoon suite for after the wedding."

"Really?" He smiled, like she'd just thrown him a morsel of hope. "Thanks. I will."

"I hope she likes them."

He gave her a wave and as he continued back down the stairs, his footsteps seemed a little livelier.

Zoe smiled, shaking her head. *To each their own*, she thought.

Freddy stood at the top of the stairs like Owen might come back for more belly rubs. As Zoe headed for her office, she called to him. Eventually, he abandoned his post. He lingered behind, double checking the doors again. Or maybe it was because he forgot he was on the same floor and had done it already.

Zoe waited in front of her door, watching him move systematically from room to room. Maybe it wasn't that he was such a poorly behaved dog, she told herself. Maybe he was actually super smart, checking for danger, protecting her. A real guard dog.

As he passed the next door, his tail whacked against the wood, making a knocking sound. He spun around and barked at it.

Then again, maybe not, she thought.

Zoe took out her key and turned toward her door to unlock it. But suddenly, there was no door, no key, no floor. Just an ear bursting *bang*.

Heat warmed her face, light blinded her, and it felt like the door just hit her in the face. Her feet lifted off the ground as she sailed backward. She was thrown against a wall.

Pain shot down her shoulder. Her head whipped back,

smacking against the door frame, hard enough to crack the wood. Or maybe that sound was her skull.

The next thing she knew, she was on the ground, Freddy frantically licking her face, wondering if it was time to play. Zoe pushed herself to a sitting position and blinked at her office—or what was left of it, anyway.

It hadn't been the door that hit her. That was lying on its side in the entrance way, blown clean off the hinges. Flames licked around the frame. Even above the ringing in her ears, she could hear the constant crackle and roar of the fire burning within.

It took her a few stunned moments to realize what she'd just been hit with: an explosion. Her office just blew up.

14

⚭

Blow This Hot Dog Stand

Zoe could see the light. No, she wasn't dead yet. Besides, she figured if she were, she wouldn't be on her way to a light place.

She watched the light go up and down, then side to side. As it drew back, she blinked away the white spots in her vision.

"Your reaction looks good," the ambulance attendant said. "Pupils equal and reactive."

As he jotted it down on his clipboard, the tiny flashlight shone down on her lap. Freddy scrambled out of her arms and dove for it, barking like it was attacking her. He dug at the light dot on her lap and she laughed as he tickled her legs.

The EMT shut it off. The moment the light disappeared, Freddy spun on Zoe's lap to face her, his tail patting her leg. *I just saved your life.*

"Look, I already told you I didn't lose consciousness," she told the attendant. Not that she could remember, anyway. But then again, she wasn't sure she could remember a thing like that. "I'm not going to the hospital, so you might as well give me that waiver to sign now."

Wouldn't that have been an adorable mother-daughter bonding experience? Lying side by side in a hospital room. How would she be able to convince her mother she could take care of herself then?

"Are you sure you don't have a headache?" the EMT asked her. "No nausea?"

"No. Just the high-pitched ringing in my ears."

He made a couple more notes on his sheet, but he'd fully assessed her already, so she wasn't sure what more she could tell him. "Okay, if that persists, make sure you see your doctor. And as for the rest of the symptoms—"

"I'll keep an eye out for them, I promise. I'll head to the emergency room if I have any concerns."

Finally, he smile-frowned and handed her a waiver and pen. He pointed to the bottom. "Sign here . . . and here."

She did as he asked and passed it back to him before sliding off the stretcher with Freddy. "Thanks for the help."

"You didn't let me do anything," he said teasingly, but maybe a bit fed up with her stubbornness too. She supposed she had that in common with her mother. And doxies, for that matter.

She waved over her shoulder. "Thanks anyway."

Zoe hopped out of the back of the ambulance and glanced up to the fourth floor of the old hotel. The window on the end had been blown out. Black char marks surrounded the brick facade around it. Even now that the firefighters had doused the fire, smoke drifted out from the broken glass.

Thankfully, no one in the surrounding offices had been hurt. The blast had been confined to her office alone.

While that was a good thing, the thought made her hands holding Freddy start to shake and her knees tremble.

A few seconds later and she and Freddy would have been walking into that office. Hell, if she'd been on time that morning, she would have been smack dab in the middle of the explosion when it went off.

For some annoying reason, she could hear Levi's voice in her head. *Life's too short.* And both Zoe's and Freddy's were almost cut short that morning.

She held Freddy close as she watched the police officers discuss the wreckage, taking photos of blown-up bits of taffeta, silk flowers, crystal headpieces, and chunks of silicone dildos. Lots and lots of colorful dildos. While she'd answered most of their questions already, she assumed that would raise a few more.

"Zoe!"

Over the ringing in her ears, she heard her name being called. For a second, she wondered if she was imagining Levi's voice again, but then she turned to see him waving at her from behind the police line. With a glance back at what was left of her business, she headed down the sidewalk to meet him.

When she got closer, he said, "There you are. Are you all right? I was so worried when I saw all the emergency vehicles."

"About what?" Zoe blinked at him.

She was surprised to even see him there, far less looking all frowny at her. He eyed her up like he wanted to dive over the police tape and hug her. After what happened between the two of them the night before—or rather, what didn't happen—she didn't understand why.

Seeing that look in his eyes kept her on the opposite side of the tape, like the thin piece of plastic would protect her, would prevent him from coming any closer.

"What do you think I was worried about?" He scowled

at her. "*You*. That's your office building, isn't it?" He pulled out her business card and checked the address on it.

"Yes, it is," she said matter-of-factly.

Zoe kept any emotion out of her voice and expression. She tried to shove it into that overfilled bottle inside. But that hadn't been working so well as of late, so she reached into her purse and groped for Merry Monkey instead.

"More specifically," she said, "that giant charred hole at the top is my office. Or it *was* my office."

Levi's mouth popped open and he glanced back up at the fourth floor, then at the card to double check, like she had to be kidding. "Your office blew up? How?" Now he did step over the police line.

Her heart thudded in her chest, wondering if he'd try to touch her, to comfort her. Like she needed his pity. Like she needed him at all.

She took an automatic step back, and she squeezed Freddy tighter, hiding behind him like backup protection. "I'm thinking combustion."

Levi scowled. "Obviously," he said a bit sharply. "Snap out of it. It's not funny. You could have been in there when it happened."

Her mask started to slip a little, startled by his dramatic reaction. Well, okay, maybe it wasn't too dramatic. She supposed when she got home and didn't have to pretend for anyone, she might actually fall to pieces smaller than the silicone bits squishing beneath her shoes.

She could feel herself begin to shake again as the reality seeped through her calm exterior. But she couldn't fall apart. She couldn't lose control. Not here. Most especially not in front of Levi.

"Yeah, but I wasn't, okay?" she said. "I was just about to go in when it blew up. I only got thrown around a little."

Levi reached out to her. Taking another step back, she

brushed his hand aside. But as his fingers grazed her arm, she felt his touch like a call, feeling the need to lean against him like she'd wanted to after her van lost control.

A police officer approached them from a cruiser. "Excuse me, sir?" he addressed Levi. "I'm going to have to ask you to leave the crime scene." It was a nice-enough request, but the firmness behind it had even Zoe backing up.

"Sorry about that," Levi told the officer. "I just wanted to make sure she was okay. But obviously she's just fine without me." He gave her a cold look before stepping over the police tape and heading back down the sidewalk.

Zoe scowled at his retreating back. Where did he get off being mad at her? Wasn't he the one that had been pushing her away in his apartment?

She stepped over the police tape and marched after him. When she caught up, she grabbed him by the sleeve and spun him around to face her.

"What happened to laid-back Levi?" she asked. "The go-with-the-flow rock and roller? You're getting awfully worked up over a little explosion."

He rolled his eyes. "Maybe because of who was in it."

"I didn't realize you cared," she threw at him. "You didn't seem to care when you were kicking me out of your apartment."

Levi tossed his head back and laughed, but he obviously wasn't amused. "I believe you left of your own free will after I asked you for more than what you were offering."

"If you didn't like what I was offering, then why are you here?"

Had he reconsidered? She wasn't sure she would sleep with him now, after being rejected. But she couldn't deny the way his touch had felt the night before.

Even now, she could still feel those talented fingers on her body, could remember the way his deep, melodic voice tickled her ear. Her body wanted him, all right. She couldn't deny that—at least not to herself. To Levi, she would deny it to her grave.

"You told me to come by to finish going over the playlist," he said. "Remember?"

"Oh" was all she could say. She'd completely forgotten about that. "I just hadn't expected you so soon."

"Well, I guess I was a little eager."

Zoe wasn't sure if he meant he was eager about playing at Piper's wedding or eager to see her. Since she was afraid she already knew the answer, she didn't bother to clarify. It was obvious they wanted two different things.

She'd been up-front the night before when she told him she didn't want to get romantically involved, that she couldn't offer him *more*. That path wasn't an option for her. And it was clear to her now that he wasn't interested in just sex. So what else was there to say?

She must have been silent for a while because he asked, "So what happened?"

"Nothing happened," she snapped, frustrated with the whole situation. "This is just the way I am. I don't want a relationship with anyone. It's not you. It's me."

"Really? You're giving me the whole 'It's not you. It's me' line?" He laughed. "I meant what happened in your office?"

The way he smiled at her then made her blush. She'd been doing that a lot lately. They were surrounded by her sex toys scattered all over Folsom Street, and yet she was getting embarrassed because a guy had a crush on her.

"Oh," she said again. After a moment, she redirected her thoughts, hoping the blaze in her cheeks would subside. "The police won't reveal the cause, but I can probably guess what happened."

"You think someone bombed your office," he said more than asked. "I take it you have some suspects in mind."

"Chelsea for starters. Either that or Juliet."

He stared up at the fourth story again. "Can you really see either of them doing something so extreme? I mean Chelsea struck me as a mean girl from high school all grown up, but this seems a little out of her league."

It was true. Chelsea was more about the mental head games, but then she recalled her threat at the expo after Zoe had caked her, and she wasn't so sure.

Screw you, Zoe Plum! I'll get you for this!

Was this how Chelsea was getting her back? Holly had told Chelsea that if she wanted to be noticed by the media then she *should do something worthy of attention.* Maybe this was Chelsea doing something to get attention, or at least to bring bad attention to Zoe.

Juliet, aka bridezilla, on the other hand, had that twitchy, unhinged look in her eyes. There was lots of potential there for a psychotic break.

All bark no bite, my ass, Zoe thought.

"When I arrived today," she said, "minutes before the explosion, I had a visitor waiting outside my office."

"Who?" Levi asked.

"Owen Wells."

"You're kidding. Owen? You think he could be a suspect?" His face kind of twisted, probably trying to imagine the man he went to university with as an attempted murderer. "If so, maybe they're more perfect for each other than anyone thought."

Zoe shook her head. "No. I don't think he's capable of something like that. He was only here trying to defend Juliet over the whole vandalism thing. It's just weird timing is all."

"Like maybe he might have been stalling you?"

"Maybe." She grew quiet as she considered him as a threat, or at least an accessory to the crime.

He seemed like such a nice guy. She didn't like to think of him in that light—or rather, darkness. However, if he was crazy about a nut job like Juliet, maybe it took one to love one.

"I don't know what to think," she said. "But I can't come up with anyone else that wants to kill me this week."

"Got a lot of friends, do you?"

She snorted but didn't answer. Freddy answered for her by trying to lick her chin. *I'm your friend. Who are you again?*

"So what are you going to do now without an office?" he asked.

Zoe laughed, but it was more like an exhausted sigh. "I don't know. I suppose I'll start searching tomorrow. I can't work out of my apartment right now. It's a disaster. I'm in the middle of packing for the move that's not happening now. You know, to the house I can't afford anymore due to lack of steady business."

He kicked the toe of his shoe against the brick wall next to them. "Well, I know someone with a pretty big flat that might have some extra space to offer you."

Zoe stared at him, like she wasn't sure if she'd understood correctly, but when he continued to act shy, she realized he was offering his apartment to her.

"Why would you do that?" she demanded. "Why would you offer me your space after last night? After you were about to walk away just now? I don't understand."

He shrugged. "No big deal. I aim to please."

"It is a big deal. And are you aiming to please anyone? Or please me?"

"Lots of people. I'm not the worst guy, you know," he said a little defensively. "But especially you."

She'd been clear the night before. She knew she had. And yet here he was, standing before her with that hopeful boy-next-door look on his face.

Part of her recoiled at the romance, while part of her was intrigued. On the outside, he looked like a bona fide rock star. But beneath all the piercings, the dark look, the ripped jeans, he struck her as the sweet, innocent guy. The boy next door all grown up. The guy who, when he told you he liked you, he meant *you*, not your tits and ass—no matter how amazing hers were. Levi could be one of the good ones. Which was very, very bad news.

"I'm not sure I can be any clearer," she said. "I'm not trying to lead you on here."

"Who says you're doing the leading?" he said with that boyish grin.

But she wasn't smiling. She wanted him to know she was serious. "You can't change my mind. Many men have tried before you."

"I know I can't. The only person that can change your mind is you." His expression suddenly matched her own, like maybe she was getting through to him. Or maybe it was because he thought he could get through to her.

"I can't offer you more, Levi." She shook her head, afraid to accept the offer. Afraid to go down a path with more temptation than she'd already allowed in. Temptation for more than just sex.

"This isn't extortion, Zoe. You need help. I can offer it. No strings attached." He gave her a slight smirk, and she realized he was using her words on purpose.

She couldn't help but smile back. She took a deep breath, unsure if she was doing the right thing. But with Piper's wedding coming up and so much to do with replacing, well, everything, she was backed into a corner.

"Okay. I appreciate the offer. It won't be for long, I promise. I'll be out as soon as I can."

Freddy suddenly squirmed in her arms—more than usual, anyway. She realized he probably had to pee, since his last walk was before they arrived at the office.

She placed him on the ground. With all the people coming and going around them, she kept his leash short as she let him lead her down the sidewalk.

Levi strolled beside her. She found she didn't really mind, but she continued to worry about their new business arrangement. And that's all it was: business.

They were quiet as Freddy searched for the perfect spot to relieve himself. Then he became distracted by a butterfly, and then a piece of grass, and then his own tail.

Zoe stared at the path of wreckage strewn about the street. It littered the sidewalk and decorated parked cars. Her eyes followed the ruined remains of her office all the way to the intersection.

On every street corner, there seemed to be plenty of people with nothing better to do than stand around and gawk. While some of them had their phones out, snapping photos, one person in particular caught her eye. He had a professional video camera honed in on the chaos.

The man's posture was tense, his attention focused as he panned across the view of the ruins. Finally, he lowered the camera to survey the scene again and Zoe got a clear look at his face.

It was, well . . . Zoe didn't actually know his name. It was Holly Hart's minion, Hey, You, as she not-so-fondly referred to him.

Zoe automatically scanned her surroundings for a sign of the annoying blonde. Hadn't she gotten enough stories out of her for one day? Zoe could just imagine the headlines she'd invent for this one.

We'll see about that, she thought.

"I'll be right back," she told Levi.

Plucking Freddy off the ground, Zoe headed for the

intersection. The light turned, giving her the crosswalk symbol and she marched across the street.

She was half way to the other side when a car squealed around the corner for a right-hand turn. Zoe saw it flying toward her as though in slow motion, yet she wasn't fast enough to dive out of the way.

Her muscles clenched, freezing in indecision. Should she run or brace for impact?

The driver slammed on the brakes, tires skidding. Zoe stumbled to the side in an awkward backpedal, clutching Freddy. When the car lurched to a stop, it rocked from the momentum, barely three inches from her leg.

Zoe glared at the driver who threw his hands in the air sheepishly and mouthed the words "sorry."

Is the whole damned city out to kill me today? But there was no time to give him a piece of her mind or she'd lose the nosey cameraman.

Looking back across the street, she caught Hey, You's eye. He'd seen the near miss and knew she was coming for him. The advantage of surprise was lost. Clutching his camera, he made a break for it.

Zoe took off after him. She weaved through the throng of people collected on the sidewalk, bobbing her head, hoping for a glimpse of muted, brown hair and undefined features. But he was a difficult man to pick out of a crowd even when he stood still.

It made her realize how perfect he was for the job of media hound. He was so very extraordinarily ordinary that no one would be able to describe him if they were looking right at him. Heck, she'd never even heard him speak.

Just when she thought she'd lost his trail, she saw him headed for an alley halfway down the block. Pausing at the entrance, he glanced around him. His eyes met Zoe's and his one free hand reached down and covered his crotch, as though subconsciously.

She grinned wickedly. Obviously he hadn't forgotten the time she threatened him when he was harassing Piper.

Pushing past a couple of guys she recognized from her office building, she picked up her pace and ran, shoes clicking like angry drumbeats. Now that she'd started to really move, she noticed new aches and pains from when the explosion sent her flying.

Biting the inside of her cheek, she pushed aside the twinges of shooting pain. The jolts coursed through parts of her body she hadn't even realized she'd injured. Her head throbbed as she forged on.

Footsteps getting faster and faster, she turned the corner, ready to grab Hey, You by the sweaty shirt collar. But as she plunged into the alley, she only caught a glimpse of him at the other end, running for his life. A second later, he rounded the corner and disappeared from sight.

Zoe swore under her breath. He'd been too fast for her. She supposed you couldn't get involved with Holly Hart for a living and not know how to run for your life—or balls, in his case.

It wasn't like she was going to catch up to him with her injuries, in heels, and carrying a dog, so she slowed down. However, Freddy's legs pawed the air, like they were still running. *Let me at him. Let me at him!*

Zoe gave his head a soothing pat. "Don't worry. We'll get him next time. Right?"

Freddy stared at her, his big ears rising a little. *Get who?*

Sighing, Zoe turned back for the main road. The sun had yet to hit the narrow back alley. The morning chill still lingered, crawling over the dampness that had

settled on her skin from the chase. Goosebumps prickled up the back of her neck.

She held Freddy just a little bit closer, for both warmth
and comfort. She'd just survived a near-miss explosion.
Someone was clearly out to kill her, and here she was
chasing a creep down a quiet alley.

She glanced behind her again, but Hey, You was long
gone. When she turned back, a tall figure was blocking
her path.

Zoe jumped. Startled, Freddy began barking. Once he
recognized Levi, his tail began to whip back and forth,
hitting Zoe on one of the many bruises she'd acquired
that morning.

"Are you okay?" Levi asked Zoe.

"Yeah, I just saw Holly's cameraman hanging around."

"Really? Is Holly around here somewhere?" He began
to scan the crowd, as though hoping to corner her for an
interview.

Zoe rolled her eyes, but before she could come up with
a sharp response, her phone vibrated in her purse. She
pulled it out and answered.

"Hello?"

"Hello, is this Zoe Plum?"

"It is." Zoe automatically held her breath, hoping for
good news.

"This is San Francisco General Hospital. Your mother
is ready to be picked up."

"Thank you. I'll be there to pick her up as soon as I
can."

Zoe hung up and automatically turned to head for her
van, but when she looked across the street, she saw that
her rental van was one of the vehicles covered in little
numbers to mark the evidence scattered all over it. There
was no way the police were going to release it to her any
time soon.

"You have to pick your mom up?" Levi asked like he was just making conversation. "It's a shame you don't have a ride."

His stupid grin held a little self-satisfied glow. He wasn't going to make it easy on her, but she supposed she deserved that. He'd done a lot for her in the last few days and what had she done? Assumed he was some easy lay, propositioned him for sex and then got angry when he turned her down.

With great difficulty, she swallowed her pride. "Levi, would you mind giving my mother and me a ride home?"

"Why, I'd love to." He batted his eyelashes at her. "You just can't seem to get enough of me, can you?"

15

Put a Dog Off the Scent

Zoe unlocked the front door to the Victorian stick-style home in Noe Valley where she grew up. "Here we are." She held the door open for her mother to enter, but Freddy barged in first, already scoping out the joint.

It was another hot day, so the air felt stifling and heavy inside despite the fact that Zoe had shut all the curtains to keep the sun from beating in.

"It's nice to be home," her mother said, shuffling inside. "Thank you very much for the ride, Levi."

"No problem," he said. "It was nice to meet you."

"You too." She gave him a little head bob, like a mini bow. It was a habit she'd never managed to fully break since leaving Japan.

Taking off her shoes, she put on a pair of slippers before heading into the living room. Zoe knew her mother often got cold feet, but she also suspected that it was another habit that had carried over, despite the fact that they had hardwood floors, not tatami mats.

Levi waited until she was out of earshot before whispering in Zoe's ear. "I think your mom hates me."

Zoe snorted, not sure why he even cared what her mother thought of him. He certainly tried hard enough to change her mind on the drive home with the small talk and the cheesy compliments like "I can see where your daughter gets her good looks."

"She doesn't hate you," she told him. "She's distant with everyone at first. My mom is very private and keeps to herself. She's probably just embarrassed that a complete stranger is driving her home from the hospital."

Levi handed her the bag of belongings her mother brought home from the hospital. Freddy gave it a curious sniff before heading into the living room after her mother.

"I won't be long," she told Levi, heading up the stairs to the second-floor bedrooms. "Or I can take a taxi home if you have somewhere else to be."

"Somewhere better to be than here with you? Impossible." He smiled at her from the bottom of the stairs.

"Then I'll just be a minute."

"Take your time." He waved her on. "I'll just be snooping around your childhood home."

She threw him a look. "Then I'll only be a second."

Zoe quickly ran through the house, checking to make sure her mom had everything she needed, but she'd done most of the preparations the day before. As she went from room to room, she made a list of things to bring the next day. It was routine by now since she regularly popped by a few times a week.

While her mother usually did her own grocery shopping and cleaning, Zoe had to do a lot of the tougher things around the old house. For being the black sheep of her family and leaving Japan at the age of twenty to marry an American, her mother was still very traditional at heart. Despite an independent life away from her family, she'd relied heavily on her husband for all those years to perform the "male" roles of the household.

When her dad died, it was Zoe who had to teach her mother how to reset the breaker, how to start the gas lawn mower, how to set mousetraps. And Zoe still ended up doing most of that herself during her regular visits to the house. She felt safer lighting the pilot light on the furnace or changing the burnt-out ceiling light bulbs than she did letting her mother do it herself.

Heading to the kitchen, she pulled out the medications prescribed by the doctor and organized them all on the kitchen counter. Each label had different instructions on how to take them and how often. Even she was confused, so she grabbed a pen from the drawer and relabeled them all in Japanese.

Zoe grabbed the mail from the mailbox and brought it inside. Heading into the living room, she flipped through the letters, scanning for junk. When she glanced up, Levi was standing in front of the mantle with a picture frame in his hands.

He waved it in the air. "Your mother says you were quite the gymnast."

She recognized the photo in his hands. A dark-haired little girl was balancing on a beam no thicker than her with a giant self-satisfied grin on her face. She'd been eight.

Zoe swiped it out of his hands and set it back on the mantle where the clean patch of dust was. "Stop snooping."

"But I'm getting to know a whole new side to you." He reached for the next photo in line.

She slapped his hand away. "Keep digging, and I'll show you a side you won't soon forget."

He just grinned, undeterred. "I like the leotard."

Zoe's mother sat down in the recliner closest to the fireplace, lifting Freddy onto her lap. He flopped onto his back like a baby in her arms, his foot jiggling with pleasure as she rubbed his belly, like *I could get used to this*.

"Zoe is very hard working," she told Levi. "She's always been very talented at whatever she's done. She could have been an excellent gymnast."

"If not for the growth spurt that landed me a foot taller than most boys in my school," Zoe said. "I blame Dad's genetics for that one."

She sifted through the mail again. Finding no more ads, she went to set them down on her father's old desk in the corner. That's when she noticed the red letters on one of the white envelopes screaming up at her.

Urgent.

She went to pick it up again and noticed another stack of letters on the desk, unopened. Her eyes couldn't help but catch the bolded red letters on an envelope. She picked it up to get a closer look.

Final Notice.

The envelope shook in her hands. She spun around, holding it up. "Mom. What is this?"

"Oh, just junk mail." She waved a dismissive hand. "Nothing to worry about."

"Mom, junk mail isn't addressed 'urgent.'" She tossed it on the coffee table in front of her. "Junk mail isn't titled 'pending foreclosure.'"

"*Zoe. Shizukani.*" She switched to Japanese as easily as she might take a breath. "*I didn't raise you to speak to your mother that way,*" she continued in her native language. "*Nor do we discuss such matters in front of strangers.*"

"No, you've just decided not to speak about it at all," she replied pointedly in English.

"Nihon-go de!" she persisted. *"What's done is done. It can't be helped."*

"Well, paying your mortgage helps." Zoe rifled through the rest of the unopened letters, all with similar messages and red-lettered threats. "Why? Why haven't you paid your bills?"

"Nihon-go de," her mother demanded.

Levi jiggled his keys in his hand, glancing from mother to daughter. "Maybe I'll go wait in the van."

She sighed and gave him a grateful look. "Sorry. I'll only be another minute."

"Take your time," he told her.

Zoe waited until she heard the front door close before asking her mother again, "Tell me why?"

But her mother's lips pressed together until they nearly disappeared in anger.

Zoe rolled her eyes and asked again in Japanese. *"Naze?"*

"I can't pay them because I don't have the money."

Zoe frowned. *"Where is all your money going? Surely Dad had some kind of life or mortgage insurance."*

Her mother turned away, speaking to the cold fireplace when she answered. *"He had a pre-existing heart condition. A congenital defect. So when he died of a heart attack, the insurance company wouldn't pay out because of a loophole. What little money I was left with hasn't been enough."*

Zoe sank into the chair across from her. *"Why didn't you tell me? I could have helped."*

"Don't worry. Once you meet Kimura-san, I'm certain you will like him. And he is rich, so once you are married, we won't have to worry about all this."

Zoe rubbed her temples, feeling the pressure build behind them. *"Mother, I haven't agreed to marry him. I might not even like him. He might not like me."*

"What's not to like?" she asked. *"Everything will work out. You will see. My sister assures me he is a very reliable man. He will take care of us."*

For wanting such an independent life away from her family, her country, her traditions, Junko Plum was the most *dependent* person Zoe had ever met.

Because her mother had needed a man all her life, Zoe understood why her mother felt that she did too. But that wasn't Zoe's view of things. That wasn't going to be her.

"But Mom—"

Suddenly, her mother clutched her head. Moaning a little, she let her head fall back against the headrest.

Zoe jumped to her feet. "Mom. Are you all right?"

Her mother sighed. "Oh, I'm fine." But she didn't sound so fine. "I just worry about you. It causes me so much grief."

Zoe crouched down beside her mother. She sighed, patting her hand. "You don't have to worry about me."

She reached out and stroked Zoe's hair like she did when she was a child. "You're all I have left to worry about."

Zoe suddenly remembered the doctor's advice. The best thing she could do was reduce stress—for her mom, anyway. Zoe's stress was an entirely different story.

"I told you I would meet Taichi. And I will. You don't have to worry."

Her mother straightened in her chair, her dizzy spell miraculously over. "Good, because you have a date with him this weekend."

A date, Zoe thought. *So soon? No stress. No stress. No stress.* Her face formed what she hoped looked like an excited smile. "Great."

Yet another reason to get things back on track with her business. So she could prove to her mother once and for all that she was fine on her own. She could take care of herself. And now it looked like she was going to have to take care of her mother too. But without many upcoming events booked, it was hard to do that.

Zoe crossed the room and swiped the other letters off the desk. "In the meantime, I'm taking these with me."

Her mother stood up. Setting Freddy on the floor, she made as if to take them back. *"I'm the parent. You're the daughter. It's not your job to worry about matters like this."*

Zoe held them out of her reach, which wasn't very hard, considering their difference in height. "Not my job? Well, too bad. You didn't raise me that way either." She threw her words back at her.

Shoving the stack of letters into her purse, she kissed her mother on the cheek and headed out to Levi's van with Freddy in tow.

16

Like a Dog with a Bone

Thud. Thud. Thud.

Levi's metal door vibrated with each beat from within, as though his studio apartment was alive, its heart beating. Zoe raised a fist to knock out of automatic politeness, but then realized it was pointless since anyone inside wouldn't hear her over all the racket—or maybe because of their acquired hearing loss.

Balancing her box of supplies under one arm, she slid the metal door open. It rolled aside, releasing the chaotic noise within like she was stepping into a nightclub from a quiet street on a Saturday night.

Freddy strolled inside like he had VIP access. He was getting used to being at Levi's. Heck, they'd practically spent more time there that week than in her own apartment.

It may have seemed like a club, but there were no bouncers here, no drunk girls taking selfies at the bar, no perverts rubbing their junk all over chicks and calling it dancing. There was, however, a band. A pretty good band by the sounds of it.

She put her supplies down on the table and headed for the music room. As it came into view, Levi noticed her, but carried on with the song. When he hit the chorus, his voice, which had been so sweet and melodic during the verse, growled with an extra grittiness. It rolled over her and through her like cool, hard marbles.

Zoe had heard him sing a few songs off the playlist for Piper's wedding, but this was different. At that moment, she couldn't see the cheesy serenading boy next door and definitely not Martha Stewart. He wasn't singing silly lyrics that he'd made up on the spot rhyming like a Dr. Seuss book.

He was rocking. Hard.

Everything about him in that moment fit the bill. The rocker look, the sexy voice, the way his body moved in time to the music, flowing through him naturally like he was born backstage at a Led Zeppelin concert and swaddled in leather.

She tried to combine this new Levi she was seeing with the guy who'd made her dinner the other night, the guy who'd wanted to get to know her as a person rather than using her for sex, who followed her around the expo like an innocent teenage boy with a crush.

He was practically every girl's dream. A hard exterior with a gooey interior. Not that she really noticed much. It's not like his performance was melting her insides like hot caramel or making her clench with yearning or anything.

Her breathing wasn't coming faster from desire. It was because she'd just carried her supplies all the way from her newly repaired van. And that wasn't her heart throbbing in her chest with lust. It was the kick drum pulsating through her.

Nope. Levi had no effect on her at all. She was so over it.

Freddy came to sit next to her heel, slapping his tail in time to the beat on the cement floor. He glanced up at her, as though he could see right through her. *Liar.*

She glared back like "Who's side are you on, anyway. Remember who feeds you."

Levi's eyes held Zoe's while he sang. She felt that powerful voice resonate deep inside her like the floor vibrating beneath her shoes. His gaze darkened, and as he held his last note, that feeling lingered, sinking lower until it settled somewhere between her thighs.

Watching him sing with his band, a rock star for real, it definitely gave him that bad boy lead singer factor. And while Zoe wasn't going to take of her bra and scream like a crazed fan, something about the way he looked behind that mic made her want *him* to take off her bra and make her scream.

As the music ended, Zoe had to take a deep breath and remind herself of what he wanted in exchange for sex. *More.*

They were just business associates, Zoe told herself. He was giving her a place to store the supplies she had to replace after the explosion. A quiet space to work with more room than her disorganized apartment. She just had to resist ripping the clothes off his tall, tight body. She could manage that for a few days until she found a new office space. Probably.

"Good set, guys," Levi said, placing his guitar in its stand. "Let's wrap it up for the day."

Zoe felt a little giddy as he approached, like he'd picked her out from the crowd. That is, until she reminded herself she wasn't at a concert, and Levi was just Levi.

"Hey. Sorry I just let myself in," she said.

"No worries. Mi casa, su casa, remember? That's why I gave you a key."

"What's in the box?" one of Levi's bandmates asked, the bass player, she thought. He was already leaning over the box on the table, peeking inside.

"Dildos mostly," Zoe said.

He leapt back like she'd just said it was a box of scorpions. "You've got a whole box of dildos?"

Once he recovered, he pushed the cardboard flap aside with a single finger as though it were contaminated. His eyebrows rose an inch at what he saw inside.

"That's nothing," Zoe told him, hiding a smirk. "I've got a whole van full of sex toys."

His mouth dropped, like he wasn't sure if she was joking. Maybe he thought they were all for her personal use.

Levi laughed. "Zoe, this is Brody."

The drummer of the band didn't seem as shy as the bass player and started digging through the box, pulling out toys. His eyes lit up as though it were Christmas morning at the Playboy mansion.

Levi shook his head. "That pervert is Aaron."

"My favorite kind of customer," Zoe said. "They tend to spend more money," she stage-whispered, not bothering to lower her voice.

Aaron's hands were full of toys, so he waved the purple dildo clenched in his fist. "Nice to meet you. What else do you got?" He gasped and dug for the bottom. "What's this?"

He drew out a long, flesh colored tube.

"That's a Beater Cheater," she said.

As Aaron turned it around, his grin widened when he realized what you'd beat with it.

"It's for my male customers," she said. "It comes equipped with a hole on either end."

The keyboard player stood back, watching on with a dubious look. He frowned, clearly trying to do the math. "Why two holes?"

Levi shrugged. "Variety?"

"Probably because they couldn't fit all three holes?" Zoe offered.

His ears turned red as he finally figured out the equation.

"And this is Jett," Levi said. "He's clearly not as quick as the other two."

Zoe could tell he was trying to act cool around his friends, but she noticed a telltale flush crawling its way up his neck. It gave her a strange sense of satisfaction. In fact, she wanted to make him blush harder.

"I've heard of those things," Jett said, still not willing to get any closer to the box. "Do they actually feel like the real thing?"

"It's very realistic," she assured him. "But nothing can replace the real thing." Her voice automatically took on the sultry tone she used for parties. People trusted the opinion of someone who felt sexy, who acted sexy, who believed they were sex on a stick. So of course, Zoe did very well in the sales department.

Shaking his head, Jett slapped Levi on the back and headed for the door. "You're a lucky man."

Zoe wasn't sure what he meant exactly. Maybe that he got to spend time with a girl well versed in sex. Or was it more specifically related to her? Had he talked with his band mates about her?

Brody followed Jett toward the door, pausing by Zoe as he left. "You know, I've got a big apartment. I'd be happy to let you play with your toys there." He flashed her a playful grin.

"Good-bye, Brody." Levi shoved his friend toward the door.

Brody threw his hands up in the air, like "What did I do?"

Aaron seemed more reluctant to leave the toy box behind. At the last second, he grabbed the Beater Cheater and waved it. "Can I have this?"

The guy was hilariously unabashed compared to his band mates, but Zoe would never laugh at someone's sexuality. Hell, she encouraged people to express it for a living. Instead, she pulled a business card out of her purse.

"Only if you tell your friends where to get one when you try it and love it."

"Woo-hoo! Thanks!" He headed after the rest of his band. "I'm going to go home to love it right now."

Groaning, Levi slid the front door shut and locked it like he was afraid they'd come back. "Sorry about them."

Zoe laughed. "They seem nice."

The blush was slowly fading from Levi's neck, but she noticed him reach for his jeans a few times to rearrange them. "Well, I'll let you get to work. I've got some errands to run for a bit." Picking up his phone, he tapped the screen a few times until music started playing through the speakers placed around his apartment. "There. Just in case Freddy gets any ideas." He looked at him pointedly.

Freddy's tail slapped against the cement floor, but he didn't seem to understand what was going on.

"Sorry about all the merchandise." She gestured to the wedding and sex toy supplies piled in the corner. "Don't worry. It won't be for long."

Aiden had offered to help Zoe look for an office for rent. With all the properties he owned in San Francisco, she hoped something would pop up soon.

"Trust me," Levi said. "There's no rush."

He grabbed his keys off the counter nearby and gave

her a wave, rearranging himself one more time before slipping out the door. Zoe grinned but tried to focus on the work ahead. The longer she went without an orgasm, the harder it was going to be to work around him. But she had to. There was still too much to do before Piper's wedding.

She spent the rest of the morning organizing her merchandise, taking stock of what hadn't been blown into a million pieces. She'd lost a lot of her event decorations both in the explosion and the vandalism at the Hilton. She brought up a copy of her records from her laptop, making a list of what she needed to replace for insurance purposes and prioritized it based on what event was booked next.

Once she'd placed a few calls and ordered replacement decor and supplies, she set it all aside to sort through her mother's bills. She'd been working on them all week. Even after tallying up the numbers, she realized her mother was right. There was more money going out than coming in. San Francisco was an expensive city, and her father's death left her with very little to survive on.

If only she'd talked to Zoe sooner. She wouldn't have been able to hold off the sale of the house forever, but she could have ensured her mother came out of it all in the black. There were years of equity built up in the home. To lose it all was an insult to her father's years of hard work and savings.

Zoe crumpled a bill and tossed it in the garbage. She felt neglectful for not intervening sooner. Finances were not her mother's forte. But she never would have guessed things would get that bad. Then again, when things got tough, her mother became a turtle and tucked into her shell, just like when it came to her health.

When numbers began to blur together, Zoe popped a

couple of aspirin and called the mortgage company. After an hour of waiting on hold, and a talk with some higher powers that be, Zoe managed to get the bills up to date and work out a payment plan—in exchange for some hefty penalties, of course.

But her mother couldn't pull money from thin air to get back on track. She needed help. She needed Zoe. But sinking money into her childhood home meant Zoe was going to have to give up on her dream of buying her own place. It meant she was going to have to buy part of her mother's house.

In the end, she called her mother and proposed putting her name on the mortgage. Being a practical woman, she agreed that it was the best course of action. That, and because it was only temporary. After all, once Zoe married Taichi, they wouldn't need to worry about it anymore.

Zoe didn't really want to get into that one, so she let it slide and ended the call. However, this new agreement opened up a whole new list of phone calls to make in order to get the ball rolling.

The first call she made was to her landlord to give notice for the end of the month. One thing was certain. Her mother was struggling to live on her own. Who knew if she was taking her medication right or eating as often as she should? Zoe's frequent visits just weren't enough anymore. She'd have to move in as soon as possible.

Her phone vibrated on Levi's desk in front of her. It was a call from an unknown number. She was tempted to let it go to voicemail, but with all the calls she'd made to mortgage lenders and bill collectors that morning, she hit the *accept* button.

"Zoe Plum here."

"Hey, girlfriend!" Holly's voice screeched through the phone. "Just wanted to catch up. How are things since the big blow up? Were there any irreplaceable items for Piper and Aiden's impending wedding that were destroyed?" she asked casually.

Zoe's head began to throb at the sound of the reporter's voice. It reminded her of her news report about the bombing that appeared on the five o'clock news Monday evening. Of course, Holly just had to slip Zoe's name into the segment.

Even though another San Fran Slayer tragedy was headlining the news—this time, a Pizza delivery boy had been attacked—it obviously didn't overshadow her small-business misfortunes. She'd already received calls from three weddings, two parties, and five Pure Passion Party bookings, wondering if they should cancel her services. Whoever said there was no such thing as bad publicity was wrong.

Now the entire city knew that her business was falling apart. Who was going to book an event with her when they saw what chaos her life was in? Not to mention they'd assume she had no resources left to work with.

Unwilling to give Holly any more to use against her, Zoe said, "Everything is on track and their wedding will be beautiful. You can quote me. Otherwise, no comment." She hung up before Holly could argue and immediately blocked the number.

She slammed the phone down on the desk. Feeling the throbbing behind her eyes intensify, she laid her head next to it. Just as she closed her eyes, the front door slid open and Levi strolled in.

He took in both Zoe at the desk and Freddy curled up on the area rug, chilling to the music in the background. "Nap time already?" He flopped down on the couch. "How are things? Making any headway?"

"It's official," she said. "I'm going to be a thirty-year-old living with her mother. I'll be taking on half of the mortgage payments in order to prevent the repossession."

"Really?" He seemed to think about that for a moment. Finally, he huffed and shook his head. "I'm not sure I could do the same thing. My parents would drive me insane. I think it's sweet you want to help her out."

Feeling anxious, Zoe stood up and started digging through her boxes of toys, pulling out the ones she needed for the pleasure party she was hosting that weekend.

Each party paid a couple hundred or more, depending on the information requested and the number of guests. And of course, she received a commission on all sales. While it was just a side gig, the two grand a month helped supplement her income—she was very good at selling sex.

She set them down on the desk, organizing them from thickest to thinnest. To keep her hands busy, she began to clean them with a gentle cleanser spray.

Zoe tried to think about it from Levi's perspective, but it didn't seem strange to her. "I guess I never thought of it any other way. She and my father took care of me for the first twenty-some years. Now it's my turn to pay back the favor. It's just happening sooner than I thought it would."

She sighed and reached for the next dildo, gripping it firm around the shaft as she rubbed with a microfiber cloth.

"I had no idea things were so bad for her," she told Levi. "She's a very private person, even with me, it seems."

"Maybe she didn't want you to worry," he said.

"Well, it backfired because now there's even more to worry about."

Really getting into the cleaning mode, she grabbed the monstrosity on the far left. Big Boy. It rotated, it vibrated, it shook, thrust, and spun. It was the Cadillac of all the Pure Pleasure line. But it clearly didn't get its name because of its superior functions. Big Boy was renowned for its girth, measuring in at a whopping six-inch circumference—the largest in the *mainstream* category.

Zoe began working it from tip to base, scrubbing harder and harder as she considered everything that hadn't gone to plan recently. It was kind of stress-relieving, like a spring cleaning would feel for someone with less sexual hunger than Zoe.

She felt Levi's eyes on her as she worked. When she turned to him, his eyebrows quirked up, and his expression was filled with amusement. And maybe something else.

"You look like you're working that thing pretty hard. Shall I leave you to, ummm, sort yourself out?"

Zoe suddenly realized that she might have been overly eager with her cleaning. "Pun intended?" she asked.

She noticed him try to subtly readjust himself. Gripping Big Boy, she gave it a couple more suggestive strokes, daring him to continue to ignore her, to turn her down. He wanted her, she knew he did. So how long could he keep his hands to himself?

Levi chuckled, but she could see a blush crawl up his neck and across his cheeks. But he made no move to . . . make a move.

Disappointed, she put Big Boy back in line. Just as she'd thought. Levi talked a big game, but when push came to shove—or at least when she wanted it to—he was the boy next door, the guy you'd bring home to meet the family. Not the guy she'd hoped would follow through on all his teasing.

Well, Zoe didn't bring boys home to do that. Not since Sean left her, anyway. Well, she supposed technically Levi had met her mother, but it wasn't like *that*.

Levi stood up, Zoe thought to leave. But then he crossed over to the desk, a curious sparkle in his eyes.

"You know, if you ever get tired of toys, you can have the real thing right here." He spread his hands like she didn't realize he meant him. "You look a little stressed. Maybe I can help you out with that."

Zoe narrowed her eyes. Now he was just being mean. "You're a tease."

"I'm not teasing," he said. "I'm being completely serious. But if you want me, you get the whole package, not just my, err," he glanced down, "package."

"I think I'll be just fine with Big Boy," she waved it in front of his face.

His eyes scanned the full, *very full*, length of it. He held a hand out. "May I?"

She dropped it into his hand and he seemed surprised by the weight of it. All the mechanisms inside that made it do everything but dance added a bit of heft.

"Why are you taking them out?" he asked. "Don't you need to sell these?"

"That's a fairly new product. The company often sends me free stuff to test. I can't sell what I haven't tried myself."

His wide eyes scanned the toys lined up across the desk. "And you've tried all this stuff."

She wasn't sure why she liked to shock him so much. His blush always made her think of things she could show him, what she could do to him that would make him blush harder. It was like she wanted to shove her sexuality in his face—literally and metaphorically—just to see how far she could push him, how much she had to tease him until he finally broke.

"These are just the beginning. I've pretty much tried it all."

After adjusting every switch, dial, and knob on the big red beast in his hands to see what it could do, Levi sat

down on the desk in front of her. He shifted uncomfortably like he needed to readjust again.

"So why sex toys?" he asked. "What made you want
to get into that line of work?"

"I didn't get into it. It got into me." She winked. "That's
how it usually works, anyway. Or do you need a demonstration. I'm a certified sexual health rep for Pure Pleasure, you know."

His sexy mouth quirked up. "I like the sound of that."

"I have a certificate and everything."

"You're practically a sexpert." He laughed. "But no,
come on. Really. Why do you like to sell this stuff?"

"Because I believe sex is important. It's important to
your physical health as well as your mental well-being.
And as a whole, society doesn't get it enough. It's a rather
neglected organ in the body. There are cardio machines
for your heart and lungs, and weights for muscles and
joints. These," she waved at her collection, "are machines
to exercise a person's sexual health."

"And do you get enough exercise?" he asked sugges-
tively.

Technically Zoe didn't get any at all, but she wasn't
about to admit that she was practically a nun. "What's
enough?" she asked vaguely. "That's why I have to supplement."

"Like a daily vitamin?" He chuckled.

"Or several times a day." She could hear her voice taking on the usual sultry cadence she used to sell sex toys.
Only, it wasn't the toy she was trying to sell him.

God, she wanted him so bad it hurt. She was sure that
it would only take one time. If she could just have him
for a couple of hours, her missing orgasm would come
back home on its own, and they could both move on with
their lives. But Levi was one tough customer.

"Several times, huh?" he said. "Then you must be really healthy."

She could hear a change in his voice too, a response to her own. Something had altered in the conversation. Maybe it was in the shifting of his body, like he wanted to touch her, or the way his eyes dropped down to the low neckline of her blouse.

"I like to take good care of myself," she said, moving a little closer.

"With Big Boy?" He flipped a switch and it moved up and down in a thrusting motion.

She ached at the sight of it. "It might be the only thing that can handle a woman like me," she joked.

He slid off the desk to stand in front of her. He was barely touching her, but she could feel his heat.

"Oh, I can handle you. The question is, can you handle me?" He moved to place both hands on the desk on either side of her hips, trapping her there.

"Honey," she said. "I would destroy you."

"I'd like to put that to the test. How about that demonstration?" He smiled, but it wasn't his usual cheesy grin. It was infused with a dare, with lust, a confidence that made Zoe wonder if he might actually be able to keep up with her.

"Well Big Boy might be a bit much for your first time, but I might have a strap on somewhere around here." She glanced in the toy box on the desk, pretending to search.

"I didn't mean for me," he said.

She fake-sighed. "Shame."

"I meant for you." He moved forward, erasing what little space was left between them.

"Mmmm," she purred as he pressed against her. "I like a giving man. But I'm a girl who likes to pay my debts. How can I return the favor?"

"I have something in mind. But it's a surprise."

"I like surprises." She tugged at the waistband of his jeans, wanting to discover what surprise he was hiding from her.

"So you're up for whatever?" he asked.

She pretended to think. "Depends if the favor's worth returning."

"Oh, I'll make it worth your while." His voice held a guarantee she couldn't ignore.

"Then you're on," she said.

"It's a deal."

The unknown made Zoe clench with anticipation. Was it really happening? Was he finally giving in? It wasn't often a man had her on the edge of her seat. She yearned for her "surprise" almost as much as she yearned for his touch.

But he didn't touch her. Instead, he stood back, groping her with his eyes, assessing every curve and swell as though deciding where to start first. Well, if he wasn't going to hurry up and decide, she'd have to do it for him.

Reaching out, she laid her hands on his stomach. Scraping her nails down his shirt, she felt the contours of his muscles. Her palms slid farther down, over the bulge beneath his pants. She lingered there, fingers exploring the shape. Levi groaned, and that was all the invite she needed.

All that talk of sex toys, his verbal teasing, it was like a tortuous foreplay. Zoe was ready to go. And by the feel of him, Levi was ready too.

Reaching for his belt, she gripped the hard leather. But before she could undo it, he grabbed her wrists and held them aside.

"Not so fast," he said.

"If we go any slower, I'm going to explode." For a second, she worried that this was going to be like the last time. That she had it all wrong again. That he didn't want her.

He chuckled. "No, you won't. But you will when I'm done with you."

"I can't wait." She reached eagerly for his belt again.

"Do I need to restrain you?" he asked.

Searching around the desk, his eyes landed on a role of thick, hot pink ribbon. Picking it up, he unwound a length of it and cut it with a pair of scissors from the drawer.

"Hey," she said. "That's for thank-you notes."

"I'm sure you can thank me some other way."

He backed her up until she sank into the office chair. Spinning it until her back was to him, he drew her arms behind her. He held her wrists, tying them together so slowly that she felt each tickle of the ribbon against her skin. It sent a surge of tingles up her arms.

As he fastened the last knot, it dug a little painfully, deliciously into her skin. He spun her chair around to face him, and her head spun with it in excitement.

"How am I supposed to join in all the fun?" she asked, testing the strength of her bonds, but they wouldn't give.

"You don't always have to be in control," he said.

"Have you met me?"

"Maybe it's time you learned to let go. To just lie back and let someone else take the wheel."

Reaching under the seat, he flipped a lever and the chair suddenly reclined. She gasped in surprise and a little eagerness.

He leaned down as though to kiss her, but before their lips touched, he paused. "You can say no."

Instead of saying no, she leaned up to touch her mouth against his, but he pulled away before she could. Holding her gaze, he reached down and began unbuttoning her blouse.

The more he exposed her, the faster her breathing became. It was both thrilling and frightening. If she could touch him, kiss him, control things, maybe it wouldn't be so scary. It had been so long since a man had seen her, had explored her.

Levi stood back, gazing down at her bound body. She couldn't hide from him. And as he pulled her blouse apart, she could hide even less. But like he'd said, she could say "no." At any moment, she could stop him. He was giving her complete control over the situation, so she relaxed into the leather chair.

Despite the fear, it made her feel giddy, enticingly naughty. She gave into the idea that she really didn't have control, and at the moment, with everything going on in her life, the brief reprieve was welcome. Levi could do anything he wanted to her, and oh, God, what was he going to do?

One by one, Levi slid the rest of her buttons free until he could pull the blouse open wide. Her breasts heaved up and down beneath a leopard-print bra as her breathing quickened.

Levi took in the sight of her, running a palm over her smooth, pale skin. Pushing her bra aside, he slid his fingers beneath the fabric and gave her nipple a pinch.

She squealed and jumped, the sensation tensing her entire body. He'd hardly done anything yet, and somehow the effect seemed to excite her even more, to build her up like a shaken pop bottle about to burst.

Finally, he stepped back. Gripping both her knees, he parted her legs and forced her skirt up until it was bunched around her hips. He slid her thong aside, running his finger down her.

Nerve endings fired in a jolt that had her back arching. He'd built her up to the point that she couldn't take much more.

"No more teasing," she panted. "I'm ready."

His fingers inched a little deeper. "I can tell."

She glanced down at his crotch, biting her lip. Instead of reaching for his belt, he reached for her erotic display on the desk. His hand hovered above each colorful, erect form, as though deciding which one to choose. When he reached Big Boy, his hand grasped it firmly, decidedly.

She gasped as he positioned it between her legs. "I haven't taken him for a test drive yet. I'm not sure I can handle it."

"Then you've really got problems," he said. "Because Big Boy's got nothing on me."

She groaned in response and squirmed in the seat. He smiled as he brought the tip closer. The moment it touched her she jumped. It felt cool against her fired-up warmth, the sensation invigorating as he leaned in, pushing it deeper.

Her breath hitched. Her muscles tightened around the soft silicone. Levi's arm flexed as he pushed against the resistance. Zoe made a noise, like a half-gasp half-moan, and he hesitated, searching her face for signs of pain.

"Don't stop," she managed to say. Placing her legs on either side of him, she braced against the desk.

And then he filled her all the way.

Her cry of pleasure was drowned out by his own grunt of satisfaction. He kneeled down on one knee as he drove it inside of her again and again.

It was so different from when she used toys on herself. Her own movements were familiar, habitual. She knew exactly how to move it, how to position it, how fast or slow to go. But this was better.

Not knowing what he'd do next made it unpredictable. It was exciting, almost torturous in the way he dragged it out. He built her up, higher and higher until she felt herself go beyond her usual self-induced pleasures. When she thought it couldn't get any better, he started playing with the buttons.

Each time Zoe opened her eyes, his were on her, enjoying the sight of her body moving, her sounds. As her moaning grew louder, his cheeks flushed. By his half-lidded eyes and his staggered breathing, she could tell he wanted to take Big Boy's place.

Was he thinking about what he had in store for her after? What was he going to have her do to return the favor? Was he going to finish her off and then have his way?

Finally, when her body couldn't hold off any longer, she cried out, arching against the leather backrest, unable to hide her explosive reaction as she fought her bonds. Levi groaned with his own sense of gratification, maybe with pride in being the one to make her shake and tremble before him.

When Zoe grew still, relaxing against the seat, he slowly pulled Big Boy out. Emotions surged through her, emotions that had been building for days, like her bottle had popped its top and flooded her body.

After it settled, she felt better than she had in a while, but she still craved more.

"I need you," she told him. She bit her lip as she realized how the words had come out. But she didn't mean it like *that*. She wanted to take it back somehow, to correct herself.

He laughed. "What? Big Boy wasn't enough for you?" His voice sounded a little thick, like he wanted his favor returned, and soon.

"No," she said. "I mean, yes. But I want the real thing." She could hear the pleading in her voice, but she didn't care enough to reign it in. "Enough teasing."

"You've had your fun," he said. "It's my turn, remember? You said we could do whatever I wanted."

She sighed, nodding readily. "Whatever you want."

"You promise?" His eyebrow arched as he held her gaze, like he didn't believe her. Just what exactly did he want from her? Was it something kinky?

"I promise. I'm all yours."

He smiled. Having the control clearly did it for him. "Good."

Spinning her chair around, he tugged on the ribbon binding her wrists. When he pulled Zoe to her feet, her knees buckled and she leaned against him for support. Eagerly, she pressed herself up against him, but Levi drew back.

"I'll give you a minute to collect yourself."

Zoe frowned. "Collect myself for what?"

"You'll see. I'll meet you downstairs at my van in five minutes."

"Why? Where are we going?"

"It's my turn for fun." He pointed a finger at her, as though daring her to back down. "You promised."

She stared at him, a little confused. He wanted to have sex in his van? To each their own, she supposed.

Levi readjusted the bulge in his pants. "Actually, I might need ten minutes." He scanned her toys lined up on the desk until he found a Beater Cheater. "May I borrow this?"

Zoe's mouth fell open. She couldn't believe it. The way he'd looked at her, the way he'd touched her, she knew he wanted her as badly as she wanted him. But apparently, he'd rather take care of himself than let her do it. She didn't get it.

Finally, she managed to answer. "K-Keep it. You've earned it."

Watching him head for the bathroom, Zoe wilted like month-old *mitsuba* and sank into the chair with disappointment. Sure, she'd climaxed. *Finally.* The pleasure that was still vibrating through her body told her that much. And yet she felt unsatisfied.

She briefly eyed the line of vibrators in front of her. But they just didn't hold the same temptation for her. Instead of being cured, instead of being able to move on from the Levi Dolson orgasm block, she knew her vibrators wouldn't cut it.

There was only one thing that would satisfy her now. Only one thing that she wanted, that she needed: Levi himself.

And she wasn't going to feel satisfied until she had him.

17

Tuned Out

Zoe narrowed her eyes, envisioning that perfect, round hole. She clenched her fist, feeling the smooth firmness beneath her fingers. She shifted it slightly, getting the feel for the weight of it.

She couldn't drive it right up the middle. No, that was too easy. She had to prove to Levi that she could keep up, that she was just as good as he was. She was aiming for that sweet spot, the hole at the far back. It was risky, but she'd get the big points for it. And if she gave Levi what he wanted, maybe she'd get what she wanted.

Zoe tightened her grip and brought her arm back. She aimed for the center, but at the last second put a spin on it. It curved up the side, popping up into the air and slipped perfectly into the hole hardest to get in.

She cried out in surprise, jumping up and down. "I did it! I don't ever remember getting it in that hole."

Levi nodded approvingly, clearly impressed with her beginner's luck. "It's a tough one. But it feels good, right?"

"Yeah. I'm getting pretty good at this. Let's do it again."

Laughing, Levi dug another coin out of his pocket and slipped it into the Skeeball machine. Their scores set back to zero and the machine rumbled as it spat out new balls.

Zoe reached down and picked one up. "You know, when you said you wanted to have fun . . ."

"I meant that I wanted to have fun," Levi said. "You know how to do that right? Fun? It's that thing that makes you smile."

She rolled her eyes and gave him a sarcastic look.

"Yeah, kind of like that, but with less contempt."

She laughed. "I know how to have fun. I just assumed that you'd put a smile on my face a different way."

He paused mid swing. "What? You didn't enjoy yourself this afternoon? You looked like you were having fun at the time. Big boy didn't do it for you?"

No, she thought. It only left her wanting more from him. But she wasn't about to tell him that in case he thought more meant *more*. "I just didn't take you for an arcade man, that's all."

"Me? I'm practically a kid at heart."

She looked him up and down. "Okay, well that I can see."

"Hmm, I'm going to choose not to be offended by that."

"That's probably best since you drove me here." She gave him a wink. "Okay, show me what you've got. And don't be too sore when you lose."

"Getting cocky, are you? Okay, you're on."

They went shot for shot. It was close, but in the end, Zoe beat him by ten points.

As they left the Musée Mécanique with its variety of antique games, they began to walk down The

Embarcadero toward Pier 39. It was scorching in the late-afternoon sun, but bearable with the breeze blowing across the bay.

Zoe felt bad for dropping Freddy off at her mother's, but it was probably for the best. With the sidewalk crowded with tourists, joggers, and dog walkers, she thought it would have been overwhelming for him. Although, he would have enjoyed the music drifting out of each restaurant they passed by.

"So why music?" she asked Levi as they walked. "What made you want to join a band?"

"My parents introduced me to music at a young age," he said. "They enrolled me in piano lessons when I was five, violin when I was eight, and trumpet when I was eleven."

"Wow. That's a lot of instruments. You must have been a natural."

"I think they wanted a one-man symphony," he said, making her laugh. "I was lucky it came pretty easily to me. But while my parents were obsessed with classical, when I was fifteen, I bought my first guitar. I broke their hearts with my newfound love for rock and roll."

"And a star was born," she said in a voice fit for the magnitude of the statement.

He shoved her playfully for making fun of him. "Yes, it's true. I've always been this amazing," he joked. "But because I'd been introduced to a wide variety of music growing up, I had an appreciation for all of it. Jazz, swing, classical, hip-hop, blues. You name it. I like to incorporate what I love about each one into my own style."

"I've noticed. You definitely have your own style." And she didn't just mean his musical tastes. She couldn't exactly pin him as a rock star lead singer, or a Martha Stewart, or anything really. He was just Levi. "Your parents must be really proud of you."

He snorted. "Not really. They wanted me to learn music to become well rounded. They didn't think I'd go and try to make a career out of it. They wanted me to be an accountant, like my successful father. They saw me following in his footsteps, joining his firm, taking over the company one day."

"I guess that's not what you saw for yourself."

"I tried it their way at first. I went to college, took the courses that they wanted me to, graduated with honors." When she gave him a surprised look, he said, "Oh, yeah, I'm not just a pretty face, you know."

She smiled, but thought it wise not to say anything in case she offended him. But honors? Definitely no pigeonholing him at all.

"But in the end," he continued, "it just wasn't me. I will always have my parents to thank for my gift and my education. They only wanted what was best for me, but I had to follow my dreams."

"But isn't that what's best for you?" she asked. "To do what you love to do? To do what makes you happiest?"

"Well, sometimes my parents thought they knew better than I did when it came to what made me happy."

Zoe snorted. "I can sympathize with that. My mom tries to manipulate my life all the time." She'd been dreading her date with her supposed future husband all week, and it was already happening the next day.

The sounds of their footsteps changed as they reached Pier 39, click-clacking on the wooden boards, sounding almost musical to Zoe's ears.

"So you went against your parent's wishes and gave into your love of music," Zoe summed up. "Admit it. You did it for the girls."

"I'm not going to say it hurt. And it eventually worked, too." He shoved his hands into his pockets. It was such a self-conscious gesture, something she didn't often see with him. "That's how I met my ex-wife."

Her head snapped toward him. "Ex-wife? You were married?"

Levi reached out and tugged her toward him just as she was about to walk head-long into an antique lamp-post. "As a matter of fact, I was," he said pointedly. "You don't have to say it like that. Like, how could I possibly convince someone to marry me?"

"No. No." She cringed at her lack of manners. "I didn't mean it like that. I'm sorry."

Zoe wasn't sure what she'd assumed. That he was some trumpet-playing band geek who came out of his shell after high school and turned into a hot wannabe rock star to make up for lost time? That he played gigs for the booze, the women, and the lifestyle?

When she'd first met him, she imagined him hooking up with groupies and fan girls who lingered after last call to get their tits signed. Although, him stumbling into the Fisher-Well's wedding with a lipstick smear on his cheek might have had something to do with that. That is, until she got to know his boy-next-door side.

But at one point he'd been the kind of man who had promised forever, who had committed to one woman for the rest of his life—or at the time, he believed so.

Was he still that man? Is that why he wanted more from Zoe? Because he was the settling-down type?

They headed up a set of wooden steps to the upper level of the pier where a series of wooden walkways zig-zagged over the busy shopping area. It was far quieter above the popular tourist shops and allowed them to talk without having to dodge people taking photos or kids racing around, vibrating due to all the sugar from the candy stores.

Maybe that's why he'd brought her there that day, she

thought. So they could talk, get to know one another. And she was certainly getting to know a lot about him. She got the feeling she'd been roped into another date. And it frightened her—mostly because she was actually enjoying herself.

This was exactly what she'd wanted to avoid right from the start with Levi. The *more*. And usually she could avoid it with men, but Levi hadn't given up like all the others before him.

"So how did you meet your wife?" she finally asked, when the shock wore off.

"*Ex*-wife," he said pointedly. "We met at a bachelorette party I was performing at."

"A bachelorette party? And let me guess, she was impressed by your instrument." She arched her eyebrows.

He didn't rise to the suggestiveness in her voice. Usually so playful and easygoing, she was surprised at how serious the topic made him. "I guess she saw something in me. At first, anyway." He laughed without smiling. "I can't tell you what that was."

As they came to another set of stairs, they descended them. Here it was considerably noisier, but not because of the people. Three hundred or more sea lions lounged on the floating docks just to the west of the pier, lined up nose to tail, sometimes thirty of them per dock.

Zoe leaned against the fence and listened to them bark. They didn't seem at all disturbed by the people snapping photos of them basking in the hot sun.

The view of the bay was amazing. To their left, Zoe could just see Coit Tower perched on its hill, and to their right lay Alcatraz, lonely in the middle of the bay.

After a few moments, they realized that it was far too noisy to talk. By an unspoken agreement, they moved on.

"How long have you been divorced?" Zoe asked.

"Five years," Levi said. "I like to think that I learned a thing or two from my first marriage."

"And what's that?" she asked.

"How to be a good partner," he said. "How to be happy in a relationship, and how to keep a woman happy."

"So what happened? She wasn't happy?" She paused, shaking her head at her big mouth again. "I'm sorry. That was rude. You don't have to answer that."

"It's okay," he said. "No, she wasn't happy. Not from lack of trying, though."

"What do you mean?"

"Well, she wanted extravagant meals, so I learned to cook. She wanted to travel, so I took her all over the world. Finally, she wanted nicer things, a bigger house, a more expensive car."

"How many gigs did you have to play for all that?"

"I had to quit music. She convinced me to reach out to my family again. To my parents. My dad got me a job in his company for a while. I was a real Aiden Caldwell type. Wore a suit and everything." He ran a hand down his faded T-shirt uncomfortably, like he was smoothing down a tie.

"You behind a desk?" Zoe couldn't keep the surprise out of her voice. She tried to imagine him without the gelled hair, the black nails, the leather wrist bands, the ever-increasing piercings—were his ears always pierced?

She shook her head. "I can't see it. So let me guess, she still wasn't happy?"

"No. She wasn't. In the end, she said she needed space to figure out what she wanted. It turned out what she wanted was my best friend. *Ex*-best friend." He pulled a face. "I guess I just wasn't enough for her."

"I'm sorry." Zoe's heart lurched in her chest. She thought of the way she'd felt when Chelsea revealed she was engaged to Sean. And Chelsea was her enemy.

She thought that had been the worst-case scenario. But she supposed it would be worse to lose your partner to your best friend.

As Levi stood in line for tickets to get on the carousel, Zoe stared at him. Maybe she'd stumbled upon that rare breed of man, the nice guy. The guy who wanted a girl for all the right reasons. Whenever she'd been pursued by a man in the past, it wasn't exactly for her sharp wit or eye for organization. But Levi was different.

They climbed the bright red stairs to the second story of the carousel where the most famous sights in San Francisco were painted over their heads. Bright, round light bulbs flashed down on them, reflecting off the shiny gold poles holding the colorful horses in place.

Levi gestured for Zoe to choose one. She headed for a fierce black horse with courage painted in the twinkle in his eye, teeth bared as it fought against its restraint. Since it had come to a stop at its highest point, she had to raise her leg to slip her foot into the stirrup—the skirt made it a little awkward.

As she went to jump, she felt Levi's hands help push her up and into the saddle. She sat sidesaddle so she didn't flash everyone that was watching from the pier below or climbing onto their own horses—it was a family-friendly place, after all.

Levi chose the one directly next to hers. It happened to be a docile mare adorned with a pink saddle and bright, girly flowers.

To be the focus of a nice guy's attentions was, well, flattering. And yet it had her wanting to leap off the end of the pier and swim as far away as she could. To make up an excuse and grab a taxi home. But since her horse suddenly jerked and the ride began to go around, she chose to stay.

"I'm sorry that happened to you," she said over the

classic carousel music playing happily around them, because she meant it. And also because she couldn't think of anything else to say that didn't sound trivial.

He shrugged, but it wasn't the same as his usual shrug, because it was a big deal. "It was for the best, because I rediscovered what I wanted. And that was music. I quit my dad's firm and started the band. Ever since then, I've put everything I've got into it because, I guess, I want to prove to my family, and especially my ex, that I'm worth something the way I am."

Zoe watched his handsome face as he spoke. By the way he said it, she wondered if he believed that he was, or if he was trying to prove it to himself too.

"None of them ever believed I could get anywhere in music," he continued. "I want to show them that I can make it without their help or support. Without selling out and doing something I hate for more money. And I guess it might feel a little cool to be staring back at my ex in a grocery-store aisle one day from the front cover of *Rolling Stone*."

Zoe laughed. "I imagine that would feel very satisfying."

She recalled how eager he'd been to gain Holly's attention at the expo. Despite how aggravating the reporter could be, an interview with her would certainly boost his career. She could see why he wanted it so badly.

"The divorce must have been a tough way to learn what you really wanted," she said.

"It was," Levi agreed. "But it also showed me that I wanted a woman who knew what she wanted. Who's direct, honest to a fault, determined."

Zoe blushed as she realized he was listing all the things he admired about her.

"I want a woman strong enough to say what she wants and is capable of getting it, of grabbing life by the balls."

"So is that how you grabbed life by the balls?" she asked. "You wanted to settle down with a wife and have a couple kids? Doesn't seem so rock star to me. What about the concert tours, and groupies, and hotel-room trashing?"

"I don't think that's what that means," he said. "Grab-bing life by the balls means following your dreams, reaching out and taking what you want, living life to the fullest, whatever that might mean to you. Maybe even doing something that scares you." He gave her a mean-ingful look.

"And you don't think that's what I'm doing?" She shifted in her saddle to face him. "I'm fighting for my business, my independence. I do what I love to do. No one gets to tell me what to do. It's the beauty of being single." Well, she relented in her head. Her mother was telling her to go on a date the next night, but that was different.

"You can't live life to the fullest by only living part of it," he told her. The calm way in which he said it, like he was some fortune cookie come to life, grated on her like the music was starting to.

She snorted. "Just because I don't want the white-picket-fence life means I'm not a ball grabber?"

"No, I mean . . ." He took a deep breath, redirecting his thoughts. "When was the last time you just let go? Laughed until it hurt? Screamed at the top of your lungs? Or gave in to your emotions and let loose?"

"My emotions are just fine where they are."

"Hidden from people?"

She stared at him, her mouth dropping open. Who did he think he was? "If you're so certain that I'm not capa-ble of knowing what I want, then why are we here, Levi? That's not what you want, remember?"

"I think you do know what you want," he said with certainty. "I'm just waiting for you to finally admit it."

"I have admitted it. Over and over again." She gripped the gold pole harder. "I've told you that I'm not interested in a relationship. So why are you still pressuring me? Are you a glutton for punishment? Do you want another failed relationship?"

"No. I want my next relationship to work." His voice was hard, matching hers. Maybe because she was pissing him off. Or because he'd never meant anything more in his life. Or both.

He sighed in frustration. "Zoe, you're ambitious, and when you want something, you go for it. You're already happy and satisfied all on your own, in here." He reached across the space between their horses and tapped her chest.

She swatted his hand away, scowling at him. He barely seemed to notice, his intense gaze boring into her. Why wouldn't he give up?

"You're not looking for someone or something to complete you," he said. "A good relationship would just be the encore act to make the show perfect. You just refuse to see that."

"You're right," she said coolly. "I am happy. Without a man. I know what I want. And that's to be alone."

Levi turned away from her, but she could see his reflection in the warped carousel mirrors. His jaw clenched as he stared ahead, clearly trying to regain control of his emotions.

"You don't mean that," he said finally. "No one wants to be alone. Everyone wants to find that special person to spend the rest of their lives with."

"I'm not everyone," she said. "I already know that I don't ever want to get married."

"There was obviously a time when you did."

"And that was a mistake," she snapped back. "A close

call. I'm better off this way. It worked out for the best, really."

"You got hurt, and now you're scared to open up." His expression suddenly changed to one of pity. And there was nothing she hated more than being pitied. "Have you even opened up to anyone since your wedding day? Have you let anyone in?"

She rubbed her forehead as the music, the lights, the spinning was starting to give her a headache. "I've let people in. You can't pretend to know me after two weeks. Because you don't."

"No, I don't." The sound that came out of his mouth was a laugh, but he didn't look like his usual lighthearted self. "That's just the point. Does anyone? Or do you keep yourself so guarded that no one knows what's really going on in there? Do you even know what you want yourself?"

"I know a hell of a lot better than you do," she threw back at him. "Who are you to tell me what I want, what I need, what will make me happy?"

Levi leaned closer so he didn't have to yell over the music or engine noises. Or maybe it was because heads were turning their way as they went round and round. "Because I think you know what you want, but for being such a straight shooter when it comes to everyone else, you sure are good at lying to yourself."

"What the hell is that supposed to mean?"

"One minute you're telling me I've got no chance, and the next you're grabbing my junk. Even when you're pushing me away, you're running after me."

"No. I mean okay, yes. I did do that." She shook her head, trying to get a grip on the conversation. It seemed to be forging on quicker than she could keep up, faster than she could defend herself. "Maybe I've been a bit

indecisive, but it's not because I don't know what I want.
I do know."

"Then what is it?" Levi reached out to her, his hand
grabbing her waist like he was pleading with her.
"Because you're sending me mixed signals."

Zoe flicked his hand away like it burned. "Maybe
because you're pushing me. You're pushing me for
promises, for more. You're pushing me for something
that I can't give you."

"Can't give me? Or refuse to? You pretend like you've
been honest, Zoe, but you've been lying right from the
start."

She gaped at him as they undulated up and down on
their horses, the rest of the world spinning around them.
She closed her eyes, feeling dizzy.

She shook her head. "That's not true at all. I've been
honest with you this whole time."

"Sorry, but I just can't believe you. I think you're lying to me, and I think you're lying to yourself."

She scowled at him. "Then that's your problem. Not
mine."

His face hardened and his nostrils flared as he took a
steadying breath. "Fine, then tell me right now, and I'll
never bother you again. Look me in the eyes and tell
me you don't want me. All you have to do is say 'no.'
Say it, Zoe."

Zoe glared at him, feeling her breathing come in nauseated pants, her heart thudding inside her chest, her
head splitting open from the music overhead. But she
couldn't seem to form the word.

"What do you want, Zoe?" Levi asked when she didn't
say anything.

"I don't know!" she yelled.

The only thing she could think of that she wanted

more than anything else in the world was to leave, to get off that ride and run as far away as possible.

She could feel things bubbling up inside of her, things she wanted to swallow back down, to tuck away in her bottle. But that didn't seem to be working so well anymore. They kept leaking back out whenever she was around Levi, like he was shaking her up, building the pressure like a can of Coke.

The ride needed to be over. Now. She was ready to jump off the second story carousel, to dive off the pier if she needed to. She couldn't wait another second.

"Stop the ride. Stop the ride!" she yelled. "I need to get off!"

But when the ride kept going and her world kept spinning out of control, she slid ungracefully off her horse, falling to the metal floor with a *bang*. Practically crawling on hands and knees, she made her way to the edge of the turning platform.

Someone shouted nearby. The ride jerked. Zoe gripped the horse next to her. Somewhere inside the inner workings of the antique carousel, gears grinded to a halt, a motor whined as everything began to slow.

When the ride thankfully came to a stop, she scrambled toward the stairs. Then she heard Levi call out behind her.

"Zoe!"

At the top of the stairs, she turned to the sound of his voice. He was still on the horse, staring after her like she'd lost her mind, and he felt sorry for her.

"You were right the other day," he said. "It's not me. It's *you*."

18

A Song and Dance

Piper swept out of the changing room in a white silk empire dress. Zoe and Addison watched from the plush Queen Anne sofa with hopeful anticipation. Would this be the one? The perfect gown to replace the one that was destroyed in Zoe's van?

Fabric swished with each step as Piper glided across the Princess Room and stepped onto the raised platform in the center. Zoe crossed her fingers, feeling guiltier than ever that Piper had to go through dress fittings and alterations all over again. And so close to the big day.

She might not have cut up her friend's dress herself, but she was the reason it happened. She just wasn't sure why yet. The police still had no leads. It was hard to narrow it down from the thousands of people who had visited the Hilton that day.

The short saleswoman, Astrid, danced around her high-profile customer like an excited puppy, rearranging her train, straightening any wrinkles. Once every square inch was tweaked, tugged, and fluffed, she stood back and spread her hands wide as though displaying Piper. *Ta-dah!*

Piper assessed herself in the three-way mirror before spinning around to face her friends. A hesitant wrinkle creased her forehead.

"What do you guys think?"

Addison sighed. "You look beautiful. It's gorgeous. Aiden will love it."

Zoe shook her head. "You look like crap."

Piper's mouth dropped. "What?"

Addison gasped, a long, drawn-out, cartoony sound. "Zoe!"

"It's true, Addy. Don't lie." She held up her hands to Piper before she became distressed. "You look beautiful, as always. But the dress isn't flattering. Your boobs are squished, your curves hidden, your torso shortened."

Piper turned her shocked gaze from Zoe to Addison, the fashionista of the group. "Addy? Is it true?"

She bit her bottom lip and kind of cringed. "Well . . ."

"It's only one week until the big day," Zoe reminded Addison. "We don't have time for sugar coating."

Piper crossed her arms, still waiting for Addison's response.

"It could be better," Addison finally relented. Which was as blunt of an answer as they would get out of her, since she was nothing if not coated in sweet sugariness.

"So, this is a no?" Astrid asked in her thick French accent.

"It's a no," Zoe confirmed.

Piper's shoulders slumped and she headed back to the changing room to try the next one.

When she was out of earshot, Addison spun on Zoe. "You don't have to be so rude."

"I'm not rude. I'm honest," Zoe said simply. "We're running out of time, and I will not let this wedding be anything but perfect."

Addison frowned, but eventually nodded. "You're right. Okay. Honesty. I can do that." She took a sip of tea out of the shop's Royal Albert teacup, as though the caffeine would fortify her. "Are you okay, Zoe? You seem a bit stressed today."

"I don't know why?" Zoe said airily. "I only have a week to be ready for Piper's wedding, there's someone out there that might want to kill me, and my business is tanking as we speak. Not to mention, I'm moving back in with my mother." And she didn't even want to get into the whole arranged marriage thing.

By now, Zoe couldn't deny that someone had it in for her. The snipped brake lines might have been a tiny hint, the explosion an even bigger one. But it wasn't just that. Whoever was behind the incidents didn't want to simply hurt Zoe. They wanted to ruin her by destroying her business, her office, her supplies. It was personal. That was why her first instinct screamed rival.

Natalie was clearly going out of her way to cut Zoe down professionally by stealing her clients. Could she have been taking things too far? She would have known exactly which dress to cut to shreds to do the most damage to her business. Hell, she'd even had a key to Zoe's office. But could she have gone as far as blowing it up?

Then again, Chelsea had just as much motivation as Natalie, if not more. She'd been trying to undermine Zoe for years. Or maybe they were both in on it since they were working together now. Maybe it was part of some grand master plan to eliminate Plum Crazy Events for good.

Then there was Juliet. And she was just crazy.

With a sigh, Zoe leaned against the sofa's backrest

while she shoved all those problems into her bottle with everything else and jammed the cap back on.

Addison was watching her closely. She was already up to date on the details of Zoe's dramas. "Can I do anything to help?"

"No. Thank you. I just need a little stress relief." She took a sip of her own tea.

Addison grinned into her cup. "Maybe Levi can help you out with that."

At the reminder, Zoe swallowed hard, nearly choking on tea. Addison gave her a strange look as she coughed and sputtered. That had been one of the main sources of her stress since she ran away from Pier 39 the day before. She hadn't spoken to Levi since.

Thankfully she didn't need to explain her reaction because the changing-room door squeaked opened. Astrid held it open for Piper to squeeze out in a tulle ball gown with heavy beading on the sheer bodice.

She barely made it to the platform before Zoe was pointing back toward the changing room and Addison was shaking her head—albeit with an apologetic frown.

Piper groaned and spun on her heel, disappearing again for round three.

While Zoe and Addison waited, a chime rang out in the tune of the wedding march. The French woman slipped out of Piper's dressing room.

"That'll be the door. I'll just go see who it is. I'll be right back!" Shoving the heavy privacy curtains aside, she headed out to the store front.

Piper poked her head out into the viewing area before shuffling out in a shapely mermaid gown. It certainly hugged her curves nicely. Approaching the raised platform, she tried to lift her fishtail skirt to step up, but her movements were stiff. She couldn't bend over far enough to reach the flared tulle.

Finally, she kicked the fabric up with her foot and caught it in her hands. Leaning awkwardly, she stepped onto the platform and spun to face her friends.

"Beautiful," Addison breathed.

Zoe nodded her head, her eyes running over the gown critically. "I agree. But it's still a no. Too impractical. You need to be comfortable on your big day. If you can't move freely, there certainly won't be any dancing. You'd have to cancel Reluctant Redemption," she realized, suddenly hopeful. "But if you really want it, I can call them right now and let them know the bad news."

Astrid's thick accent drifted through the curtains as she returned. "I'm sorry. I'm booked for the day," she was saying. "You'll have to make an appointment and come back another day."

"Oh, it's fine. They won't mind." Zoe recognized the voice only a second before the heavy pink curtains swished apart and in burst *The* Holly Hart.

"Ladies!" Holly cried. "What a coincidence!"

Piper gaped. "Holly?"

Zoe got to her feet, blocking Holly from coming into the private viewing room any farther. "Coincidence, my ass."

But Holly had obviously learned to be quick to get all those breaking stories, and she dodged Zoe's outstretched arms. Slinking to the platform, she shoved her phone up to Piper's mouth, the screen displaying a recording app.

"So, any talks of honeymoon destinations?"

"Why? Will I find you lurking in the bushes?" Piper narrowed her eyes.

"I don't lurk. I stake out. It's a professional term." She held a hand to her chest. "I'm a professional."

"What are you doing here?" Zoe demanded.

"I didn't think you'd mind, you know, considering our

little arrangement." She gave a subtle eyewink. Or about as subtle as Holly could be.

Zoe eyed her up and down. "What arrangement? We don't have an arrangement." Grabbing the reporter by the arm, she began to drag her back through the curtains.

"Oh, you remember," she said lightly, like she was used to getting manhandled. "I scratch your back, you scratch mine."

"Zoe, what is she talking about?" Piper stepped down off the platform to get into Holly's face. She crossed her arms below the sweetheart neckline. "What are you talking about?"

Holly looked at Piper as though she were a simpleton. She spoke very slowly so she could follow. "Where do you think I've been getting all my delicious facts for my blog articles?"

Piper spun on her friend. "What? Zoe, you didn't."

"I didn't. Well"—she hesitated, wincing a little—"I guess I did, but—"

Holly gasped and held a hand over her mouth. "Was that supposed to be a secret? Oops. My bad." Stepping back, she held up her phone to take a photo of Piper in the dress, but Addison slapped it away before she could take the shot.

"Zoe. How could you?" Piper asked.

Zoe cringed at the tone in her voice, at the hurt, the betrayal. And she wished she could deny it, but she had let a few things slip. A lot of things, now that she thought about it. But she most certainly didn't tell her about their appointment at the bridal shop.

"You knew Aiden and I wanted a low-key wedding," Piper said, storming back to the changing room—more like teetering in her tight dress. "No media, no public, and especially no Holly Hart," she said like the name was poison in her mouth.

"Hello. Right here." Holly held up a hand and waved. "Still in the room."

Zoe pulled on Piper's arm before she could slip away. "It wasn't like that. You know what Holly is like."

"Overbearing, obtrusive, nosey . . ." Addison counted the amazing qualities out on her fingers.

"Again. Right here," Holly said.

Zoe spun on her, her hands balling into fists. "Yes. You are still here. Let's do something about that, shall we?"

Holly held up her hands in a gesture of surrender. "Now, now. Let's not be hasty. We're all friends here."

"No. We're friends," Zoe gestured to the three of them. "That doesn't include you."

"Friends?" Piper repeated. "That depends on your explanation as to why you've been leaking info to Holly."

The shop owner's eyes shifted uncertainly between the girls. Finally, when the tension was thick enough to jab one of her stick pins into, she clapped her hands. "Shall we try on another dress?" she asked hopefully.

"Ooh. Yes! Let's." Holly plopped down on the sofa and settled in like she was replacing Zoe in the "friends" category.

And by the fierce expression on Piper's face, it looked like there might very well be an opening.

"Not you." Addison shoved the reporter off the velvet sofa and onto the hardwood floor.

Huffing, she picked herself up and brushed off her coral pantsuit. "I don't have to take this. I'm leaving," she said, like it was entirely her choice.

"*Allons-y!*" Astrid said as she shooed Holly toward the exit.

They disappeared through the curtains together. Zoe relaxed as the fabric fell still, but then a moment later, Holly's head popped through the slit again.

Her eyes narrowed in Zoe's direction. "Tit for tat, re-member." She waggled her fingers in farewell. "Chow!"

Silence fell around the girls. They heard the distant chime of the Wedding March as Holly was kicked out of the store.

"Zoe, how could you?" Piper asked again.

Zoe's face screwed up as she tried to find some kind of explanation that would make sense, but she couldn't. "I didn't mean to. I'm sorry."

The curtains parted and Astrid ushered Piper back into the changing room, determined to sell a dress that day. "Next dress. Here we go!" She shut the door firmly behind them, and a moment later the frantic swishing of silk and organza could be heard through the door.

"So what?" Piper called through the door. "Wedding details just fell out of your mouth by accident then?"

"The day I was kicked out of the expo, Holly was there with her cameraman. They caught it all on film. It wasn't good." Zoe lingered nearby, speaking through the door's louver slits. "She threatened to run a smear campaign against my business. Between my assistant stealing clients, and Chelsea slandering my name all over town, and Juliet's tantrum at the expo, I couldn't afford the bad publicity."

"So you sold me out."

"No. I mean, yes." She ran a hand over her face, banging her head against the wall. "But I only gave her information that she could dig up herself if she really had a mind to, and you know she would have. I didn't tell her anything that would get her anywhere near the wedding, or allow her to stick her nose into it."

"Except for my wedding-dress appointment," Piper shot back through the door.

Zoe placed a hand against the door, wishing she could talk to Piper's face, so she could know how sorry she was, so she could see it in her expression. "I swear I didn't. I have no idea how she found out."

Addison had been listening from the other side of the room, but now she came to stand near Zoe. "Piper," she spoke to the door, "to be fair, I know first-hand how manipulative Holly Hart can be and what kind of damage she can do when she doesn't get what she wants."

Addison frowned, probably remembering how close she'd come to losing her business the year before. Holly had been creative with the facts about a dognapping case in the show-dog circuit and turned it all around on her.

Piper went quiet on the other side of the door. Zoe and Addison exchanged a glance as they listened to the scratch and swish of fabric against skin.

Finally, Piper replied. "It's not like I don't get it," she said. "I do. And I don't want your business to suffer, Zoe. But I only get one wedding, and if she can ruin a business, then she can ruin our wedding."

"She won't. I promise," Zoe said. "I won't let her. Look. It's done. Holly Hart isn't getting any more information from me. I swear it. Or I'll find you a new wedding planner myself."

"It's not like I haven't had offers." It was almost a mutter, but it was clear enough that Zoe heard every word.

"What?"

Piper went quiet inside the changing room, like she was deliberating whether to say any more. "I didn't want to tell you this because you already have so much to worry about, but . . ."

"Tell me. What is it?" Zoe resisted the urge to whip the door open.

"I got a call from your old assistant yesterday."

The tea in Zoe's stomach turned acidic, eating away at her insides. "What did Natalie want?"

"To be my wedding planner."

Zoe stepped back from the door like Piper just swore at her. "She tried to poach you? With only a week left to go?! You're my best friend."

"Ahem," Addison made a fake coughing noise.

"One of them," Zoe amended eliciting an angelic smile from her friend.

Astrid stepped out of the changing room, a curious look on her face. "Natalie? Natalie Evans? She's no longer your assistant?"

"No," Zoe said. "She left me for the competition. Enchanted Events."

The woman frowned. "That is so strange. She just called here on your behalf this morning to confirm your appointment."

Zoe laughed, in an I'm going to kill someone kind of way. "You're kidding."

"I guess we know who let the cat out of the bag," Addison said.

Zoe shook her head, already pacing the room, ready to take action. Her heels clicked angrily on the hardwood. "Holly must have gone to Natalie after I refused to talk to her anymore. Natalie knows I use this shop a lot."

The changing-room door opened as Piper finally came out. "Zoe, please do something before she tells Holly anything more."

"Oh, trust me, she won't be doing any more talking once I'm finished with her . . ." When Zoe turned around, she gasped at the sight of her best friend—one of them, anyway.

Next to her, Addison squeaked and covered her mouth. "Oh, my gosh."

Piper hesitated, like she wanted to slink back into the change room. "Is it that bad?"

Zoe shook her head. "It's perfect."

"Really?" Piper's face lit up as she rushed to the platform.

Astrid appeared with a shoulder-length double veil. Sliding the combs into her hair, she fluffed it out like a tulle frame around her pretty face.

Piper's breath hitched a little and her eyes began to glisten, something that had never happened with the original dress. "This is *the one*."

Addison skipped over to the platform and did a little happy dance with Piper while Zoe gave a little relieved sigh and thanked the wedding gods. Despite all the last-minute roadblocks with the wedding, she might actually pull it off.

She turned to Astrid. "We'll take it."

The woman smiled, very pleased with the sale. "Certainly. Let me just go grab an order form."

Turning, she headed for the front, but Zoe stopped her. "No. I don't think you understand. We want *this* dress." She pointed, like there could be any mistake.

Astrid blinked, glancing from Zoe to her friends. "You mean the one off the rack? No. No. I'm afraid that's not possible. We can put a rush order on it. It can be here in three months."

Three months! They didn't have time for that. "Try a week," Zoe said.

Astrid gaped at her. She looked about ready to argue, but Piper hoisted her skirts and hopped down from the platform.

"I'll take *this* dress, please," she told her. "Just name your price."

Astrid finally closed her mouth. Her eyebrows rose, as though in question, and Piper responded with a nod.

A grin spreading across her face, Astrid slipped through the privacy curtains, calling over her shoulder as she left. "I'll just go ring it up!"

Zoe waited until the drapes swished closed before laughing. "Impressive, Piper. You're practically a Caldwell already."

But Piper spun on her with a firm look, shoving her fists on her hips. "Now promise. No more Holly."

Zoe held up her hands in surrender. "I promise. And I'm really sorry."

Piper smiled, seemingly placated. "Me too."

"Group hug!" Addison threw out her arms and encircled both her friends.

Now that the dress dilemma had been solved, Zoe was going to have to pay a little visit to Chelsea's office. Holly's visit reeked of her underhanded guidance.

It was one thing when Natalie had simply left her high and dry. People quit jobs all the time. And considering everything that had happened in Zoe's life recently, confronting the traitor had been low on her list of priorities.

But Natalie had gone too far. Zoe was done standing by while her backstabbing assistant continued to undercut her and hijack her business. Clearly, she was going to have to remind Natalie who was boss.

19

Make the Canary Sing

Zoe stood in front of an office space in South Beach, reading a sign embossed in a delicate scroll print—a very nice font for thank-you cards. *Enchanted Events.* She sneered before turning the handle and barging in.

Natalie was making coffee at a shabby-chic table in the corner. As the door swung open and banged against the wall, she gasped and spun around. The pot slipped from her hand. Dark roast splashed down the table linen, and leapt out of her cup to land on the front of her pale blue blazer.

Then Natalie saw who it was and the cup dropped from her hands. It broke and the rest of the contents splashed over her suede shoes and onto the cream area rug.

Zoe smiled, pleased at the results of her visit so far. She always knew how to make an entrance.

"Natalie." She drew out her name in false affection. "How are you? It's been so long."

"Zoe! W-What are you doing here?" she stammered.

"I thought we could catch up. You know, have a little

girl talk." She strolled casually through the office, wrinkling her nose at the over-the-top romance decor. There were heart and kiss symbols, cheesy quotes about love and marriage, and stock photography of people holding hands. It was so clichéd, like cupid just exploded in the room.

Natalie shrank back as Zoe got closer. "I haven't done anything wrong," she said.

"Then why are you so nervous?"

Natalie made an attempt at drawing herself up. Straightening her coffee-stained blazer, she lifted her chin. "If those clients wanted your business instead of mine, they would have stayed with you."

At least she wasn't trying to deny what she did. Zoe had to give her that. "Hard for them to refuse the prices you've been advertising. No one in the industry is going to look kindly upon you when you've been undercutting every planner in the city."

"This is a cutthroat business. You taught me that."

"I also taught you to make friends, not enemies," Zoe said. "It's a very interdependent community. Everyone benefits when the wedding business thrives. It works off word-of-mouth, reputation. It can be very damaging to your career to make enemies."

Natalie narrowed her eyes. "You're one to talk."

Zoe took a step forward, and Natalie automatically backpedaled, bumping against the shabby-chic table and spilling the creamer down the back of her skirt. Zoe smiled, and Natalie flinched.

It's not like she'd ever hit the poor girl—mostly because that would be an unfair fight. However, it was too tempting to not toy with her a little, like a cat would a mouse.

Natalie's eyes flitted to the French doors on the other side of the room. The golden lettering swirling across the frosted glass said *Chelsea Carruthers*.

Zoe had come to get answers, and not just about how Holly Hart had known about their appointment at Love and Lace bridal shop that day. She had bigger questions to ask first. And as much as she disliked Natalie at the moment, she knew she wasn't capable of blowing up her office or cutting her brake lines.

Chelsea, on the other hand, was a wild card. She just had that vindictive, underhanded, sociopathic feel to her. So far, the cops had turned up nothing in their investigation. If they weren't going to get the truth, then Zoe was going to have to.

She so hoped Chelsea was guilty. The satisfaction of seeing her behind bars while simultaneously eliminating her most annoying competition was a two-birds, one-stone scenario.

Zoe backed away from Natalie who now stood in a puddle of hazelnut creamer. "I'm not done with you." Leaving Natalie to sweat a little, she headed for Chelsea's office.

"You can't go in there," Natalie said, her voice a little squeaky.

"Don't worry," Zoe said. "I just want to talk."

Natalie took a step forward, like she wanted to stop her, but then thought twice about it. "She's not in."

But Zoe knew she was lying because she could see a figure move behind the frosted glass. "Nice try."

Gripping the handles, Zoe flung the doors open. She strolled into Chelsea's office like she owned the place, a smug smile on her face. Only Natalie hadn't been lying. Chelsea wasn't in, but someone else was.

The person turned, and suddenly, she was staring down at her past.

"Sean."

"Zoe? Zoe Plum, is that you?" Sean got to his feet. "Oh, my God."

Zoe winced, like his geniality just slapped her in the face.

He smiled that brilliant smile of his like he was so happy to see her. Too brilliant, too white, too friendly for how she'd imagined him over and over again during the last six years. She'd imagined him ugly, and mean, and not worth missing for even a second. But he was just as good looking now as he was the day he'd dumped her.

Sean laughed in disbelief. Zoe recalled his laugh like it was a name she'd heard a million times. It used to sound so musical to her ears. Now it sounded like the wedding march—so overdone.

"It's been so long," he said. "How are you?"

He crossed the small office and reached out as though to give her a hug, as though they were a couple of old friends, as though he hadn't turned her life—and her heart—upside down.

Without meaning to, Zoe found herself backpedaling into the reception area, just like Natalie had done a minute before. Her heart had stopped dead in her chest. In fact, part of her thought that would be best. Yes. She could just keel over right there on the *Live, Laugh, Love* carpet and then she wouldn't have to come up with a response.

But when she didn't die soon enough, her heart began to ache from lack of oxygen. She took a gasp of air, continuing to stare in disbelief. Sean's expression never wavered. He still looked like he was an old friend wanting to catch up.

Zoe wasn't about to pretend that this was some social call. She wasn't one to hide her feelings at the best of times, far less the worst. And this was the worst.

But Sean was good at hiding his feelings. Because he'd pretended that he'd loved her, that he'd wanted to spend the rest of their lives together. Pretended right up until the last possible moment. The moment when it really mattered.

Suddenly, Zoe remembered where they were: a wedding-planner's office. That's right, he was getting married—or at least trying to again. She felt her fingers and toes go numb as her body shunted all her blood to vital organs just to keep her alive. The ugly office went dark around the edges and she felt like she was going to pass out. Her upside-down-heart was struggling to keep up.

Out of some sick masochistic need, she heard herself ask the obvious. "What are you doing here?"

"Waiting for Chelsea."

"Of course." She nodded, not unlike a bobble head. "She . . . she told me that you're getting married."

"You're obviously here to see her. She won't be long if you wanted to wait." He gestured to the other chair in her office, as though inviting her to sit with him.

She wondered why on earth he would invite her to wait for Chelsea. Didn't he know they were practically enemies? *Of course,* Zoe realized, *he doesn't know.*

Why would Chelsea tell him about their run-ins, about what a bitch she was being to his ex-fiancée? Zoe imagined that to get anyone to marry her, Chelsea probably had to hide her maliciousness. Lie about who she really was.

"No. Thank you. I think I'll be going."

"Are you sure?"

Right. Like she wanted to be near him for any longer than she had to be. Like she wanted to be in the same room with the two of them. As if Chelsea wouldn't take full advantage of the situation, rub it in Zoe's face just how much in love they were.

And what was wrong with Sean? Was he completely

oblivious? No. Not oblivious, she thought. Just over it. He wouldn't think twice about why this would be weird. Just like he probably hadn't thought twice about her since their wedding day. She'd been the only one dwelling on it this whole time.

Zoe turned to leave, but Sean lurched forward. "Wait. Please. I think . . ." He ran a hand thought his thick, dark hair—and she'd so hoped that he'd be sporting a cul-de-sac by now. "I think that maybe we should talk. You know. Get things off our chest. Out in the open. Some closure."

She stared at him as though he just told her he was a professional wrestler now. "Closure," she repeated numbly.

"Maybe we can go grab a coffee. Catch up." He smiled. God, he could be so damned charming when he wanted to be.

But not charming enough for her. Ever again. "No." She shook her head, forcefully. The very idea nauseated her. "I can't. I'm busy."

"Too busy to catch up with an old friend?" he asked hopefully.

Zoe's lip curled at the word "friend." "Yes," she said. "I-I've got a date."

Natalie snorted. "A date?" She was still standing frozen by the coffee table, cream dripping onto the carpet as she watched the scene between Zoe and Sean unfold. Zoe had forgotten she was even in the room. That she even existed.

"*You* have a date?" Natalie asked pointedly.

They'd worked closely together for two years. Hearing no talk of a boyfriend, or having a date with a man, or even any mention of being interested in one, Natalie had probably made the assumption that Zoe was a hardened spinster—which wasn't far from the truth, though Zoe preferred the term *seasoned bachelorette*.

Zoe glared at Natalie, daring her to challenge her story. "Yes. A date."

Sean's eyes took on that look of a hurt puppy, the one that prevented her from ever being able to stay mad at him for long—with the exception of his last screw-up. "With who?"

Between Sean's undeserving look of betrayal and jealousy and Natalie's disbelief, Zoe felt her face harden into a smooth mask. She wasn't that hurt twenty-four-year-old anymore. She'd gotten over it—sort of.

She raised her chin. "My fiancé."

Turning on her heel, she marched toward the door. On her way past Natalie's desk, she spotted a turquoise daily planner lying next to her laptop. Zoe's determined footsteps slowed as she considered it for a moment.

It was the same daily planner Natalie had used while working for Zoe. With Zoe's favorite contacts, her favorite vendors, and her favorite suppliers—including wedding-dress shops. It would have had all the info for Piper's wedding in it. Every last detail.

Reaching out, she swiped it off the desk and flipped through it. "Did you tell anyone about the wedding venue for Piper Summer's wedding?" she asked Natalie.

Natalie looked affronted. "Of course not. Being professional means maintaining client confidentiality."

"Except she's not your client and you haven't acted the least bit professional so far. Did you tell anyone?"

She scowled. "No."

"Good. Keep it that way, or we'll have to have another little chat." She waved the daily planner in the air. "I'll be confiscating this. And if you have a problem with that, take it up with Holly Hart."

Natalie opened her mouth, an argument on her face,

but before she could speak, Zoe turned her back on her two exes—assistant and fiancé. Marching out of the office, she slammed the door behind her and went to get ready to meet her future husband.

20

Changing Her Tune

Slurp.

The noodle whipped around like it was struggling for its life as Taichi Kimura sucked it into his mouth. He grinned across the table, his pasta-filled cheeks puffing out in a smile. Zoe gave her best resemblance of a smile before drinking deeply from her wine glass.

"How is your pasta?" she asked.

"Very good. Thank you." He gave a slight nod of the head, like a mini-bow.

According to Zoe's mother, he'd recently moved from Japan, but she'd expected him to have already been acquainted to, if not adjusted to, American life, having gone to university in the States.

But the habits were as strong as his accent: the bowing, the politeness—*slurp*—the slurping. Her mother still did the same thing when she ate soup or noodles, a long-ingrained courtesy to show respect and appreciation for the chef's hard work.

Growing up with it, she found the habit endearing. It

made her feel at home, as though she were dining with her mom and not on a boring date. If you weren't slurping it, you weren't enjoying it. And if Taichi's noises were anything to go by, it must have been the best meal of his life. At least one of them was enjoying their date.

She took another swig from her glass. "So, how is your new job going?" she asked. "Are you settling in?"

"Yes, thank you. It is very good. Everyone is so nice."

The conversation died off for the rest of the meal. When he finally finished his fettuccini, and Zoe her second drink, she was hoping the date would be over and so would her obligation to her mother. She anxiously glanced around until she caught the waiter's attention.

When he noticed her, he gave her the head tilt and approached their table.

"Will there be anything else for you?" he asked very slowly and a few decibels too loud, like that somehow makes English easier to understand.

While Taichi's accent was strong, his English was impeccable. Zoe almost took offense on his behalf at the waiter's assumption. But if her date noticed the unintentional slight, his manners were impeccable too, because he answered politely enough.

"Yes, please. I had my eye on the chocolate cake."

"Cer-tain-ly!" He turned to Zoe, and even though she'd ordered in a perfect American accent, he spoke the same way. "And for you, madam?"

"Make that two. And another glass of wine, please."

"You like chocolate too? We have that in common," Taichi noted with delight, as though that would have been a deal breaker.

She'd forgotten how boring dates could be. Then again, she'd been spending a lot of time with Levi lately. One could even consider some of those encounters as dates, if one wanted to—which she most certainly did not. And at no time would she consider their interactions boring.

But Zoe wasn't on a date with Levi—not that she wanted to be. In fact, they hadn't spoken since she left him on the carousel on Pier 39 the day before. No, she was on a date with Taichi Kimura, and because she'd promised her mother she would consider him as a potential husband, she put thoughts of the rock star aside.

But the nonexistent small talk was slowly eating away at her sense of propriety. It may have been a first date, but Zoe didn't like to waste her time. Besides, they both knew why they were there. What was the point in dancing around the subject? Or maybe that was her third glass of wine talking.

"Tell me, Taichi," she said. "Why did you agree to this date?"

"I'm new to town. I thought it would be nice to meet someone and get to know you. Your mother said you were beautiful, but her description didn't do you justice."

"Thank you." She smiled. "But you're aware of both our mothers' intentions, are you not? Of the arranged marriage?"

"I am," he said blankly.

"And you still came?"

"You came as well," he indicated her thereness with a hand gesture, but she knew he understood what she was getting at.

"Touché, I guess." She frowned into her empty glass. "I'm just trying to understand. You're coming to America, land of the free. I assume you want to live here because of the lifestyle, the freedom of choice."

"That is one of the reasons."

"Doesn't that include the freedom to choose your own wife?" She was afraid she was being too blunt, considering they'd just met, so she tried to explain. "Being from a younger generation, I'm surprised you would consider such a traditional arrangement."

"It's true, I enjoy many things about America and look forward to many years discovering it. However, who better to do it with than someone who understands me and my own culture as well as this one?"

Even to her fuzzy, wine-befuddled brain, his succinct answer surprised her. It actually made a lot of sense. "But why me? I'm more American than Japanese. Not to mention I'm brash, I'm blunt, I swear too much, and I'm stubborn. Don't expect a docile, subservient wife."

What was she saying? He shouldn't expect anything, because it wasn't like she was going to marry the guy. Maybe it was her fight about marriage with Levi that had started her thinking. Or maybe it was running into Sean so unexpectedly after all these years, but she wanted to know what Taichi saw in her that was worth marrying, even if he'd only just met her. What did he see that Sean didn't? That—if Levi was right—*she* didn't see? Was she marriage material?

"In all your mother's descriptions of you, she never said you were docile." Taichi chuckled good-humoredly. "You know who you are. You are independent. I like that. We are just two similarly minded people that are willing to come together and form a mutually beneficial union. I'm simply looking for someone to enjoy my life with. So why not you?" he asked simply.

Thankfully, the waiter came with their dessert, preventing her from having to respond.

Why not? That was a good question. Zoe certainly thought she was a great catch. But marriage material?

Taichi seemed perfectly pleasant, mild mannered, and polite. She could never see him mistreating her—mainly because she could kick his ass if he did.

As she stared at him over her new glass of wine, he

certainly looked attractive enough. And to have someone to lie next to every night meant no more vibrators for her.

Scratch that, she thought. Of course there would be vibrators. It only makes things more interesting.

An arranged marriage seemed a lot less messy than hopping back into the dating-scene again. It made her cringe to think of the uncertainty of it all, the self-consciousness, the doubts, all to possibly end up left at the altar again. Taichi, on the other hand, was a sure thing. He already knew he wanted to marry her.

Taichi dug into his chocolate cake. "Why are you considering an arranged marriage?" he asked. "As you say, you are more American than Japanese."

Zoe's own candidness suddenly turned around and bit her right in the butt.

A week ago, she would have laughed at the question. Her? Consider marriage? Ha! She'd never have thought it possible. Not until she'd met Levi, until he'd made it impossible not to take a good hard look at the choice she was making to be alone.

He'd made her think about things, feel things she never thought she would again. Things she'd put behind her a long time ago. Or at least, she'd thought she had.

But Levi only wanted to date her. There was still that uncertainty, the unknown if it would all fall apart one day. Levi was a wild card. Whereas Taichi was a safe bet.

She recalled the way that Levi looked at her on the carousel the day before. He'd asked her *What do you want?* And quite frankly, she didn't know anymore.

Levi had been questioning her, pushing her to explore her beliefs over the last two weeks, but she couldn't run away from that question anymore. Not seated across from a man who could be her fiancé.

Taichi was giving her his time, his honesty, and can-

didness about marriage. She owed it to him to be honest.
With him and with herself.

"I guess," she said, "because it would be nice to have
someone there by my side. Someone to share my day
with that could do more than just bark. Someone to wake
up next to every day that didn't have doggy breath. Someone who could be an equal partner."

And there it was. The truth. Maybe she didn't have
everything she needed. Maybe she wasn't entirely sold
on being alone forever, just her and Freddy. As she
thought more and more about it, there were a lot of holes
in her life that a dog just couldn't fill. But was Taichi the
man to fill them?

"Those are good reasons," he nodded affably. "Partnership, dependability, mutual respect."

Smiling, she tucked into her dessert, allowing herself
to really enjoy the date for the first time that evening.

Was she seriously thinking about it? Maybe everyone
was right. Maybe even Levi was right. Life was too short.
It was too short to be alone, too short to spend it hiding
her heart away.

Later that night, she got home and crawled into her
empty bed. And when she cuddled up next to Freddy and
her Fuzzy Friends, she knew for certain it just wasn't
enough anymore.

The only remaining question was, who was the right
person? The man she knew would never break her heart,
but at the same time might not ever make it whole again?
Or was it the man who had found the opening to her
heart, who had the potential to fill it again, but could also
leave it shattered?

21

Singing a Different Tune

The warm scent of gourmet food and the comforting undertones of fish wrapped around Zoe like a blanket. It reminded her of her childhood, since it had always been her mother's go-to dish. Her mother said it brought back memories of her own childhood growing up in Uji.

Today, however, Zoe didn't find it comforting enough. She paced back and forth nervously in the empty restaurant. Of course, part of her was concerned with Piper and Aiden's upcoming wedding. What if the food wasn't spectacular enough? What if they didn't like the dishes Chef Glazier had prepared? Enough had already gone wrong with her wedding plans. But at the moment, all she could seem to worry about is whether or not Levi would show.

Zoe had invited him to the lunch the caterer was preparing as a sampling for Piper and Aiden's wedding. She'd been thinking about him ever since her date on Friday night. About the things she'd said to him on the pier, how angry she'd gotten. When all he'd said was the truth.

She wanted to apologize in person, but she wasn't sure he'd show up since he never texted back. So she paced back and forth in the reception area while the servers set up their table for nine, worrying he wouldn't show.

Maybe he didn't want to hear her apology. Or worse. What if he simply didn't care?

She began to make a list, putting her worries about the day in order.

Will Levi show?
Will he forgive me?
Does he still want to date me?
Do I want to date him?
Would I marry Taichi?
Do I want to get married at all?

Ever since her fight with Levi, or maybe since her date with Taichi, she'd realized just how much of an influence Levi was on her. Even in the two short weeks they'd known each other. She just didn't know what that meant yet.

The front door opened. Street noises filtered in as someone entered. When she turned, she was able to cross one worry off her list.

"Levi."

"Hi." He stood in the doorway, as though unsure whether to come in. But at least he'd come that far. And he'd even cleaned up for the brunch with a shirt and tie—not tucked in, but somehow it just worked for the rocker.

"I'm glad you came," she said.

"Free food? I can't say no to that." He shrugged, but it wasn't with his usual *no big deal* attitude. "How was your weekend?"

"Busy. I had a Pure Pleasure Party last night with twenty guests." She waved that conversation away for later. She hated delaying things with idle chit-chat. She wanted to get to the heart of it.

"Look. I want to apologize for the other day. I didn't like what you had to say so I got defensive and took it out on you. I guess I'm used to dishing it out, just not receiving it."

"Thank you. I'm sorry for what I said." He took a hesitant step inside.

"Don't be," she said. "Don't ever be sorry for being honest with me. Because you were right. Maybe I am afraid to let people in. To let them get too close." The words hurt to admit out loud, but she also felt lighter, her bottle a little emptier.

"I get it," he said. "You were hurt. And you're scared it's going to happen again."

"I guess, I'm starting to realize that being alone might not be the answer. You always say that life is too short. But maybe it's also too long to spend alone."

"It's also a long time to spend with the wrong person, trust me." He laughed, glancing down at his shoes. "I guess that makes me scared of choosing the wrong person again."

Zoe's chest felt like a corset had just been tightened around it, squeezing. Her breath whooshed out. Did that mean he now thought of her as the wrong person? She certainly wouldn't blame him after how she reacted on the carousel. Did she want to be the right person?

She thought back to her date with Taichi and their conversation. "How do you know? Who's the right one?"

"I guess that's the hard part. You don't know. You just do your best to keep your eyes wide open, but also your heart." He looked away for a few seconds, as though thinking. "It's like when the band and I jam. We just pick up our instruments and start to play."

"Play what?"

"Anything. Random notes, tones, riffs. You just hope it all harmonizes together. The drums, the base, the keyboard, the lead guitar. Sometimes it works out. Sometimes it doesn't. But when it does, it's a real hit. And you'll never know unless you take chances."

She nodded, understanding where he was going. "Grab life by the balls."

He smiled, really smiled like he usually did with her. "Yeah."

Zoe hesitated. She wanted to say more, something about him. About them. But she didn't know what or where to start. She couldn't even understand her own feelings right now. How was she supposed to explain them?

The front door opened again, and she lost her chance as Piper and Aiden walked in.

"Hey. Sorry we're late," Piper said. "We got stuck in traffic."

"That's okay," Zoe said. "The food is just coming out as we speak."

Obviously Levi liked what Zoe had to say because he stayed. They gathered around the only table set in the restaurant. While the place normally didn't open until five, apparently they did private meals—if you're Aiden Caldwell, that is.

Not long after, they were joined by Addison, Felix, and Naia. When Bob and Marilyn showed up, the soup was served.

Now that they were all seated around the table, their group felt whole. Zoe thought it was nice of Aiden to pay for the extra settings so they could still be together, even if it wasn't their usual Sunday pancake brunch.

Their group was certainly getting larger than it used to be. All her favorite women were paired off and in happy relationships. And to Zoe's surprise, she even had her own plus one for once. Well, sort of. It wasn't really a date. But Zoe had never really had any men in her life to bring around her friends. And come to think of it, was Levi even "in her life?" And was that what she wanted?

Levi reached for his water and caught her eye. She quickly glanced away. She hadn't even realized she'd been staring at him. But then she looked around and realized that everyone else was staring at them.

It felt juvenile, like they were all a bunch of awkward teenagers standing in the halls at school, trying to act cool but being so damned obvious about what they were really thinking.

Zoe rolled her eyes and dug into her appetizer, and yet, something like a high school girly giggle bubbled up inside her.

"So tell me, Levi," Aiden said. "Are weddings big business for live bands these days?"

"It's not too bad. Not steady work, but with other weekend events and gigs at the local bars, we're almost full time." He reached for a butternut squash tart. "We're actually booked to do a week-long tour around California this week. I leave tomorrow."

"Tomorrow?" Zoe nearly dropped her tart. She tried to rearrange her surprised features into one of mere interest. She recalled Levi mentioning something about the tour to Holly Hart.

Levi ate his appetizer like he didn't hear her anxiety. "We're starting in Sacramento and working our way down to San Diego. Don't worry. We'll be back in town for a gig Friday night, so it won't interfere with the wedding. And of course," he told Zoe, "you can continue to use my place to work."

Surprisingly, that wasn't Zoe's first concern. In fact, instead of the wedding being her first thought, it was about him. She wondered if they'd be able to talk about things a little more before then. Or maybe time away from him was what she needed. Time to think.

"You're the lead singer of the band, right?" Addison asked, although she knew that perfectly well by now.

Next to her, Felix's eyebrows rose in appreciation. "Wow, that must get you lots of"—he hesitated, suddenly remembering his audience—"gigs," he finished lamely.

He flinched, and Zoe assumed it was because Addison just kicked him under the table.

"Maybe I should hire you guys to play at my pub," he said to cover it up.

"That would be cool," Levi said. "I do a lot of solo stuff too, even for the fancy events. Soirees, fundraisers, black-tie events, that kind of thing. I know a lot of classical and jazz standards. Apparently I make good background noise."

This got a chuckle out of everyone around the table. Zoe most of all.

"I can't see you blending into the background," she said.

The laughing stopped and everyone stared at her like she'd just done a backflip.

But Levi didn't seem to notice. He gave her a familiar look. And then it struck her. His looks were starting to become *familiar* to her. That was something new.

"Hey," he said. "I can behave myself, you know. I clean up pretty good too."

"Oh, I remember." But when she tried to recall how he looked at Juliet's wedding the day they met, her mind automatically produced the memory of him with nothing but a dress shirt on. And from there she tried to imagine what he looked like beneath it, as she'd been doing a lot ever since.

His eyes were smiling, like they were sharing some

kind of inside joke. Was it her imagination, or was he thinking about the same moment?

When she finally looked away, there were more familiar looks, but from her friends this time. Could they be any more obvious?

Zoe felt like throwing one of her salad croutons at them, but then she would be stooping to their level of immaturity. So instead, she settled for sticking her tongue out at them when Levi wasn't looking.

Addison set her glass down with a bang. Everyone jumped and turned to her. "Why do you want to date our Zoe?"

Zoe gasped, her mouth dropping. "Addison!"

"What?" she said like an innocent angel. "Normally you'd be the one asking the blunt questions, so someone's gotta."

"Because she's a great catch," Levi said, not skipping a beat. "But I don't think I need to tell her best friends why she's amazing."

Good answer, Zoe thought. Did that mean he was still interested? She supposed he was still there, so that was a good sign.

Addison seemed to think so too, because she nodded. "Touché."

"What are your intentions?" This time it was Piper demanding an answer.

"Piper!" Zoe hissed across the table.

"Purely honorable," Levi said.

A little too honorable so far, thought Zoe.

When the main course was served, conversation turned to their usual Sunday chit-chat and Levi seemed to fit right in. But of course he would. He was so easygoing that Zoe could see him slipping into any situation effortlessly.

"Bob," Levi said. "What is it that you do?"

"I'm a detective with the San Francisco Police Department."

Levi whistled. "Now that's an interesting job. I bet it keeps you busy."

He chuckled, as though that was an understatement. "That it does."

"Bob is following the San Fran Slayer case," Zoe told him. "He's on TV all the time to make the official statements."

Levi stared across the table at Bob. "Now I know where I've seen your face before."

"I heard the killer just struck again last week." Addison leaned in, as though they'd be overheard in the empty restaurant.

"I saw that on the news," Piper said. "Didn't he kill some jewelry designer?"

"A pizza delivery driver was just found the other day," Zoe said.

Marilyn tutted, setting her fork down. "This isn't really a discussion for meal time, is it? Can't we discuss something more pleasant?"

"My ears are burning!" A voice sang out. Everyone turned to find Holly Hart poised at the entrance. "Now don't stop chatting on my account. Go ahead. Talk about how pleasant I am."

Jaws dropped in shock as she grabbed a chair from a nearby table. She dragged it over, metal legs scraping on the floor, and spun it around to straddle it.

Wedging herself between Aiden and Piper, she scooted herself closer to the table like she was one of the gang. She placed her chin on her fist, batting her eyelashes at Aiden.

Aiden's jaw clenched. He dropped his fork on the plate and it clattered noisily. Pushing himself away from the table, he wiped his mouth on a napkin. The look on his face said he'd lost his appetite for the desert spread that was being carried out at that very moment.

When Zoe caught a glimpse of Piper's expression, she was ready to tell the server to clear all the knives off the table, just in case.

"What the hell are you doing here?" Zoe demanded.

"Now, now," Holly said. "Is that any way to treat a guest?"

The server hesitated as she set the last of the truffles on the table. "But the reservation was for nine. I'm not sure there's enough food left. I could always go check with Chef Glazier."

Holly held up her hands. "Oh, I don't want to be a bother."

"She's not staying," Zoe said. "The word 'guest' would imply she was invited and *she wasn't*." She glared across the table at the reporter.

"Oh, but I was." Holly aimed a conspiratorial wink at Zoe so all could see.

Piper's eyes widened, and her head snapped as she gaped at her friend. "Zoe. You didn't."

Holly bit her lip. "Oops."

Piper threw her napkin on the table and stood up. "How could you? You said you would stop feeding her information."

Zoe flinched at the anger in her voice. "I wasn't feeding her information. I gave her a few useless hints."

"Except when she showed up at my bridal gown appointment, it wasn't so useless."

Zoe got to her feet, leaning over the table as Piper scowled at her. She wasn't going to back down. She didn't do anything wrong. "I didn't tell her about the dress fitting. Natalie did it. Or maybe Chelsea. I thought you said you believed me."

"I did believe you. But you said you stole her planner,

and now Holly just magically happens to show up at our sample meal?" Piper threw her hands up. "How did she find out about this one, huh?"

Zoe banged the table with a fist. "I swear I don't know how she found out."

Holly stood up now too, as though she were ready to put herself between the two of them if need be. "Ladies. Ladies. You know you wouldn't have to fight about me if you'd just give me an invite already."

Zoe ended the angry staring contest with Piper and turned her murderous gaze on Holly. "Why bother when you seem to invite yourself to everything anyway?"

"I don't blame her," Piper said.

Holly placed a touching hand over her heart. "Thank you."

"I blame you." She jabbed a finger in Zoe's direction.

"Oh, drama, drama, drama." Holly took a seat again, as though getting comfortable for a show.

Zoe grit her teeth. "I didn't tell her anything," she spat. "What? Do you think I'm lying?"

With a deep breath, Piper seemed to make an effort at calming herself as the whole situation was getting out of hand. "Look I'm just saying that you haven't exactly been on the ball lately. I understand." She held her hands up before Zoe could reply. "You've got a lot of things on your plate and—"

"So you don't believe me," Zoe said. "I thought you were my friend."

"Friend?" Piper scoffed. "You're the one leaking wedding info to the paparazzi."

"I'm not a paparazzo," Holly corrected her. "I'm the people's voice. Their champion. Ooh, are these peanut butter chocolate balls?" She popped one in her mouth and rolled her eyes in ecstasy. She held up the platter to Piper. "You should really try one of these babies."

Marilyn seemed to be fidgeting, anxious about all the yelling. She hated when there was discord among the group. In fact, everyone seemed uncomfortable, eyeing one another like no one quite knew what to do. How could they possibly choose sides?

Levi, however was snacking away on the chocolate and truffle tray, tossing one to Naia every once in a while, making her giggle. Much like he tried to make light of the Fisher-Wells disaster. It's not like he didn't think it was a big deal. Zoe was beginning to realize it was his way to bring balance to stressful situations.

Bob placed a hand over Marilyn's to still them, but his no-nonsense response was directed at Piper and Zoe. "I'm sure there's a perfectly good explanation as to why Holly is here. And if we all just settle down, I'm sure we can sort it out."

Aiden stood up and rubbed Piper's back. "Let's all just sit down and try the desserts so we can make our choices for the wedding menu and go, okay? This chef has been booked for months and we've been waiting for this appointment. There's no time to come back."

Piper huffed a breath through her nose. "Fine."

But Zoe had lost her appetite. "I wouldn't want to throw off the chef's numbers. I'll go."

"Zoe, wait!" Addison yelled out.

But Zoe stared straight ahead as she grabbed her purse and marched out the front door. The summer air was thick and hot after the air-conditioned restaurant, but it suddenly felt easier to breathe.

The door squeaked open behind her, and footsteps slapped the pavement as someone ran after her. They slowed when they came up beside her. It was Levi. Shoving his hands in his pockets, he stared ahead, strolling casually like he'd been there the whole time.

"Well, the salmon was delicious," he said.

Despite her anger, Zoe felt herself smile. He'd just walked out of a luncheon with the people who hired him for a high-profile gig. Not to mention, he didn't even try to stay behind to schmooze Holly Hart for a segment on his band. Instead, he'd chased after her.

"You should have tried the dark chocolate caramel balls." He continued to chat as though they had a perfectly pleasant meal. "The chef's a genius. I never would have thought to pair sesame seeds with salted caramel."

Zoe's footsteps faltered, and she came to a stop. "What did you just say?"

When Levi noticed she'd stopped, he turned around. "Caramel balls?"

"Sesame seeds." Her voice was barely a whisper. The air left her lungs like she'd been punched in the gut. Piper was deathly allergic to sesame seeds. "Shit!"

Zoe spun and raced back to the restaurant. She just hoped she was in time to stop Piper from eating them before she wound up in the hospital. Or worse.

22

A Barking Dog Never Bites

Zoe wrenched the restaurant door open and ran back to their table. She scrambled past chairs, tripping over them in her haste, bumping tables decorated with fresh flowers, knocking their vases over. She could hear Levi right on her heels.

She was panting by the time she got to the private back room. Addison and Felix turned to her, surprised by her sudden appearance, but her focus was on Piper. Chocolate being her comfort food during times of stress or joy or boredom or any time for that matter, Piper was reaching for one of the sesame balls.

As she brought it to her mouth, Zoe screamed "No! Grab that ball!"

Zoe leapt across the table, slapping it out of Piper's hand. The chocolate ball flew across the room, bouncing off Holly's cheek, and landed in someone's water glass.

Dishes slid off the table, busting apart as they hit the floor. Marilyn screamed in fright. Felix spun Naia away to safety. Bob stood at the ready, unsure of who to protect. Piper gasped.

When everything settled, and the dishes finally stopped crashing, and people stopped yelling, the moment seemed to freeze like some bizarre tableau from a comedy sketch, because no one seemed to know what to do.

Piper stood frozen, her mouth hanging open. Zoe just stared back from her sprawled position across the tabletop, trying to catch her breath. She could feel soup soak through her dress.

Levi was the first to speak. "I feel like you just don't get this whole ball-grabbing concept. You've still got the wrong balls."

Naia giggled in her dad's arms. Holly started to take photos with her phone, snapping them off from different angles in the room until Addison grabbed it. Drawing her arm back, she tossed it clear across the room.

"Have you lost your mind?" Piper finally asked Zoe. She looked furious. She began to dab at the spray of tomato basil soup across her front.

"Sesame seeds"—Zoe gasped—"in . . . balls." She slumped onto the table

Piper's glare shifted to the chocolate ball floating in the water glass. The black powder that had coated the ball floated on the water's surface. After a moment, the furrow lines on her forehead relaxed and she gaped at it like it personally tried to kill her.

"Oh, God," she said. "How—"

"Levi had one," Zoe explained. "He told me outside that it had sesame seeds in it."

Aiden frowned, automatically reaching out for Piper. "Are you okay? Did you bite into it at all?"

"No. No. I'm fine." She rubbed her fingers off on the front of her dress as though there might be remnants on them.

Zoe inched her way off the table, trying to do as little damage as possible, or at least no more than what she'd already done.

Levi helped her off the table to prevent it from tipping over. When she stood up, all manner of desserts and drinks dripped down the front of her dress.

"Wow," he said. "You really must hate sesame seeds."

"She's highly allergic," Zoe told him as she tried to wipe herself off with a napkin. "Like anaphylactic allergic."

He rolled his eyes. "Yeah, I gathered that," he said with an ironic twist to his smile.

"Piper Summers," Holly said in her reporter-like voice. She marched over, holding her phone up to record Piper—with a newly cracked screen, Zoe noted. "Your wedding planner, has dropped the bouquet at every turn of planning your upcoming nuptials to rich CEO, and ridiculously fit, Aiden Caldwell. Is it time to look for a new planner?"

Piper stared the phone down. "Not a chance. I couldn't do it without her. I wouldn't." And Piper's expression looked so sincere, so earnest, that Zoe's arms were suddenly wrapped around her friend.

"Thanks," she said. "I needed to hear that." And it seemed she'd needed a hug too, because she lingered in Piper's embrace a moment longer, transferring remnants of brunch onto her friend's outfit.

"I'm sorry I didn't believe you," Piper said.

"I'm sorry too." When Zoe pulled away, she glared at the metal doors to the kitchen. "I specifically told the chef no sesame seeds. He knew you had a severe allergy. This is inexcusable." Her fists balled at her sides as she became more worked up, as the reality of what just about happened hit her. "Excuse me while I go have a few words with the chef."

As she turned for the kitchen, she nearly ran into Holly. The reporter stuck the phone in her face, but she pushed her away.

"You, don't go anywhere," Zoe told her. "I'll deal with you in a minute."

Holly gaped. "Me? What did I do? I'm just doing my job."

Zoe turned away from the reporter in disgust and started for the kitchen doors, but the server cut her off.

"Excuse me, but it's staff only in the kitchen. You can't go back there."

Zoe unleashed the force of her eyebrow on the girl. With a quirk and a twitch, the server backed off as though Zoe had physically, pushed past her.

Zoe swept the stainless-steel door aside and blew into the kitchen like a storm. She certainly felt as thunderous as one. "Chef Glazier?"

How careless. How irresponsible.

This was no small oversight. She'd had to fire caterers before for overcooked vegetables or cold soup, but this mishap wasn't just going to put a bad taste in someone's mouth. It had put her friend's life in danger. It could have killed Piper.

The door swung shut behind her, muting Holly's screeches as someone clearly tried to forcibly remove her from the restaurant. But as silence fell over the kitchen, there was still no answer from the chef.

She strained her ears, but she heard nothing, no signs of life in the spotless kitchen. No clanging dishes or knife chopping. "Chef Glazier!?"

When she rounded the stainless-steel counter, his station was still a mess, so she knew he couldn't have gone far. Fresh tomato juice ran across the counter. Yam peels slid under her foot. The knife he'd used for the steak bites was thrown to the side of the cutting board, both still partially covered in streaks of blood.

Maybe he was in the washroom. Or maybe he'd heard all the commotion outside and realized his mistake, then took off to let the servers deal with the customer complaints. Well, Zoe wasn't going to let him get off that easily.

She spotted a second cutting board covered in the dark cocoa powder used to sprinkle over the chocolate balls, but when she looked closer, she saw it was much darker and chunkier than powder.

Swiping a finger over it, she rubbed the black stuff between her fingers. It was gritty, something finely chopped. She tasted it. Sesame seeds.

He'd chosen a black seed color, which blended into the cocoa powder. No wonder no one had noticed it.

The garbage was full of discarded onion peels, containers, and mushroom stumps. Zoe grabbed a spatula and shifted the garbage aside. Hidden beneath a watermelon rind was a half-used bag of sesame seeds. A small package that one would find in a grocery store aisle.

Did he misplace her prioritized, itemized, color coded list of allergies, preference, and favorites? And just where was he?

"Renowned chef, my ass," she mumbled.

Zoe headed farther into the back where it looked like deliveries were accepted. On the way, she came across a small room off to the side with the door cracked open. The label said *Office*.

Well, there's a start, she thought.

She brought up a fist and banged on the door, but there was no answer. When she tried the handle, it was unlocked. The door creaked open, but she couldn't find the toque blanche or double-breasted jacket of Chef Glazier.

Searching the room for signs that he was still there—keys, coat, wallet—she spotted the check she'd given him as a deposit months before when she first booked him as the caterer. It was stuck to the wall with a thumbtack. He might have been a good chef, but he was a terrible record keeper.

Reaching out, she ripped it down. She'd rather scramble to find a replacement caterer at the last minute than use his services again. She went to tear it up, but then she thought of something even better. Something that would send a clear message.

As she stomped back to his station, her body still shook with adrenaline, with the close call of seeing her friend succumb to anaphylaxis. And Chef Glazier wasn't even man enough to own up to his mistake.

She swiped his bloody steak knife off the counter and placed the check on the cutting board with the sesame seed debris. Raising the knife, she stabbed the slip of paper right through the middle.

There, she thought. *That message should be clear enough.*

Zoe left the kitchen, ready to get out of there. She found the others waiting at the front door.

"Did you find him?" Aiden asked her.

She shook her head. "No. Unfortunately."

"Well, I think I'll be having a talk with him when I get to the office tomorrow." He wrapped a protective arm around Piper as they went to leave. "Or maybe my lawyer will."

"Don't worry," Zoe said. "I'll be finding a new caterer for the wedding. One that's even better. It will be perfect. I promise."

There was that word again, "perfect." But so far, nothing about this wedding was anything close to it. First the entertainer broke his leg, then the gown was shredded, her décor blown up, and now this. But so far, she'd met every challenge. And she'd meet this one head on too.

Levi held the door open for Zoe, grinning down at her.

She hesitated, suddenly self-conscious. "What?"

"You're a force to be reckoned with, Zoe Plum. First, you dive across a restaurant like a superhero and save your friend. Next, you storm into the back and give the chef a piece of your mind. One would almost say that you're close to finding those balls to grab."

She scraped by him, closer than she needed to in order to walk through the door, rubbing her body against his. "Maybe those balls are closer than I thought." She smiled at him. Not seductively to match her innuendo, but earnestly.

He must have understood her meaning because his look softened.

Standing so close to him in the open doorway, she suddenly realized that despite their two steamy encounters, they'd never actually kissed. At least, not on the lips.

At first, she hadn't wanted to. She'd thought it was too romantic, too intimate. But suddenly, she found herself leaning toward him, tilting her face up to meet his.

A smile lit his face and he dipped his head, but just before their lips could touch, they heard a noise nearby.

Squeak . . . squeak . . . squeak . . . squeak.

Exchanging a glance, they looked around. The noise was coming from a white van parked three cars down. Even from there they could read the decal on the side. *Channel Five News.*

Squeak . . . squeak . . . squeak . . . squeak.

It rocked gently on its wheels, increasing in tempo as they watched, which could mean only one thing.

Zoe snickered. "Do you think . . . ?"

Levi wrinkled his nose. "Holly and the cameraman?"

They stifled their giggles as the noise persisted, changing in rhythm and gusto. Zoe clutched at her stomach as it began to hurt, bracing herself against the restaurant doorframe. Even Bob and Marilyn who were lingering on the sidewalk had noticed.

Marilyn clicked her tongue. "Well, I never."

The shocked look on Marilyn's face sent Zoe into a whole new cycle of giggles.

"Help! Help! Someone call the police!"

Footsteps slapped the restaurant floor, growing closer. With a look, Levi and Zoe pulled apart and headed back inside to see what the commotion was. A moment later, the server appeared from the back and skidded to a halt in the waiting room.

"You!" She pointed an accusing finger at Zoe. "You did it, didn't you?"

Something red dripped from her hand, blood, Zoe realized.

"I did what?" Zoe asked. "What's wrong?"

"Chef Glazier is dead. And you killed him."

23

Bad Dog

The wall on the clock ticked loudly, counting the painfully slow minutes as Detective Warner glared at Zoe from across the metal table. She'd been stuck in the room for six hours already, her mind going in circles as she answered questions over and over again. Every once in a while, the detective would leave and come back with a new batch for her. She felt as dizzy as she had on the Pier 39 carousel.

He tapped his fingers on the table and stared at her expectantly. She thought it must be her turn to start the line of questioning from the top again. "Am I free to go yet?"

He inhaled, as though he were seriously thinking about it. "There's still the issue of a dead chef."

Zoe moaned, as though she were in physical pain. And she was. After so many hours, the detective's voice was scratching against her brain like stiff, cheap lace. "I've already answered your questions. I've told you all that I know. What more do you want?"

He crossed his arms and sat back to stare at her again, belly protruding above the table. "I'm still not satisfied."

She threw her hands up. "You think I killed this guy?"

"I'm the one asking questions around here, Miss Plum," he said. He leaned forward, planting his elbows on the table. "How's business?"

Zoe blinked at the sudden change in direction. "Okay, I guess."

"Now be honest." He shook a warning finger at her. "Your business hasn't been doing so great recently. You've been losing clients. Isn't that right?"

Zoe rolled her eyes. So they had interviewed Chelsea at some point, after all. "Any clients I've lost lately has been all Chelsea's doing. Her and my ex-assistant, who's now working with her."

"So you admit that business has been suffering," he said, like he'd caught her.

She shrugged. "Yeah, but I'll get back on-track soon enough."

"Remember that little explosion at your office?"

"Remember it? I was practically in it." Now he was really throwing her for a loop. This was the first time he'd brought that up. What was his new angle?

"Turns out it wasn't a gas leak," he said. "It was a bomb, Miss Plum. Someone blew up your office intentionally."

She snorted. "I could have told you that."

"Of course you could have," he said. "That's my point."

She held up her hands. "Wait a second. Are you implying that I did this to myself? Why would I blow up my own office when I needed everything in there for events over the next couple of months? Do you have any idea how this has set me back? How much work I have to do to replace everything in time?" She ran her hands through her hair, tugging on her long locks just thinking about it. "Why would I risk my business?"

"Insurance fraud, Miss Plum. Instant cash in hand." The detective rubbed his fingers together in her face, close enough that she could smell the stale smoke on them. He must have been going crazy without a cigarette for so long.

As though reading her mind, he popped a piece of nicotine gum into his mouth. As he chewed, she saw his extra pointy incisors, like some balding, middle-aged vampire. "I called your landlord. He says that you've given your notice. That you're moving in with your mother."

"That's because *her* finances are a mess, not mine," Zoe responded coolly, which was getting harder and harder to do as the hours went by. "That and her health has been failing. She needs help—"

"I called her too," he cut her off. "She says that everything is just fine."

Zoe groaned, exasperated. *Thanks, Mom,* she thought. "Of course she said that. She's an incredibly private person. Why would she tell a complete stranger about her life? She barely keeps me informed. Besides what does all this prove?" she asked. "If you think I'm so hard-up for money, why would I do anything else to jeopardize my friend's upcoming wedding? A good paying gig."

With a burst of energy, he stood up, knocking the chair back. "You've been losing clients left, right, and center. Your office just blew up, your company van went in for repairs, and you can't even afford your rent so you have to move in with your mother." He succinctly summed up each crappy thing going wrong with her life lately, counting each one as he went.

She crossed her arms. "And I suppose I cut my own brake lines too? What was that? Attempted suicide?"

"You're down on your luck," he said, like he didn't

hear her. "You need this wedding to go well. With all the public exposure for your friend's big, high-profile wedding, it could really boost your business again." He smiled like he was rooting for that to happen.

He circled the table, walking behind her. She spun anxiously in her seat to face him.

"But everything's not going perfectly is it, Miss Plum? First the wedding dress, then you blow up the decorations to get the insurance money, and now the caterer goes and tries to put your bride in the hospital. That was the last straw. You lose it. You snap." He snapped his fingers in her face. "You march into the kitchen—"

"But I didn't find Chef Glazier when I was back there," Zoe interrupted.

"So you say." Detective Warner began to pace, as though he was onto something. "Or you did find him and things got out of hand. You argued. It turned physical. Then you grabbed a nearby knife and killed him. In a moment of panic, you dragged the body to the loading bay where you stashed it amongst the storage boxes, then you went back to your tea party like nothing happened." He spread his hands, like *That's it. I just solved the case. Book her.*

Zoe leaned back in her chair like she was relaxing, taking a page out of Levi's book. *No big deal.* She smiled. "That's a nice story you just made up there. It makes me sound pretty devious."

"You can't fool me, Miss Plum," he said. "I have an ex-wife." Grabbing his chair, he spun it around and straddled it to face her.

"I didn't kill him," she said simply.

"Then why were your fingerprints on the murder weapon?" At her look of surprise, his incisors flashed. "Ahhh, that's right. We found your little deposit check stabbed with the knife."

"The steak knife? Yeah? So what?" Zoe frowned in confusion. "I was letting him know he was fired. It was my way of sending him a message."

"Oh, you sent him a message, all right. It was a little sloppy of you. His DNA was practically still dripping from it when we found it."

Her body suddenly grew cold, her fingers and toes tingling. She didn't feel so relaxed anymore. "What?"

"His blood, Miss Plum." He spoke slowly, like she was a complete idiot. "The knife was covered in it. As well as your fingerprints."

She remembered seeing the blood on the knife. She'd assumed it was from the steak bites. But there wasn't that much blood on it. Had some of it been wiped off?

Leaning forward, she gripped the table like she was going to be sick. "Oh, God. But I-I just found the knife lying on the countertop. I swear—"

The door to the room burst open. Zoe jumped, tipping over her cup of water. It ran across the table and spilled onto the detective's lap. He leapt out of his seat, swearing as he tried to wipe it away.

"I'm in the middle of an interview here," he barked. "What the hell is going on?" Scowling he turned to the door. His face fell slack when he saw the trim woman walking through the door.

Without waiting for an invite, she strode across the room, heels clicking on the linoleum floor. "There's nothing going on because you're done here."

When Detective Warner got to his feet, she towered over him. Fist on her hip, she looked down her nose at him like she ate balding vampires like him for breakfast. She stood between him and Zoe as though protecting her.

"You've got to be kidding me." The detective turned to Zoe. "I thought finances were tight. How can you afford a lawyer like her?"

Zoe was still staring at the powerful female like she was Wonder Woman come to save her. "They are. I can't. I have a lawyer?"

"Michelle Johnson with Wright Law Office." She held out a hand.

Zoe shook it a little robotically. "How—?"

She smiled at Zoe's reaction. "Aiden Caldwell sent me."

Of course, she thought. She should have lawyered-up immediately once it was clear where the detective's finger was pointing, but she supposed she hadn't thought of it. Why should she need a lawyer? She was innocent. She had nothing to hide. At least she hadn't thought so, but it seemed they were finding enough dirt on her.

"Don't say anything more," she told Zoe.

Detective Warner barked a laugh. "She's said plenty enough already."

"Well, unless she's said, 'I'm guilty,' then I assume 'plenty' isn't quite enough." She stared down at the detective while he sucked on his teeth.

Finally, as though he were agreeing to a colonoscopy, he waved a hand at Zoe. "You're free to go."

Zoe got to her feet. "Really?"

He pointed a stern finger at her. "Don't leave town."

Michelle gestured to Zoe's cup sitting on the table. "Take that with you. They can get your prints off of it after you leave."

Zoe grabbed it and followed her lawyer out of the room. "But I already gave them my fingerprints." She wondered if she shouldn't have done that. She really should have called a lawyer sooner, but she'd used her one phone call to make sure someone checked in on her mom.

"That's fine," Michelle said. "But you don't want to give them anything else."

Zoe nodded, assuming she meant saliva or something.

Once they were both standing in the reception area, Michelle gave her a business card. "Go home. Get some rest. I'll speak to you first thing in the morning. Do not discuss the incident with anyone."

Zoe nodded numbly. She liked this woman. Focused, direct, confident. Everything she didn't feel herself at the moment.

By the time she got her purse back and signed some papers, the clock on the wall said it was seven o'clock. As she was pulling her cell phone out to call a cab, she was accosted from behind.

Arms wrapped around her, squeezing her like bridal undergarments. She gasped and spun around.

"Zoe!" It was Addison. "Oh, my gosh. Are you okay?"

Zoe gripped Addison's sweatshirt, relieved beyond words to see a friend after that experience. But instead of admitting that, she said, "Of course. Why wouldn't I be?"

"They didn't try to throw you in the slammer?"

"No." Zoe couldn't help but laugh. "They just interrogated me."

Addison gave her a serious look. "How does it feel, you know, now that you're on the other side of the law?"

"I didn't break any laws, Addy."

"Oh, I know that." Her one eye closed in ridiculously slow wink.

"No winking. Stop that." She swatted at her. "I never killed the chef. You actually think I'm capable of that?"

"No way. I'm totally behind you a hundred percent." She gave another wink. "Let me know if there's anything I can do for you. Just name it. A file baked in a cake, boxes of cigarettes for trade, conjugal visits."

Zoe's shoulders relaxed as she exhaled in a half-laugh half-sigh. Addison was obviously trying to cheer her up. "Thanks. I appreciate it. How about we start with a ride?"

"That I can do," she said. "And no law-breaking necessary."

Zoe glanced sidelong at her as they descended the front steps of the precinct. "You seem to forget that I've seen how you drive."

Addison just laughed but didn't deny the insinuation.

"Did someone check on my mom or Freddy?"

"Yes. Freddy is fine but missing you. And Piper went to your mom's earlier, and she's all good."

Zoe thought that if she wasn't okay, she likely wouldn't say anything to Piper or anyone else for that matter. "Do you mind if we check in on her on the way to pick up my van?"

"Of course. And don't worry. She knows we were all brought in for questioning, so she doesn't know you're suspect numero uno."

"Good." Zoe thought the stress of that news might actually kill her mother on the spot.

As soon as Zoe crawled into Addison's Mini convertible, she called Aiden and Piper and thanked them profusely for the help. When she got to her childhood home—or rather, her future one—her mom seemed to be in relatively good spirits for someone whose daughter was involved in a murder investigation. And even more so when she asked about Zoe's date with Taichi.

Maybe it was her guilt about being the kind of daughter who gets arrested on suspicion of murder, but she told her it went very well.

Naturally, she was pressed about marriage, and Zoe, very honestly, told her mother that she was considering it. Which was completely true, just maybe not to Taichi. But she'd give her mother another week out of the hospital before she had that talk.

By the time Zoe trudged up the stairs to her apartment, she was not only facing a possible future of incarceration for a crime she didn't commit, but if that didn't happen, she'd be consulting the *koyomi* to determine the best day to get married to Taichi. She didn't know which was worse.

But assuming Aiden's kick-ass lawyer could keep her out of jail for the next week, she still had a wedding to plan, which also meant finding a replacement chef—a live one. That's if whoever was out there trying to take her down didn't get to her first.

She wondered if the sesame-seed poisoning was connected to all the other recent incidents somehow. Was someone trying to discredit her as a planner? Maybe it was a way to get rid of her as competition. To create bad press in the media about her biggest wedding of the year?

The only person who might have sent Holly there at just the right time—or the worst—would have been Natalie. But then there was the whole murder aspect. Natalie wasn't capable of that, surely. Zoe recalled how she'd cowered simply from Zoe's presence in her office.

At the thought of competition, Chelsea popped into her mind. Was she capable of murdering the chef? Maybe it had been Juliet. Maybe everyone was about tit for tat lately.

As she slid her key into the lock, all she wanted was to fall into bed with Freddy and at least a dozen Fuzzy Friends to keep her company. But when she opened her front door, she had more company than she'd expected.

A figure stood on the other side waiting for her. She gasped and opened her mouth to scream, but the sound was suddenly blocked by a mouth against hers. Levi's mouth.

Her scream turned into a moan as he sucked hungrily on her lips. Not removing his mouth from hers, he pulled her inside.

Shoving the door closed with his foot, he backed her

up against the door. His body pressed against her like he didn't want to leave an inch of space between them. And neither did she.

She'd held him at a distance for so long, refused to let him near. Now she wanted to get her fill of him, gorge like a bride after a hardcore wedding diet.

Zoe ran her hands around the back of his head and gripped his hair, pulling his face, his kisses, closer. He grunted and drove his tongue into her mouth greedily. She met it with her own, wanting to taste him, to have every part of him inside of her. She wanted it all.

It must have been her moaning as he rubbed against her, or maybe her panting as she lost herself in the make out session, but Freddy began to bark wildly like she was being attacked.

Reluctantly, Levi pulled away. Even in the dim entryway, Zoe could see the lust in his eyes as they scraped over every inch of her, like he'd thought he'd never see her again.

When Freddy's barking died down, Zoe said, "I've been wanting to do that since this afternoon."

He ran a thumb across her lips, biting his own as though he wanted another taste. "I've been wanting to do that since the moment we met."

Tired of waiting for his turn, Freddy circled her leg three times before jumping up and pawing at her shin.

She picked him up and welcomed his frantic kisses. She ignored the fact that he'd get excited over anyone and was probably thinking, *I feel like we've met before. Do I know you?*

Zoe had never been so happy to come home. And not to just one male in her life, but two.

"How are you?" Levi asked.

"A free woman. Thanks to Aiden." She slipped off her shoes and headed for the living room.

"Yeah, I know," he said, following her. "I saw him at the station after the police were done questioning the rest of us. We waited around, hoping you'd be released, but when it was clear it wasn't going to be that simple, Aiden made some calls."

The news made her feel both guilty that her mess had disrupted everyone's day and grateful for such good friends. "I'm glad he did or I'd still be in there. It seems I'm suspect number one." With a groan, she flopped onto the couch and put her feet up while she snuggled Freddy.

Levi sat down next to her, apprehensive for a man that just had his tongue down her throat. "I hope you don't mind me being here. Since Aiden was dealing with the lawyer and Addison was still being questioned, I offered to come check on Freddy. She gave me her spare key to your place to get in. I figured your mom would be more comfortable with Piper. Besides," he scratched behind Freddy's ears, "he and I seem to have a pretty good thing going."

As though in agreement, Freddy gave a quiet "Woof."

Zoe cradled him against her chest, soaking in the comfort after her long day. But despite the plentiful kisses he gave her, something told her not even that would be enough that night.

"I didn't know how long you would be held at the station so I thought I'd stay with him," Levi said.

"I don't mind at all," she said. "Thank you for keeping him company."

"Actually, that's a lie." He smiled kind of sheepishly. "I hung around to see you. I wanted to make sure you made it back all right."

"I'm all right."

He seemed disappointed in her answer, like he was hoping for more. Hoping she'd expand a little. Open up to him.

"Good. I'm glad." He got to his feet to leave. "Well, I'd better be going. You're probably tired. I'll see you at the wedding?"

Before he could head for the door, she grabbed his hand. "No. I mean . . ." She took a deep breath and tried again. If Levi was going away with his band for an entire week, this wasn't how she wanted to leave things. "I'm okay, but I could be better."

This news seemed to make him happy despite the seriousness of it. "I don't doubt it. Can I do anything to help?" She could see he was trying not to push her too hard for more.

"I don't want to be alone tonight," she said, finally. "Stay with me." Zoe held his gaze, pleading with her eyes as though she'd never wanted anything more in her life. In fact, the way she felt right then made her think that maybe she never had.

Levi winced like he was in physical pain as he searched for an answer. He squeezed her hand tight. "Zoe, I—"

"I don't mean sex," she corrected. "I just want to sleep. Nothing more."

The hesitation erased, and his expression melted with pleasure. "That's definitely something more. A lot more," he said. "Of course I'll stay."

24

Three-Dog Night

Zoe led the way into her bedroom as though it were the grand tour of the White House and they were entering the Oval Office. It felt momentous, like the moment held a certain reverence.

Beyond the odd plumber or repairmen, she'd never had a man in her apartment, far less her bedroom, since she'd lived with Sean. The only wiener she'd had in her bed was the four-legged kind. And maybe she'd had it wrong up until now. Maybe the answer wasn't swearing off all men for the rest of her life, but was about finding the right man at her own pace. One step at a time.

Levi had said he'd wanted more. For Zoe, this was so much more than she'd ever thought she could give again. And it felt good. Maybe good enough to find even more within herself to give.

Zoe turned on the bedside lamp and plopped Freddy down on the bed. "I'm just going to get into something more comfortable. And by that," she said, "I actually mean something more comfortable. There's a spare pillow in that cupboard over there."

She headed for the washroom, but then she heard a creak of a door behind her and her stomach dropped.

There was a pause. "What the . . ."

She lunged for the wardrobe. Slamming the door shut, she braced herself against it. "Not that cupboard."

But it was too late. Because by the mixture of confusion and amusement on Levi's face, he'd already seen what was hidden inside. There was a moment when he just stared at her, like *are you serious?*

A smile tugged at his lips, as though if he'd seen what he thought he'd just seen, he was going to burst out laughing. And just to be sure, he reached behind her and gently pulled on the door until she gave in and stepped aside.

What was the point? He'd already seen it.

"Are these . . . Fuzzy Friends? I remember these from when I was a kid." He picked up Happy Hippo. "I didn't even know they made these anymore."

"Well, they're not just for kids, you know," she said defensively, snatching it back. "They're collector's items too."

But he gave her an eyebrow arch that said he wasn't falling for it. He picked up Tricky Turtle. "You know they lose their value once you open the package, right?"

"They never came in packages," she said. "And this cupboard protects them from both dust, and UV light, and—"

"Zoe. Stop. Stop." Levi kind of laughed and sighed at the same time. "Come on. Let me in."

Zoe ducked her head. She was doing it again. She was shutting him out. Putting on her cool persona, both emotionally and physically. The ice queen. "You must think this is pretty silly."

"No, I don't," he said with the biggest smile she'd ever seen on anyone.

"Then why are you looking at me like that?"

"Because beneath that tough exterior, beneath all those layers of armor you've built up"—he tapped her chest—"I'm starting to get glimpses of that soft, fuzzy, bean-filled center beneath. I feel like I'm finally getting through. Not that I'm pushing or anything." He threw his hands up and took a step back. "I'm being pushy again, aren't I? I'm sorry. I just"—he sighed—"I really like you. The bits of you that you've let me see, anyway."

She made a noise like she was about to say something, but nothing came out. It had been so long since she let anyone this close.

"How can I get in there?" He tapped her chest again. "See what's inside?"

"Oh, they're called buttons," Zoe said. "See, you just slip this round thing through this hole—"

He held a hand over hers to stop her from undressing further. "You know what I mean."

She nodded. "It doesn't come naturally. Not anymore. Just be patient. Give it some time."

"Does that mean you're giving me the time?" he asked. "That you finally know what you want?"

"I know that I want to try," she said honestly. "I'd just convinced myself for so long that being alone was the best thing for me. That I'd be happier that way. You were right. I was scared."

"I'm sorry I pushed you so hard. I guess I thought you could take it. You didn't seem like a woman who would be scared of anything. But I should have let you come to that conclusion on your own." He stared down at his feet as he chuckled. "I guess I'm not a very patient man."

"You grab life by the balls."

He gave her a surprised look. "Exactly," he said.

"But you know, I'm not the only one hiding behind a mask," she said.

Levi's eyes widened. "What? I know you don't mean me, because I've been annoyingly me right from the start."

"Oh, I'll agree to that." She laughed. "Your mask is more literal. The nail polish? The makeup? The piercings?" Zoe tugged lightly on his eyebrow ring. Under the light pressure, it came away in her fingers.

She gasped, dropping it in surprise. "I'm so sorry!"

However, when she glanced up to assess the damage, there was no blood. There weren't even piercing holes left behind. Just two red marks where the ring had been.

Zoe bent down and picked up the metal hoop at their feet, but it wasn't even a complete ring. It had a chunk missing. She wrinkled her nose in confusion. "What?"

"You've caught me." He reached up to the spike in his upper ear and pulled it apart like two magnets. "I'm a fake."

She gaped at him. "They're not real?" Now she knew why they seemed to move around his face all the time.

He shrugged. "I'm not a big fan of pain. I know I'll never get a tattoo, that's for sure. But I have used some stick-on ones. It was pretty bad ass," he joked.

But she wasn't laughing. She was still staring at the ring in her hand. She finally asked, "Why do you do it?"

"I guess I'm trying out some new looks," he said. "Seeing what suits the whole rocker vibe. I need to fit the part, right?"

"I don't think your fans care about what you look like. They care about your music, and your music is amazing," she said honestly.

Levi bit his lip and sat on the end of her bed. "But what if that's not enough?" he asked her, but he was staring at his painted nails. "What if I'm not enough?"

The words tickled at a memory. Zoe recalled what he'd said about his ex-wife. *I guess I just wasn't enough for her.*

Grabbing his earlobe piercings, she pulled them off impatiently and tossed them on her dresser. She slid her hand into his and dragged him into the bathroom where she took out her nail polish remover pads.

The acetone stung her nostrils as she began scrubbing his nails, one by one. Levi watched her with an amused look on his face, but never said a word.

When his nails were clear again, she handed him a makeup remover pad. Levi glanced at it and chuckled, but then she gave him a look and he dutifully turned to the mirror.

Wiping away the dark eyeliner, he washed his face and patted it dry with a cloth. When he finally turned back to her, he was less dark and brooding, less intimidating, and just as handsome. But now she could see *all* of his handsome face. All of Levi. He might have even passed for the boy next door.

"There," he said. "Are you happy? Is there anything else? Maybe my jeans, perhaps?" He reached for his fly, but for once, her focus wasn't down there.

Placing her hands on either side of his face, she stared at him for a moment until he shifted uncomfortably, maybe feeling as naked as she sometimes felt beneath his piercing gaze.

"It's more than enough," she said.

"So what does this mean for us?"

Zoe bit her lip. She wished she could say what he wanted to hear, but in the end, she turned away. "I can't make you any promises. I can't tell you that I'm a for-ever girl, that I suddenly believe in 'till death do us part.' "

He grabbed her arm and gently forced her to face him.

"I'm not asking for a promise of forever. Just a promise of more."

She searched his hopeful eyes. "More than what?"

"More than a night."

And it was surprisingly easy for her to say, "I can do that."

"Then that's good enough for me." He held her face and kissed her. "For now."

She kissed him back, relieved that they were on the same page. That she could even be on a page at all and for it to feel right. And kissing Levi felt so very, very right.

He pulled back and returned to her cupboard. "Look. We can pretend that I didn't see any of this until you're ready for me to know that stuffed-animal-cupboard side to you." He tossed Tricky Turtle back inside and shut the cupboard doors firmly. "See? What collection of stuffed animals?"

Zoe snorted. Despite her racing heart, she opened the cupboard again. Reaching in, she drew Courageous Cat out. "This was the first Fuzzy Friend I ever received. He was a gift from my dad. He gave it to me on my first day of elementary school and said it was to give me courage. I used to take him everywhere with me."

"You can tell." Levi rubbed the ratty fur.

Zoe pointed to the back of the wardrobe. "That's Merry Mouse. Dad gave him to me the day I won my first spelling bee. Noble Numbat was for graduation. Lucky Lynx helped me through my grandmother's death." She continued to point out each one as she went. "Broken arm. Passing my driver's exam. My first broken heart. He gave me this one after my wedding day."

She grew sad as she considered the meaning behind each one. The collection was a furry representation of all

the biggest life moments that her father had been there
for. She swallowed hard before closing the doors.

"My dad was a pretty stoic man, the strong silent type,
you know?"

"Yeah, I know." He gave her a pointed look.

She relented with a little shrug, but continued. "It's
not like he always knew what to do or say during all the
good and the bad times, but he remembered how much I
loved my first Fuzzy Friend. It became his way of showing me he cared, even long after I was too old for stuffed
animals."

She sat down on the bed and Freddy instantly wormed
his way across it to seek out her attention. Levi sat
down next to her, barely blinking, like if he moved, if he
spoke, if he blinked, this more open Zoe would disappear.

"When my dad died, I felt so lost in my grief," she told
him. "I didn't know how to deal with it. I'd already started
shutting people out after my wedding the year before,
bottling things up. When I searched for something to help
ease my grief, I didn't know what else to do but buy a
Fuzzy Friend."

"So you collect them," he said. "That's not strange at
all. People collect all types of things."

"Well, I do more than just collect them. Sometimes I
use them as a way to help lower my stress or anxiety during situations. I carry them around in my purse and
I . . ."

She paused, trying to think of exactly what she did or
why. She automatically reached out for Kissing Koala
and began to rub its soft fur. She couldn't look Levi in
the eye as he listened to her try to explain.

"I guess knowing it's there is comforting," she said.
"Maybe it's my way of remembering all of those other
hard times"—she gestured to the wardrobe—"knowing

that if I got through them, I'll be able to get through whatever it is I'm currently facing, you know?"

She finally managed to meet his intense gaze. He was nodding, a look of understanding on his face.

"That sounds exactly like a worry stone," he said. "Some people keep a stone in their pocket, and any time they begin to feel stressed out, they reach in and touch it. In fact," he said, "I always have my lucky guitar pick in my pocket during gigs. I never use it. I just like knowing it's there."

"So you don't think it's stupid?"

"Of course not. But you know"—he glanced back at the wardrobe and then lowered his voice as though the fuzzy bags of beans could hear him—"you could talk to someone when you have a bad day instead of a stuffed animal."

Zoe laughed. "I don't talk to them. I just, you know, hold them." She rolled her eyes at the ridiculousness of it. She'd never actually said it out loud before.

But Levi wasn't laughing. "You could talk to me. I'd like to be there to support you."

"I guess that wouldn't be so bad."

His nose wrinkled. "You guess?"

"Well, we'll have to see," she said in mock seriousness. "Tonight is your audition."

"Now I'm nervous. And me without my lucky guitar pick." He repositioned himself on the bed, sitting up straighter like he was in the middle of an interview. "How am I doing so far?"

"Not bad, but I think we definitely need some snacks. I haven't eaten in hours." Zoe grabbed her stomach. "I'm pretty sure they were trying to starve a confession out of me."

"Snacks. Okay, I can totally support you in this endeavor." He hopped to his feet, ready to snack her.

"Great. I've got some food in the kitchen. Why don't you dish something up while I go wash the jail off me?"

"Are you sure you don't need support in the shower too? Because I can totally be there for you if you do."

Giggling, she waved him away. "I've got this. You get the snacks."

Levi grabbed her, nuzzling her neck. "But you look good enough to eat."

His stubble tickled her and she squirmed and slipped out of his arms. Yet, she wanted nothing more than to stay wrapped in them, to feel his facial hair tickle over the rest of her body. Suddenly, she was afraid that sleeping wouldn't be enough that night.

Ducking into the bathroom, Zoe shut the door, smiling to herself, something she didn't think she'd be doing after the day she'd had. Stripping out of her clothes, she jumped in the shower. When her hand twitched toward the massaging shower head, she turned the water temperature right down until she got a blast of cold.

Just sleep, she reminded herself. *Just sleep.* But even that had her breathless with excitement.

She felt like a whole new person. Or maybe just a *whole* person. By opening up herself, it was opening up all new possibilities. She'd shut herself off to men for so long, to the idea of finding someone new. But now, she almost felt giddy with hope. It made her want to shout or dance, to grab life by the balls.

She considered how she'd gotten to that point in such a short time. Levi had strolled in and turned her life upside down. Or maybe right side up. It's not like she didn't have plenty of men chase her over the years, so what was it about Levi that drew her out of her shell? More like punt-kicked her out of it.

But maybe that was it. Maybe she just needed the push. A push from the right person.

Once she felt the last of her day wash down the drain, and those immediate sexual urges subside for the time being, she climbed out of the shower. As she was brushing her damp hair, she heard a knock on her front door. Or rather, she heard Freddy bark and howl like a clan of ninjas had broken in, so she knew someone must be at the door.

Throwing on a robe, she slipped out of the bathroom. As she made her way to the entrance, she heard Levi open the door.

"Hello," he said.

"Is Zoe home?" The familiar male voice hit her body like a tsunami. She reached out for the wall to steady herself.

Fighting the desire to bolt, she put one foot in front of the other. She had nowhere else to go. This was her home, after all. So what the hell was he doing there?

"Yeah. I can go grab her," Levi said. "Who can I say is here?"

But Zoe already knew before the door came into view. "Sean?"

"Zoe." Her ex's eyes briefly ran over her robe before flicking to Levi in an unspoken question.

Levi shifted uncomfortably. "I'll just go finish up in the kitchen."

He disappeared around the corner to give them privacy. But Zoe could clearly hear the gentle clinking of dishes from the kitchen, so she knew he'd be able to hear them.

Finally, Sean spoke. "Zoe—"

"Sean, what are you doing here?"

He hesitated in the open doorway. "After I saw you the other day, I don't know . . ." He held his breath, like the words just wouldn't come. "I just had to see you."

She crossed her arms over herself, aware of how

underdressed she was. "Why? You haven't needed to see me for six years."

"It's not like I didn't try, at first." He took a tentative step inside her apartment, like the fact that she hadn't kicked him in the balls meant she was willing to talk things out. "I called, I e-mailed, I wrote, I popped by. You wouldn't talk to me."

"You left me standing at the altar."

Sean took another step forward. "But if we could have talked—"

"There was nothing to talk about," she said, much slower this time. *"You left me at the altar."*

"I had my reasons. If you just let me explain—"

"Unless it was that you were being held hostage by pirates, I don't want to hear it."

But he tried anyway. "I was young and stupid—"

"You got that right," she snapped.

"And I didn't understand what it was I wanted or what I had." Sean's hands rose as though he wanted to touch her, to hold her.

She flashed him a severe warning look, and they dropped to his sides.

"I took you for granted and I'm sorry. I freaked out." His forehead creased as his eyes filled with pleading. "I've always regretted that day. I've always wondered . . . Wondered what it would have been like if I'd turned up."

She wrapped her arms even tighter around her body, like she could hold in all the things he was trying to bring up again. The things she thought she'd pushed down inside a long time ago. "Why are you telling me all this now?"

"Because I thought that was all in the past, and then I saw you the other day, and it was like a sign. It all came rushing back to me." He shook his head, as though trying to sort out his thoughts. "Look. I know we can't start over, but God . . . I don't know, Zoe."

Zoe wasn't sure if this was all very funny or not, but she suddenly had the urge to burst out laughing. Or maybe crying. No, yelling would definitely have been better.

"What about Chelsea? You're marrying her."

Sean pulled a face. "I called it off. Please." He fell to his knees in front of her. "Just give us another shot. Just a date. Coffee even. Some place we can start over."

He inched closer, reaching for the hem of her robe, but Freddy seemed to sense that Zoe wasn't enjoying her visitor. He began to growl and snarl, hackles raised as he crouched between them.

Zoe's shocked gaze was so focused on the prostrate figure before her that she hadn't noticed the man in the hall until he spoke.

"Zoe? What is this?"

She blinked at the newcomer as though the accent didn't give him away immediately. "Taichi. What are you doing here?"

"Your mother said you were home. She told me that I should come to see you." He looked from Zoe to Sean and back again, trying to make sense of it.

Hell, so was she.

Sean pushed himself to his feet, blocking him from entering the apartment. "Well, you'll have to come back, pal. We're kind of in the middle of something."

It annoyed Zoe how he spoke for her. As if she were a child. As if he had any more right to be there at that moment than Taichi. In fact, Taichi had more right.

Taichi scowled at Sean, straightening up like he was actually taller than her ex, not five-foot-seven. "And who are you?"

"I'm, well . . ." Sean hesitated. "I'm hoping to be her

boyfriend." At this, he turned a hopeful gaze at Zoe before turning back to Taichi. "And who the hell are you?"

"I am her fiancé."

Oh God, he said it. She slapped her forehead.

"Fiancé?" A hushed voice asked behind her.

Zoe spun around. Levi stood there with a bowl of chips and dip in his hand. Her focus had been so consumed by the two men at her doorstep that she'd nearly forgotten he was even there.

But Levi's focus was entirely on her. "You're engaged?"

"Who's he?" Sean and Taichi asked.

The hurt in Levi's expression suddenly faded until it was hidden beneath a cool mask. "I'm nobody."

"Levi, I—"

Shaking his head, he put the bowls down and slipped on his shoes. Without a backward glance, he left.

Zoe couldn't move. She couldn't speak, not even to tell the two men arguing back and forth in her doorway to shut up and leave. All she could focus on was Levi's angry footsteps thumping down the hallway, hoping they would slow, hoping she would hear them change direction and come back this way.

Zoe pushed past Taichi and Sean, stumbling into the hallway. "Levi, wait!"

She headed after him, running down the hall, robe swishing around her thighs. A neighbor poked their head out of their door and shushed her. Then they took one look at her and gasped.

Her hair clung to her neck and face in wet tendrils. Her robe flapped open, giving them a glimpse of her naked body beneath. She hadn't even bothered to put on a pair of shoes.

Zoe scowled at them as she barreled past, ignoring the shocked look they gave her, like she'd absolutely lost her mind. And if she let Levi get into his van and drive away, she worried she may never find it again.

Her footsteps echoed in the stairwell as she chased him down to the exit, her bare feet slapping with each step. One hand on the rail and one hand keeping her robe shut, she flew after him.

She rounded the next landing and saw down to the doors. A glimpse of his backside gave her hope that she could catch up. The doors slammed shut before she could yell after him.

Stumbling down the last few steps, Zoe shoved the front door open and lurched onto the sidewalk. She hissed at the cold on her bare feet and the cool night air sweeping around her legs.

The last time she'd felt this desperate, this helpless, had been on her wedding day, when her entire future had blown up in her face. All the plans, the promises, the hopes, and dreams were tossed away by the individual she'd trusted most in the world. Like they were garbage. Like she was garbage.

But it wasn't the same at all. That day, all those feelings, the grief, the resentment, the humiliation, and rejection had burst out of her because the one person she needed most in the world had betrayed her. But now that she'd finally found someone she needed more, *he* felt betrayed by *her*.

She rounded the corner of the alley and spotted Levi climbing into his van. He slammed the door and started the engine.

"Levi, wait!" she screamed out. She ignored the pain and cold in her feet as she pushed herself harder, faster.

But then the engine revved, and the van took off. Suddenly she was just a crazy person wearing nothing but a robe in a dark alley, screaming a man's name. Zoe was alone.

25

All Bark and No Bite

Zoe set her box of vibrators down on the hardwood floor and took in her new office space with pride. She'd only moved in on Monday and already it was coming together nicely.

Aiden had really pulled through for her. She knew he had properties all over the city, but he'd really out-done himself. The office was spectacular, with a view of the bustling shopping area out front to match.

The building had retained the rustic charm of late 1800s Italianate, with the bonus of being on 24th Street with ample parking nearby and only a ten-minute walk from her new-slash-old house. She could run home and check on her mother whenever she needed to.

It had taken some major hoop jumping with the lender, but she'd been approved to be added to her mother's mort-gage. In addition to the lump sum of savings she'd already had for a down payment, she also had an impeccable credit score, thanks in part to her OCD tendencies.

They'd been to the lawyer, and the papers were signed. Zoe was officially a home owner.

The feeling was strangely foreign, and yet it felt natural to be moving back into her childhood home, even though she was regressing to a point before she'd moved away and found her independence. It had been a time and place where she was dependent on others, where she needed her parents. Only now it was her mother who needed her.

Zoe checked the time once again. It was nearly 10 A.M. She began rearranging her decor in the bay window for the tenth time that morning, fluffing up her bridal mannequin's wedding dress, angling the groom's top hat just so, anything to keep busy. To keep from imagining how her first appointment of the day was going to go.

After Levi stormed out on Sunday night, she returned to her apartment to find Taichi and Sean still bickering— well, mostly it was Sean.

She'd sent her ex away to cool off for a few days. She didn't know what to say to him at the time, anyway. Then she'd had a talk with Taichi, explaining that an arranged marriage just wasn't going to work for her.

Now that she'd had most of the week to calm down, she agreed to meet Sean in—she checked her watch again—fifty minutes. And although she'd been imagining their conversation all week, making lists of the things she wanted to tell him, she still wasn't sure what she would say.

To kill time, she perched on the edge of her antique desk, an office-warming present from Piper and Aiden— like they hadn't done enough already. Raising her phone above her, she snapped a selfie, making sure to get the big bay window in the shot. She sent it to the both of them, along with a text.

See you guys at the wedding rehearsal tomorrow night. XOXO.

The office couldn't have come at a better time. She didn't exactly feel comfortable using Levi's apartment when they weren't even on speaking terms, even though he'd been gone on his rock tour all week.

At the thought of him, she picked up her cell and called him. *Again.*

Ring, ring, ring.

She held her breath. After having called him so many times that week, the noise had become as aggravating as the Chicken Dance to her ears.

If she could just talk to him, explain that things weren't how they seemed. But it wasn't the kind of thing she wanted to leave on his voicemail either.

Three weeks before she didn't even know the man existed and now she couldn't seem to go five minutes without thinking about him. She missed talking to him, missed hearing his voice. She'd even downloaded his album and played it on repeat just to hear him sing.

Surprise, surprise, there was no answer. Zoe waited until the voicemail kicked in to hear his voice.

"This is Levi Dolson with Reluctant Redemption. Sorry I missed your call. Please leave your name and number, and I'll get back to—."

Zoe quickly hung up before it finished, as she always did. Or else he'd have gotten ten silent voicemails by now, like she was some creepy mouth-breathing stalker. Okay may be fifteen . . . or twenty.

Yup, nothing crazy about Zoe Plum. She was as cool as a cucumber.

There was a knock on the door. A thrill of excitement rang through her. Was it her first customer in her new office?

But when she swung the door wide with a welcoming smile, she nearly slammed it back shut.

"Zoe!" Juliet Fisher squealed. "It's so good to see you."

Zoe gaped at the woman beaming in her doorway. Expecting a setup, she took an automatic step back and tried to close the door. But the ex-bride wedged herself inside like she thought the wind had blown it shut. Her look of euphoria didn't change.

"I wish I could say the same, Juliet. And . . ." Zoe did a double take. "Owen? What are you doing here? Together."

She remembered the last time she'd seen Owen, which was just before her last office blew up. Her eyes automatically flitted toward the window—her nearest exit.

"Look." Zoe held her hands up. "I already told you that I won't be held responsible for the cost of your wedding. You can check our contract."

"No. No." Juliet's titter sounded so sweet that it hurt Zoe's teeth. "We're not here for that."

Zoe's heart was racing, Juliet's uber-sweet disposition freaking her out. "Then what is it? Because I'll call the cops if you try anything funny."

Juliet gave her a look like she thought Zoe was adorable and pushed past her until she was deeper inside the office. Zoe put up a fight, trying to block her path, but she didn't seem to notice.

"About the expo. I'm sorry," Juliet said. "I was hurt, and angry, and hadn't slept in days. I was losing my mind without my munchkin." She reached up and pinched Owen's cheek.

Owen grinned, and Zoe wondered if it had been the chocolates that had won Juliet over.

Zoe eyed the two of them like psych-ward escapees. "I see you two have worked things out. When did this happen?" She hoped she sounded casual enough as she dug for information to feed the police.

"Just the other day," Juliet said like she was gushing. "Monday, I think it was. Wasn't it, pookie?"

Monday. So Juliet would have still been pissed at Zoe for ruining her wedding on Sunday when Chef Glazier was killed. Which meant she wasn't out of the running for potential suspects. Zoe mentally tucked that note away for later. It wasn't like she could just bust that question out and hope Juliet would answer honestly.

"When you say that you're sorry about the expo," Zoe began, "are you talking about the van?"

"No, the van wasn't me. I swear." Juliet shook her head. "I mean that I'm sorry for yelling at you and making that announcement over the PA system."

"Right, well I think that's best for the police to determine." Zoe casually inched toward her desk where her feathered pen rested next to an inkwell. It was purely decorative, however the pen's metal tip was sharp enough to be an improvised weapon, if needed.

But Juliet didn't seem to notice. "I came here because I wanted to put all that behind us. To move on."

Zoe narrowed her eyes. "Move on to what?"

She slid her hand into Owen's, batting her eyelashes up at him. "To our wedding, of course."

Zoe gaped at the two of them. But it was Owen she addressed. He was the only one who was ever reasonable. Well, except when it came to his fiancée, she supposed. "Your wedding? You're going to try to get married again?"

It was Juliet who answered. "Of course. We're not going to let one bad day ruin what we have."

Zoe thought Juliet and her family had done a fine job doing that all on their own. "Well, congratulations. I'm thrilled you two worked things out." She went to the door and held it wide open, hoping they would take the hint.

"So you'll do it?" Juliet asked hopefully.

She glanced from bride to groom. "Do what?"

"Plan our wedding?" Juliet squealed happily again.

"Plan your . . . No. No way. I can't possibly." Zoe began backing up, wanting to leave her own office.

Juliet grabbed her arms, squeezing hard like she was desperate. Or maybe because she wanted to rip Zoe's arms off and beat her with them. "But you already know our tastes and our must haves. It would be a piece of cake."

"I'm actually booked solid."

"But it's not for another year. We'll offer you double."

Not even for a million dollars, Zoe thought. "Yup, sadly booked for the next two . . . make that three years."

Juliet's hands dropped in disappointment. "Oh, well that's too bad."

"If you want my advice," Zoe said. "Elope. So much cheaper." But as the couple trudged out of her office, Zoe thought of even better advice. "On second thought. I know of someone who might be able to help you."

She ran to her purse and dug her way to the bottom. Things had been so crazy that she hadn't had time to clean it out since . . . yup, there it was. Natalie Evans' scrunched-up business card from the expo. Straightening it out as best she could, she handed it to the Juliet.

"Natalie Evans?" Juliet read. "Isn't that your assistant?"

"Natalie works for Enchanted Events now. And she worked very closely with me on your wedding, so she understands all your needs." *As in, everything under the sun,* Zoe added in her head. She gave the couple a cheerful wave as they headed out her door. "Tell her I sent you."

"Thanks. I will!" Juliet called back.

"Good luck, you crazy kids." *Emphasis on the crazy.*

Rushing over to her bay window, she watched them walk down the street, mostly to make sure they left, but also staring in amazement. At both the fact that Juliet had actually believed Zoe would say yes to planning her wedding, and at the fact that there would *be* another wedding.

Once they were out of sight, she shut the door and locked it, just in case they came back. Grabbing her phone, she ran through her list of contacts and found the one for Detective Warner to let him know Juliet had popped by. She didn't know if it was important, but the more information to absolve her and figure out who was making Zoe's life hell, the better.

She was about to hit the *call* button when there was another knock on her door. She gasped and spun to face it.

For a moment, she considered pretending she wasn't there, but of course where else would she be? Juliet was crazy, not stupid. When the knock came again, she sidled closer.

"Who is it?" she called through the door.

"It's Sean," came the muffled response.

Now her heart was racing for a whole different reason. With a shaking hand, she flicked the deadbolt. Gripping the handle, she took a deep breath and opened the door.

Sean was grinning from ear to ear, clutching a bouquet of flowers like they were about to go on a first date. He handed them to her. "For your new office."

"Oh." She blinked down at them in surprise. "Thank you. You're early."

"Sorry," he said. "I was just anxious to see you. I'm

so glad you called. Can we go somewhere? Maybe grab a coffee? Some lunch?"

"Look, Sean. I wanted to talk to you about Sunday night. What you said—"

"Was all true. Every word of it." He grabbed her hands in his, squeezing them. "I was an idiot to ever let you go."

"You mean stand me up." She tugged her hands away. "You didn't let me go. You didn't respect me enough to be up front with me. You just ran away."

"I know. I owe you an explanation."

"No. Don't." She held up a hand. "I don't want to hear it. I don't really care. All I wanted to say is that you can't just show up at my apartment like that. You can't just come waltzing back into my life unannounced. I don't know you. You don't know me. Not anymore. I'm a different person."

Maybe he'd forgotten how blunt she could be, or maybe she'd grown less patient for subtlety over the last six years, but he winced at the no-nonsense tone in her voice. "I know. And I want to get to know that person."

Zoe tried to remind herself that she'd loved this man once, and that, despite the sheer insanity of it, he'd come because he clearly had feelings for her still.

Uncrossing her arms, she softened her tone. "But that person doesn't want to get to know you. I've moved on. I'm over it."

Walking over to her desk, she slid open the top drawer and grabbed the ring box she'd dug out of her closet that morning. She'd never been able to get rid of her old engagement ring—she supposed in the way she'd never let go of her wedding dress. Or that day.

She handed it back to Sean. "I've moved on with my life. You should too."

Sean didn't quite know what to say after that. Hell,

neither did she. Her revelation came as much of a surprise to her as it probably did to him. Maybe more so.

Zoe had been dreading this moment all week, and probably for much longer than that. It was as though she'd been afraid of the memory of him.

And yet, as he finally stood there in front of her after all these years, she found she was rather tired of wasting her time on him, on their past, on her memories and fears. After six years of letting that one day control her life, she didn't want to waste another minute on it.

She held the door open for him. "Thanks for stopping by. And for the flowers."

Sean took a deep breath and nodded. "Take care of yourself."

"Thanks. I will," she said, and meant it. And when she finally closed the door on that chapter, she knew the first place to start.

Picking a pair of scissors off her desk, she took care of that hideous old wedding dress, once and for all.

26

Face the Music

Zoe, Piper, and Addison strolled down Folsom Street like they owned the town. Heck, with all the properties Aiden owned in the city, once Piper became Mrs. Caldwell, maybe she would. And by the way the men lingering outside the SoMa bars eyed them, the girls were definitely owning their dresses.

After the rehearsal dinner, they'd raided Zoe's closet for the sexiest, slinkiest numbers while Addison worked her magic on hair and makeup. And, damn, were the results tempting—at least they seemed to be tempting the bouncer at the next bar. He was practically licking his pierced lips.

And why the hell not? Wasn't that what a bachelorette party was for? Saying sayonara to all the single men. Giving them one last look at what they'd missed out on? *Look out San Francisco,* Zoe thought.

Zoe glanced at Piper in her red cocktail dress and thought the men of San Francisco would be weeping that night. And Addison? Well, she was taken too. She was practically a step-mom now, but she loved any excuse to doll herself up.

But Zoe had nothing in her way. No memories of Sean, no fear of getting hurt, and definitely no Levi. By all the calls he didn't return that week, he'd made it clear that she was the last thing on his mind. And she was ready to prove that he was the last thing on hers.

She felt six years of repressed emotions and desires ready to burst out of her. There was no holding her back. Or maybe that was the shots they'd had at Felix's bar earlier talking.

Piper dragged her friends into the bar with the pierced bouncer. Zoe gave him a wink as she flashed her ID. He swung the door open and they stepped inside.

A wave of stale booze hit Zoe's nose like a sucker punch. She could feel the heavy bass pulsating through the floorboards, thumping inside her chest.

It wasn't exactly the kind of club she'd envisioned for Piper's bachelorette. Since it was the night before her big day, she'd suggested something quiet and subdued. Zoe had expected maybe a few rounds at a classy wine bar.

But this dive wasn't quiet nor subdued. In fact, among all the ripped jeans, leather, and chains, their sexy cocktail dresses stood out like the only single girl at a bouquet toss.

Zoe sidled closer to Piper. "Are you sure about this place?"

"Oh, I'm definitely sure," she said. "Besides this is the last place Holly Hart will think to look for us. And I'm getting really tired of dodging her."

"True." she relented. A guy smiled at them as they walked by. The black lights glowed off his teeth, which were all filed to points.

"But maybe that's also a bad thing," Addison said.

"Because no one will think to look for us here if we, you know, don't turn up."

"Oh, come on. It will be fun." Piper grabbed both their hands and dragged them deeper into the noisy, crowded bar.

Zoe eyed up a guy dripping with chains, a studded dog collar cinched around his neck. "Something tells me I'm not going to find my dream guy here."

Piper rolled her eyes at Zoe. "You've been saying you're going to find your dream guy all night, and I haven't seen you talk to a single guy yet."

"Yeah, what's stopping you?" Addison asked, skirting around the studded collar guy. "Could it be the fact that you're waiting for a certain musician to call?"

Instead of scoffing, Zoe barked a "Ha!" to be heard over the music that was growing louder the deeper into the heart of the bar they went. "What musician could you possibly be referring to?"

"Still haven't heard from him, huh?" Piper asked.

"Nope." Following Piper, Zoe squeezed through the people around the edge of the dance floor who were too cool to dance.

"Maybe he never saw the letter you wrote for him," Addison suggested.

Zoe regretted writing the damn letter now that he'd clearly read it and ignored it. What had started out as a list of things she'd wanted to say to Levi, a way to organize her thoughts, ended up as a three-page detailed letter explaining the night at her apartment and how she really felt about him.

Absence hadn't made her heart grow fonder, it just allowed her to listen to what was really in it, and that was deep feelings for Levi. She missed him. She wanted to be with him. And not just for a night.

She wanted him night after night after night. And the mornings too. She wanted to go on dates with him, to show him stupid childhood photos of her, to make dinner with him, and listen to him serenade her. It turned out that her heart wanted *more* of Levi.

He hadn't returned any of her calls all week, so the night before, she'd driven over to his apartment. Using the key he'd given her, she left the letter on his kitchen cupboard. Of course, after coming to her senses moments later, she'd wanted to take it back, but she'd slid the key under the door after locking up. There was no getting it back.

"Maybe it slipped under a sofa, and he never even saw it," Addison said. "Just like when Leo DiCaprio didn't get Claire Danes's letter in *Romeo and Juliet*." She jumped up and down excitedly, as though that must be it. A guy in a Nirvana shirt clearly misinterpreted and began jumping around her, trying to dance.

Zoe dragged her away, blocking the guy with her own body. "And all the calls he never returned?"

"Maybe he lost his phone," Piper said.

"Maybe he accidentally dropped it into a mosh pit and someone stomped on it," Addison said. "That must happen. Occupational hazard."

"Or maybe he just doesn't want to talk to me," Zoe yelled over the music. It was clear she'd already been rejected. Her friends just couldn't see it.

"But—"

"It's for the best. Trust me," she said with finality.

"Come on. Let's dance," Piper yelled, dragging her friends farther onto the dance floor until they were right beneath the stage among sweaty bodies pushing and jumping.

The next song began, slowly at first, then it built up in heat and rhythm, infecting Zoe's body. Her hips began to sway and her hands reached for the sky. As the intro peaked, out of the corner of her eye, she saw the lead singer lean into the mic to belt out the first verse.

The smooth, deep voice froze her gyrating body. Her head whipped toward the stage and she glanced up, but she already knew who she'd see: Levi.

Zoe suddenly felt exposed on the dance floor, static among a sea of waving hands and wriggling bodies. She wanted to hide. She wanted to run, but before she could move, his gaze that was scanning the crowd found her, as though he could sense her there.

His voice faltered and he hesitated before picking the tune up again, making it seem as though it was on purpose. He closed his eyes as he focused on the song.

Their connection broken, Zoe found she could move again. She pushed against jostling, sweaty bodies. They pressed back, surging forward to fill her space at the front.

As she scrambled to get away, she got an elbow to the ribs, a heel to her shin, a flailing arm to the face, but she forged on, not paying attention to the crowd or the music.

She'd pretended she didn't care that Levi never called. But she did care, and she couldn't deny it when it was right there in her face, all around her, girls screaming his name.

"Levi! Levi! Levi!"

Someone grabbed her arm from behind. "Zoe!" It was Piper. "Don't be upset. When I saw he was playing a gig here tonight, I thought that if we came, you could talk things out."

"Now you can tell him how you feel," Addison said.

Zoe was already backing away. "I'm sorry. I just need to get out of here."

She turned and finished weaving her way through the crowded bar, resisting the urge to start throwing punches to clear the way. After avoiding these feelings for six years, now that they'd returned, all she wanted to do was run away from them.

Finally, she broke through to the back of the dance floor where the bodies spread out. She picked up her pace, heels sticking to the beer lacquered floor.

With each step that brought her closer to the exit, she could breathe a little easier. Then the band hit the chorus, and the familiar words rang clearly through her head. Her breath caught in her chest.

> *"You drive me plum crazy.*
> *Now it's 20-20.*
> *You are the one for me.*
> *So why can't you see?*
> *Miss Plum Crazy.*
> *You drive me Plum Crazy."*

It was Levi's limerick he'd serenaded her with at the expo. But he'd improved it. He'd actually made it into a real song.

The sticky floor seemed to make it impossible to keep moving. Her feet were frozen to the spot. And as he sang on, his voice thickened with emotion, with importance, emphasis. His heavy words weighed down on her, holding her there.

And despite her desire to avoid him, to hide herself and her heart, there was a pleading tone in his voice that made her turn around. When she did, his tortured gaze was locked on hers above the crowd as he sang the song he'd written about her.

Suddenly, the crowd faded away until it was just the two of them. And Levi was singing only to her, telling her how she felt through his lyrics.

"Why do you hide behind your mask?
I still see you.
Take off yours and I'll take off mine,
To be near you.
So just let me in and we'll be all right.
I need you.
Miss Plum Crazy.
You drive me plum crazy."

Zoe found herself slowly drifting back toward him, eager to hear more of the song, until she was standing below him again. It was like those piercing blue eyes were undressing her, not in a sexual way, but as though he were removing her armor.

Since she'd met him, it felt like he could see her for who she was, the insecurities, the hiding, and yet he still cared for her. *Her.* Not the woman she let people see. He saw the woman underneath the mask.

The song drew to an end, but he still didn't remove his gaze from hers. "Thank you, everybody. We're Reluctant Redemption. Thanks for coming out. Have a good night!"

The bar erupted into cheers and whistles, but Levi didn't wait to take a bow or soak it all in. He leapt off the stage, landing in front of Zoe.

He grabbed her hand. "Come with me."

Hands patted his back, congratulating him on a good set. He tossed head nods and thank-yous but didn't slow as he led Zoe around the side of the stage and through a door that said *staff only.*

The door slammed closed behind them, muffling the raucous sounds, shutting out the rest of the world. Their quick footsteps clicked loudly in the silence backstage as they slipped past spare mic stands and stepped around old speakers stacked against the wall.

Zoe could finally hear herself think about what she was going to say to him, how she would explain her feelings, her fears, her uncertainty. Yet despite all of those things, her heart raced to have her hand clasped in his, to know that he hadn't stopped thinking about her the entire time he was gone. Instead he'd been writing a song about her, singing about her.

Neither of them spoke as he opened a door with their band name scribbled on a taped piece of paper. Not verbally, anyway. His eyes said everything she needed to know as he cast glances over his shoulder. The way they drank the sight of her in, scraped over every inch of her tight purple dress, she knew he couldn't wait to peel it off of her.

The moment they were inside the small dressing room, their lips came together. Her hands caressed the contours of the face she'd missed seeing. Stubble scraped her fingertips.

His arms locked around her, crushing her body against his. Pressing his tongue into her mouth, he moaned as she caressed it with her own, hungry to taste her again like he'd been starved all week.

Raising his foot, he kicked the door closed. It slammed shut like a gunshot going off for a race to have more of each other, touch more, taste more. They tugged at clothes and pulled at buttons.

Levi's hot hands slid down her back. Her cocktail dress was so tight, he might as well have been feeling her naked body.

Cupping her butt, he hoisted her up. Her legs automatically wrapped around him, locking behind his back.

He pressed her up against the door. The cool metal stung her back, making her realize how hot she was. Hot for Levi. Her skin blazed beneath his touch, his mouth like fire against hers, his breath like steam as he ran his kisses down her neck.

Levi carried her to a vanity on the other side of the room. Glass bottles crashing to the floor as he swept the clutter aside with one quick swipe, before sliding her onto the counter.

She gripped his hips and pulled him closer. He pressed himself between her parted legs, tugging her long hair aside as he ran his hot kisses down her neck to the top of her low-cut dress.

Greedy for more, he tugged down on the stretchy fabric until her perky breasts popped out the top. With the built-in support in the dress, she'd skipped the bra, so when her tight nipples popped out, he groaned in surprise. He brought his mouth against one, swirling and flicking with his tongue.

"I need you," she breathed. Her desperate, grasping hands reached for his belt and unhooked the leather, sliding it free.

Levi's hand clasped over hers, and he pulled away. His face screwed up, and he groaned as though it pained him to stop her. He tilted his head back and took a few labored breaths before answering.

"I want to, but—"

"I don't mean sex," she said. "I mean . . . okay, I want that too. But it's because I want *you*."

His eyes closed for a moment. Clearly everything that remained unsaid was suddenly coming back to him. "What about your fiancé?"

Zoe laughed, still a little breathless. "I'm not engaged. My mother, she wanted to arrange a marriage for me, and because I didn't want to upset her in the hospital, I agreed to a date. I don't know what she told him, but knowing her, she probably already had the venue booked. But I'm not marrying him," she assured him.

"And your ex?"

"Still an ex. I accidentally ran into him the other day, but I barely even talked to him. I don't know why he got it in his head to show up at my place." She widened her eyes, as though she could hypnotize him into believing her.

"It's just, I've been thinking about you all week. Obviously." He kind of laughed. "And then I saw you here, and I just thought, I hoped that you came because you were thinking the same things."

Zoe winced. "Actually, it was a set up. Piper brought me here." When his expression dropped and he began to back away, she held him there. "But I'm glad she did," she said softly. "So does that mean you didn't get my letter?"

Levi frowned. "What letter?"

"The one I left in your apartment."

"I haven't been back there. We got in from San Diego this evening and came straight here." He rubbed a hand over his face, considering everything she'd just said.

"Well, I could have explained it all over the phone if you'd answered my calls."

He shook his head. "The band has a no-cell-phone policy while on tour. It keeps our heads in the game. All emergency calls are screened through our manager."

She groaned. "That would have been good to know before you left. That's the dumbest thing I've ever heard of."

Levi ducked his head. "Yeah. I'm starting to think that has to change."

He stared at her, cringing with apprehension like he was imagining that moment in her apartment again. And maybe because it still hurt to think about it. "It just looked like—"

"Like I was a woman who didn't know what I wanted?" she finished for him.

"Exactly."

"Well, I know what I want now. I want you," she said. "I want you after I thought I'd never want anyone again. I just wanted to be alone so I could avoid the pain. But nothing could be as painful as not having you. I want you," she said again. "I *need* you."

And there it was, when less than two weeks before she'd told her mother she didn't need a man. But she needed one, and not just any man. She needed Levi.

The admission was like removing a fifty-pound wedding dress from her body. And it wasn't just the acceptance of it within herself. It was the act of expressing it. Tipping that bottle that she'd been filling for so long and letting it pour out.

He cupped her face gently and brought it close to his until they were nose to nose. "I'm all yours." As he brought his mouth to hers in a gentle kiss, the door opened.

They jumped, as though they'd forgotten where they were. Zoe quickly rearranged her top just as a red-headed girl in a blue polka dot vintage dress swept into the room. Zoe tugged her dress back into place and slid awkwardly off the vanity.

"Oops." The girl laughed. "Sorry to interrupt." She practically bounced across the room, a little ball of energy. "Levi, you were amazing."

She stood on her tip-toes, and he automatically bent down so she could kiss him on the cheek. She made a loud "Muah" sound as she slapped one on him, leaving a bright red stain on his skin. Then she turned her bright eyes on Zoe.

"Is this her?" she asked.

"This is her," Levi said as though it filled him with pride to say it.

The girl gasped. "You're the one in the song."

Before Zoe could react, she slapped a kiss on her cheek too. "It's so nice to meet you."

"Zoe, this is Candi," Levi said. "She's our manager."

Zoe gave a wave, still holding her breasts in place. "Nice to meet you."

"And as your manager, I'm ordering you to get back out on stage. They're calling your back for another." She threw him a stern look before twirling out of the room.

"I'll be right there!" He turned back to Zoe and gave her an apologetic look. "We've never refused on encore."

"It's okay. Go." She waved him away. "I'll be waiting right here."

Levi gave her one more lingering kiss before he headed back to the stage.

Once he was gone, Zoe checked the mirror behind her. She grabbed a tissue from her purse and wiped the lipstick off her cheek. When she pulled it away, she smiled at the shade of red. It was the same one he'd wore when he turned up at Juliet's wedding. Something told her she didn't have anything to worry about there.

She readjusted her dress and ran her fingers through her long hair. She was blotting her cheeks when the door opened behind her again.

She smiled to the reflection. "You'd better not keep your public waiting," she teased.

When there was no response, she shifted her focus to the door. It wasn't Levi. It was Chelsea Carruthers.

27

A Shaggy Dog Story

Zoe stared at the reflection in the mirror in disbelief, as though that must be someone else's pinched face scowling at her from the dressing-room doorway, not her rival. Maybe she'd had one too many shots earlier.

She closed her eyes to blink the image away, and when she opened them again, what she saw was a glimpse of metal raised above her head. A mic stand.

Zoe's body recognized the threat before her brain did. She dropped to the ground just as the mic stand came crashing down where she'd been standing. It caught the vanity, taking out the rest of the knickknacks sitting on it.

Cans of hairspray and brushes rained down on Zoe's head, and she threw her hands up. When she looked up, the stand was raised to come down on her.

Kicking out, Zoe caught a heel on Chelsea's knee. The kneecap shifted beneath the force, and the *crunch* ran up Zoe's leg. She shuddered. Chelsea screamed out.

Zoe tried to scramble away, but Chelsea recovered and

she drew her weapon back again. Zoe rolled to the side. The stand smashed down, sending the trash can across the room. It whistled as it sailed past her head.

Picking up one of the fallen hairspray cans, Zoe took aim and fired. The mist hit Chelsea in the face, and her eyes clamped shut. Coughing and sputtering, she tried to wipe away the sticky film.

Zoe clambered to her feet and lunged for the door, but a half-blinded Chelsea swung the stand. It went wide, taking out a lamp. Zoe leapt out of the way just in time.

"Somebody help!" Zoe screamed, but she knew no one would hear her over the band's encore.

Chelsea hopped on her good leg, wincing slightly each time. She took a swing, and another, and another, forcing Zoe away from the exit.

With nowhere else to go, she darted to one of the folding chairs and threw it at her rival. Chelsea stumbled, catching herself on her bad leg. Groaning in pain, she braced herself against the wall.

Taking the chance, Zoe dove for her. Her fingers wrapped around the metal stand, clamping on tight as she tried to wrench it away. But while Chelsea was in sneakers, Zoe's heels set her off balance.

The stand twisted to the side and Zoe tripped toward a tattered armchair. She landed awkwardly on the seat, but held on to the metal stand. As Chelsea gripped either end of the stand and pressed down, putting all her weight behind it, it became too much for Zoe's arms to handle. Inch by inch, it sank toward her throat.

Chelsea's teeth squeaked as she ground them together, face contorting with the desire to squeeze Zoe's neck until her head popped off.

The cool metal pressed against Zoe's windpipe. She swallowed and felt it rub.

With Chelsea's hands wrapped around the stand, her

side lay wide open. In a last-ditch effort, Zoe whipped a knee up. It connected with ribs in a *pop* and Chelsea grunted, wheezing.

The pressure on Zoe's neck relaxed. She twisted the rod with a sudden movement and it sent Chelsea flopping to the ground, holding her side, cringing in pain.

The chair tipped over, Zoe along with it. But now Zoe was on top and had the advantage.

Ripping the mic stand from Chelsea's grip, Zoe tossed it aside. Throwing her weight on top of her rival, she tried to restrain her. She wrapped her long legs around the ones trying to kick her, and her arms around the ones trying to claw and punch and grab any part of her, until all Chelsea could do was jerk and buck awkwardly beneath Zoe's body.

Chelsea gave a few more futile wiggles before she gave up and settled on yelling and swearing in frustration.

Zoe made sure to keep her face away from Chelsea's in case she decided to bite or head butt. Over the swearing and screamed threats, she heard laughing and chatting voices drawing closer through the door.

"Help! In here!" she yelled.

Footsteps quickened. The door burst open. Levi's eyes swept over the destruction before they landed on the heap of tangled limbs on the floor.

"Zoe."

"Help me," she grunted. "I can't hold her much longer."

Levi dropped to the ground, replacing her hands with his own. As she began to untangle her legs she saw Brody and Aaron grab Chelsea's ankles to prevent her from kicking out.

"I'll go grab the bouncers," Candi said before taking off, vintage heels clicking down the hall.

Jett stood out in the hall, plugging his one ear to hear his phone over Chelsea's screams. Zoe assumed he was calling the police.

Zoe rolled away and onto her back, gasping for air, feeling her pulse throb in her already-blossoming bruises. Her limbs shook and she couldn't find the strength to stand until a couple of hands reached down to help her up. She looked up to see Piper and Addison above her.

She let them help her to her feet and into a chair where she could catch her breath. It might have only been a two-minute fight, but she felt as though they'd been wrestling for hours. She supposed that's what happened when your body gave it everything it had in order to survive.

Chelsea was successfully pinned, but she continued to thrash on the floor like she wanted to finish what she'd come there for.

"What the hell happened?" Levi asked Zoe.

"After you left, Chelsea came in here with a microphone stand wanting to play a game of T-ball using my head."

Bodies shuffled out of the way. The bouncer with the lip piercings pushed his way in, kicking the toppled chair aside. Another bouncer followed him in and they took over for the band. As they stood Chelsea up to get her out, she jerked wildly in their grip and released a carnal scream.

"You bitch!" she yelled at Zoe. "You just couldn't let me be happy, could you? You have everything, your successful business, your rock-star boyfriend, your connections throughout the city. Why did you have to take what little I have?" Her hair escaped from its usual tight bun, falling over her face, making her look wild.

"What the hell are you talking about?" Zoe asked.

"Sean. My *fiancé*," she spat. "You just couldn't stand to let me have him, could you? You had to steal him from me. Natalie said you came by the office the other day, that you spoke with him. What did you say to him to make him leave? Huh?"

Zoe closed her eyes, trying to gather herself. "I went there to tell you to back off and stop trying to sabotage me. I had no idea he was going to be there. I don't even care if you marry him. You two deserve each other."

The rims around Chelsea's eyes had started to turn red, and when she spoke, her voice cracked with emotion. "Then why won't he marry me?"

Zoe sighed. She rubbed the bridge of her nose, feeling a headache form. She felt a hand land on her back and start to rub it comfortingly. It was Levi. She smiled up at him gratefully.

Chelsea's emotional outburst tugged at something inside of her, drawing forth memories of her own wedding day when Sean's sudden abandonment threw her off the deep end.

She hated to admit that she had anything in common with her rival, but she could certainly sympathize with her. Zoe was almost tempted to throw Chelsea a bone, to tell her it would get better again if she let it.

"I don't know why he's not marrying you," she finally said, a little calmer. "But considering Sean's track record, I'd say it's him and not us."

"Everything was fine until you started meddling in my life. You've ruined everything!" Chelsea burst into tears.

Zoe laughed, getting fed up with the conversation. Everything hurt, and she suddenly yearned for bed. "I haven't done anything to you. You've slandered my name all over town, you stole my assistant and my clients. And don't even start with your booth being wrecked, because I didn't do that."

"Of course you didn't," Chelsea said like Zoe was a complete idiot. "I did!"

"What?"

"I was supposed to get that interview with Holly Hart. I was supposed to be on the news. But instead, all anyone cares about is you. Everyone's just so *plum crazy* about Zoe, Zoe, Zoe." She rolled her eyes.

"And you thought you'd blame me for it, get me kicked out of the expo, and ruin my reputation."

"Two birds, one stone," Chelsea said, like anyone would have done the same thing in her position.

Zoe narrowed her eyes, thinking back to before that day, when all her troubles seemed to begin. If she'd been willing to do that, then what else was she capable of?

"Did you sabotage the Fisher-Wells wedding?" she asked.

"How could I? I wasn't even there. But Natalie, on the other hand, was in the perfect position. And she was so eager to get a job in my company that she was prepared to do just about anything."

Zoe got to her feet, suddenly finding the strength for round two. "Were you the one who broke into my van? Did you cut up Piper's dress?"

Levi stiffened next to her. "Did you cut her brake lines?" He blinked. Obviously everything was coming back to him at the same pace it was to her. His hands balled into fists at his side. "Were you the one responsible for the explosion in her office?"

Addison gasped. "Did you try to poison Piper?"

Piper crossed her arms, eyes narrowing with a promise of violence. And Zoe didn't blame her. If Chelsea had really been the one to cause all their grief in the last few weeks, then she was to blame for Piper's wedding nearly derailing time and time again. Zoe might have been her target, but Piper had also paid a price each time.

Chelsea's head whipped around the room to greet each accusation that was hurled at her, as everyone tried to put the puzzle together. But then her face suddenly transformed, from anger, hatred, and outrage, to hilarity.

While her face was smiling, Chelsea's eyes were dead, lifeless. Her body sagged against the bouncers. She'd lost her fight. Maybe because she had nothing left to fight for.

Zoe remembered that anger, that unquenchable anxiety and turmoil just bursting to get out, and the frustration of not knowing where to place it—strangely, not at the man who deserved it for so recklessly toying with someone's heart. But in Chelsea's case, she'd clearly found a target for that anger: Zoe.

The bouncers dragged Chelsea's listless body outside to wait for the cops. For now, her fight was gone, but it wasn't over. Zoe knew all too well that that kind of anger wouldn't just go away. It would linger and fester if Chelsea let it.

Chelsea was out of sight, but in the silence, Zoe could still hear the scraping of her shoes along the floor as she was dragged down the hallway. Then her sharp voice rang out, echoing backstage.

"Just wait, Zoe!" she screamed. "You'll get yours! And I'm not talking karma!"

28

Singing the Same Tune

Zoe peered out of Levi's apartment windows for the fifth time since they'd arrived there. She wasn't sure what she expected to see. Maybe Chelsea standing down on the street in the rain, just waiting for Zoe to go to sleep, to drop her guard.

She shivered, feeling overly exposed by the floor-to-ceiling view. Gripping Levi's bathrobe closed around her, she backed away.

There was a knock on the door and she jumped, but when she checked the peephole in the metal door, she sighed in relief. It was just Freddy, or more specifically, Levi holding Freddy up so all she could see was him.

She unlatched the door and slid it open. Poking her head out, she eyed Levi up and down. "Secret password?"

He chuckled "Sex in pan?"

"Mmmm, please." Smiling she stepped aside.

Freddy raced inside before Levi, still geared up from their walk. He ran a few laps of the apartment as Levi slipped off his shoes.

After Zoe's battle with Chelsea, everyone kind of dispersed for the night. Piper and Addison went home for their beauty sleep for the big day. But Zoe wasn't all that eager to return to her small apartment. Even though Chelsea had been arrested, Zoe was still worried the police wouldn't have enough to hold her for long.

Levi had driven Zoe home after the cops questioned them both outside the dive bar, but he'd refused to let her be alone that night. In the end, she didn't put up much of a fight and packed a few overnight things for her and Freddy.

It was more than just a safe place to rest her head that she was eager for. However, just in case her stress remained unrelieved, she'd brought Big Boy along in her purse.

"Thanks for taking Freddy out while I showered," she said. "I think the hot water helped my sore muscles." She rolled a shoulder, getting a sharp reminder of where Chelsea dug her elbow in.

"Come here." Levi drew her toward the leather couch.

Once she was sitting, he positioned himself behind her. She moaned as he began to massage and knead her aching back, wincing as he found each new knot.

"She really did a number on you, didn't she?" he asked.

"She was definitely going for the kill."

A noise in the kitchen startled her. A moment later, Freddy skittered out, a guilty tail curled under him.

Levi reached for the stereo remote and switched on the local radio station. Like he'd been shot with a tranquilizer, Freddy jumped up on the low armchair across from them, worming his way beneath Levi's leather jacket for a nap.

"You have nothing to worry about tonight now that Chelsea's behind bars," Levi said. "Besides, you seemed to be able to handle yourself pretty well."

Zoe gave a huff like a weak laugh, but even that hurt. "Because if I hadn't, I think I'd be in a coma right about now," she told him. "It took a lot out of me."

She could feel him lean in close, his body warming her back. "I'm sure I could rouse a little energy in you." The words tickled her ear and she could already feel that energy tingling.

"I thought you, you know, didn't want to do that," she said.

He took up his kneading again, but after a moment, he said, "You think it's weird that I turned you down for casual sex."

She shrugged, thinking it wasn't weird so much as a blow to her pride.

When she didn't answer, he said, "I'm just not a no-strings kind of guy. I think sex is more important than that. What two people have should mean something, and sex is an expression of that."

Hand it to a songwriter to be good with expressing himself verbally. She closed her eyes as his hands loosened the tension in her neck.

"Don't get me wrong, though," he added quickly. "I think it's super sexy that you're comfortable with your sexuality."

Her eyes fluttered open. Stiffening, she looked over her shoulder. "What do you mean?"

"Well, look at you." He waved his hands over her like that was enough explanation right there. "You practically exude sex. Every man's jaw drops when you walk by, and you know it. And then of course there's your sex-toy business."

"Hold on a second." Zoe gaped. "Oh, my God. You think I'm a slut!"

He held up his hands in surrender before a fight even

began. "I didn't say slut. I definitely didn't say that. I'd say . . . enlightened."

"You do. You think I'm easy." Her voice was rising, but she was smiling at the incredulity of it all. The irony.

He laughed. "Nothing about you is *easy*."

"I don't know what to say. I'm not sure whether to be offended or not." She slid away from him on the couch to face him, not sure how to begin explaining that the truth was the complete opposite. "I'm anything but."

"I'm not trying to insult you. I'm just trying to explain my own personal views on sex and that they might be different to yours," he said hastily, reaching out across the distance between them. "But you're a sexpert, are you not? One would assume you'd have to have sex to claim that title."

His expression was so apologetic as he tried to clarify, but she certainly didn't blame him. That was what most people assumed. Hell, her friends probably suspected the same thing. And maybe part of her wanted people to believe that. To believe that she was some kind of sex goddess, confident and comfortable with her sexuality. Which she was, but she just hadn't been comfortable using it with just anyone.

"Oh, I'm a sexpert, all right," she told him. "I know tricks that would make your toes curl . . ." she leaned in, suckling on his lower lip before giving it a nip, "in theory."

He was reaching inside her robe, but his hand froze. "In theory?"

She cleared her throat, suddenly finding it difficult to breathe. Was it hot in there, or was it just her? "Practice is an entirely different matter."

"What do you mean?" he pressed.

"I'm all talk," she said simply. Unable to meet his

probing gaze, she stood up to move around the living room. The words threatened to choke her, but she swallowed and blurted them out. "I haven't had sex in six years. And even before then, well, I was with Sean, the same guy, for four years."

"Hold on. Hold on." Levi jumped to his feet, coming close like he must have heard wrong. "You haven't had sex in six years? B-But you're a sexpert," he stammered. "You have a certificate and everything."

He ran a hand through his hair, staring at her with wide eyes as though for the first time, seeing the girl who was too heartbroken to open herself up to anyone, to connect with people emotionally or physically.

Suddenly, she was someone who maybe bordered on the sexually innocent, not the "enlightened" woman she pretended to be. It made her more uncomfortable than when people assumed she was promiscuous.

"I-I just assumed," he said. "I'm sorry. I know I shouldn't have but—"

She waved away his visible guilt. "I'll let it go, since I'd assumed the same thing about you."

He continued to stare at her in disbelief. "But why has it been so long?"

She fidgeted beneath his shocked gaze and moved away again to the other side of the sitting area. "Because for a long time, I told myself that I didn't need a man. And maybe because I think sex is special too. I wasn't just going to give it away to someone I didn't need in my life."

"But that night in my apartment, you wanted to give it away to me." He moved to be near her.

"I suppose it's because I need you in my life." She reached out a tentative hand and laid it on his chest. "It was like my body knew before I even wanted to admit it to myself."

He took her hand and kissed each finger distractedly while he thought it over. Or maybe it was because her honest statement had hit something deep inside of him, because he closed his eyes and inhaled, as though breathing in her words.

"Six years," he finally said. "Well, I certainly don't want to deny you any longer." Even in the dim apartment, Zoe could see his eyes darken, his pupils drink her in.

She leaned into him, running a hand over his jeans. "Good. Because I don't think there's enough batteries in this apartment to take care of me if you don't screw me tonight."

She pressed her lips against his, sucking on them with the same hunger she felt at the dive bar. Her hands ran over him, finally free to explore, like she'd been given a green light. When they reached his fly, she stroked her finger up and down the front of his pants. His response was clear enough by the growing bulge, but when she reached down for his belt, he inhaled sharply.

Grabbing her hands, he gently held them away. "I'm not going to screw you tonight."

She groaned and flopped back on the couch. Muscles clenched between her legs, and desire ached low in her belly. After the physical yearning had been building for six years, the disappointment was suddenly too much. Her eyes began to prickle with frustrated tears.

"I can't handle it," she said. "You can't tease me like this."

Levi chuckled, the sound deep and rumbling. She could hear the desire behind it. *So then why . . . ?*

Reaching down, he pulled Zoe to her feet. Taking her by the hand he led her toward the spiral staircase to his loft bed.

If he wasn't going to screw her, how could he just expect her to sleep now?

At the base of the stars, she yanked her hand out of his grasp and backed away, shaking her head. When she heard the soft *ting* of the drum set behind her, she stopped. Staring up at him in disbelief, she felt ready to scream.

Levi patiently took her face in his hands and ran a thumb over her cheek, calloused from so many years of guitar playing. The touch was so soft and gentle compared to her desperate, greedy groping that she felt ashamed, embarrassed.

Forget that sexpert certificate on her wall. She felt like a fraud. Hell, after six years, maybe she'd forgotten how. Isn't that the saying? Those who can't do, teach.

"Why are you torturing me?" she asked.

"I'm not trying to torture you. But I'm not going to screw you," he said firmly. "I'm going to make love to you."

Dipping his face to hers, he kissed her slow and tender, his lips as gentle as silk running over hers. His fingers caressed her face then moved to her neck, following the collar of his bathrobe down her chest. Sweeping the collar aside, he exposed her to slide his warm palm over her.

Her skin seemed to tighten beneath his touch as his fingers trailed between her breasts. When he reached the tie around her slim waist, he unfastened it before pushing it back. It slid off her shoulders and landed in a heap at her feet.

Levi pulled back, soaking up every swell, every curve of her long, lean body. He bit his lower lip, his breathing changing rhythm at the sight of her.

After six years of loving her own body, Zoe had long since let go of any self-consciousness. She let him gaze at her, watching his appreciative expression, his eyes growing heavy with desire until he couldn't resist any more and reached out to touch her.

Hands explored her perky breasts, lingering around her nipples until they hardened and her breathing quickened. Those hands slid down her flat stomach and around the contours of her back. Those hands that knew what buttons to press, what strings to strum, what keys to stroke. And stroke her he did.

His mouth followed where his hands had touched, his stubble tickling her body, raising goose bumps. As he lowered himself to his knees in front of her, desire had Levi moaning with that sweet voice that made her melt each time he sang, that made her knees weak. He crooned his soft groans against her stomach and down her thighs, strumming those deft fingers between her legs like she was a guitar.

Her knees began to shake, threatening to give out beneath her. She reached out to hold herself up, her fingers landing on piano keys.

Their tinkling filled the room, matching the high pitch of her tense body as her toes curled. Her hand came down again to make a different sound, as though trying to find their harmony.

Levi suddenly pulled away. Her breath hitched. But then he took her hand and dragged her to the music room carpet only to begin the real performance. He'd only been warming her up before, tuning her. Now, his mouth and fingers moved in unison, playing her like an instrument until her moans and sighs crescendoed to her climax.

And in that moment, she felt like she might explode. Wave after wave of pleasure washed over her, and instead of bursting inside, she felt that bottle of emotions, which had been filling for so long, empty completely.

It left her body relaxed and yet strangely full even as those bottled emotions began to leak in the form of tears. She blinked them away. They weren't unhappy tears, but blissful, relieved. Tears of joy.

No vibrator could do that. Only Levi could leave her feeling so full, and yet so empty and free at the same time.

As he kissed his way back up her shaking body, he saw the tears running down her smiling face. He kissed them before kissing her lips. She could taste the salt mixed with the taste of her on his lips.

Pushing him onto his back, she straddled him.

"My turn."

With the same level of reverence, she removed each piece of his clothing, revealing a rock-hard rock star beneath. She ran her hands over him exploring it all, the tight abs, the toned chest, those little dips above his waistband, taunting her like arrows pointing to what she really wanted.

This time, when she reached for his belt, he didn't stop her. Instead, he laced his fingers behind his head and relaxed beneath her touch, her kisses.

As she unzipped his pants and tugged them down, she gasped.

"You weren't kidding." She grinned happily. "The Big Boy's got nothing on you."

He chuckled as she eagerly dragged his pants off the rest of the way. She tossed them aside, and they swished against the cymbal on the drum set.

She knelt between his legs. Her foot thumped against the kick drum like a drumroll building anticipation.

Grasping his instrument lying stiff and hard against his stomach, she decided to play with it a while, teasing, massaging until he squirmed and moaned. When he couldn't take it anymore, he ran his hands through her hair and pushed her head down gently while raising his hips. Deciding he'd had enough, she put her mouth on him.

His beautiful voice sang out with every stroke, every flick of her tongue as though she were tuning him now. She may not have had much practice, but it was clear that all those years of honing her sexpertise hadn't gone to waste, because it wasn't long before he was pushing her away.

"Not yet," he said. "Not like that."

Reaching for his pants, he pulled out his wallet. Like he'd read the guy handbook, he had his emergency condom tucked into one of the credit card slots.

She took it from him, ripping it apart. With steady fingers, she rolled it on like the expert she was before she crawled on top of him. Levi grabbed her hips, guiding her down.

Zoe closed her eyes, feeling each sensation as though for the first time—all the things her body had forgotten, and that her heart had forgotten, everything she'd denied herself for so long and had refused to let in.

She couldn't deny herself any longer. Not just the sex, but most important, the love. She wanted all of it. All of Levi. Even if it meant opening herself up to pain, to hurt, to rejection.

Levi's touch spoke of tenderness, his kisses were filled with understanding, acceptance, his eyes with love. With every roll of her hips and squeeze of her thighs against him, she tried to return those feelings, to harmonize with him in a soulful duet, until it burst out, a chorus inside of her.

Her body thrust against his like a striker against a bass drum, deep and rhythmic. With his thumb, he began to strum her again until her moans became breathless.

Together, they increased in tempo, banging and strumming faster and faster, their bodies making beautiful music together. And as their song climaxed and they sang out together, Zoe knew she'd finally found her jam.

And they were going to be a hit.

29

Tail Wagging the Dog

Zoe rolled over in bed, hand automatically groping for the soft feel of her Fuzzy Friends. When her hands fell on empty sheets, she opened her eyes in surprise. The night before came rushing back to her.

For so long she'd gone to bed imagining she was with a man while she sufficed with her toys, so at first she thought she was imagining things. But she couldn't imagine the feeling between her legs, the tingling in her body, as she remembered her jam session with Levi in the music room the night before. Her body was still singing.

She heard Levi's front door slide open and a jingle that told her Freddy was downstairs. Crawling out of bed, Zoe picked up Levi's crumpled shirt from the floor and slipped it on. As she wound down the spiral metal stairs, she inhaled eagerly. Coffee.

Levi was in the kitchen setting down a takeout bag and a tray with two steaming coffee cups. Freddy spotted her and skittered across the cement floor, racing around her legs.

Levi grabbed the remote off the counter and a second later the speakers came alive with Aerosmith. Freddy trotted over to his favorite armchair—mostly because it was low enough that he could jump up on it. Grabbing the throw blanket on the back, he tugged it down onto the seat and crawled under it.

"You're up early," Zoe said to Levi as she slipped onto a stool at the island.

"I thought Freddy and I would go out for some break-fast and leave you to sleep in for a bit." He gave her a lingering kiss, and a look that told her he'd read her letter that morning. "Big day, remember? I figured you needed your rest after last night."

She felt a warmth spread all the way to her toes. "It did take a lot out of me."

"I was talking about the attack." But by the cheesy grin, she knew he was kidding.

"So was I," she said.

He slid his arms around her from behind, dipping his head to the crook of her neck. "Was it worth the wait?"

"The attack?"

He chuckled, his breath warm against her skin. "The sex."

She leaned back into his embrace. Tilting her head up, she pressed her mouth against his. "Every second. But now I'm not sure I can wait to do it again."

He smirked. "Why wait? There's plenty of time to screw this morning."

"Screw? But I thought we didn't screw," she teased. "We make love."

"We? I like the sound of that. *We*," he tested the word again and nodded. "There'll be times we make love, and there'll be times when we screw. And ever since I saw you lying naked in my bed this morning, I wanted to crawl in behind you and bang you like a drum."

Zoe groaned. "That's like music to my ears." She sighed. "But I've got a busy day ahead of me. I should get to the venue to start setting up. I'm both wedding planner and bridesmaid today. Not to mention, I have to be on the lookout for sabotage."

"You have nothing to worry about. Chelsea's behind bars. And with everything she's done over the last couple of weeks, I'm sure she'll be staying there."

Zoe took a sip of comforting coffee and frowned. "I'm not so sure I'm out of the woods yet."

"Are you kidding? Vandalism, attempted murder— two times? Three if you count Piper's balls."

Zoe laughed at the wording. "But we're not sure all that stuff was even Chelsea."

"She wasn't exactly denying it either. Besides, how many enemies could you possibly have?"

She snorted. "You'd be surprised."

"Well, they'll have to get through killer over there first."

Zoe glanced at the lump under the blanket. It shifted for a moment as though Freddy sensed them talking about for him. His head snaked out just enough for his snout to show.

"And they'd have to get through me," Levi said. "I mean, if you really feel uneasy, maybe you should stay here for a little while longer. You know, just to be safe." He gave her a playful look, but she could see the hopefulness in it.

Before she could answer, the song on the radio faded, replaced by the announcer's voice.

"That was "Dream On" by Aerosmith, and you're listening to San Fran's best mix of today and yesterday. Popping into the station today we have Channel Five's very own Holly Hart. Holly, what's on the agenda today?"

Zoe's coffee churned in her stomach. She picked up the remote and turned up the volume.

"Well, if you've been following me on my blog and social media, you'll know that today is the biggest wedding of the year, Stan," Holly said. *"And I'll be working tirelessly throughout the day, giving you hour by hour updates on the latest gossip and news about the Summers-Caldwell wedding."*

"Tell us, Holly, are you on that exclusive guest list?" Stan's voice was flat with fake interest.

Holly sighed. *"Unfortunately, no. But I've got all the insider info on this doggy dream come true. My source tells me that that they'll use their dogs as the ring bearers. Wouldn't that be sweet, Stan?*

"Adorable."

"I'm sure there will be some surprises throughout the day, so I encourage everyone to follow along!"

"Well, thanks for keeping us informed about the important matters in the world, Holly. Up next, we've got No Doubt. Stay tuned."

Zoe turned the volume down. "Something tells me that Chelsea is going to be the least of my worries today." She chugged her coffee to boost her fortitude. "I should get going. I'm already running behind schedule."

"Zoe Plum running late? Who are you and what did you do with the OCD girl I first met?" He leaned in for another kiss.

"You must be rubbing off on me."

Levi made a throaty sound. "Maybe later I'll rub off on you a little more."

She gave him a wink. "Sounds like a date."

"A date? Now I'm really starting to worry." He chuckled, glancing at the time on his phone. "I'd better get going myself. I have to meet up with the guys to plan for tonight."

Zoe raised her wrist to glance at her watch, already in planner mode, but then she remembered she was wearing next to nothing, far less a watch.

"Take your time and get yourself dolled up here," he said. There was a metallic clink as he set a key on the counter in front of her. The key to his apartment she realized. "You can lock up when you leave."

"All right. Thanks," she said. "I'll slip it under the door when I'm done."

"Or you can hold onto it. You know, for emergencies."

She gave him a look, and he threw his hands up.

"No pressure. Not pushing. Totally relaxed." He gave her a quick kiss before he grabbed his coffee and a breakfast sandwich from the takeout bag and headed for the door. "And don't forget to eat." He pointed to the bag.

"Sure thing. Thanks for breakfast."

Once he was gone, she turned up the tunes for Freddy and started getting ready. Instead of her bridesmaid's dress, she slipped on some comfortable clothes. She could change at the venue with the other girls once they arrived, but first she wanted to get there early to start setting up.

Throwing her bag over a shoulder and grabbing Freddy—who seemed unwilling to leave his warm blanket burrow—she slipped out of the apartment and locked up. But as she bent down to slide the key under the door, she hesitated.

She stared at the silver thing in her hand for a second. It felt much heavier than it had before. It was more than a key to a temporary office space.

After a moment, she slipped it in her purse and headed to her van.

Zoe headed for Pacific Heights, anxious to get started. Although she'd set up most of the decor the day before, there were always little things to address. An askew tablecloth, a row of chairs that was out of alignment. And of course, she needed to be there before the florist delivery so she could direct the placement of the flowers. This day had to be perfect. It was going to be perfect. Even if it killed her.

30

I'll Get You and Your Little Dog, Too

Zoe headed through town to Broadway Street for the Beaux Arts mansion. Not only was it going to comfortably fit the two-hundred plus guests invited to the wedding, but it was going to kick off Aiden and Piper's married life in style and luxury. She'd dragged Piper to nearly twenty potential venues to get just the right one. Because they deserved nothing but the best. Absolute perfection.

When Zoe tried to pull onto Broadway, she couldn't get anywhere near the place. The street was blocked off by police cars with their lights flashing.

She whipped into a free spot along the street and got out of her van. The day was heating up already so she grabbed Freddy and approached the police line with him in her arms.

Thinking of how Addison would tackle the situation, she tried to empty her mind of any negative thoughts. As though pure positive thinking could prevent any hiccups that day. But her heart was already picking up speed.

Like any crime scene, it had gathered quite a crowd. Zoe joined the rest of the curious onlookers in front of the yellow tape fluttering in the morning breeze, and leaned over it to see down the street. Her fingers were crossed as she thought *Please don't be the venue. Please don't be the venue.*

But, of course, it was.

First, she saw the two fire trucks parked outside. *It's okay,* she told herself. *Maybe it's just a false alarm.* Then she saw the hoses stretched up the grand stairs, snaking around the thick columns and through the double doors. *Maybe it was contained to just one area,* she reasoned. *A small kitchen fire, I'm sure.*

No one was yelling or rushing into the imposing building, so it was clear the danger was over. Well, everyone just needed to wrap it up and leave so she could fix whatever damage they might have done to her perfect decor. *And God help them if anyone has so much as sat on one of my pristine white silk-covered chairs.*

Then her eyes ran up the stone edifice, and that's when she saw black marks of soot marring the facade above the upper windows and along the ornate cornices. Windows were blown out, blackened curtains drooping out of them, dripping with water.

Cosmetic damage. That's all. Nothing a well-placed topiary can't fix. Zoe swallowed hard, but her throat had gone dry from her sudden panicked breathing.

"Excuse me, ma'am."

Zoe tore her eyes away from the scene and found a police officer coming toward her. "You need to stay behind the tape please."

Zoe glanced down to find that she wasn't just leaning anymore. She'd taken a full ten steps into the middle of the street, dragging the police line with her. *Well, technically I'm still behind it,* she thought.

"Oh, sorry," she said, backing up a few inches. "What happened here?"

"We're not releasing any information to the public yet," he said on autopilot.

"But I'm not just the public," she said, like clearly he didn't understand who she was. Didn't he know she was planning the most important wedding of the year? She should really get a badge for this sort of situation. "I'm with the wedding party."

The police officer looked at her in confusion. Zoe didn't have time for this. Hadn't he been following Holly Hart's announcements all over the internet as the morning went by? Zoe certainly was, but mostly so she could stay a step ahead of her.

"There's a wedding taking place in that building today," she explained patiently. But she felt the panic return when an incredulous look crossed his face.

The officer snorted, but more in an apologetic way. "No one will be getting married in that building today or anytime soon."

She wanted to grip him by the uniform and shake him. What the hell was she supposed to do now? The venue doubled as the ceremony and reception location, not to mention there were romantic photo ops galore. And what about her newly replaced décor? She had practically nothing left now.

Zoe had worked so hard over the last year to give Piper and Aiden the perfect wedding. She'd taken on so much of it herself, so much of the stress, the details, right down to the hand-folded origami flowers carefully placed in each invitation.

God, Piper and Aiden were going to be so crushed. And all those people coming from all over the state. Piper's mother and brother had already come all the way from Washington. In Aiden's case, people were flying from all over the world. And for it to be canceled all because of a tiny little fire?

Freddy seemed to sense her anxiety rising. He frantically licked her neck like he was helping. Zoe stared at the damage, at the chaotic collection of emergency vehicles. "But . . . But what am I supposed to do? The wedding is today."

The police officer shrugged. "I guess you'll have to switch to a different venue."

"But that's impossible." She laughed. "This is the best wedding venue in the city. Do you know what kind of strings I had to pull to book this place? It *has* to be this venue."

"Why?" he asked. "Either they get married somewhere else or not at all. If they choose the latter, then I guess I'd be questioning their priorities."

Her mouth fell open as his words sank in. She blinked, mentally shaking herself and took a step back. "Oh, my God. You're right."

She laughed as she realized that she sounded exactly like Juliet. She'd been so focused on making everything perfect that she was getting all wrapped up in the details rather than looking at the bigger picture.

The most important thing about this day was Piper getting married to the man of her dreams. Not where they did it, or how, or what dress she was wearing. It was about them. It was about love.

"Thank you." Zoe told the officer. She hugged Freddy to her chest. "Come on, Freddy. We've got a wedding to save." And with less than four hours before go-time.

She spun to head back to the van, nearly running over someone. She started to apologize before she saw the camera in her face.

"Zoe Plum," Holly said. "You're the wedding planner in charge of this year's most anticipated wedding. The

Summers-Caldwell wedding. Now that the venue for today's momentous celebration has gone and blown up—"

"It blew up?" Zoe froze mid-swat at Hey You. "Are you sure?"

Holly rolled her eyes, like *Who do you think you're talking to.* "I have my sources."

Zoe stared back at the destruction with new eyes. The glass, the chunks of stone, the bits and pieces of opulent furniture all scattered across the road with little numbers marking them. Of course. It looked just like the scene after her office blew up.

But that didn't mean . . . Could it?

Destruction seemed to follow Zoe wherever she went lately. Chelsea's threat was still echoing inside her head since the night before.

Just wait, Zoe! You'll get yours! And I'm not talking karma!

But Chelsea was supposed to be in jail. Or had she been released?

Was it possible the answer lay in the puzzle pieces they didn't have yet? Like the other attempts on her life, could this explosion have been meant for Zoe too? Had she somehow put the people closest to her in harm's way?

"So tell us," Holly said. "What will the lovebirds do now?"

Zoe shoved the mic out of her face. "No comment." Holding Freddy to her chest, she marched back to her van, but Holly gripped her by the arm.

"Don't tell us that the happy occasion is canceled." She smiled delightfully into the camera lens like she was from an entertainment show, not Channel Five News.

Some of the people lingering around the crime scene started to gather around, attracted by the camera and Holly.

"Okay, I won't," Zoe told Holly. "Because it's none of your business."

Holly covered the microphone and lowered her voice so she wasn't overheard by her adoring fans. "Come on. You've gotta give me something here. I've been building this thing up for weeks. It's going to be an embarrassment if I don't pull through on some kind of drama."

"Well, maybe you should have been minding your own business all along," Zoe said.

"The things happening in this city *are* my business. It's my job to keep the good people of San Francisco informed." She raised her voice so the surrounding crowd could hear.

A few cheered at the false passion in her voice. Clearly they'd been following her minute-by-minutes notifications too.

"I'm a vessel," Holly said humbly. "A medium. San Franciscans want to know the latest gossip on their favorite couple. I'm just giving them what they want."

"Gossip?" Zoe narrowed her eyes. "And here I thought you were a hard-hitting reporter. I guess you'll always be a lowbrow gossip columnist. Maybe you should go back to that tabloid, *The Gate*?"

Holly's face hardened and she shook the mic in Zoe's face threateningly. "Tell me what I want to know, or I'll start a smear campaign against you that will keep you from any event this side of Nevada!"

"Bring it on," Zoe said. "But you're still not getting anywhere near this one."

Holly's eyes lit up. "So it's not canceled then."

"There *will* be a wedding, if it's the last thing I plan. But you're not going to have a clue where it is." With a triumphant grin, Zoe wrenched out of the reporter's grasp and walked away.

"Mark my words, Plum!" Holly yelled after her. "It *will* be the last thing you plan!"

If there really was someone out there wanting Zoe out of the picture, the last thing she needed was Holly Hart discovering the new location of the wedding. If she did, it would be posted all over the internet within seconds. And if anything was certain, it was that whoever was behind the attacks would be following Holly's announcements. For both her sake and everyone else's, Holly Hart needed to be kept in the dark.

Zoe stomped back to her van, feeling the muscles in her back start to knot up where Chelsea had bruised her the night before. She craved the touch of her Fuzzy Friend in her purse, but her hands were currently full of a much larger and fuzzier friend.

"Can you believe her?" she asked Freddy.

In answer, he leaned up and gave her another lick on the neck.

Zoe laughed and tried to pull away from the incessant tongue bath. "You're a special dog, Freddy. Always good talking to you."

While she was being sarcastic, it was true. It may not have been like talking to Levi, but there was something so comforting about having a friend always there, always happy to see her, to listen, to hug. And as she held him close, she found that by the time she got back into her van, her anger at the reporter had evaporated and her muscle knots had melted away.

The moment she crawled behind the wheel, she tossed her purse aside and stared out the windshield at the emergency vehicles. What was she supposed to do now? How would she break the news to the happy couple?

She glanced over at her passenger who fidgeted in the seat. Even when she turned on the radio, it didn't settle him much. With everything that had been going on in the last few days, she hadn't been able to give him much exercise.

She gave him a scratch behind the ear. "I'm sorry, buddy. Not much time to play today either, I'm afraid. You need somewhere to run around, don't you?"

He whined, like he understood her. And after two weeks, it felt like they really were starting to understand each other. Maybe seeing eye to eye wouldn't be so impossible, after all.

"I know, you need to play, don't you?"

She thought about all those guests and how they'd been encouraged to bring their dogs. Not only did she have to find a new venue for the wedding in—she checked the time again—three hours and fifty-two minutes, but it also had to be pet friendly. That's if there should be a wedding at all. And if there was, maybe it was safest for everyone involved if Zoe was nowhere near it.

She glanced out the windshield again. It was forecasted to be a beautiful day. They could make it an outside wedding. Maybe at the Presidio where Piper and Aiden had their first pseudo-date, but then they would need somewhere with the facilities to serve dinner and for the wedding party to get ready ahead of time. Since it was last minute on a Saturday, getting ahold of the venue director would be difficult.

As Freddy whined again from the passenger seat, it suddenly hit Zoe. There was a place that ticked off everything on that list and was still meaningful to the bride and groom.

Digging her cell phone out of her purse, Zoe called Piper. It rang three times before she picked up.

"Hello?"

"Good morning, blushing bride," Zoe said.

"Hello, maid of honor!"

Zoe heard the excitement in her best friend's voice and

cringed as she said the next words. "Listen, Piper. There's no time to sugarcoat things. I've got some bad news for you. The venue is a no-go."

There was a moment of silence on the other end. "What?"

"It blew up."

"Blew up?" Another long pause, followed by a noise like Piper was blowing out a long breath, sifting through all the questions to the most pertinent one. "Can we find somewhere else?"

Zoe smiled. "I thought you might say that. It's doable, but Piper . . . I'm worried about everyone's safety. This explosion, after everything that's happened—"

"Zoe, Chelsea is in jail right now," she said, knowing exactly where Zoe was going.

"We don't know that for sure, and this explosion can't be a coincidence. I was supposed to be in that building early this morning. I was running late. What if that bomb was meant for me?" Zoe laid her forehead against her steering wheel, as the thought hit her belatedly. Her head spun. "What if they try again and people get hurt? People we love?"

"Then they'll have to deal with me," Piper said.

"I'm serious. Maybe I shouldn't be at your wedding. Not if it means putting everyone in danger."

"I will not have a wedding where my best friend isn't there," she said, her voice firm on the other line. "We'll hire security. We'll keep the new venue quiet. Do what you need to do, but I'm going to marry this man today no matter what. And you're going to be by my side."

Zoe took this all in and finally relented. "Okay. That's all I needed to know."

"What do you need me to do?"

"Do your bride thing. Remain on standby. Relax, envision your perfect day, have some chai tea, and leave the rest to me. I'll let you know the plan as soon as I've got it all set up." Zoe pulled her tablet out, already opening Piper and Aiden's file. "But I've got to go. I have an entire wedding to move in three hours and . . . forty-six minutes."

She just hoped that once she did, this blow-out event wouldn't be a blow-up event.

31

Put on the Dog

Call all the guests to relocate
Photographer
Inform caterer and band of venue change
214 chairs
Ribbon
Flowers
String lights
Lanterns
Fabric
Order dance floor

Zoe scanned her list for the tenth time, ensuring she hadn't forgotten anything. Who was she kidding? Of course she'd forgotten something, but as long as she had the bride and groom, that's all that mattered.

Fifteen minutes until go-time and by some miracle, she'd pulled off the venue change. She cast an eye over the scene before her and smiled at the early 1900's home, turned Dachshund Rescue Center, turned wedding venue.

The two-story canary yellow farmhouse was draped with sweeping panels of organza at every entrance and tied back with ribbon. Flowers exploded from every space around the wraparound porch and dripped from the thick tree branches arcing over the yard. Twinkling string lights hugged every post, every tree, and even the fence for the dog enclosure where the guests' pets were free to enjoy the celebration.

Since most of Zoe's stock decor had been obliterated in her office explosion, and then replaced, only to be destroyed in the explosion that morning, she picked up what she could on the way to the center. What she couldn't scrounge up from her new office and random stores, she had to beg, borrow, and steal to get.

Addison and Felix had called everyone on the guest list, giving them strict orders not to tell *anyone* about the new location. Marilyn, Bob, and a few other center volunteers helped prepare the house and yard for the influx of over two hundred people, some of whom she could see still making their way up the long driveway to the center.

Since the parking lot wasn't big enough to accommodate many vehicles, the guests had to park along either side of the driveway and walk to the house. However, it wasn't an unpleasant walk beneath the mature acacia trees arcing over them like a lush tunnel. Zoe had even decorated the branches with glowing lanterns and pink flowers so they dangled above the guests' heads.

All things considered, it had actually turned out pretty well. Zoe took a deep breath. The worst of it was over.

Arms slid around her waist and she felt a kiss on her neck. She leaned back into the embrace, welcoming the reassurance.

"You really pulled off a miracle today, you know that?" Levi said.

"Thanks," Zoe said. "It's not perfect, but it feels good."

"They're getting married, and that's all that counts."

"You're right," she said. "Got your violin all tuned up for *Canon in D*?"

Levi's face went slack. "Crap. I was supposed to bring a violin?"

Zoe's heart officially stopped in her chest. It began to pack its bags, ready to give up on the whole ordeal when an angelic look crossed his face.

"Just kidding."

Zoe slapped him on the chest, and after a good-luck kiss, she hurried up the stone steps as fast as she could in her dress.

Sweeping through the French doors into the reception, she found Aiden and his two groomsmen seated around the hearth. They glanced up at her as the brass bell announced her entrance.

"Okay, gentlemen," she said. "We're almost ready. Please go take your places under the gazebo."

As they filtered out, sounds of clinking dishes drifted from the kitchen in the back where the caterer was making do with smaller facilities than expected.

Aiden remained behind until it was just the two of them. He reached up to tighten his tie self-consciously. "How do I look?"

She automatically reached up to tweak it. "Like Mr. Right."

He leaned in to give her a hug. "Thank you for everything."

"Don't thank me. You might have been better off with a different planner."

"It couldn't have turned out better," he said.

"Better hurry," she told him. "You don't want to keep Piper waiting."

He gave her a look like "here we go" and slipped out back. Zoe checked her watch. Ten minutes until go-time.

She headed upstairs, her heels clicking rapidly. When she made it to the second floor, she beelined it for the room at the end of the hall. Piper sometimes used it to nap when she had to stay overnight at the center to monitor sick pups. But today, the little wooden sign that Zoe hung around the door knob said it was *The Bride's Room*.

The door squeaked open, and in the dim hall light, she saw Piper's mother coming out. She'd never met her friend's mother before that day. They looked so much alike, except her hair was darker and contained none of the natural red highlights that made up Piper's auburn locks.

She squeezed Zoe's shoulder on the way by. "She's all ready for you."

"Thanks." Zoe knocked and waited until she heard, "Come in!"

Zoe turned the handle and headed inside. The corner room was bright with both windows open, and she squinted against the afternoon light bouncing off the bright ivory dress in front of her.

Piper turned to her, and she was literally glowing. The sun caught the delicate beading along the bodice, making her shine like the beauty she was.

Zoe gasped. "You look perfect."

"Thank you." She spun to take another look in the floor-length antique mirror.

Addison watched from the bed. "I went with a half-updo."

"Very nice." Zoe ran a hand over the soft curls. "Your auburn hair complements the champagne lace on the skirt." She picked up the veil. "May I?"

Piper nodded and spun around. Zoe set the comb into

her hair and fanned the veil around her shoulders. As Zoe stood back and took in the finishing touch, she sighed.

She'd seen a lot of brides, but when she said, "You're the most beautiful bride I've ever seen," she'd never meant it more.

Piper's eyes widened. "Zoe! Are you crying?"

Zoe blinked, the droplets getting caught in her lashes. "I-I guess I am." She laughed, dabbing at her eyes with a tissue. "I've been having all sorts of emotional revelations lately."

Piper laughed and grabbed Zoe for a hug.

"Wait! Me too. Me too," Addison yelled, wedging herself into the huddle.

When they all pulled away, they were sniffing and laughing.

Addison started throwing tissues at them. "Don't ruin the makeup, ladies."

As Zoe dabbed at her tears, there was a knock on the door. Zoe checked the time. Five minutes to go.

"Come in!" Piper called.

Zoe didn't know who she expected to be on the other side, but when the door opened, it was the last person she would have guessed.

And obviously Piper felt the same because her mouth fell open. "Ethan?"

Piper's brother hovered at the threshold. "I wanted to come tell my little sister good luck."

"Thanks," she said.

He looked stiff, but Zoe didn't think it had anything to do with his designer suit. She had to hand it to him. The man knew how to dress. But she supposed he had to, being a high-priced lawyer in Washington. It kind of went hand-in-hand. They probably offered classes about it in law school—Law*suits* 101.

An awkward moment passed, and Ethan stepped into

the room cautiously, as though the floor was made of marbles. His arms rose jerkily, unsure if he should hug her. Piper eventually gave in and moved into the uncomfortable embrace. Zoe and Addison shared a look.

Piper and her brother weren't exactly on hugging terms. Zoe wondered how long it had been since Piper had last spoken to him. Since their father's funeral ten years before, Piper had only seen him once or twice. Their relationship was strained to say the least.

Zoe remembered sending out his wedding invitation, but she didn't think Piper had even called her brother to ask him to attend. Maybe she'd been hoping that he wouldn't.

When the siblings pulled away, Ethan shoved his hands in his pockets. "I also came up here to, well . . . see how you're getting down the aisle."

Piper's forehead creased in confusion. "My own two feet."

Undeterred, Ethan tried again. "Well, I was just wondering, you know, since Dad isn't here, if maybe I could be the one to walk you down the aisle."

Her eyebrows shot up. "You?"

"Yeah. I mean, I know we aren't exactly close anymore, but you know, we're still family and . . . I don't know." He shrugged, and Zoe hoped he was better at his closing arguments in court than that. "I guess, I thought it would be nice if I could walk with you."

Zoe noticed how he didn't say "give you away," which was probably a smart idea since nobody owned Piper Summers. For Piper's sake, she hoped that Ethan's offer was the start of them building a bridge, and not just because Piper was marrying a man with a butt load of money.

Piper crossed her arms while she considered him with a skeptical look. "Did Mom put you up to this?"

He shook his head. "No. I'd really like us to be closer. I've actually been talking with Mom. We're considering moving down here to San Francisco. I think it would be nice if we were all together."

Piper's eyes hardened. "Why?"

"Because we're all we've got left."

Piper's harsh gaze lowered to the floor, and when it came back up it was less daggery, if still a little guarded.

Zoe's gaze flicked from Piper to her brother. Unable to help herself, she checked her watch. Two minutes. Through the open windows, she could already hear Levi start up a classical piece on his violin.

Finally, Piper nodded. "All right. That would be nice. Thanks." She attempted a smile.

Zoe clapped her hands, startling everyone in the room. "Great. Now that's settled, it's time."

Piper took a deep breath, and then they were off. Their anxious footsteps thudded down the stairs and through the house until they were all lined up with everyone else at the back door. Marilyn was waiting with Picasso by her side to guide all of them. She was practically glowing with excitement for Piper.

Since Zoe was one of the ones walking down the aisle, she'd given Marilyn instructions regarding who goes when. Piper's mother had already made it down the aisle so Zoe threw Addison a thumbs-up to let her know she was up. She stepped out the back door and onto the porch before sashaying down the aisle.

When it was her turn, Zoe turned around to the bride. "Good luck."

Piper smiled, all teeth, but seemed unable to find her voice to answer.

As Zoe made her way down the peony-lined path, she spotted a few guests out of place, a toppled vase, and a bow on a chair that needed retying. However, she focused instead on Levi's playing, and by the time she was half-way to the gazebo, she'd forgotten all about the details.

Head tilted against his violin, Levi grinned at her as she passed. She winked back before climbing the gazebo stairs and taking her place next to Addison.

Next out the door was Naia in her flower-girl dress. While she tried to toss the odd petal here and there, she was mostly concerned with the tougher job of controlling the two ring bearers who stopped to sniff nearly every guest they passed.

Aiden and Piper's dogs, Sophie and Colin, carried the rings on little bows tied around their necks. With difficulty, Naia gradually coaxed the doxies down the aisle where Aiden helped her untie the rings.

The porch door squeaked open and the congregation turned around. Zoe swore that even the dogs had stopped rolling around in their enclosure to watch. But as Ethan and Piper crossed the property, it might as well have been just Piper and Aiden there.

Her best friend looked magnificent, off-the-rack dress and everything. The way Aiden stared into her eyes, Zoe could see that he wouldn't have cared if she'd worn a dog-food bag to walk down the aisle in.

Zoe watched as though she'd never seen a ceremony before or heard vows exchanged. Maybe it was because this ceremony involved two of the most important people in her life. After what they'd over come to be together at the start of their relationship, how could even the biggest skeptic continue to believe it wouldn't work out? Or that every marriage was doomed to fail—or in Zoe's case, not begin at all?

How could she have denied it for so long? How could she have lied to herself for so many years, when there was love in the world like theirs? Or maybe, just maybe it was

her new growing hope for her own future with Levi that
had her singing a different tune.

"I now pronounce you husband and wife," the justice
of the peace said. "You may kiss the bride."

As Aiden smiled and reached out for his new wife, he
kissed her as though for the first time. When they finally
pulled away, Levi started up another happy tune on his
violin and the couple unceremoniously made their way
down the stairs of the gazebo where they ate pancake
brunch every Sunday morning.

The congregation stood and clapped, while some
barked, as they walked down the stone path. Zoe even
saw Freddy running the length of the fence.

Aiden's best man offered Zoe his arm, and she took
it. They followed behind the couple, making it as far as
the porch before the crowd swallowed the happy couple
to congratulate them. It was chaotic and spontaneous.
And utterly perfect for Piper and Aiden.

It was the kind of intimate, laid-back wedding Piper
had told Zoe she wanted, or at least had *tried* to tell her.
It seemed that despite all the setbacks and obstacles that
had been thrown at her, Zoe had pulled off Piper's perfect wedding—even if it was accidental.

As Zoe maneuvered through the crowd, Piper caught
her eye and mouthed the words "Thank you."

Zoe waved and moved toward the dog enclosure.
Seeing her come for him, Freddy pushed to the front of
the cluster of dogs vying for attention, like *My ride's here,
guys!*

Appetizers were already being served on the other
side of the house, drawing the guests away from where
she needed to get the band set up on the wrap-around
porch. Then there was the dance floor that needed to
be assembled, chairs gathered, and dinner tables set.
But if she was really going to be able to hop into the

wedding-planner role, first she needed to grab her tablet from the van.

Clipping Freddy's leash on, she headed for the parking lot. When she unlocked her van and reached in to grab her tablet from the console, the screen glowed with a long list of recent notifications from Holly Hart. With a flick of a finger, she scrolled through them. She opened the latest one.

Hey, Holly's Hounds! Have I got a treat for you! The wedding is back on track with a new locale. It's the perfect fairy-tail ending for this puppy: The San Francisco Dachshund Rescue Center.

Zoe snapped her tablet cover shut. *Dammit*, she thought. Now all the gossip mongers around the city were going to converge on them. Good thing she'd called in the best security company in town. Hopefully they'd sent enough guards to cover the large property.

When she headed to check in with the head of security, she spotted two guests who had strayed from the rest of the wedding group. But when she got closer, she did a double-take. What she'd mistaken as a dark suit was actually a police uniform. And the other guest that was speaking with the cop was Bob, Marilyn's detective boyfriend.

Zoe glanced around. There was no one else nearby. They obviously didn't want to be overheard, whatever they were discussing.

The presence of a cop at the wedding couldn't mean anything good, especially after recent events. But things were going so smoothly—other than Holly's announcement. What could possibly be going on?

This was supposed to be Piper and Aiden's perfect day. Nothing was going to go wrong. Well . . . nothing else. Not if Zoe had anything to say about it.

Zoe plucked Freddy off the ground and tucked him

under her arm. "Now behave," she told him. She held a finger to her lips like he would understand, hoping that they'd finally be on the same team.

Holding him close, she slipped off her noisy high heels. The hot pavement burned the soles of her feet. Wincing with each step, she crept closer until she was hidden behind the closest car to them, a silver Mercedes— obviously a guest of Aiden's. But they were still too far away for her to hear.

Crouching low, Zoe inched her way to the front of the car, careful not to be seen over the hood, or more important, soil her dress. The angle gave Freddy plenty of opportunity for kisses. She ignored him—whatever kept him quiet.

". . . we have patrol units parked out front," the cop was saying.

"Do you think anything will happen tonight?" Bob asked.

"We're not sure. It's just a precaution for now. We'll keep an eye on things, but after the reception we'll take Miss Plum into police custody."

Zoe gasped, but covered her mouth before she could make another noise. They were going to arrest her? But what for? Did it have something to do with Chelsea? Maybe she was setting Zoe up again. Or it could have been about the venue bombing that morning on Broadway. They thought she might have been responsible for the first one. What if Detective Warner had yet another breakthrough that pointed straight at Zoe as suspect number one?

"Don't you think you should take her in sooner?" Bob asked.

Zoe scowled. *Thanks, Bob.* Whose side was he on anyway?

If Bob was coordinating with them, whatever they had

on her must have been incriminating. But still, as her friend, she'd expected him to back her just a little.

"We've got the place surrounded," the cop said. "No one gets in or out without our knowing. We don't want to alarm anyone in case it affects the investigation. We'll take her quietly after it's done."

"All right. I'll keep an eye on things in here. Thanks for keeping me informed."

Freddy began to struggle in Zoe's arms, clearly bored of her little spy mission.

"Shh, Freddy. Stop," Zoe whispered as she tried to keep a hold on him. "Stop."

But Freddy's calm limit had been reached and he wanted to play. Squirming out of her arms, he flopped on the ground and made a break for it.

Zoe lunged for the leash, but it slipped out of her grasp. He skittered out from behind the Mercedes right toward Bob and the cop. Obviously they weren't on the same team yet.

Even though Freddy had just blown her cover, she couldn't let them know that she'd overheard, in case they decided to slap on some handcuffs and take her away right then and there. If she hadn't ruined Piper and Aiden's wedding so far, then that would surely top their wedding cake.

Stooping low, she ran back a few vehicles, further away from the men, until she was hidden behind her van again. She slipped on her heels and hopped from foot to foot to make some fake running sounds before rounding the bumper and heading in their direction.

She slapped a smile on her face, hoping that she was a good enough actress to pull one over on a cop and a veteran detective. She slowed down when she passed the Mercedes and huffed a little like she'd just run all the way there.

Bob was holding Freddy's leash. "Lose something?" he asked, without even a hint that anything was amiss. Like he wasn't just talking about her incarceration with the officer.

Well, two could play that game. "Yeah, thanks. I don't know where his energy comes from." Now that she was at the top of the driveway, Zoe could just see flashes of movement outside the distant gates. Zoe nodded. "What's going on out there?"

"Just some party crashers," the officer told her. "Someone called to complain that they're getting a bit riled up, so we came to check it out."

So that was the story they were going with. Zoe's eyes automatically flicked to Bob. His face remained pleasant, like they were all just having a casual conversation.

Zoe laughed. "Holly's got the city as amped up about the wedding as she is."

"Don't worry," the officer said. "We'll be sticking around to keep an eye on things."

I'm sure you will, thought Zoe. "Great. Thank you. Well, everyone's here that's supposed to be here."

"No one will be getting in those gates on our watch."

Or out, she thought. But that was okay with her. This day was about Piper and Aiden. She planned to do what she needed to do to finish it off. Then she'd go quietly.

"I'm sorry you have to waste staff watching our party," she said.

He shrugged. "We do this kind of thing at public events all the time."

She pulled a face. "I just wish it were a little less public." Taking Freddy's leash from Bob, she began to back away toward the house. "Well, thank you. I'd better get back. Lots to do."

She left the two men behind, who most likely began

talking about her the moment she was out of earshot—hopefully not about what a terrible actress she was.

But Zoe knew how to act cool—she'd had years of practice under her fanny pack. She was confident she'd pulled it off.

She sashayed back to the wedding party like the only things on her mind were centerpieces and photo ops. And right about now, that's all she could worry about, because despite socialite wannabes banging on the front gates, someone wanting to blow her to bits, and cops poised to arrest her for God knows what, she was still the best damned wedding planner in San Francisco. And she had a wedding to oversee.

32

⚭

Hear of Marriage and You'll Dream of a Funeral

"At last my love has come along.
My lonely days are over and life is like a song."

Levi belted out the most rock and roll version of "At Last" that Zoe had ever heard. But it was strangely catchy and had her glad that she'd opted for the extra-large dance floor because it seemed as though everyone was on it. Even Marilyn and Bob were shaking their tail feathers. Reluctant Redemption seemed to know all the crowd pleasers.

Piper danced her way over in Aiden's arms. "Aren't they great?" she half-yelled over the music. "I'm so glad we hired them."

Addison spun by with Felix. "I bet Zoe is too!" She grinned devilishly at Zoe as she carried on by.

Zoe ignored the comment, but had to bite back a smile. She wandered over to the snack table where she was keeping her purse and bridal utility bag hidden. For the hundredth time that night, she pulled out her tablet and scrolled through the recent notifications.

There hadn't been much from Holly since she'd leaked the news about the new venue. The only other comment was posted when the band began to play and she critiqued the newly married couple's first dance. Obviously she was part of the crowd outside the front gates, but other than that, things had been quiet—which Zoe took as a bad sign. What was Holly Hart up to?

Holly would probably stay all night, if need be, lurking outside the property, waiting for guests to leave so she could accost them with questions. Zoe wondered if the cops would have arrested her by then. Would they arrest her in front of everyone? She preferred to hand herself over quietly and save the newlyweds any embarrassment.

She was staring across the property at the driveway, half expecting them to come for her any second when she heard a shout or a cry. Or maybe a whoop of excitement for the band. But it sounded like it came from around the side of the house.

She peered into the darkness outside the circle of light created by all the lanterns and string lights. It could have been one of the guests. Perhaps a dog got out of the enclosure or off a leash. Zoe knew it wasn't hers because he was at her heels enjoying the tunes.

As Zoe went to investigate, someone grabbed her hand and tugged her back. She half spun until she landed in Levi's arms.

"Hey, rock star." She smiled. "Intermission already?"

"No. But the band was playing our song, so I thought I'd come steal a dance." He gave her a wink. The string lights nearby sparkled in his eyes, and she got lost for a moment.

"We have a song?" she asked. "And what song is that?"

He hooked Freddy's leash on one of the many dog-minding posts she'd pounded into the ground around the dance floor and swept her away. "Any song that will get you into my arms."

And being in his arms felt so right.

She laid her head on his shoulder to soak it all in, him, them, that moment. The band was playing an instrumental version of "We Are the Champions" by Queen as Levi took her for a twirl on the dance floor. He spun her and when she came to a stop, she was facing the house.

Her half-lidded gaze landed on the bar. Something caught her eye. A flash of platinum blonde hair, almost white beneath the twinkling string lights strung from tree to tree.

Levi led her around to the other side of the dance floor and the person was lost from sight. Zoe craned her head this way and that to see past the other dancers. When a couple moved, she caught sight of the woman again.

She gave Zoe a cheeky smile and raised her martini glass, like a greeting to Zoe, or maybe a big old "screw you!"

Holly Hart.

"Is everything okay?" Levi asked, as she stopped dancing.

"Holly's here," she said, not taking her eyes off the reporter.

She was dressed head to toe in black, as though this was a funeral, not a wedding. Maybe that was for the best, since there was about to be a funeral. *Hers.*

"I'm going to kill her."

"I see the claws are coming out." He shrugged his shoulders and she realized her nails were digging into them.

"Oh, sorry." She sighed. "I need to go deal with this."

"Shall I call for backup?"

"Yeah. Maybe go get Bob. There's about to be a murder."

Zoe maneuvered her way across the dance floor, all smiles at the surrounding guests until she reached the bar. Holly waited patiently for her, not even bothering to look guilty or like she didn't belong there. Instead, she sipped her drink and waved to her good friend Zoe.

The moment she was in reach, Zoe gripped her arm, ready to drag her to the front gates herself. "What the hell are you doing here?"

"Why, I'm enjoying the festivities." She brushed her hand away. "This is quite something. I have to admit, I had my doubts after what happened to the first venue. But you really managed to pull it off." She gave her a sly wink and lowered her voice to a whisper. "That's why you're my favorite."

"Bite me."

Holly clicked her tongue. "Is that any way to treat a guest?"

"You're not a guest," she spat. "How did you get in here?"

"Oh, it's a big property." She waved the details aside. "You didn't think a couple of police officers and some incompetent security guards were going to stop the likes of Holly Hart, did you? I always get my story."

Zoe plucked a leaf out of her blonde hair. "Yeah, I'm sure you get around."

Grass swished behind Zoe and she turned to find Levi and Bob marching over. Even in dress clothes, Bob could look official. It was in his rigid stance, his hard expression. He carried authority even when he didn't have his gun.

"What's going on?" he asked. "Everything all right, here?"

"Miss Hart here seems to have lost her way," Zoe told him.

Bob turned to her. "Will you come with me? Or would you prefer I get one of the officers outside to escort you out in cuffs?"

"Oooh, handcuffs." She bit her lip. "Sounds kinky. A couple of them were pretty cute. I'll take that option." She giggled. "I like it rough."

"Now don't make a scene," Bob said like he was chastising a little girl.

"Who's making a scene?" She pouted. "You ain't seen nothing yet. Just call your boys and then we'll see what happens," she said, the threat as clear as Swarovski crystal.

Zoe took a step forward, glaring down at the reporter. "I will take you down myself, so help me God."

Holly raised her chin. "Let's go, stretch."

"Zoe, just leave her be."

Zoe turned to the voice she recognized as Piper's, but it couldn't possibly be. She'd never stick up for Holly Hart. "What?"

Piper stood in front of Holly, looking her up and down as though she were a wild animal not yet tamed. "She'll do more damage to the evening if we kick her out." With a sneer, she addressed Holly. "You can stay, on one condition. You hand over your phone until the night is over and delete any photos you've already taken."

"Deal." Reaching into her clutch, she drew out her phone and handed it over to Zoe.

"I don't trust her," Zoe said. "She probably has a hidden camera on her somewhere." She eyed her skin-tight dress.

"Who do you think I am? James Bond?" She threw Zoe a withering look. "But if you're really that worried, I'm sure Aiden could always frisk me." She bobbed her head around, searching the crowd for him. "Where are those handcuffs when you need them?"

"Don't make me regret this," Piper warned her.

Holly drew an imaginary halo above her head with a finger. "I'll be on my best behavior."

"That doesn't exactly ease my worries."

"Oh well, you can't please everybody." Holly downed her drink and popped the olive into her mouth. "Excuse me. I'm going to go mingle." She threw her black paisley wrap over her shoulder and left.

Zoe watched her walk away. "I don't trust her," she said again.

"Neither do I," Piper said. "I just figured it would be less hassle to leave her be."

"I'll keep an eye on her." Zoe made shooing motions with her hands. "Go dance with your husband before Holly tries to."

Piper smiled. "Thanks."

Levi wrapped an arm around Zoe. "I'd best get back on stage. Any requests?"

"Britney Spears," she joked.

"Done." He kissed her cheek before sprinting back on stage.

Zoe glanced down at Holly's phone in her hand. Holly was up to something. She handed it over too willingly. There was no way she wasn't going to record every moment she could. Which could only mean she had another way of recording the event. And since Zoe had rarely ever seen the reporter without her cameraman to boss around, she had a hunch he was sneaking around there somewhere too.

Holly was busy rubbing elbows with a few of Aiden's guests. While she was distracted, Zoe headed for the thick tree line that encircled the property.

From this distance, the music was a soft, steady beat

in the background. After the dazzling lights around the house and dance floor, it was like she was walking into a black hole.

Zoe resisted the urge to go back and grab her tablet to light her way. She couldn't very well sneak up on Hey, You if he could see her coming a mile away. Then again, considering the Channel Five News team she was dealing with, he probably had night vision goggles to do his late-night snooping.

She shivered, wishing she'd brought her wrap. Not wanting to take her leather heels into the forest, she began to skirt around the edges of the underbrush.

The distant glow from the lights and paper lanterns caught on the leaves around her. She imagined they were eyes watching her, blinking when they rustled in the wind, winking at her. She certainly felt like she'd had eyes following her everywhere for the last few weeks.

Her ears strained for any sounds in the woods, a cracking twig, the zoom of a lens. But all she could hear was the distant sounds of Britney Spears. She chuckled, but kept moving. She had a job to do.

The breeze picked up again. The leafy bushes began scraping and hissing as they rustled all around her. When it died down, she heard the rhythmic swishing of grass behind her. She'd been so focused on the search before her, that she wasn't watching her back.

She spun around, squinting against the party's lights, but she saw nothing. The swishing drew closer. She took a panicked step back. It was right in front of her and yet she still couldn't see a damn thing.

A scream crawled up her throat.

Then it struck.

It pawed at her shins and licked her exposed ankles, relentless in its attack. Zoe let her scream out in a quiet grunt.

Freddy had somehow gotten free from the post she'd hooked him to, because his leash was still attached, dragging through the grass behind him.

"Freddy," she hissed. "Go back. Go." She snapped her fingers and pointed, unsure if he could see her. But even if he could, she realized that he would have done the complete opposite of what she said, anyway. So, she pointed at her feet and said, "Okay, stay."

Naturally, Freddy took off. Only, instead of returning to the party, he dove for the trees.

"No. Freddy!" she yell-whispered. "Not that way!"

Crap, she thought. *So much for being inconspicuous.* She was tempted to yell "Hey, You! Ready or not, here I come!"

Zoe could hear Freddy rustling through the underbrush, crunching dead leaves, snorting and digging in the dirt as he sniffed around. *There's a mouse. I know there's a mouse. It's around here somewhere.*

Although, if there had been mice, he would have scared them all away with his stealthless attack.

"Freddy come back here. There's no mice in there. Come." But Freddy was being Freddy and doing exactly what he wasn't supposed to be doing.

Sighing, Zoe hiked up her floor-length dress and went in after him. She swore she was putting obedience classes on her to-do list. Just as soon as she got out of jail.

Zoe peered into the darkness, picking her way over hidden roots and fallen branches as she followed the sounds of excited prancing in the leaves. She doubted he'd found anything but a stick. The sounds grew louder just behind the next bush.

"Freddy. Come here, boy. I'm making my voice sound really fun and lighthearted right now, but you're actually in big trouble," she sang.

Crouching down, she began groping along the damp

earth to grab his leash. But from her new point of view,
a bright light caught her eye. A flashlight maybe, hidden
beneath the bush. She'd likely discovered Holly's path
through the property.

She held the branches aside and reached in, but it
wasn't a flashlight. It was a screen. As she explored, her
hand landed on the object. It was heavy, whatever it was.

She dragged it out to discover it was Hey, You's camera.
But there was no sign of the weasel himself.

The camera was still in the midst of recording. She
wasn't sure what he'd hoped to capture all the way out
there from the bushes. Squinting against the screen's
light, she found the stop button.

She'd helped enough videographers film weddings
over the years, due to poorly timed washroom breaks or
illnesses, that she knew her way around professional
equipment. Using the buttons, she managed to find the
playback menu.

A selection of past footage popped up on the screen.
Footage that looked very familiar. Hell, it was practically
her last three weeks all laid out in video clips. Out of curiosity, she checked some of the previous footage.

She searched back to the expo, when Holly first began screwing with her life. Her fight with Chelsea popped
up on the screen. She pressed play and watched as she
threw the pink champagne cake in her rival's face.

Zoe cringed. Watching it from the outside looking in
was even worse. That hadn't exactly been her brightest
moment, nor one she wanted to relive, so she moved onto
the next clip.

It was just more footage from the expo. Not exactly
riveting stuff. Hey, You was scanning the underground
parking lot, taking in a panorama of the parked cars.
Then it zoomed in on a van. *Her van.*

It was post break-in because she could see the tendrils

of Piper's shredded dress fluttering out the open back. But there were no people gathered around it. It was before the vandalism had even been discovered. Had it been Hey, You who first reported it?

As she continued to watch, the van wiggled and rocked. Seconds later, a figure leapt out. But it was too dark, too far away to see who it was.

Zoe flipped to the next video. Of course, it was her gaping at her destroyed van, at the dress, and Holly was pestering her with questions. She skipped that one.

The next footage was something Zoe had watched on the news, along with the rest of the city. Holly Hart stood in front of the camera, checking her teeth in the lens's reflection before introducing the night's top story.

"This is Holly Hart coming to you from North Beach, where the San Fran Slayer has taken his next victim."

But the mention of the serial killer made Zoe shiver with the creeps. Zoe scanned through the rest of the footage. It was practically a montage of her life, one epic disaster after another. And the news team had been there for everyone. Every single one.

Her hair stood on end, and it felt like something was crawling up the back of her neck. She rubbed at it and spun around, her chest thumping.

Suddenly on alert, she peered through the dark woods, straining to hear anything out of the ordinary. But the only sounds were Freddy's grunting as he tried to drag his "mouse" out of the bush—which, knowing him, was likely a root.

Mouse, mouse, mouse, mouse . . .

Zoe shook off the sudden anxiety. This was the rescue center, after all. It was practically a second home to her, a place where she spent much of her free time. A safe haven. Not to mention, she was surrounded by a collection of professional security guards and San Francisco's finest. Besides, she could hear Levi's voice drifting over from the speakers in the distance, and it comforted her.

She searched the menu for any clips filmed on the day of their brunch at the restaurant. She found one. It had been created half an hour before they left. And Holly Hart was interviewing a very much alive Chef Glazier.

"This is Holly Hart reporting from the restaurant House of Glass. I'm with Chef Glazier, world renowned chef and caterer for this year's biggest event, the joining of our favorite devoted doggy duo, Aiden Caldwell and the Dachshund Rescue Center spokesperson, Piper Summers." She turned to the chef. *"Chef Glazier, can you give us a sneak peek of the wedding menu?"*

"Well, they haven't made a final decision yet. As we speak, they are sampling my signature dishes—"

Zoe frowned and pressed fast forward, skipping over their banter. She'd had no idea this had been going on in the kitchen while they ate lunch. Holly must have come in after the interview, pretending like she'd only just arrived.

Zoe slowed down again when it looked like Holly was giving her sign off. In the next video, Hey, You was still in the restaurant kitchen. Chef Glazier was showing him around. By the looks of it, they were in the delivery area where the body had been found.

"What kind of stuff do you get delivered here?" a man asked. Zoe realized it was Hey, You. She'd never actually heard him speak.

He continued to ask mundane questions about the delivery area while the chef insisted he return to his guests. Zoe supposed that was why Holly asked the questions and he was stuck behind the camera. But when he continued to press the chef about wanting to see the bay door open, it was obvious. He was distracting the chef.

Fed up, the chef turned back to the kitchen. Zoe's view

of the scene jiggled as Hey, You chased after him. *"Wait!"*

But then the chef paused on the threshold of the kitchen. *"What do you think you're doing?"*

All she could see was the chef's back blocking the view of his work station, but Holly answered.

"I thought I might contribute to the momentous occasion," she said. *"You know, I'm not half bad in the kitchen. I make a mean soufflé."*

But the chef wasn't buying it. He swiped at something on his cutting board. *"What is this?"* He smelled it and touched a finger to his tongue. *"Sesame seed?"*

"This isn't what it looks like," she said.

He glanced from her to the dessert balls, freshly powdered with the deadly stuff. *"You know about her allergy,"* he said, more like an accusation. *"You plan to poison my customer."*

"Okay, it's exactly what it looks like," she said. *"But it's not like it's going to kill her,"* she reasoned. Zoe still couldn't see Holly's face, but there was no hint of remorse or guilt in her voice.

"Both of you stay right here." The chef shook a finger at her. When he turned to face Hey, You, his cheeks were flushed, his eyes bulging with fury.

Hey, You wasn't bothering to aim the camera. The chef's chest filled the frame, the buttons of his coat shaking as he continued to rant, threatening police and lawyers. Then mid-sentence he trailed off, his voice gurgling in the back of his throat.

Chef Glazier fell forward. He crumpled at Hey, You's feet. Holly stood behind him, holding the steak knife. It dripped with the chef's blood.

Zoe yelped and covered her mouth with her hand. She sank to her knees, feeling the damp earth soak through her dress. She wanted to scream, to run. She suddenly felt so alone and exposed, but she couldn't seem to drop the camera. She couldn't tear her eyes away.

"Jesus. Holy Shit, Holly. What did you do?" Hey, You asked. *"What did you just do?"*

But Holly still didn't look sorry. In fact, she looked irritated, like someone just brought her a Pepsi instead of a Coke. *"Well, I didn't plan for this to happen, did I?"*

But Zoe couldn't help but notice she'd put on leather gloves at some point. That was why only Zoe's fingerprints had been found on the knife.

Holly hastily wiped the knife on the chef's pant leg before putting it back down next to the cutting board.

"Shit," Hey, You said. *"You just stabbed someone."*

The world tilted like Hey, You just about dropped the camera, and Zoe got a glimpse of Chef Glazier's body lying face down. Blood seeped through his white coat, the stain growing bigger.

She shut her eyes and when she opened them again, Hey, You had placed his camera on the counter. He was bent over the body.

When he stood back up, he said, *"Oh my God. He's dead. We have to do something."*

His words seemed to change something in Holly. Her face went blank for a moment. *"You're right. You're right. Oh, my God. We have to do something."*

"Good, okay. We should call the police and—"

But Holly wasn't listening. She reached down to the body. *"Come on. You grab his upper body. I'll grab his feet."*

"What?"

"Well, I can't very well get blood on me. This is Dior for shit's sake." She tugged at her outfit. *"Use your brain."*

"But I don't understand," he said. *"He's dead. We need to call the police."*

"The police?" Now Holly did look affected. She looked downright scared. *"But then they're going to blame me."*

"Yes." He nodded. *"Because you killed him."*

"You were here too."

"Tricking someone into eating a few seeds is one thing," he said. *"But this? This is cold-blooded murder. I mean, shit, Holly."*

Holly covered her face with her hands. A sound not unlike a sob came out of her, but Zoe thought it was far from the real thing.

"After working together for all these years," she said. *"After everything we've been through, you'd turn me in just like that?"*

Holly stepped over the body until she was close enough to place a hand on Hey, You's chest. When he didn't move, she laid her head against his shoulder. *"I thought you'd do anything for me. We're a team."*

"Team? You do nothing but boss me around." But he sounded less panicky and more confused as he stared down at the top of her head on his chest.

"That's only because I've been fighting my true feelings for you."

He swallowed. *"Feelings?"*

"Don't deny it. I know you've wanted me since the first day we worked together. I've wanted you too."

Her hand slid down his chest to his crotch. He jumped as she clutched it.

"Ooh. See? You can deny it all you want, but your true desires are obvious." As she rubbed the front of his pants, Zoe could see his eyes roll into the back of his head and his resolve begin to waiver.

"I need you," she said. *"I want you. And you want me, too."*

"Yes," he said.

She rubbed faster. *"But we can't be together if I go to jail."*

"No."

"I can't take it anymore," she said. *"I want you. Now."*

"Now?"

"Yes."

"We can go to my place," he said.

"No. I can't wait that long. We can do it in the van." She leaned in close, like she was about to kiss him. *"But first . . ."*

His eyes closed and his lips quivered as they searched for hers, but she pulled away, disappearing beneath the counter. When she popped back up, she was holding a pair of feet.

"Grab his arms. Hurry. Before someone comes back here."

He did as she asked, grunting from the dead weight. *"Where are we going to hide it?"*

"Just shut up and lift with your legs."

They moved off camera. A moment later, the kitchen's double doors swung open, and the server came in with her tray.

"Chef Glazier!?" she called, scanning the kitchen for signs of him. When no one answered, she shrugged and loaded the desserts onto the tray.

The moment the doors swung closed behind her, Hey, You, and Holly returned to clean up the blood on the floor. Hey, You reached for the camera and the screen went blank.

Zoe now knew Holly was the one behind everything. Her van, the bombings, the murder. Everything. Hey, You had known she was up to something, or at least, suspected it. She recalled chasing him down an alley after her office was bombed. He'd been gathering footage of her. Evidence.

Zoe knew she should take the camera and run. Run to the police. Run to Bob. Run to someone and tell them what she'd found, but something made her click on the most recent video. The last one.

With a shaking finger, she hit play.

By the heavy breathing, she could tell that Hey, You was hiding in the woods. In the very spot she was standing on, she realized. He was filming the dance floor.

A twig snapped.

Zoe spun, thinking it was behind her, but she was still alone. It had been behind Hey, You. The camera spun to face the sound. It was Holly.

"What are you doing here?" she asked.

"I came to stop you," he said. *"You can't do this."*

She took a step forward, but he blocked her.

"Get out of my way," she said.

"Give it up. It's over."

"It's not over yet," Holly told him. *"I've tried too hard to fail now."*

Zoe's breath left her in a grunt. The camera shook in her hands. It wasn't her. It wasn't Zoe that Holly was after. It never had been.

"You've failed," Hey, You said with finality. *"You can't undo it."*

"There's one way."

And by the tone of her voice, Zoe knew what that way was.

The whole time, she'd assumed someone was out to get her. Was sabotaging her. But it wasn't about Zoe. It was about Piper. It was about stopping the wedding by whatever means necessary, by ruining the dress, hurting the wedding planner, landing the bride in the hospital.

But nothing had been able to work. And now that the wedding had taken place, there was only one way to "undo" it.

Zoe dropped the camera. "Piper."

She didn't watch the rest. She didn't find out what happened to Hey, You because Holly had gotten past him. She was already at the reception. Nausea rose hot inside her, and she had to fight the urge to pass out from the overwhelming panic.

Scrambling to her feet, she was already moving to grab Freddy, stumbling with anxiety. Was she too late? Would she find Piper in time?

The screen had been so bright, the woods so dark. She tried to blink away the images of Chef Glazier's body, his blood.

She reached down to grab Freddy, but her heel caught on something. A plant, or maybe a root. Unable to find her balance, she fell forward.

Pain exploded in her knee. Her shins scraped against rough bark. Her arms flew out, and she braced herself for impact. But her chest and face landed on something soft, cushiony.

Groping through the dark, she pushed herself up and found herself nose to nose with Hey, You, his sightless gaze facing her. He was dead.

A soundless scream escaped her, like a high-pitched whistle of wind through a broken window.

She clambered back, clawing at the ground, kicking the stiff body. It flopped away from her, the lifelessness making her panic all the more.

Freddy found her in the dark, his tail wagging happily, like he'd found the biggest mouse ever and deserved a treat.

A sob escaped Zoe. Grabbing her doxie, she half-crawled, half-stumbled out of the woods, back toward the party. She just hoped she wasn't too late to warn Piper.

33

Bird-Dog

Zoe rushed onto the dance floor with Freddy clutched in her arms. Her muddy dress, wrapping around her legs with each frantic step, threatened to trip her.

Barging past dancing couples, she clipped a shoulder, sending someone spinning. She ignored their cry of surprise and pushed her way through the bodies. Finally, she spotted Bob dancing with Marilyn.

She gripped his arm and he turned, eyes wide. "Oh, Zoe. You startled me."

Marilyn pulled away from her dancing partner and gave her the once over. "Zoe, dear. You look like you've been dragged through a hedge. Literally. What's wrong?"

"Bob," her voice was raspy from running, from fear. Her grip tightened on his arm. "Bob, you have to go get the police."

"Why? What's happened?"

The gentle, older man transformed before her. The lighthearted sparkle that had been in his eyes while he was dancing with Marilyn faded and his look became unreadable. He wasn't the man she spent every Sunday pancake brunch with. He was the law now, and in his eyes, she was on the other side of it. A criminal waiting to be arrested.

Despite the urgency of the situation, she became aware of the dancers slowing down around them. They were forced to step past their frozen group. They eyed her with curiosity. Bob seemed to notice too, and drew her away from the dance floor, out of earshot.

It occurred to Zoe that what she was about to say could cause mass panic among the happy wedding guests. She lowered her voice and leaned close enough so not even Marilyn could hear. "There's a body in the woods. He's been murdered."

Bob stepped back in shock. His mask from earlier slipped. The one that he'd worn when he pretended he didn't know she was going to be arrested, like she was some common criminal to be deceived.

The expression hidden beneath tore at her. Horror, disgust. Did he really believe she was capable of the murder? He obviously believed she should go to jail.

When she took her next breath, it almost sounded like a sob. "Look, I know the police are waiting to arrest me. But I didn't kill the man." She gripped him by the shoulders. "You have to believe me because there's something more important—"

Bob held up a hand. "Wait. Arrest you?" Understanding dawned on his face, as he was clearly reviewing their encounter in the parking lot. He shook his head. "They're not here to arrest you. They're here to *protect* you."

Zoe blinked, trying to make sense of what he was saying. "From what?"

Glancing around, he slid his arm through hers and led her around the side of the house where the music was quieter. Marilyn anxiously followed, but Bob held up a gentle hand. The woman watched them leave, picking at a thread in her wrap.

When they were far enough away, Bob took on the stance of a man just having a nice chat with a friend. He placed his hands in his pockets casually, as though everything was normal. But what he said next was anything but normal.

"They're here to protect you from the San Fran Slayer."

Zoe's legs trembled. She braced herself against the porch railing, but her arms were shaking so violently that she slid ungracefully onto the steps. Freddy slinked to the ground in front of her, but she held his leash tight.

"What?" she managed to breathe.

Bob took a seat next to her, as though they were taking in the night air together. It felt so wrong. As though they were relaxing while Piper's life was on the line.

"They found evidence on Chef Glazier's body consistent with the slayer case," he said. "They know it wasn't you."

"Are you sure it's the slayer that killed the chef?" She shut her eyes. The images she saw on Hey, You's camera were still there, forever burned onto her retinas, of Holly killing Chef Glazier. If the chef was killed by the slayer, that meant Holly . . .

"Yes, we're sure. Considering the attempts on your life recently, they're taking you into police custody for your protection after the wedding." He eyed the trees surrounding them. "But if you found a body, maybe the slayer's already here."

"She is."

Bob's head whipped toward her. "How do you know it's a female? We've never released information about the sex."

Zoe could feel time slipping away. Every moment they

sat there was another moment lost. They had to find Piper before Holly did something to her. Before she was murdered by a serial killer.

"Listen to me Bob. The slayer is Holly Hart."

"How—"

"There's no time to explain. But it's not me she's after. It's Piper."

Bob's wide eyes scanned the party, but his gaze was distant, as though realigning all the facts, all the evidence in his mind.

"And she's here now," he said, stunned.

He sprang to his feet with the energy of someone half his age. "I'm going to go get the police from the property gates. You stay here." He made as though to leave, but at the last second, he turned back. "And Zoe? It's important that no one knows anything is wrong. If Holly is alerted that we're on to her, it might make her act sooner."

"Act?" Zoe swallowed. She was suddenly on her unsteady feet. "I have to go find Piper." She began backing away, dragging Freddy with her.

Before she got far, Bob grabbed her arm. "Zoe, it's too dangerous."

"She's after Piper, not me."

"But if you get caught in the middle—" he began.

"Bob," Zoe said. "It's Piper."

"You can't help her if you wind up dead yourself." She felt Bob squeeze her arm, as though trying to relay the importance of what he said.

But his words didn't convince her to stay behind. It only made her more desperate to find her best friend.

As Bob went for the police, Zoe took a deep breath and pushed it all down—the fear, the anxiety, the guilt that somehow she could have prevented this. If only she'd figured it all out sooner.

But at that moment, all that mattered was saving the

bride from a serial killer in Manolo Blahniks. She never thought she'd miss the normal wedding woes, like ill-fitting wedding dresses, and drunk uncles.

Zoe spotted Aiden near the dance floor. Picking Freddy up, she crossed over to him, in a totally not-jittery or too-anxious way.

She laid a hand on his arm. "Aiden."

He turned with a smile but then he took in the state of her. "Zoe, what happened to your dress?"

"One too many tequila shots. Have you seen Piper?" she asked, sounding too loud and slightly terrified even over the rock music.

He frowned, glancing around as though expecting her to be nearby. "Not for a little while now."

"Okay, no problem," she said as normally as she could. "She's probably in the washroom. I'll go check on her."

Before she turned away, she gave his arm a squeeze, because she was afraid it wouldn't be that easy. That she wasn't simply going to find Piper reapplying her makeup.

Zoe calmly made her way to the snack table. She grabbed her purse and slung it over her body. It was the easiest way to keep her tablet with her while freeing up her hands. She would need to keep in contact with Bob somehow, in case she found Piper. Or in case Holly found Zoe first.

Pushing that thought aside, she headed into the house, systematically checking each and every room and closet. She wished she had a Fuzzy Friend. Instead, she held Freddy tight. Not for a moment did she consider putting him down. Not with a serial killer on the loose.

His presence kept her calm and focused. She could get through this, just like she'd gotten through every other terrible moment in her life. But this wasn't a spelling bee or a broken limb. This was life and death.

Her frantic search probably took less than two

minutes of racing through the house, but she was sweating and panting by the time she reached the porch again.

Piper was nowhere in the house. And as Zoe scanned the yard, there were no signs of her white dress. There was nowhere else the bride would be.

Zoe closed her eyes. She knew Holly had gotten to Piper.

But Zoe did spot her friends. Not just friends. They were practically family. Addison, Felix, Naia, Marilyn, Aiden. They were all laughing, having a good time, while a tragedy played out under their noses that only Zoe and Bob knew about.

As she stood there, heart rate increasing with each passing second, she racked her brain for places where Holly might have taken Piper. Her eyes moved over the tree line. Could they be in the forest? Away from prying eyes?

Levi caught her eye from the makeshift stage on the porch. He gave her a wink and a smile between verses. Zoe felt her face move in what she hoped was a smile because no one could know, no one cold suspect. Raise the alarm and Piper could pay for it.

Of course, somehow Levi could see right through her usual calm veneer, because a little wrinkle formed between his brows, and he stared at her a moment too long.

Before she could give anything else away, she turned toward the dog enclosure. Freddy was squirming in her arms—maybe he sensed her anxiety too. If she was headed into the woods in search of a murderer, she'd need her arms free.

The moment she set him down in the enclosure, he raced away from her. *How's that for loyalty?* Zoe thought. *First sign of trouble and he runs.*

There was only a small group of dogs milling in the large grassy area. She assumed they were all hiding in the longhouse where the cages were, maybe hiding from the loud music. Obviously they weren't the music aficionados Freddy was.

But instead of heading for the other dogs, Freddy zipped toward the giant doghouse. Without a backward glance, he ducked through one of the unlocked doggy doors leading into the building.

Now that he was safe, Zoe scanned the enclosure and the dark wall of trees on the far side. But the soft glow from the hanging lanterns and string lights didn't reach very far. She hesitated, unsure where to begin her search. The property was so big. How was she ever going to find them by herself?

A moment later, a doggy door swung open and Freddy returned, dragging something behind him. It was long, whatever it was, because his short legs became tangled. He went head over tail until he was a sausage in a blanket. Literally, Zoe thought, as she realized he'd found a long piece of fabric.

Squinting through the dark, she unlatched the gate and went to untangle Freddy. Frowning, she held the fabric up to the dim light. It was a shawl. Not unlike the one that had been wrapped around Holly's shoulders when she'd arrived.

Beneath the vibrating bass, Levi's warm voice humming through the speakers, and the steady drum beat, Zoe could hear chaotic sounds pierce the air. Shrill, urgent barking.

It was coming from the doghouse. The only place on the property where no one would hear anything over all the dogs' barking. No one would think twice about all the racket.

Freddy took off without waiting for Zoe. Glancing over her shoulder, she tossed the pashmina aside and headed across the dog enclosure.

Thankfully, the music drowned out the noises of her approach so she could sneak up. But she quickly realized that if Holly really was in there, Zoe wouldn't know until she was in the middle of whatever was going down. She needed to scope it out first, but bursting through the door wasn't exactly covert. Without any ground-level windows, there was only one other option.

As she snuck closer, she could see the light from inside glowing around the edges of the doggy doors. Getting on her hands and knees, she crawled up to the one Freddy had just gone through. With a hesitant finger, she cracked the door slightly and lowered her head to peer inside.

She was met with a blast of excited yipping and crying from the collection of dogs within. By all the fur blocking her view, it seemed most of the dogs had gathered there, agitated by whatever was going on. They'd clearly all crammed themselves into the few stalls not locked from the outside.

Between furry bodies jostling in front of her, she caught glimpses of Holly Hart's blonde hair. She had her back to Zoe. Her arms flailed wildly, like she was talking to someone, but Zoe couldn't hear over the dogs.

A border collie skittered out of the way and she saw what they were so excited about. On the other side of the chain-linked enclosure, in the open area between kennels, Piper was gaged and bound with dog leashes to one of the wooden center posts.

The sight of her friend had Zoe's body sagging onto the dirt ground in relief. She was still alive. Then Zoe saw a flash of a knife in Holly's clenched hand.

34

Putting the Dog Down

I found Piper. Holly's got her in the doghouse. I'm going in.

Zoe's fingers shook as she sent the text message to Bob. Her stomach flipped, taking her heart with it. She felt like throwing up. Gritting her teeth against the nausea and fear, she tossed her tablet beside her purse.

She didn't wait for a response from Bob, because she knew what it would be. But she wasn't about to sit by while her best friend's life was in danger.

She rummaged through her purse again, looking for something to use as a weapon. Her hand hit something weighty and she gripped it. Its familiar thickness and shape told her what it was before she drew it out. Big Boy.

Well, she thought. *It's all I've got.* Besides, it had taken care of Zoe, so hopefully it was enough to take care of Holly Hart.

Slowly, Zoe wormed her way through the doggy door. It was built to fit even the largest dog the center might ever see, but between her long dress, her heels, and the dogs anxiously licking her, it was difficult to get inside without making a noise.

No matter how she turned her head, Freddy kept kissing her face and chewing on her earlobe. His tail was tucked between his legs as he followed her slow path inside the kennel. He was letting her know *I think there's danger.*

Thanks for the tip, she thought sarcastically.

The chain-linked enclosure didn't exactly offer much cover, but the reporter was still facing away from the kennel, and Piper was too distracted by the murderer threatening her life to notice her arrival. Between the dogs barking and Holly busily bantering with a gagged woman, Zoe slipped in without notice.

"You know," Holly was saying to Piper, "Aiden was quite the player back in the day. But I told you that once before. He and I were practically made for each other. What a team we were," she gushed. "Those were some of the best articles I ever wrote." She pointed the tip of her knife at Piper's throat. "But then you came along."

Piper's eyes widened and her jaw moved as she tried to scream, but it was muffled beneath the duct tape slapped over her mouth. Zoe got ready to spring into action, even if it meant losing the advantage of surprise. But then Holly sighed and waved the blade around dramatically like she was gesturing with it.

"So I waited and watched ever since." She laughed like she was remembering all the good times they'd had together. "Honey, I saw it all. You've got some moves in the bedroom, girlfriend. Very carnal. Kudos."

Zoe kept low, hiding among the shifting fur as the dogs continued to dance inside the partitioned enclosure meant only for one. Inching her way to the gate, she reached up to the latch and slowly began to lift it, careful to prevent the metal from squeaking.

Holly leaned her head on Piper's shaking shoulder, her filler-injected lips sticking out in a pouty face. "I never in a million years thought Aiden would actually go through with the wedding. Not with his scandalous background." She began to scrape her knife back and forth along the base of Piper's neck. "I always assumed he'd come to his senses. That he'd finally see what's been right there in front of him the whole time." The blade changed angle, the edge puckering Piper's skin.

Zoe flung the kennel door open, the dogs flooding into the open space. "And what's that? A narcissistic egomaniac?"

She raised Big Boy just as Holly turned in surprise. It came down with a loud *thwap* across Holly's face.

Holly shrieked, stumbling back against the kennel, metal rattling. The knife clattered to the floor.

As Holly found her balance again, Zoe brought her foot up and kicked her square in the chest. The air left her lungs in a grunt and she was thrown back. She half stumbled, half slid into an open kennel.

Zoe slammed the door and dropped the latch.

With shaking hands, she unlocked the supply closet and used the padlock on the kennel door to ensure Holly would stay put for the police. The metal snapped home with a click of finality. The nightmare was over.

Zoe picked up the knife and ran to Piper. She began sawing away at the dog leads digging into her wrists. Her hand gripping the handle was wet with sweat, and Piper was shaking so badly that she was afraid to cut her.

Freddy pawed at their legs. *I'm helping. I'm helping. Am I being helpful?*

Finally, the last strands gave way. Piper rubbed her wrists before ripping the tape off her mouth. "Zoe!"

"Come on," Zoe said, not wanting to waste time. "Let's go find Bob."

Holly's cage rattled and they spun around to see the reporter leaning casually against the chain links. Through one of the holes, the barrel of a gun jutted out.

"Do you seriously think I came unprepared?" She snorted at their ignorance. "You, in the white." She curled a finger toward Piper in a come-hither motion.

Zoe and Piper shared a glance. From this close range, Holly would be able to hit one of them, if not both. Piper was probably coming to the same conclusion because, after a moment, her jaw clenched. Zoe could have sworn she heard teeth squeak as they ground together in anger, even above all the dogs barking at random around them.

Finally, Piper took a deep breath and reluctantly crossed over to the cage.

"I prefer using knives to guns, of course," Holly said conversationally. "There's just something so personal about it. Reporting on the gruesome things I see day in and day out, you get a bit desensitized to it, you know? The murders, the rapes, the car accidents. But taking someone's life with nothing but a piece of steel between you, now that's stirring. You can almost feel the sinew rip, the organs pop." She shuddered, a delicious smile warming her face. "But only an idiot leaves home without a gun. It's my plan B."

Piper didn't answer. She looked calm as she entered the passcode into the lock, but it rattled in her hands as she unhooked it. Zoe could tell some of it was fear. But most of it would have been rage.

Holly stood back, the gun trained on Piper's chest as she opened the kennel door. When she stepped out, she waved the gun to the side and Piper moved to join Zoe.

Holly looked at Zoe as though she were a disappointment. "You just had to come find her. You don't know when to quit, do you?"

Zoe kept her eyes on Holly's, and answered as coolly

as she would any other day. "Should I have quit after you broke into my van and ruined Piper's dress? Or cut my brake lines? Or tried to land Piper in the hospital?"

"Hey," Holly held her hand up, "at the start, I tried to derail this wedding without anyone getting hurt."

Zoe scoffed in disgust. "You blew up my office."

"Oh . . . right. Okay, so you would have been a little crispy." She waved a hand like a trip to the spa could have buffed that right out.

Piper crossed her arms over her beaded bodice. "And the sesame seeds?"

"You would have been fine in the end. It's just a little anaphylactic shock. Nothing a little modern medicine wouldn't cure."

"Chef Glazier wasn't *fine*," Zoe shot back.

"Well," Holly relented with a shrug meant for stealing the last cookie. "That was a little complication. I didn't plan for that to happen." Because that made it all better.

"And how about your cameraman in the woods? Or that jewelry designer a couple of weeks ago? Or the pizza delivery boy?"

Piper frowned, her head whipping to Zoe, catching up to the conversation.

"You know about those, huh?" Holly pursed her lips. "Listen, that jewelry designer was a crook. I swear she swapped out my diamond for a fake. And the delivery boy?" She groaned. "Thirty minutes or less, my ass."

Piper gasped, taking an automatic step back until she hit the kennel behind her. "*You're* the San Fran Slayer?"

Zoe dared to take a step forward. "And all those other innocent lives you've taken in this city over the last couple of years? What were your excuses for those?"

"Look," Holly said very reasonably. "I have my reasons for every one of those deaths, and they're all very good, I can assure you. But I don't need to defend myself to you."

"You're right," Zoe said. "You just need to defend yourself to the police."

"The police? Okay. Clearly, this is your first time being held at gunpoint. I have the gun." She waved it in the air, and Zoe took an automatic step back. "That means I have the power. You don't have the gun. That means you die."

Piper let out a breath that sounded almost like a laugh. She threw her head back, rolling her eyes at the ceiling, as though at wit's end. Zoe had seen enough bridezillas to know what that looked like. But standing right next to her, she could see Piper was using it as an excuse to look around. Maybe for a way out.

"Holly, he already married me. Just accept it." Piper raised her chin bravely, calling the reporter's bluff. She narrowed her eyes as though daring her to do something about it. "It's too late."

But Holly laughed, a barking sound similar to the anxious noises coming from the dogs circling around their legs. "Honey, do I need to go through the whole gun explanation again? It's not too late."

"So what, you think you can just kill us both and get away with it?" Piper demanded, but Zoe could hear the tremble of panic in her voice.

Holly pulled a face, like she was talking to the two dumbest people on the planet. "Uh, yeah. I've gotten away with it every other time."

"The police already know about your cameraman in the woods," Zoe said, trying anything to make her second-guess her plan. However, she wasn't about to reveal that she sent a text to Bob, in case Holly got trigger happy out of desperation.

Holly didn't look too worried, though. "Really?

Because if they did, they'd be ripping this place apart looking for me." Holly tilted her head, as though listening for sounds of them ripping. "And I can still hear your glee club boyfriend singing out there. Sounds like the party's still on."

"Rock band," Zoe muttered.

She automatically tuned into the faint music. It was a song by 3 Doors Down. But Holly was wrong. It wasn't Levi singing. It was the real song, which could only mean the band was taking a break. Was Levi looking for her? That meant he'd be in danger too.

The look on Holly's face radiated confidence. She had it all figured out. Probably right down to where she was going on her honeymoon with Aiden. The fact that she had to murder people to get what she wanted seemed like a minor inconvenience.

"Don't worry," Holly said. "I've got plenty of time to kill you and dispose of your bodies in the woods."

Zoe's eyes flitted around the longhouse. She could see no way out of the simple building. There was nothing to hide behind in the long aisle that ran between the two rows of kennels, nowhere to run. They had to get out in the open where they had a better chance of getting away.

But Holly was smart. Zoe knew she'd catch on if they tried to lead her, so she snorted, as though she didn't think Holly could pull it off. "How are you going to drag our bodies out to the woods? I mean, now that you've killed your sidekick, there's no way you can manage it all on your own."

Holly frowned, glancing between the two of them, maybe estimating their weight. "You're right. It will be a lot of work dragging your carcasses out there. Thanks for pointing that out." She picked up her knife and waved her gun toward the back door. "Get moving."

As they headed for the exit, Zoe glanced back at

Freddy among the other dogs. He tried to follow, but Holly kicked him aside.

"Hey!" Zoe yelled.

He yelped, but skittered away to safety, out the doggy door to the enclosure. At least he'd be safe from Holly.

Zoe watched the door swing shut behind Freddy, wondering if this was the last time she'd see him.

Piper threw Zoe a look, like *what's the plan?*

Zoe grimaced and shrugged. *I guess we'll wing it.*

Holly jabbed Zoe in the back with her gun as a reminder. "Run and I shoot. Yell and I shoot. Do anything I don't tell you to do and I shoot. Got me? Now open the door."

As Zoe turned the handle and opened the door, fresh, clean air swept over them. She inhaled deeply until she felt her mind clear a little.

Holly wasn't going to shoot right then unless they forced her to. They were too close to the party. Everyone would hear. They still had time to figure something out, to come up with a plan. And Zoe was nothing if not a good planner.

Holly marched them around the side of the building so they were completely blocked from the view of the house. Zoe could hear people cheering, the music blaring, but Levi still wasn't singing. Was he searching for her?

Zoe pretended to stumble in her heels. As she lurched forward, catching herself on the enclosure fence, she tore off the pink sash around her waist. She balled it up in her hand. When Holly shoved her forward again, Zoe tossed the fabric back so she wouldn't see.

But Piper saw. And while Zoe didn't exactly have a surplus of outfit to leave behind as breadcrumbs, there was plenty to tear off a delicate bridal gown.

As they hit the tree line, Piper began stumbling herself, blaming the cumbersome dress. Each time, she tossed a little something aside, too small for Holly to notice in the dark: a string of beads, a ribbon, a chunk of lace.

It was so dark after the warm lights inside the doghouse. Hardly any of the moon's glow reached them beneath the thick canopy above. Surely Holly would have a hard time hitting her targets when she could barely see, Zoe reasoned. But each time she gathered the courage to make her move, Holly would jab their backs with the cold barrel of the gun, reminding her that at such close range, she'd be able to hit them with her eyes closed.

Eventually, the music faded to a dull beat in the distance, muffled by the thick trees, but they were still too far away from the other side of the property to hear street traffic. Where could they go? How could they get someone's attention from out there?

Zoe's eyes had adjusted enough to see Piper's expression. It didn't look like she had any ideas either.

Holly's footsteps began to slow, and Zoe's heart began to pick up speed again.

"Stop here," Holly said. She tossed Zoe a leash. "Tie Piper up to that tree over there."

Zoe stared at the lead in her hands and then at Piper. All thoughts fled her brain. There was no plan, no impromptu solution. This was one wedding catastrophe she could never have predicted.

When she took too long to respond, she felt cool metal press against her neck. Enough said: do it or die.

Piper slowly began backing up to the tree. Her eyes never left Zoe's, as though she was waiting for a cue. But Zoe just stared back, her forehead creasing with the effort of focusing her frazzled mind.

As she approached her friend, Zoe gripped the leash so tight it bit into her soft palms. Her breaths came faster, and her eyes prickled with tears.

This wasn't how it was supposed to go. The good guys were supposed to win. Holly was supposed to lose. It was Piper's wedding day, for God's sake. Was Aiden going to lose his wife of only six hours?

And what about Levi? Zoe had finally found the man she wanted to be with, who made her whole again. And that was it? Was she simply going to disappear into the woods, never to be seen again? Would he even know what happened to her?

No. It wasn't going to end like that. Zoe could handle anything, including *The* Holly Hart.

Zoe closed her eyes and imagined every ounce of her energy building in her limbs, tensing her legs to spring, flexing her arms to attack.

Just as she prepared to spin on Holly, there was a rustle of leaves and sticks behind them. They all spun toward the sound.

"Who's there?" Holly demanded.

But when they saw no one out there in the dark, Zoe knew who had come to save her. Freddy.

She could almost hear his innocent excitement. *Hello! It's just me. Is this hide and seek? I found you. I win!*

Holly was turned away, eyes searching. Zoe lunged for her. Grabbing Holly's arm, she drove her knee up, forcing her elbow to bend back. There was a pop, a grinding of the joint that Zoe could feel echo all the way up her leg. Holly screamed and dropped the gun.

Piper yelled out, "Help!" before dropping to the ground. She scrambled through the underbrush, her hands groping along the dirt for the weapon.

Holly dove for Piper, hands outstretched for her neck. But before she could so much as touch her friend, Zoe took the leash in her hands and looped it around the reporter's neck. She yanked on either side of the lead, cinching it tight.

Choking noises sputtered from Holly's mouth. Her hands flew to her neck, frantically clawing at the nylon cord. She jerked, struggling to get away, but Zoe held on.

Piper groaned in frustration as she continued to search, crawling on the ground. She threw aside leaves and tossed dead branches in search of the gun. When her hunt brought her closer, Holly raised her foot and kicked out.

It connected with Piper's chest with a dull thump and an "oof" as Piper's breath whooshed forcefully from her lungs. She tumbled back in a swish of leaves, coughing and wheezing as she clutched at her chest.

Heaving tighter on the ends of the leash, Zoe felt it dig deeper against Holly's soft neck until she imagined her head snapping right off. Holly resisted, her neck muscles straining as she pulled forward. Inch by inch she drew away from Zoe. Then her head came whipping back.

Zoe heard a crack. A flash of light burst in front of her eyes. She could almost smell the pain stinging her nose.

Hot liquid ran down her face and she tasted metal in her mouth. She stumbled back in surprise, holding her nose as she coughed and choked on her own blood.

Holly wheeled around on her. Her fist drew back. Before it could connect with Zoe's already-throbbing face, something flashed in the dim moonlight.

A musical twang filled the woods, and Holly cried out, falling to the ground. Freddy hadn't come alone. He'd brought Levi.

Levi's face twisted with fury as he came to Zoe's rescue. He raised his guitar over his head in true rock-star fashion, ready to bring it down on Holly.

Beneath the hollow vibrations humming from the guitar, Zoe heard a rustle. A *click*.

Holly's arm rose, a finger wrapped around the gun's trigger. She aimed for Levi's exposed chest.

35

⚭

A Live Dog Is Better Than a Dead Boyfriend

As Holly pointed the gun at Levi, Zoe's breath left her in a sob. Her eyes filled with tears, already grieving for what was about to happen. To have her heart made whole again, only to be ripped out once and for all. She couldn't stand it. It wasn't fair.

Not willing to let Levi be taken from her, she reached out to him, as though she could hold him there, keep him in her life.

A split-second later, the shot pierced the night air, echoing through the woods surrounding the rescue center. She could feel the sharp loss almost as though she'd taken the bullet herself. As though Holly had aimed for her newly repaired heart and blown it wide open.

Zoe cried out with the pain and the loss. She wrapped her arms around Levi, holding him tight.

Somehow, even after being shot, he found the energy to bring his guitar down on Holly. Again and again it twanged, and rung, and thumped until all he held was the neck, dripping with dark liquid that glinted in the dim moonlight. Panting, he tossed it aside and fell to his knees, Zoe along with him.

That ache, it burned inside her. It was almost too much to bear, but she held onto it as she held Levi. She didn't want to bottle anything up anymore. She didn't want to hold back. Because without the fear and pain of losing him, she couldn't give him her love. And she had so much to give him. And she wanted it all, every feeling, every last painful second she had with him.

"Levi," she sobbed. "Stay with me. Don't die."

"I won't leave." His voice broke, as though he could barely get the words out. "I'm not going anywhere."

She heard Piper's screams fade as she headed back toward the center. "Help! We're over here! We need a medic!"

Levi seemed to be holding Zoe as much as she was holding him. Like he needed her as much as she needed him. She felt the damp soil seep through her dress, making her shiver.

"I can't lose you," she said. "Not now. It's just . . . too short." She choked on her tears as another wave of grief ripped through her.

She was shaking now, breathing in short gasps, unable to get enough oxygen between her sobs and that terrible heartbreak.

"Don't leave me," she said.

Levi laid a hand on her face, wet and hot with his own blood. Or maybe it was that her face felt so cold. He held her gaze, the moonlight reflecting in his blue eyes. His expression looked so pained that it hurt her to see him suffer.

Between her quick breaths, he kissed her. "I will *never* leave you. I promise. Never."

Those words made it a little easier to breathe. The constriction in her chest eased. After all the excitement,

Zoe could feel the energy trickle out of her body. She relaxed in Levi's arms, feeling very tired all of a sudden.

The sound of ripping fabric made her drooping eyes flutter open. Her blurry gaze landed on Piper. She was balling up a piece of her dress. *No, her beautiful dress,* Zoe thought. She laid it against Zoe's chest and pressed firmly.

Zoe screamed out as hot, white pain shot through her body, rippling down to her cold toes. She bit her lip to stop from screaming again.

Her vision was no longer blurry. Sleep no longer called to her. How could she sleep when it felt like Piper was stabbing her through with a hot poker? The pain seemed to pulse with every beat of her heart. Which at least told her that she did, in fact, still have her heart.

"Can you carry her?" Piper asked Levi.

Instead of answering, Zoe felt his hold on her shift. Then the world spun as he stood up, or maybe that was just her head. Every step that Levi took felt like a fresh stab to her chest.

Levi grunted and huffed as he headed back for the center, holding her protectively to his body as he picked his way through the rough terrain. She watched his face, focusing on the effort, the strain, the worry that creased it.

It struck her as odd that he was carrying her when he was the one who was shot. And when the dim lights from her wedding decorations glowed up ahead, it was even stranger that everyone was calling her name and not his. Especially when he was covered in so much blood. It was smeared all over his shirt, his hands, his neck.

The music had stopped, replaced by agitated chatter, cries of exclaim, tinny voices over two-way radios, and distant echoes of sirens.

The light brightened and Levi set her down on a cold,

hard surface. She blinked around the room and saw she was in Piper's veterinary operating room.

Piper set something over Zoe's face. It hissed at her, blowing air.

Annoyed, Zoe raised a hand, trying to swipe it away. A hand clamped over hers and held it still. Her head swiveled toward the person. It was Levi.

There was a clink of metal on metal as Piper set tools down next to Zoe. She then hung a bag of liquid above her head and Zoe watched it swing back and forth, almost hypnotized.

Her eyes began to droop until something pinched the skin in the crook of her arm. She hissed at the sharp pain. Levi held her hand tight, as though afraid she would fight back, but she no longer had the energy to react. Instead, she watched Piper fuss over her from the end of a really long tunnel.

The pain had dulled. She wasn't sure when. Or maybe she'd become used to it. In fact, she felt like she'd left her body entirely. The only thing that remained was the buzzing inside her head like a swarm of cicadas had gathered in there and the feeling of her hand in Levi's.

Only now did it occur to her that Levi hadn't been shot. *She had.*

But that didn't seem like the most important thing right now. The only thing that seemed to matter was that Levi had kept his promise. He hadn't left her. Only, as her eyes began to droop, she wasn't so sure she could promise the same thing.

36

In Tune

Slimy wetness rubbed Zoe's cheek over and over again, working its way toward her nose. She groaned, swatting it away. But this only seemed to make it worse. It increased in both speed and enthusiasm.

She brushed her hand in the general direction of her face, but her limbs didn't seem to be working as well as they should be. She ended up slapping her face instead. Her nose throbbed as she hit it, taking her breath away.

Slowly, she half-opened an eye to peek at her attacker. It was Freddy dancing on top of her blankets— although, they couldn't be hers because she didn't recognize them. His wiry goatee tickled her face as he persisted in kissing her.

As she squirmed weakly away, pain shot down her chest and left arm. She froze, holding her breath, bracing against the pain. Her body may not have been cooperating, but she managed a very serious quirk of her eyebrow at the doxie.

Freddy jerked like he'd been shot then flopped against her, exposing his belly in surrender.

Sleepily, her eyes blinked one at a time while she took in her surroundings. A white ceiling and ugly green curtains stared back at her. Her nostrils stung, both from the scent of antiseptic and the dry air hissing into her nostrils. There was beeping and whirring and chiming and . . . snoring.

Zoe raised her head, grimacing as fire spread through her chest like she'd inhaled hot ashes. She found the source of the snoring half way down her bed. It was Levi.

He sat on a stiff, plastic chair, head resting on her raised bed. His arm stretched across her legs as though still holding on since . . . well, since the wedding. Whenever that was.

She reached out a tentative hand and ran her fingers through his locks. She noticed he had none of his usual gel making it stick up. He inhaled deeply and his eyes fluttered open. They were bright and clean, not ringed in dark makeup.

Those eyes met hers and he smiled sleepily, like they'd just woken up after a crazy night together. Well, they had, but not the kind of night Zoe would have preferred.

Levi blinked, as though he suddenly realized where they were—which Zoe was only just staring to figure out.

"You're awake." He reached for her face.

She closed her eyes, enjoying the sensation of his touch, the gentleness welcome after so much pain. The pain . . .

As she took a few deep breaths, her head began to clear and images accosted her. Memories, sights, sounds, smells, fear. She recalled the wedding, the body, the woods, Holly.

Someone dropped something nearby and the *bang*

made her wince. Her chest spasmed as though reliving the moment the bullet tore through her. Once she caught her breath, she raised the scratchy hospital blanket, tugging at the neckline of her gown to peek under it.

She wasn't sure what she'd expected to see. Blood and gore? A gaping hole in her chest, maybe? Instead, there was an oversized white bandage on the left side of her chest. A thick clear tube ran out from under it.

"The doctor said you were very lucky," Levi said, startling her. She still felt a little dopey. Maybe the IV dripping into her arm had something to do with that.

"I should buy a lottery ticket." Her voice croaked, and when she swallowed, her throat was dry.

"It was just a small handgun, so it didn't go all the way through," he said, ignoring her joke. "It hit just below your collarbone. Any lower and it would have hit your lung."

Her eyelids fluttered for a moment, imagining the bullet was still in there, rubbing against her lungs with each breath. She'd had a lot of close calls in the last couple of weeks, but nothing could have been closer than that. A centimeter, maybe a millimeter, and she wouldn't have been there.

She dropped the blanket, unwilling to look at it anymore, to imagine how close she'd been to not having, well . . . what did she have? Sure, she and Levi had only just begun, but she was acutely aware of the potential she would have missed out on, the hope of so much more.

She'd practically put her life on hold for six years, like she'd been holding her breath. And now that she'd found Levi, had found that hope, she could finally move forward. She could finally breathe again. And she was more grateful than ever that she had the lungs to do it.

"How do you feel?" Levi asked her as his thumb caressed the side of her face.

"Like I've been shot."

"I can't say I know how that feels." He frowned, his hand cupping her face like he wanted to grab more of her but was afraid to hurt her. "But I almost did." He shook his head, his face screwing up. "Why? Why did you do it?"

She shrugged, but then grimaced as a fresh wave of pain spread through her. "What can I say?" she choked out. "I grab life by the balls."

Levi passed her a cord with a red button on the end. "Hit this. It will give you pain medication."

She jammed the button three times. Her IV machine whirred, and a few moments later, she felt a little woozy. It wasn't enough to take the pain away, but it certainly sanded down the edge a little.

"Well, it was definitely ballsy," he said at last. "But I wish you wouldn't have. It should be me lying there. It hurts to see you like this."

She gave him a wry look. "I'm so sorry for your pain."

He chuckled, but the humor in his expression didn't last long before he turned grim again. "You saved my life. If it had been me, I might not have made it."

"That's true. I know how you feel about pain." She reached up and ran a thumb over his naked eyebrow. There was not a glimmer of metal anywhere on his face. "But I'm tough. I can handle it."

"I know you are." Sighing, he turned his head to kiss her wrist, stubble tickling her sensitive skin. Those blue eyes held hers for a moment, as though waiting for something, searching.

After a moment, he sighed. "You're hiding from me again. You've got your mask on."

"No." She shook her head until it made her dizzy. "No more mask. It's gone. I think you've proven that I can't hide from you. No matter how hard I try. It's just . . ."

There was so much to say, but she wasn't sure her foggy brain could put it in the right order.

"You're right," she said at last. "Life is too short. Maybe it's the drugs talking, but right now I'm just happy I'm here. I have my friends, my life," she laid a hand on his cheek, "and I found my heart."

He pressed his palm over her hand to keep it there. "Thankfully that's still intact."

She smiled. "It's better than ever."

Tired of being ignored, Freddy snaked his way up the bed, trying to lick the oxygen tubing laying across Zoe's cheek. *I came too. I came to see you. Pay attention to me.*

She giggled, wincing as each shake sent shooting pains down her arm. "How did you get Freddy in here?"

"The nurse let me smuggle him in," Levi said. "He is a local hero, after all."

"Is that so? Freddy, do you have an alter ego I should know about?"

He tucked his tail between his legs, but wagged it back and forth, unsure if he was about to get praise or heck. She gave him a scratch beneath the chin, and he sat in the crook of her good arm, jutting his barrel chest out to make sure she got every last spot.

Levi pulled out his phone and cued up a video from the Channel Five News website. In front of the camera, as usual, was Holly Hart. Only, this time, she was in handcuffs. And lying on a stretcher.

As the camera panned out, the brunette who normally did the weather segment stepped into the shot, microphone at the ready. Although the scene was grim, her smile was so big you could see her molars. She'd obviously been promoted.

"What does a wedding, a wiener dog, and a rock star have in common?" she asked. *"They were the keys to un-*

covering the identity of the serial killer, our local tormenter, the San Fran Slayer. AKA our own beloved Holly Hart." She turned, inviting the viewers to watch the downfall of Holly Hart's regin as she was placed into the back of an ambulance.

"I am happy to report that the Slayer mystery has finally been solved at the location of this year's most anticipated event, the Summers-Caldwell wedding."

A recent photo from *The Gate*'s announcement section popped up on the screen. It was a snap of Piper and Aiden shortly after news of their engagement went public.

"After murdering her cameraman and crashing the bash, Holly Hart attempted to take out the blushing bride in the hopes of replacing her as Mrs. Caldwell." The reporter walked slowly and the camera panned with her until she stood in front of the Dachshund Rescue Center.

"As we already know, the deranged ex-reporter had an obsession with the CEO of Caldwell and Son Investments. As it turns out, the obsession went beyond your average red-carpet crush. She's been stalking him for months, possibly years."

"That I can believe," Zoe said.

"Thankfully the bride's maid of honor and local wedding planner, Zoe Plum, of Plum Crazy Events, found Holly before she could do any harm. But when things didn't go as planned, local rocker and front man of Reluctant Redemption, Levi Dolson, tracked them down with the help of Zoe's dog, Freddy." She smiled as though it was the cutest thing in the world.

The scene cut away. Her youthful face was replaced with a photo of Freddy. It was the one Zoe had posted on the center's website. Next to it was a video clip of Levi's band on stage.

"Tonight, the lead singer performed the biggest hit of

his life by taking down Hart, but not before Zoe Plum
was shot and seriously injured." She paused dramatically. *"I'm happy to report that she's in stable condition*
and will recover from her injuries to plan another day."

Behind the weather girl-turned-reporter, the ambulance sped off down the rescue center's long, winding
driveway. *"With Holly Hart on her way to prison for a*
long time, our city is safe once again, thanks to a wed-
ding planner, a rocker, and a wiener. Reporting this
rockin' ending for Channel Five News, I'm Fiona Fair."
She gave a sassy wink to end the segment, looking over-
joyed. But that probably had less to do with the positive
resolution of the mystery than it did her sudden promotion.

Levi tucked his phone away in his back pocket. "Did
you hear? The reporter called me a rock star."

"I call you rock star all the time," Zoe said.

"Yeah, but now the whole city knows. And she men-
tioned your business. Imagine all the brides that will
want to hire you if you're willing to take a bullet for them.
You can have a slogan, like 'Zoe Plum, wedding planner.
For when things don't go to plan.'" He used a deep, movie
trailer guy voice, like she was the Arnold Schwarzeneg-
ger of wedding planners.

She snorted. "That's great. But I'm not sure I want to
take bullets on a regular basis." The idea brought back
the image of Holly's gun trained on Levi's chest. She
swallowed hard thinking how close he'd come to being
shot straight in the heart.

"So how did you know where to find us in the woods?"
she asked to take her mind off it.

"It was Freddy," he said. "The boys and I were taking
a break. When I couldn't find you, I texted you. I heard
the chime from your tablet and followed the noise, but
all I found was your purse by the doghouse. That's when

Freddy found me. He was able to follow your breadcrumb trail through the woods."

"Freddy. Did you hear that?" she asked him. "You're my hero."

Freddy's ears perked up at his name, but he was too busy shoving his snout beneath her arm, trying to find a hole to crawl into. She could tell he was growing restless.

"So does that mean you're going to keep him?" Levi asked.

"Yeah," she said. "I think we're good for each other. A perfect match."

Freddy began to wedge himself beneath Zoe's blankets, burrowing down where it was warm. His tail slipped under until all she could see was a lump fidgeting beneath the linen.

Every time he crawled over her shins or nudged her thigh, he seemed to find a bruise. She winced, but laughed.

Levi chuckled. "You'll need to get used to having music in your life to keep him happy."

"That's okay. I planned on having music in my life to keep *me* happy." She gave him a meaningful look.

His face warmed, but it was like he was holding back a little, maybe trying not to be too pushy. "You know, I just so happen to be a musician. I could help you out with that."

"That's good. I'll be needing a lot of music, for a long time," she said seriously. "Maybe forever."

His face erupted in a smile. "I can do forever." He leaned over the bed to kiss her gently.

The green curtain behind him swished aside. When they turned to look, her mother stood at the foot of the bed. If she was surprised to see Zoe in the midst of a lip lock, she seemed too happy to see Zoe awake to comment.

She rounded the bed, spreading her arms wide to

embrace her daughter. Then she thought better about it and held her face instead. "Zoe."

"Kaasan." Zoe reached up and hugged her mom, ignoring the pulling sensation from her chest tube.

By the way the arms around her tightened, she felt like she was comforting her mother more than the other way around. When they pulled away, the look on her mom's face said enough. She'd obviously been very worried.

"Gomennasai, Kaasan."

"Don't apologize to me," she said in English. "You were very brave. Stupid. But brave."

She smiled. "Mom."

"Baka," her mom said with a teasing smirk.

"Mom! I'm lying in the hospital. You're not allowed to call me names." But Zoe was laughing. And somehow she'd started crying at the same time.

"I'll leave you two alone for a while," Levi said. "Your overnight bag is in my van. I'll go grab it."

He began to pull away, but Zoe squeezed his hand, as though afraid to let him go. She hadn't even realized she'd done it until he squeezed back. Wasn't it only three weeks earlier that her instincts had her shoving him away?

"I'll be back," he told her.

Zoe's mother watched him leave with a shrewd look. "I see you and the musician are getting closer. What about Kimura-san?"

Zoe could tell her mother was broaching the conversation cautiously. At least she could show some restraint while her daughter was laid out in the hospital. Now that she was definitely going to live, Junko was right back to worrying about the long term.

"I told him it wouldn't work," Zoe said.

Her mother sighed. "I had hoped . . . Maybe if you give it some time?"

"I don't think he's the one for me. I'm sorry."

Zoe worried that the conversation was about to become as painful as getting shot. *Actually, I think I'd rather be shot again,* she thought. But she became even more concerned when her mother began . . . smiling.

"Why do you look so happy? I thought you would be upset."

"Because you make it sound like you think there is one for you," she said. "That's more than you thought a few weeks ago. It means we're making progress."

Zoe chuckled. "I guess you helped me to start seeing it as an option. I'm sorry that there won't be anyone to save us from money issues." Not that Zoe would have let a guy bail her out, but her mother had certainly been hoping for it.

"It's not about the money," she said. "I didn't raise a daughter who depends on other people to do everything for her. I raised an independent, competent woman. A woman who can take care of the bills, who can even take care of me."

She took Zoe's hand in hers, much like the way Zoe had when the roles were reversed. "All I wanted was for you to have someone who will take care of your heart. Who will be there for you during tough times, as you have been for me."

Zoe smiled as she realized that's exactly what Levi was doing. What he'd been trying to do all along. She'd just needed to learn to let him. Instead, she'd fought it right from the start. But it wasn't because she didn't want him. It was because she'd wanted him too much. Now that she'd embraced her growing feelings, the affection, the love, it was enlivening.

"Mom, how did you know dad was the one?" she finally asked.

Her mother's mouth curled into a smile as she gazed

at nothing in particular. "I remember the first time I met your father. He was brash, and loud, and arrogant, and thought himself very charming."

"Well you obviously thought he was charming too," Zoe teased.

"No. I thought he was ridiculous." She chuckled at some memory. "I tried to ignore him, but I couldn't. I told myself that he was wrong for me, that I was happy where I was, with my family, surrounded by everything I'd ever known and loved." She sighed. "And yet, despite all the reasons why I couldn't be with him, why it was hard to be together, it was impossible to be without him."

"Were you scared?" Zoe asked. "To let yourself fall, I mean?"

"Oh yes. But I was more scared to let him go. How can you ignore a feeling like that, like . . . destiny?"

"Destiny?" Zoe huffed a quiet laugh so it wouldn't hurt her chest. "How very Western of you, Mom."

Zoe's mother had given up everything to be with her father. Except for her sister, her family had cut all ties with her. To have leapt into the unknown, put her heart and her life in the hands of someone else, to have trusted him completely, that had been bravery. Meanwhile, Zoe had been afraid to even go on a date with Levi because she was afraid to get hurt.

Maybe her mother had known more about love than Zoe all along—not that she'd ever admit that out loud. And here she'd been worried that her mother needed her because she was getting older. But it turned out that maybe Zoe needed her mother more than she'd thought.

"So does this mean you are considering Levi?" her mother asked. "Is he your destiny?"

After only a few weeks, Zoe couldn't imagine being without him. How could she ever go back to her old self, to suppressing her emotions? Now that Levi had freed her from that prison inside herself, had smashed her bottle-o-crazy, she could never forget what she felt for him. Like her mother had said, it felt "impossible."

Before she could answer, the curtains swished as Levi returned. Her mother assessed him as he rounded the bedside to resume his post next to Zoe. After a moment, she nodded, as though it were decided.

In Japanese, she whispered, *"He will make me beautiful grandchildren."*

"Oh, Mom!"

"Look who I found on the way here," Levi said. He nodded toward the parted curtain.

The ugly green fabric shifted with movement before a parade of people filtered into the space: Piper, Aiden, Addison, Felix, Naia, Marilyn, and Bob. Gentle hugs were given before everyone stood back, circling her bed.

They were still dressed in their wedding attire. Piper's hair was falling out of its half-updo, her dress tattered and stained from their trip through the woods and with Zoe's blood.

Zoe wondered how long it had been, if it was still the same night. Or maybe it was the next day.

She took in the group of people who were the nearest and dearest to her, who knew her better than anyone, and also who she'd hid so much of herself from. The very things she'd hid from herself. And yet there they were, by her side to support her. Taking them all in, Zoe realized that they were the people she needed.

Maybe it took facing death to realize how much there was to live for, to recognize the things she'd been taking for granted for so long, had been hiding from. But now she knew. She could admit it and felt her repaired heart overflow with their presence.

"Thanks for coming, you guys," she said at last.

Piper crossed her scratched arms, dirty manicured

nails digging into her skin as she hugged herself. Her red eyes began to tear up as she took in the sight of Zoe. "Holly was after me the entire time. I should be the one in that bed. I'm alive because of you."

Aiden wrapped a protective arm around her, as though needing the reassurance of physical contact with his wife to know she was safe. "Thank you," he said to Zoe.

"It was a joint effort," Zoe said. "Besides, I wouldn't be here if you hadn't taken care of me after I'd been shot," she told Piper. "Holly had been there all along, popping up each and every time something went wrong. I just assumed she was being her nosy self. I should have put the pieces together a long time ago."

"You mean I should have," Bob said. "This city owes you a debt for uncovering the San Fran Slayer. Holly was the last person we would have considered. She was a respected member of the community, a figurehead. She was supposed to be reporting the crimes, not committing them."

Marilyn slipped her arm through Bob's, and his tensed shoulders relaxed. Clearly, he'd been beating himself up over it.

He inhaled long and deep through his nose before speaking again. "Holly had access no one else would have, she had people's trust, a reason to be lurking around every crime scene. She had us all fooled."

The furrow between his brows relaxed as he struggled between his professional role to inform her of events and his personal concern for Zoe. "We'll have a lot more questions for you, but for now, on behalf of the city police department, and San Francisco, thank you."

"Well, it was really in my best interest at the time," she half-joked. "I thought I was the one being carted away to jail. Then I stumbled on her cameraman's footage."

She suddenly realized all the things she'd have to review with the police. "Did you end up finding that?"

"Don't worry," he said. "We found it. And the body."

Addison gasped and covered Naia's ears. She gave a playful glare at Bob and Zoe as though in warning. Felix chuckled next to her.

"Sorry," Bob told her.

"What happened to Holly?" Zoe asked.

"She's recovering. She . . ." He glanced at Naia, as though choosing his words carefully. "She won't be the same. But either way, she'll never be a free woman. We won't have to worry about her ever again."

Zoe frowned, remembering the clang of the guitar strings as Levi had brought it down on the reporter. She shook it off, trying to focus her drug-heavy mind. "And Chelsea?"

"She'll definitely face charges for attacking you. And while she wasn't directly involved with Holly, she did provide her with copies of your ex-assistant's planner, knowing full well the harassment that lay in store for you. Maybe not the attempted murders," he said, "but she might be considered an accessory. At the very least, she actively aided in sabotaging your business. Your lawyer will have more suggestions regarding her."

Zoe rubbed her forehead like she could massage the thoughts from her mind. She tried to work through all this new information, tying it into the events of the last few weeks—which was tough to do while on whatever was in that IV.

"So Natalie didn't have anything to do with it?"

Bob shook his head. "Apparently not."

Natalie probably hadn't even been the one to call Astrid that day at the wedding dress shop. It easily could have been Holly posing as her ex-assistant. Well, Natalie may not have had anything to do with the attempted murder, but from Chelsea's confession, she knew her ex-assistant wasn't exactly innocent, either. But that was a much smaller concern for another day.

Zoe's eyes must have been drooping, because she couldn't remember anyone talking for a little while. Then Marilyn said, "Well, we'd best let you get your sleep." She laid a hand on Zoe's foot, squeezing warmly. "We're so happy to see that you're all right."

People began to give hugs, preparing to leave. Addison's hug was especially long. She still hadn't said anything but by her pink nose and bloodshot eyes, Zoe suspected it was because, if she did, she might just start crying.

When Felix dipped close for a gentle hug, he whispered in Zoe's ear. "You'd better hurry up and get better. You'll have another wedding to plan soon enough."

Zoe gasped, and her mouth fell open. "Have you?"

Felix subtly shook his head, tapping his finger to his lips to say it was just between them. He was going to propose soon.

The secret had Zoe grinning stupidly, happy for Addison, who was officially going to get the family she'd always wanted. Fairy-tale themed wedding ideas were already flitting through Zoe's head.

"And don't worry about a thing," Aiden told her. "You're going to get the best care money can buy. Physiotherapists, chiropractors, acupuncturists. You name it, I've hired them. The next few months of your rehab have already been coordinated."

Taking out his phone, he began flipping through screens rapidly, opening documents. "The schedule has been set out in a calendar, color coded, labeled, and alphabetized as per your preferences." He gave her a facetious look, as though daring her to ask if it came with footnotes.

But she smiled gratefully. "Thank you."

Zoe's mother had been silent, maybe a bit shy among the large group, but now she automatically bowed to Aiden in thanks.

Being a handshake guy, Aiden stiffened a little before giving his own awkward bow in return. When he stood up, his hand reached for his tie—a self-conscious tic he had.

"It's the least I can do," he told Zoe. "I owe you"—he kissed the top of Piper's head—"more than my life. I've got a printout of your rehabilitation schedule in the car. Do you want to see it?"

"That's okay," Zoe said. "I trust that you did a great job. I'm sure it will all work itself out."

Levi's head snapped to her, but he didn't say anything until everyone had said their good-byes and left. When they were finally alone, his eyes narrowed as he laid a hand on her forehead. "Maybe you're not doing so well, after all."

"Why? What's wrong?" Zoe craned her neck to look at the monitors, as though the numbers and squiggles flashing across them were announcing her impending death.

"You're clearly very sick," he said with a smirk. "You're not yourself at all. What happened to things working out because you make sure they do?"

She laughed, recalling how laid back Levi had been the first day they'd met, how much it had irritated her. But despite everything that had gone wrong that day— hell, over the next few weeks—everything really did turn out for the best.

Piper's wedding turned out fantastic—well, except for

the whole attempted murder thing. Zoe had cleared her name, she was finally a property owner, had adopted a lifesaving doxie, and she'd found her heart in the form of a rock star.

Zoe laughed in disbelief. "Turns out, life doesn't go as planned. Sometimes, it's better."

Catch up on the Rescue Dog Romance series!

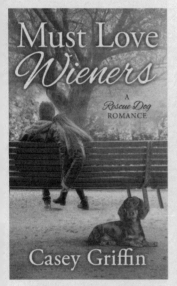

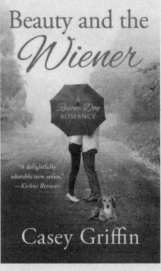

Must Love Wieners

Beauty and the Wiener